S0-BRX-377

THE GATES OF HELL

AN HISTORICAL NOVEL
OF THE PRESENT DAY

7358

BY

ERIK R. v. KÜHNELT-LEDDIHN

TRANSLATED BY

I. J. COLLINS

Theodore Lownik Library
Illinois Benedictine College
Lisle, Illinois 60532

NEW YORK
SHEED & WARD, INC.
MCMXXXIV

FIRST PUBLISHED MARCH 1934
BY SHEED & WARD
63 FIFTH AVENUE
NEW YORK CITY

PRINTED BY
THE NATIONAL PROCESS COMPANY, INC.
NEW YORK CITY

Copyright in the U. S. A.

833.9
K96§

MANUSCRIPT COMMENCED: SUMMER, 1931, IN THE KRISTILLINEN
MATKAILIJAKOTI, HELSINGFORS.
COMPLETED: NOVEMBER 1932, IN THE PESTI SZENT IMRE-KOLLÉGIUM,
BUDAPESTH.

25461

THE GATES
OF HELL

MAY 3 - 1934 Herder 221

CONTENTS

CHAP.   PAGE

PROLOGUE: THE STAGE IS SET   9

PART I

I   BEHIND THE SCENES   17
II   THE HOME FRONT   24
III   A NEW JESUITRY   39
IV   TWO KINDS OF ARGUMENT   51
V   AND TWO DEVELOPMENTS   64
VI   A SILLY BUSINESS   72
VII   SUBURBAN PRELUDE   79
VIII   TALKING OF CHAOS   83
IX   A COUNCILLOR DIES   99
X   TWO HUMAN BEINGS   108
XI   PREAMBLES TO DECISION   116
XII   GOODBYE TO ALL THAT   130

PART II

I   INSTRUCTIONS FOR DYING   137
II   THE EDUCATION OF A RUSSIAN   142
III   DROPPING THE PAST   148
IV   THE PROMISED LAND   159
V   INCIDENTAL ETHICS   168
VI   DISCUSSIONS IN DISGUISE   175
VII   MOSCOW   193
VIII   LENINGRAD   207

CONTENTS

8

CHAP.					PAGE
IX	UNDER ARREST	..	..	..	228
X	THE BIRTH OF A MURDERER	..	..	..	232
XI	THE LEFORTOVA PRISON	..	..	..	249
XII	A TRANSFER	..	..	..	263
XIII	CONVERSATIONS OF A CONVICT	..	..	..	271
XIV	DEATH, AN INDIVIDUALIST	..	..	..	293
XV	DELIRIUM	..	..	..	316
XVI	DELIVERANCE	..	..	..	343

PART III

I	THE PROSPECT OF ENGLAND	..	..	365
II	COUNTRY HOUSE CONVERSATION	..	..	372
III	BACK TO ALL THAT	..	..	..	383
IV	A DIFFERENT BERLIN	..	..	..	396
V	EUROPEAN SCRUTINY	..	..	..	402
VI	OUT OF DARKNESS	..	..	..	408
	EPILOGUE	..	..	..	428

PROLOGUE

THE STAGE IS SET

AT this date, many thousands of people in Europe fell victims to Bolshevism.

This sect did not come, like Protestantism, of the revolution of the nobles, or the syphilitic imitators of the swaggering robber barons, of the stamp of Hutten or Sickingen, or the powerful dilettante Luther, or the royal barbarian Henry VIII; it grew up like a fungus on the wall, in the darkness of decay. It spread outwards from the embassies and trade delegations, dreary-looking buildings where ill-dressed men with academic habits of thought and severe eye-glasses, and soft, tired voices, dictated business-like-sounding letters to snub-nosed typists with shapeless feet. And one day the movement grew up suddenly and passed from the big houses of the big people to spread among the masses, where it ate its way in like a cancer. People simply looked on the movement as a disease, which it was. They isolated the districts where it was rife, scrutinised passports, and looked askance and suspiciously at back-sliders.

Men with white collars, ill-shaven chins, bitten finger-nails, and little cigarettes between their thick lips, suddenly began compiling lists of adherents; girls with low foreheads were suddenly standing at the corners of the parks, blaring short, blustering sentences to the winds. Young workers with fair down sprouting on their faces, were led, after working hours, by broad-shouldered men with deep-smouldering

eyes, to out-of-the-way pubs; officials' sons in slovenly attire,
whose fathers boxed their ears, sat with bent heads at night
under the instruction of high-cheek-boned metal-workers.
White-haired, elderly, Anglo-Saxon-looking women-intellec-
tuals, with dried-up, hawk-like faces, flat bosoms, and wad-
dling gait, decked themselves with red carnations in the
button-hole, bit policemen's arms in street brawls, and gave
lectures on Darwin, Fourier and Marx. A morbid, neurotic
unrest took possession of the property-owning classes; they
held telephone conversations with "Central 6521," dined
with silent, soft-spoken men at a certain house in Unter den
Linden, in the Rue de Grenelle, in New Bond Street,
eating caviare, drinking Napareuli, and muttering, with
wryly smiling lips and creased cheeks, brief phrases of
adulation, expressive of a deadly and contemptuous affectation of cordial friendliness. Meanwhile, among the masses
outside, the sect grew and expanded more and more; blasé,
sport-wearied young women, slightly Lesbian, from the west
end of Berlin, with short hair and fashion-plate faces, instead
of reading the latest number of *Die Freundin*, sat up at
night, bleary-eyed and bored, over novels by Pilnyak, or
Ilya Babel. Thousands who had been dispensed with in their
employment, who were out of humour with the world, or a
prey to venereal disease, or tuberculosis, or neglect and
loneliness, sought gropingly for contacts, and suddenly
found something glamorously attractive and significant in
the romance of water-pipes, of electric light, of wireless
receivers, and visited "instructional films" that showed the
engine factories and gas works of Soviet Russia.

In the editorial offices of the newspapers men and women
with threadbare cloaks forced their way in with a bashfully
insistent importunity—or impudent, bellowing fat terrorists,
with attaché cases and portfolios, with reports, articles,
galley-proofs—and demanded publication. Trains came and

went from Russia, "liberal"-minded savants weighed the bright and gloomy sides of the movement, crowds whirled in procession with red flags, bawling, singing, hiccoughing, and marched stiffly on, from square to square, carrying bright red banners about in the open air hour after hour. Relays of speakers, with men in rowing vests, shook clenched fists; presses were bought up, children's newspapers were printed on cheap duplicating paper; in temporary exhibitions, the non-existence of God was demonstrated by long-haired, neurotic homosexuals—who had been visited with malignant rashes—to fat chauffeuses, ploughed students, and dope-traffickers who had got off their sentences. The masses of ordinary folk sympathised with them; people grew enthusiastic on their behalf, with shamefaced, mental reservation, read their books and papers, went to see their films, praised their practical ideas and their zeal, waxed lyrical over the "usefulness" of their work. Old maids gave them credit for their outspoken freedom in certain matters; middle-class families became divided into "reformist" and "orthodox" groups; schoolboys' Red Indian complexes changed, as by a Darwinistic process of evolution, into collective hysterias— boys in their teens were infected with the urge to march in military formation, and zealous work began in the way of collecting money for fighting funds, revolvers, life-preservers, knuckle-dusters, armlets, rifles, clasp-knives, bandages, stretchers, pistols, gas-masks, and uniform caps. Fathers of families began spending their evenings filing away the points of cartridge bullets; old women with sagging bosoms dusted little statues of Lenin; four-year-old urchins flung stones through car windows and spat at clergymen in the open street. And with it all they were gloomy and simple, intellectual and neurotic, brutal and lazy-minded. There grew up a peculiar race of sectarians, and they put the world to unrest and clamour. The most idyllic corners of Germany became overrun with them—the Hartz mountains, Vogtland, Thuringia. Foreign specialists came from Russia and reported as to the progress of intellectual enlightenment and material wretchedness. Everywhere the number of their adherents was swollen from the ranks of heresies venerable with age—in Lombardy, in Bohemia, in Thuringia, in Scotland, in Russia, in the Balkans—everywhere, where once there had been Bogumils, Waldensians, Lollards, Puritans, Lutherans, Raskolniks, Orthodox Greeks, they rose to fresh power.

In the U.S.S.R., building went on, arming went on, work went on at sweating pressure; horse-power, and more and more horse-power, was wrung from the water; tractors, and more and more tractors, were turned out by the factories; proletarian children, and more and more proletarian children, were produced in the maternity clinics. Pamphlets were published by the Pan-European Society, elderly Excellencies wrote warning articles, heretics of all shades put their heads together, men with bulging paunches, sausage-like fingers, and flat feet uttered little cries of pained dismay.

Only in Rome was there calm recollection and composure; only in Rome were principles formulated, and century-old acts delved out. There, there was experience, and assurance, and self-restraint. The short-wave transmitter of the Vatican City worked clearly day and night, the slightest vibrations that stirred the web of the central organisation registered their effect; reports were examined, co-ordinated, analysed and compared. Nobody was locked up, nobody was put to death, enlightened powers did not conclude any pacts and compacts. There, there was simply the determination to have correct information—and correct information there was. While Capitalists grew desperate, and eagerly sent their wares and their credits to their heretical antipodes—to the realms of the U.S.S.R.—Rome, Rome alone and single-handed, took upon herself the whole responsibility for this world. While everybody else was in despair, fighting hysterically, turning up their eyes in horror, whining for mercy and making suicidal pacts, the Church went her way alone, striking ever deeper and deeper blows, through quiet, indirect channels, at the heart and the head and the marrow of the new, terrible, mortally unhappy heresy of a levelling-down of humanity.

PART I

BEHIND THE SCENES

WENDEL, the man-servant, entered and announced briefly:
"Herr Korinski of the Berliner Morgenpost to see you."

"Good," said Eugen Döring. "Ask him in."

With that he laid down his pencil, and leaned back in his hard chair. He was tired out with writing; he pushed his copy-paper to one side, together with the coloured pencils, rolled-up photographs, newspaper cuttings, the gum-pot and brush, and the long scissors that were already clammy with use. The interruption annoyed him at first, but subconsciously he was immensely glad of it, for now he had a good excuse to put aside all that mass of work with a clear conscience and to spend a good quarter of an hour chatting, giving and getting tit-bits of news and gossip. He had a premonition that one who was charged with a mission was to enter that door, to give him his orders, for some strange task. The hissing of steam in the radiator seemed to stir him in a mood of excited expectancy.

A rap on the door.

"Come in!"

Korinski strode through the doorway. Without rising, Eugen Döring held out his hand.

"Good evening, revered colleague!" he greeted him, chaffingly. "And to what do I owe the exceptional honour of seeing a member of the staff of the Berliner Morgenpost in the blessed apartments of this Rapsikai rag?"

CHAPTER I

BEHIND THE SCENES

WENDEL, the man-servant, entered and announced briefly: "Herr Korinski of the *Berliner Morgenpost* to see you."

"Good," said Eugen Düring. "Ask him in."

With that he laid down his pencil, and leaned back in his hard chair. He was tired out with writing; he pushed his copy-paper to one side, together with the coloured pencils, rolled-up photographs, newspaper cuttings, the gum-pot and brush, and the long scissors that were already clammy with use. The interruption annoyed him at first, but subconsciously he was immensely glad of it, for now he had a good excuse to put aside all that mass of work with a clear conscience and to spend a good quarter of an hour chatting, giving and getting tit-bits of news and gossip. He had a premonition that one who was charged with a mission was to enter that door, to give him his orders for some strange task. The hissing of steam in the radiator seemed to wrap him in a mood of excited expectancy.

A rap on the door.

"Come in!"

Korinski strode through the doorway. Without rising, Eugen Düring held out his hand.

"Good evening, revered colleague!" he greeted him, chaffingly: "And to what do I owe the exceptional honour of seeing a member of the staff of the *Berliner Morgenpost* in the blessed apartments of this Papistical rag?"

Korinski hastened to accept the invitation to be seated, and drew out notebook and pencil.

"It is about the Balkan crisis and the Macedonian question," he said in a low voice. "If you could give me a few pointers about it—for instance, how that is connected with the Kossovo Committee in Vienna . . . . Here in Berlin people are telling the most amazing stories of how well posted you are in Balkan affairs. You are said to be the veritable *Doctor Rerum Balcanicarum!*"

He glanced a moment at Eugen's face, to see if he were smiling, but went on at once when he saw that there was no change in him. Secretly, however, Düring was highly flattered by Korinski's compliment.

When the latter came to the end of his recital of Düring's fame in newspaper circles, Düring took his turn. First he discoursed on the events of the last few years in Albania, of Fan Noli and Essad Pasha, of the assassination of Essad Pasha in Paris by Achmed Rustem Vrioni, and the part played by the Toptani family. It gave him a curious pleasure to be able to display his superior knowledge of such matters. It was as if he were having his revenge for painful years in the schoolroom at the hands of teachers in wearisome, specially hateful, and dreaded subjects; somehow, the recollection of that experience stirred in him again, across the gulf of the years. So he kept the direction of the conversation in his own hands, interrupted only occasionally by questions from Korinski, about the later developments of the situation—Achmed Zogus's seizure of power, and Bishop Fan Noli's journey to Moscow, the constitution of the Kossovo Committee by Hassan Bey Prishtina, and the unsuccessful attempt on his life. He spoke of the assassination of Zena Beg, by Zia Vulciternas, and of the Bashkimi Kombetares, of the Serbian policy in Albania, and Giani Beg in Diakovica, of the attempted assassination by Ndok

Gjeloshi and Aziz Cami of the King, in Vienna, and of the parts played by the Miridites, and by the Catholic tribes, Hoti and Gruda.

It rather tickled him to rattle off all the unpronounceable names. He went on to say something, finally, of the organisation of the *Imro*, the Inner Macedonian Revolutionary Organisation.

"You must tell me more about this," said Korinski, when Düring suddenly broke off, after speaking of this body somewhat cautiously.

"There is not much more to be told," countered Düring drily.

"That is very unfriendly of you," said Korinski, importunate and challenging. "There is a great deal more that you know! And we—we of the *Berliner Morgenpost* are sufficiently well informed to know that you are so far a sympathiser of the *Imro* as to spend your spare time in that part of the world, to take your weapons down from the shelf, and to side with the plotters. . . ."

"Indeed!" said Düring, suddenly stiff and abrupt. He glanced up at the picture of St. Ignatius Loyola, where it hung above his desk, and made a successful attempt to look unconcerned.

But Korinski would not be evaded.

"We know it all well enough!" he repeated. "We are the best-informed paper in the country—it is only in these Balkan affairs that your clerical paper has handicapped us— which is a scandal. But no wonder, either, since you—yes, you yourself—are no other than the famous Ivan Michailoff, the head of the *Imro*. Yes, here from your desk in Berlin you pull the strings of Balkan politics. You yourself. . . ."

At this point Düring was neither unpleasantly disturbed nor yet flattered. He laughed unrestrainedly. He knew Ivan Michailoff himself, and knew that he bore not the faintest resemblance to him. In fact, he turned a little to one side and glanced in the mirror, merely to see what the *Berliner Morgenpost* leader-writer's mental picture of Michailoff was like. But he saw only himself, tall and fair, with slightly tousled hair, blue eyes and high forehead, clean-shaven, with carelessly knotted tie. He would have represented perfectly the ideal of those who picture a Nordic racial type but for a round, tip-tilted nose set in the exact geometrical centre of his face, bequeathed to him as a belated reminiscence of some Wendish or Polish ancestor.

Korinski cleared his throat. That roused Düring from his day-dream, and he turned back, with the smile still on his lips. Only now it was an indulgent, gentle smile, and it did not fade when Korinski, with many professions of thanks, had closed the door after him with much circumspection.

For a while Düring gazed vacantly before him, then took up his work again. He wrote a sentence, and then another, but now nothing seemed to come right. The great, over-whelming grief that had fallen upon him the previous evening was something he could never shake off again. He racked his brain for some way out and could find none. He kept reminding himself again and again that only the savage paganism of worldly society was to blame for everything and that nobody dare set any obstacle in the way of the dictatorship of the proletariat. Once more he took up his pencil and tried to write, but to-day it seemed as if ideas would not come.

The door of his room opened to admit Medek arm-in-arm with Stegelin. Medek, like most of the journalists who were not of Berlin, had arrived a few years before from Vienna. He wrote mystical romances, and contributed to the news-paper snippets about the life and doings of the capital, which he dealt with in a dryly cynical and satirical tone which

any communistic pamphleteer might have envied. Only
slightly older than Düring, he was distinctly handsome and a
brilliant talker; sentimental only over women, a weakness
which he was always ready to confess sorrowfully. Stegelin,
on the other hand, was elderly, sickly, and slow of movement. Although over sixty, he seemed to be ageless in his
spiritual outlook, in which he was uncompromisingly
Catholic. He had never married and was much concerned in
youth movements.

"How goes it?" called Medek.

Düring looked up annoyed.

"Your blonde Teuton tresses are all tousled and ruffled.
We've just got away from old Uncle Paul, who is writing a
pseudo-Catholic novel for some obscure Bavarian press. Of
course, that'll compromise us beautifully again. That old
agent provocateur seems quite unaware that the very word
'Catholic' comes from the Greek *'kat holén tén gén'* ('all over
the world'). He ignores the universality of the thing, and
writes, in a clumsily archaic, peasant patois, some lumping
book where people address each other as 'Ho, good man!' and
'Ho, good wife!' and live a life of 'frugal fasting', on 'herbs
and nature's wine,' and wear coarse woollen waterproofs.
The whole served up with a sauce—beg pardon, a 'relish'—
of Satanic idolatry of the soil, of the most vilely materialistic
and geocentric brand imaginable. You may take the net
result as a stewing concoction of all the Catholic literary
bogeys!"

Hugo Stegelin had favoured Düring, while the other was
speaking, with his special, patronising but cordial smile.
He was somehow pleased at the engrossed and worried
expression on Eugen's face, but the latter felt himself
watched.

"Work is certainly not getting on!" grumbled Düring.
"Stegelin, will you just look at the stuff? This Polish corridor

has cropped up again. I started loathing these attacks on Poland ages ago!"

"You're right!" said Stegelin. "That has nothing to do with the Catholic Front!" And as Düring glanced enquiringly at him his manner grew more serious and he went on, as though delivering a lecture: "The Catholic Front—the Black Front—is a new complex of mine. I saw a Communist demonstration yesterday. Two echelons met, and greeted one another with clenched fists and cries of 'Red Front!' But the Black Front is much broader. It is a front that is within and around us. We lie in dry trenches, camp shoulder to shoulder, but in front of us lie all the Dragons—the pleasures of the flesh, the tendency to compromise, and tepidity, materialism, liberalism, deification of the State, nationalism, individualism, superman-snobbery; in a word, all the philosophical and political illusions that we have been fighting wildly and confusedly for two thousand years. We are driving them into a corner, to set up the authentic Millennium. But the enemy is encamped not only in front of us, but within us, so that our battle-front is doubled. All these anti-Christian ideas have their outposts in ourselves, striving to persuade us to go over to the foe, to give ourselves up—us, hungry, weary, and wretched as we are. Unceasingly the battle rages—by night, we are riddled with the rapid fire of dreams, by day temptations rage, the enemy propaganda kindles into flame, the world allures us, while we are being inwardly undermined, shaken, betrayed; stabbed. And the saddest part of it is that we are all merely a fragment of a sector of the infinite firing line; we never see the end. One day or another we are born, in the midst of the hail of shots; somewhere or other we find ourselves placed in the firing line; we battle for a few decades; and then in some way or other we go down under the fire."

Without waiting to give Düring any opportunity of reply

he was on his feet and away again, Rudolph Medek again hanging on his arm, on their way to the next room in the long corridor, to utter their unending speech of gloomy meditation.

Düring, however, began to ponder a little over what had been said while he cut strips from the hectographed newssheet of a press agency, puckered his brows, and dipped the brush in the gum-bottle. Then he stuck the cuttings on long strips of paper, and crossed his pencil through superfluities. To do this he lowered the lamp, so that only his hands lay within its pallid radiance.

It was now nine o'clock, and one by one the various members of the staff were leaving the building. When they had come, at six, the offices were still painfully clean and orderly in the bright glare of the electric lights; the warmth of the corridors had seemed "civilised" and polished. But now the windows of various rooms stood open, and the damp cold air of Berlin seeped in unchecked, whirling clouds of newspaper cuttings about on the writing tables and mingling with the chilled smoke of dead cigarettes, that still hung above the acrid-scented ink-wells. The whole editorial department seemed suddenly to have become aged, decrepit and decayed, and the very furnishings showed flaws and breakages that a few hours before had passed unnoticed.

Eugen Düring slipped into his coat, slapped on his hat, and hurried to the lift.

In the hall he stopped and looked for a moment at the pallid and restless hurrying throng that passed him, left the doorway, and hastened into the brilliant night, drenched with the heady radiance of the world without.

CHAPTER II

THE HOME FRONT

As he trod the wet asphalt, with the lights shimmering in its mirror-like surface, and glanced overhead at the cloudless, deep black of the night sky, there came over him a vague love of the night and of the darkness. "Perhaps we are really and truly the 'Black' party," he mused. "We may well be proud to be called 'Black.' It is day that is transient—but night is the primal beginning and the final end of things!" And then, as his mind harked back to his past life, it seemed to him that he was almost completely a man of the night— it was by night that he prayed, laboured, thought, meditated, worked; but by day simply hurried unreflectingly from one occupation to another, with idle talk and aimlessly directed activities.

Engrossed in such reflections, he crossed the Belle-Alliance-Platz, to the Hallesches Tor, where he took the overhead railway. Among strangers reeking of rain-drenched clothes, he thought again, "One gets so sick of it, with so many battle-fronts! The fight with an enemy ideology, confronting one and within oneself, is all very well, but the fight in one's home, with one's family—the Life-Front—there's the real horror of it. . . ."

At the Nollendorf-Platz he got out. He walked on from one street to another. The roads became ever more lifeless, quieter, darker, more deserted by the world. "The battle-front—the battle-front," he kept repeating to himself. Then he remembered the editor, Dr. Schlüter, again and the

trifling matters about which he had been gossiping that evening. "You can be proud now, Düring! The *Berliner Morgenpost* comes to you for information! You seem to be frightfully
close to the fountain-head!" It was true enough, he was very
close to the fountain-head. He was not only well up in the
political side of things; that would not have been enough. He
was young, eager for life and adventure. Others of his age
had affairs with women, wrote poetry, played hockey and
football, sped with weeping petrol-tanks round the dirt-
tracks, or pasted up Communist posters in the night. He had
turned in other directions. He had allowed himself to be led
willingly into the midst of the conflict. When the Great
War ended he was a child, a boy with long, lanky limbs,
untidy hair, and a malevolent disregard for everything that
was definite and ultimate. He had felt inwardly that he was
simply like a charcoal sketch scrawled on a white wall.
And years after the world-wide conflagration was over, and
people, morose and soured, returned aimlessly and apatheti-
cally to their homes, there was born in him the urge to make
up for what he had missed. Many young men not unlike
himself would perhaps have joined the Foreign Legion; but
he was far too restless and unruly for that—ever since his
schooldays he had been full of a fanatical hatred for all
routine and regulations. Till one day, a year after peace was
signed, suddenly and without confiding his intention to
anyone he went off to Morocco. It was when Abd El Krim
was waging his fight against the French and Spanish. Above
Tangier he joined the Riffs. For two months he lay in the
hills, thirsty, wounded, with shoulders bruised and aching
from his Mauser, then in September the Spaniards captured
him, near Melilla. In the camp a priest passed him, and he,
the former prefect of the Sodality of Our Lady at his college,
greeted him with the "*Nos cum prole pia.*" Ten days later he
was back in Berlin.

He did not study—he had not the inclination, and would not have been able to. Whereas others had become embittered and deadened by years of hard service on the Western Front, those eight brief weeks in the Riff country had sufficed to produce the same effect on him. He wrote articles on the Battle of Kabyle in the *Katholische Reichswarte*, and Dr. Schlüter invited him to join the staff of the paper. That appealed to him. The pay was scanty, but what did that matter? His father, whom he hardly remembered, had left him a considerable income, so that he was almost ashamed to be depriving others of a livelihood. He did not greatly concern himself about his mother and sister. They were extraordinarily alike, were dressed by the same dressmakers, and led a hollow society life. His mother, moreover, was a Protestant, not by faith, but by baptism; but Helga professed a luke-warm Catholicism, acquired during her convent education. The tepid pallor that coloured her faith was one of her most characteristic traits. In body, mind and soul she was feeble, pallid and vacillating. To this was added an appalling, unsuspecting simplicity and childlike lack of understanding of the phenomena of life. . . . Düring forced himself to stop thinking of his mother and sister. Automatically he drew the belt of his trench-coat more tightly about him, gaining an illusory sensation of military uniform, and thrust his hands more deeply into his pockets.

"I shall never be free from the Moroccan poison!" he reflected. "That was the beginning—and no man can foresee the end!" A year later he had been in Macedonia, then among the Druses, then again among the Kurds. He had fought against many European states; against France and Italy, against the Turks, the Serbians, and the Spaniards. Was that reconcilable with his conscience as a Catholic? His confessor had answered the question vaguely. In Sophia a Franciscan had given him a penance of three Our

Fathers; others had refused him absolution, with the exception of the German priests. When he confessed to them, it was treated as, at the most, a venial sin. But this did not satisfy him. The last time a Soviet agent had approached him in Berlin for the Afridis on the Indian North-West Frontier, he had repulsed him—but with a pang of reluctance.

Certainly one might be killed. He certainly did not do it solely from pure idealism. There was the sporting element as well. How near one often was to death, how wildly he had often had to fight, like a beast, for his life. But it was good, with all its plotting and stirring excitement. The Berlin streets had nothing like that to offer. Memory pictures swarmed before his eyes.

The streets through which he walked were empty and silent. Only now and again a car rolled by with a noise of tyres on the wet road. Behind their gardens stood the villas, and his thoughts turned reluctantly towards these—the houses with their white-walled nurseries, with their smell of varnish, milk, cambric, india-rubber.

He turned down a broad side-street, and came in sight of the villa where he lived with his mother and sister. It had been built not long before the war, and the first symptoms of a new style of art showed themselves in its design. The carefully tended gravel paths in the front garden, the garage behind the cropped bushes, the wide English sash-windows, the looped curtains in the hall, all contributed to give an impression of prosperity. He opened the wrought-iron gates and entered the garden. Then he let himself in at the front door with his latch-key, and was on the point of going straight up to his own room, when from the stairway he noticed a light in the small drawing-room, and heard voices there. He went in, and saw his mother and sister. Both were in evening-dress, smoking long Russian cigarettes; they lay indolently on deep-cushioned ottomans, their knees drawn up, and turned hostile and startled eyes on Eugen. His mother was about to say something, but checked herself and remained silent. She would not be the first to open the conversation.

Eugen stood there, on the deep pile of the carpet, stiff and erect. There returned to him in full strength and vividness the recollection of the ghastly scene of the previous evening; his mother's fright, and his sister Helga's confused evasions. And as he felt the two women's hostile gaze fixed on him, he knew that they had taken a decision with which he could not and must not agree. He would have preferred to turn round and go at once, but his conscience kept him. He flung his hat carelessly into a corner, and let himself fall into an arm-chair.

"What does the doctor say?" he asked his mother, without any preliminaries.

"The doctor?" her tones were carefully studied and cautious. "He confirmed our opinion!"

"Well! And what—what have you decided to do?"

"We are taking the only course that is possible," his mother replied, coldly reserved, as if she were conversing with a stranger rather than with her son. But he could feel that they were trying to make him understand that this was a matter concerning the women, in which it was not for him to interfere.

"And what is *your* view, as to the only possible course?" He turned in exasperation to his sister.

"Oh, don't torture me any more!" she cried, and buried her face in her hands.

"And so you intend to do murder. Just simple murder. Simply do away with an innocent life—just kill somebody in the most hygienic manner; 'do him in' antiseptically in an operating theatre, unbaptised, and perhaps, as a brilliant example of a civilised humane modernity, preserve him in a glass jar!"

He had spoken passionately, rising to his feet.

"You are excited and vulgar!" retorted his mother, angrily. "How can you even allude to things like that in Helga's presence? Any other brother in your place would have sought out his sister's seducer, and——"

"Rubbish!" he cried with contemptuous bitterness. "There is nothing to be done about a seducer, but there's a whole ostensibly Christian and really utterly pagan society to be converted from a foul double standard of morality and an uncharitableness towards sinners!"

"That is sheer hysteria," his mother broke in.

"Moreover," he went on, "moreover, it is a criminal offence. If you are caught you and Helga will be placed in the dock, and taken from there to spend six months in gaol. Councillor Schelling's lady will never shake hands with you again, Madame Gaillard of the Legation will never invite you to her teas, the *Vogue* won't publish your photos any more!"

His mother shrank back. She was suddenly seized with a frenzied terror of the proceedings in court, a case slowly unrolling like a film-play, of the publicity, of the State Prosecutors, of unfeeling, masculine wardresses, of police-inquiry clinics reeking with chloroform, and then a cell with the odour of decay. But she forced her mind away from these pictures, and frowned, forgetting to drop the ash from her cigarette.

"As it happens, Madame Gaillard herself found she was going to have a child six months ago. She did not want to have that spoil her season, so she went to Dr. Bauer," she retorted, cool and collected, letting each word fall separately in its place, as if laying out dominoes.

"But that same Madame Gaillard would return your letters

unopened if you had spent as much as two days in prison for the same crime," he scoffed.

For a while there was silence; then his mother in persuasive, pacific tones, said: "But I really cannot see, even from your religious point of view, what you have to say against it. After all, when it comes to the point, it is not a *person* that is going to be 'done in,' as you put it, but just a tiny little thing, a——"

"Ah, now I see it!" he interrupted bitterly. "The malice of murder depends on the measurement in inches; if I were to murder a dwarf from Sarrasani's or Busch's circus to-day, that would not be so disgraceful, by a long way, as if I were to go and drop strychnine into the morning coffee of some giant on show in Luna Park."

"Oh, what nonsense!" she interrupted. "You know perfectly well that a creature at that stage of development cannot feel."

"So one could slay with impunity a man rendered unconscious by drugs, on the operating table!"

"Mere sophisms!" cried his mother shrilly. "If the drugged man wakes, he feels and has intelligence. Intelligence, mind! What we have been discussing has no intelligence!"

"What we have been discussing will also feel and think in course of time. But according to your argument, one could strangle and poison almost all the inmates of the asylums. What you are trying to argue is absurd, but. . . . Oh, let's drop it!"

He stood up, took up his hat, and went off to his room without saying good-night. Alone, he flung his overcoat across a chair-back, sat down on the window-sill and looked out over the empty street. In the villa opposite dark shadows could be seen on the thin silk curtains moving rhythmically. Several cars were parked outside the door. The sight filled

him with an obscure, silent fury. He hated all wealth—even
his own—and pleasure, and bourgeois prosperity; women
making a parade of their femininity, Chinese lap-dogs,
refined social usages, and everything that had its source in
an unwritten, unspoken convention that had become empty
and meaningless. And yet his sister's misfortune touched
his heart more nearly than either of the women imagined.
He saw Catholicism's ancient enemy "Society," perpetrating
a fresh deed with its imperious edicts. And this time the
shells on that front were bursting very close to himself. He
knew, too, that the middle-classes would not be at his side
on that front, that to them also the sister with the illegitimate
child would somehow seem a disgrace, because all of them,
to the lowest of the proletariat, were infected with the same
poison of "Society"; and also, because all their own womenfolk would allow any cad to kiss their hands, so long as he
had neatly-creased trousers and well-groomed hair, while
they would give venomous and hostile looks to a girl if the
consequences of her sin took their natural course.

He did not know how long he sat there. Suddenly he
jumped up from the window sill and returned with swift
strides to the small drawing-room. It was in darkness. He
knocked at his sister's door. As he opened it he saw her, half
sitting up in bed, half crouching forward. A light burned
on the bed-side table. He sat down on the edge of the bed
by her.

"Have you come to torture me again?" she cried.

But he picked up her hand and pressed it. She felt the
warmth of his affection for her, and as if she could read his
thoughts, she began to tell him how it had all happened.

He heard her out without once interrupting. The sorrowful candour with which she spoke made him hopeful of
the strength of her conscience and her faith.

"Poor little Helga!" he said, with a depth of sincere

affection. "Now you must cast yourself for a while in the rôle of the martyrs. It will not be so terribly hard as you fancy. I am almost convinced, that even on our Black front there are those who will love and welcome you. But let's let this fellow go. There is no sense in trying to hold him. I know him slightly—he's a vapid, petty-minded provincial trying to be smart. But you are very weak and impressionable; he would get you into his own ways, and that would be terrible!"

"I simply dread all men! And women! And the papers! They'll all be down on me like vultures, like——"

"Now then, Helga, don't lose your head! You're not going to do what they've been advising you. That is rubbish from the nineteenth century. Be objective about it, and Catholic!"

"I shan't do it—but it would be so simple, Eugen, so simple. Think of the war—nearly everybody did some killing. Nearly all the men we meet who are a little older than you are——"

Then the mental picture that he had been seeing all the evening came before his eyes again in all its vivid reality. He saw himself again in front of that village inn in East Macedonia, with the small bombs in his hand, his features distorted, his burning eyes seeking out the illuminated targets. And then again he felt the connection, in primary responsibility, between those nights of death in the Balkans, in Africa, in Asia Minor, and his sister's catastrophe.

When he spoke again his voice had become dull and sad. "But you are giving me your promise to remain firm?" he asked her, a little more sternly than before. She gave him her hand, feebly. Her brown hair hung over her eyes, and the lamp-light outlined her features in delicate, vivid tracery, with the play of lights and shadows. He had got up, but at the door he turned.

"But if Mother takes you to the sanatorium you will weaken!" he cried suddenly. "When the car drives up to the hospital you will go up the steps, and not turn back, despite the promise you have given me, won't you?"

"Yes," she said. There was no sign of sorrow or desperation to be detected in her tone.

He sighed. "Good night," he said quietly, and turned to go. The door closed softly behind him, and his feet fell soundlessly on the thick carpet.

Up in his room he sat upon the bed, obstinately racking his brains for resources. He thought of several. Now he was definitely resolved to take action. "Scapinelli will help me," he mused, "Scapinelli!" On the table by his bed the telephone stood. He picked up the receiver, and dialled the number. Nobody replied.

Well aware that there was no more rest for him that night, he went down to the hall again, put on his trench-coat, drew the belt tight, shut the front-door after him, and hastened through the storm to the Nollendorf-Platz, where he just caught the last train on the overhead railway; half an hour later he reached the editorial offices of the *Katholische Reichswarte*, where he found Stegelin and the Jewish convert Sirower. He managed to detach his mind completely from all that happened at home, and entered forthwith into the pleasure of conversation. With Sirower the talk drifted on to the topic of Judaism.

"You don't understand a thing about Judaism," he told Stegelin. "You only look at it from without, instead of from within. When I look back at myself in childhood, at six or seven or eight years old, or later as a growing lad—with an inferno in the brain—one grew up amid a crowd of little, inflammable, embittered, unhappy frondeurs, the whole lot, people with the beggar's pride, typical emigrants, like the Russians in Paris or Berlin. All split up into small parties, all opposing one another—Zionists, Orthodox, Modernists; youth taking part in the problems of the immense Christian majority, in a process of progressive assimilation—defection, betrayal of the Fronde, ruled by the constant fear of expulsion. . . .

"Judaism is a religion that can be compared to a party of travellers waiting for the Messiah as one waits for a train. They come to the station, and ask when the train will start. The stationmaster tells them that the train started on its way long ago. But they will not believe it; in their hearts, deep in the ultimate depths of their hearts, there burns the frantic thought that the stationmaster must indeed have told them the truth, though they dare not admit it to themselves. With a feeling of fear and heavy aching feet they stay in the station, waiting, sit on the rails, settle their families into the waiting-rooms. The railway company's officers come and urge them to go home—but they refuse to have anything to do with that, to hear it—they stop their ears, and go on waiting, waiting, waiting. And whenever one of them creeps quietly away, they revile him. The world outside goes on, the Messiah has appeared there long ago, theological treatises are written about Him, He is worshipped in churches, in places of pilgrimage, in chapels. He has become the permanent, prevailing factor in the collective consciousness of the world; but the people in the railway station, out of all that, don't want to know anything about it. They gnash their teeth, they rummage in old books, and the time of the Messiah does not come back again. They have gone astray. Recognition often cries out aloud in their hearts, but they remain hardened, dumb, despairing. Nobody can understand anything of this torment, who has not lived with it. . . .

"And then there is something more. Till the birth of Christ we were the only valid Nationalists. The whole of the

Old Testament shows the one red thread running through it:
we see the Jews, with their kings becoming a nation, and
then openly sacrificing to idols; they return to their obedience to the one true God, and then lapse again into sacri-
fices to Baal. The punishment: war, captivity, sins, repentance. They return to their monotheism and to their country
—it was a magnificent battle for the preservation of the
nation, of the true faith. Its object—the birth of the Son of
Man among the believers in Jahweh. Keeping the place
ready for Him. The whole history of the whole world is only
for Him, and about Him. He is the real axis round which
everything revolves. Then comes Christ, and our passive
rôle is played—to be the platform for His teaching. Then
ought we to have gone forth into the welter of the nations,
surrendered ourselves, our mission completed, demolished
the irrational wall of ritual principles—for it no longer had
any meaning, none whatever.

"For eighteen hundred years we remained beneath the
surface, kept ourselves to ourselves. But then those who had
gone out from the ghetto into the world took up the Christian principles and teaching—externally, perhaps humanly,
but not divinely. To be Jewish meant, in the days of our
sacred mission, to be warlike, national and exclusive,
intolerant; David with his sling, the Pharisees, Samson with
the jawbone of the ass were our symbols, and Christianity
had obliterated the distinguishing mark of the Chosen
People. Peter was reprimanded by Christ for wounding
Malchus. Equality, freedom, brotherhood, forgiveness, were
preached.

"People are always talking about the influence of Judaism
over Christendom—they never speak of the Christianising of
Jewry. All the highways of thought in modern Judaism are
Christian in their origin; 'Liberal Judaism' is the reaction
against a harsh, terrorist Pharisaism, and is the realisation

of a misapprehended redemption; internationalism is the reaction against the 'nationalism-of-the-Chosen-People' idea; pacifism, a reaction against the national Samson-and-David complex——"

"The ardour of the convert!" interjected Stegelin.

"You're quite right," retorted Sirower. "There *is* also an ardour of the convert. Jewry came to realise that the ideas of Christianity should be sound, but not only 'sound', but essential for the continued life of the world in general. Only the conversion itself was not thorough, but merely superficial, merely a matter of externals. From Charity, from supra-national ideals, from the idea of Redemption, there grew noisy 'isms.' Without Christ! That is why these ideals, carried forward by Jews, are lifeless. Out of the advance towards the material, there at once came Capitalism. Christian ideas without Christ! In Freemasonry, in the Second International, in the League for the Propagation of the Rights of Man, in the Society for the Abolition of Capital Punishment, among the pacifists, in the movement for Prison Reform; in short, wherever benevolent humanitarian ideals of supra-national scope have been developed, the Jews have been in the forefront. It is true that every one of these ideas was originally Christian and non-Jewish; the Old Testament stood for nothing if not for authority, strictness, and nationalism. The Christian ideas were seized on by international Jewry, and so it comes about that side by side with official Christianity there has arisen a Judæo-Christian 'church' . . . and here comes the utterly Satanic tragedy: Christendom withdraws from these originally Christian principles simply because the Jews accepted them, just like the Yankees who abandoned Harlem when the negro invasion began. Christianity takes Pagan lines, it defends the gallows, uniforms, Chauvinism, and contributes its quota to the decay. But the Jewish 'church,' too, succumbs to its soullessness, to its unorganised weakness—to its Christless humanism, its fallacious democratic principles—and now pure paganism, pure Satanism, pure barbarism, comes to the top—Chauvinism and Bolshevism. And against all this there only stands one breakwater, the 'complete Church,' the Christian ideals *with* Christ. But as you can't bring Christ and the sacraments into the lodges, into the anti-war organisations, into the party headquarters, but can build a social, supra-national church, and fashion an instrument of world-peace, all humanistic Jews must absolutely, from the point of view of sheer reason, be converted *ex toto corde* . . . whole-heartedly——"

"And this Christlessness of Christian ideas," broke in Stegelin, "makes the Jews unpopular. Out of the supra-national ideals of Christ they have created an internationalism which simply denies the right of nations to claim existence."

"Exactly!" exclaimed Sirower. "But to a large extent it is many Catholics themselves who are to blame for that, because they have not bothered about the conversion of the Jews. If, instead of going into the capitalistic, or liberal, or socialist camps, we had been gathered into the Mystical Body, our position would have been very different! We should have become the storm-troops of the Church."

Stegelin blew his nose, and entered a protest against this peroration. He had nothing to say against it if one individua or another from the East lived to see his Damascus, but when it came to a wholesale migration—why, he saw cause for some cautious consideration.

Then Eugen had to enter a protest. He could not concede to Catholicism any monopoly of race—people were more than sufficiently fettered by local narrowness, and if there was a certain amount of stimulation and quickening by contact with people who were more engrossed with daily

life than with fundamental principles, that was not altogether
to be regretted.

But Stegelin was in full swing; he provided Sirower with a
few personal remarks, which the other did not allow to pass
unanswered, and then argued exhaustively with Eugen.
When the talk had altogether sunk to a shallow level,
Sirower let his chin fall on his chest and made sleepy faces.
Eugen yawned even more, and Stegelin let his speech drift
away in a grumbling murmur.

Before he left, about 4 a.m., Düring rang up the Jesuit
again. Once more the telephone buzzed unheard in an
empty room. Then he left the building with the two members of the night staff. When he opened the garden-gate of
the villa it was still dark. He put his shoes, worn down
with walking, outside his door for cleaning. Then he slept a
deep, sound sleep till nearly midday.

CHAPTER III

A NEW JESUITRY

The Jesuit Giovanni Battista Scapinelli had not been home at all that evening. He had been rushing from one quarter to another collecting material, details, and statistics for his work on the "Psychological Classification of Places of Amusement." Having cast his notes into form on his typewriter, he went into the bathroom, washed himself thoroughly, letting the cold of the water drive out the growing weariness from his limbs, rubbed his limbs till the skin was red and glowing, and put on fresh linen and black clothes.

Before the glass he hastily adjusted his Roman collar. His features smoothed themselves out. They had now completely lost that watchful, intent, cautiously defensive expression that they had worn as he went from one tavern to another in the East End of Berlin, by the Silesian Railway station and the Rudolph-Platz.

Now he was once more the man of culture who supped in the evening at the Nuncio's palace or in the houses of the rich, spoke from the pulpit in the Hedwigskirche or into the microphone of the broadcasting station at Königswusterhausen. He had one of those disconcertingly open, lofty, austerely benevolent, and yet regularly chiselled faces that seem peculiar to the majority of Catholic statesmen and politicians—such an expression as Brüning wears in the uproar of the Reichstag, a vivacious and clear-cut face, such as St. Ignatius displayed to the world.

Before he left his room—it was at an hour when Eugen
Düring had long been asleep—he put his notebook into his
overcoat pocket, then locked the door and ran down the
steps. He rode on the top of a groaning motor-bus, hair
fluttering in the wind, hat in hand; stood on the step of an
electric train, jolted from side to side, and waited impatiently
on crowded platforms; then looked at a certain tram-driver
and the way he whirled the lever in nervous circles, dashed
across busy crossings at the double, was carried high over the
roofs of the neighbouring houses by a buzzing lift, till at last
he stood in a corridor through the windows of which he
looked down over the morning life of Berlin. Involuntarily
he became aware how orderly and harmonious the houses
looked when seen from the streets, and how desolate-looking
now were the irregular masses of pits of light blacked out by
sooty pinnacles, the tangle of wireless aerials, the shadowy,
silent courtyards, the rusty gutters of the roofs, the broken
tiles, gaping attic fanlights, tinny screeching wind-vanes, and
filthy reeking chimneys. "That is the mind of the world!" he
reflected. "In the worm's-eye view, everything is fair and
beautiful. . . ." The wind moaned gustily through the
network of telephone cables, rousing him from his musings.
He turned and hurried on to a brown door that bore no name.

Shuffling steps were heard, and a transom opened.

"Who is there?"

But Scapinelli merely answered with a curt, "I . . . open
the door, anyhow!"

The door gave, little by little. He saw first a crevice; then
it widened, till a front parlour smelling of coffee and petroleum and paraffin was visible, and a woman of uncertain age,
peering through large, horn-rimmed glasses.

"Do you know me?" asked Scapinelli, quietly and un-
assumingly.

"Yes—indeed!" said the woman, with unfeigned pleasure.

"I certainly know you—from descriptions and church papers—your picture, I mean—you are Father Scapinelli."

"—of the Society of Jesus," he completed dryly. "I want to speak to you. That is if you are Frau Knunke? You are? The Prefect of the Sodality of Our Lady of the Immaculate Conception?"

With many bows and curtseys and circumlocutions she led him into the "best room."

"I must go at once—so I won't sit," he explained to begin with. "I have just one question to ask you: What would you do if you found that a member of the sodality had illicit intercourse with men?"

At first the question disconcerted her terribly—then she pulled herself together and replied, definitely and emphatically: "I should immediately secure her expulsion from the sodality!"

"Indeed!" said Scapinelli icily. "So that is how you would imitate Christ! Don't you know that there is a possibility that—let us call the child by her name—Malva Selbig may be proclaimed a Saint, and you not? Mary Magdalen was proclaimed a Saint! Don't you know, then, that you turned out Malva Selbig precisely at the moment when she had the most need of the sodality's charity?"

Frau Valerie Knunke had turned white. From anybody else she would not have withheld her rage and indignation at such an attack. But with such an "important person" she dared not give free rein to her feelings, so she replied with great restraint and caution: "But I can't demand of my young ladies that they should go on working with Selbig; my young ladies——"

"You talk about your young ladies and forget altogether to include yourself!" he answered sternly. "You seem to be very thoroughly convinced that none of those young ladies has ever committed any sin in the same connection."

"I know nothing about that!" she cried, quivering with agitation.

"You don't know, and I don't know either! Only God knows. . . . But you, you must know about yourself; have you never sinned, even in thought, in the same way? *Never?*" His voice rang out stern and threatening.

For a space, there was silence in the room, and only the singing of a canary could be heard, hopping thoughtlessly about in its narrow prison.

"Yes," came a toneless murmur eventually.

"You will not seek re-election at the next election of prefects," said the Jesuit, "but on Saturday go to your Director to confession."

He turned to go and walked mechanically down the stairs. Flight after flight. At the bottom, he was welcomed by the sun, shining out in broad streaks—it was a brilliant, glittering spring sun, like a water-colour on some carton. He blinked at it abstractedly, glanced at his notebook and at his watch, hailed a taxi, jumped in and eventually reached the Georgenstrasse. Scapinelli paid the man. On the door of the house was affixed an array of characters, strange and meaningless to any but the initiate: S.S.S., C.F.A., K.K.K., A.A.A., S.S.Z., and a lot more. Here, up two flights of stairs, worked Sonnenschein.

Sonnenschein was the "Pope of Berlin." That was how he was satirically dubbed by the Liberals and the Communists. He lacked the cool repose of Scapinelli. He was full of temperamental exuberance, and the enthusiasm that filled him expressed itself unrestrainedly in his work. The restless energy with which he was filled never failed him. Scapinelli worked with directions from Rome, with the most complete method and order, always looking well ahead, in his work and thoughts following an almost unbroken routine—vigorously dividing his time between attack, defence, sleep, prayer, and examination. Sonnenschein, on the other hand, was rushed, muddled, deeply engrossed one moment and breaking off the next. Thus he seemed the more human, and in society at large was the more popular; he was always indulgent, confiding, ready to cross any gulf. Scapinelli was more of the Grand Inquisitor, the man who looked relentlessly at faults, who punished, judged, threatened; the man who gave definite instructions and always examined afterwards whether they had been scrupulously carried out, and who only busied himself with details when he was arranging tests. Sonnenschein's tragedy was well known—as was everything about him. He had come to Berlin to inhale a Catholic spirit, and the doctor, with the callous stethoscope at his chest, had given him ten years to live. He had been grateful for this information. Of Scapinelli next to nothing was known. It was known that he had been in almost every European capital, that he bore powerful recommendations from the former Nuncio—and nothing more.

Sonnenschein sat at his desk, on which lay a whole heap of papers, letters, cards, telegrams, documents and pamphlets. Here in the office of the S.S.S., the Secretariate of Students' Social Work, he was like a spider in its web. Hither came for assistance all the stranded, impoverished, hungry, sick, of the educated classes in Berlin; those who passed the night in the *Palme*—as the Asylum for the Poor in the Fröbelstrasse was called—the venereally diseased, the tuberculous, the broken-down, the unemployed, the frauds, the pick-pockets—newcomers straight from the prisons of Berlin—professors, artists, farmers, students, clergy—anyone and everyone. And for all he had help, a kind word, a piece of bread, a shelter, a job.

As Scapinelli entered, Sonnenschein, who had just set the telephone receiver to his ear, beckoned him forward to take a seat. "Hallo!" he said at last. "Dr. Sonnenschein speaking. Is that you, my dear lady? Delighted to speak to you! You remember telling me about three months ago at a meeting of the Historical Society for Catholic Brandenburg that it would be an infinite pleasure to you to be able to offer shelter to starving students? You do? Splendid! Well, I'm coming this evening with six other hungry men to your place. Er——? Oh, you won't be at home this evening? What a pity. I shall not be able to see you. So it will have to be your maid or your cook who will take us in and look after us. . . . What's that? You gave your cook and maid a holiday? Oh, then you will have ample time to put us up for the night and arrange for us. And the keys you can leave with the caretaker. Can't you? You are afraid she will not know me? Tell her that I wear the badge of the Sodality in my buttonhole. Good-bye!"

He glanced for a moment nervously at his visitor, reluctantly roused from his thoughts; then: "Only one more call and then I'm through." And again his finger tugged at the telephone-dial.

"Hallo! Dr. Sonnenschein speaking. How do you do, Councillor?—I've got to come on you for those 350 marks —you know the circumstances—the man embezzled. To-morrow is the audit. If the defalcation is discovered he'll be thrown into the street. Wife and children will starve. Besides, he'll be in the mud; . . . he'd never get a job again. I mustn't repeat the name over the telephone. You haven't the money at home? That doesn't matter. Your credit's good. You have acquaintances. Do please see that I have the cash here at the very latest by six o'clock this evening, here at the S.S.S. Good-bye!"

Breathing heavily, with sparkling eyes, he set the receiver on its rest.

"Scapinelli," he said, "you've always got money. I want thirty marks. Recently I attended a couple of married students. The man died. The Poor Society have arranged about the funeral, but we've got to find thirty marks extra for the coffin, because the man was six-foot-two, and it has to be made a special size."

Scapinelli wrote him a cheque for thirty marks. Sonnenschein lit a cigarette. The tobacco fumes rose acrid and sharp, and then Scapinelli began talking. He spoke at length about the notion of property.

"Private property does not make for holiness. . . ." he began. But Sonnenschein was bent over his notebook, writing. Streaks of sunlight fell across his high forehead. His lips were drawn tightly together, the lines from the corners of his nostrils drawn thin and taut.

Sonnenschein needed Scapinelli's views for an article in the *Katholische Reichswarte*. As he ran rapidly through the notes of this his mind reverted unwillingly to the *Kirchenblatt* for which also he was due to write an article for Sunday. "Well, I shall have to write in the express to-night," he mused. "I must just make sure I don't forget the portable typewriter." The Church paper was his pride. His articles were read everywhere—even in the editorial offices of *Vorwärts* and the *Rote Fahne*. They were written with a verve, a terseness, and an incisiveness that might have come from a Communistic and prolific pen wielded by a guard in charge of patients maddened with drink or frenzy. Whether he was dealing with the structure of Catholicism itself, with the process of beatification, with a Communist outrage, with the lights of an electric sign, with the sitting of a committee, a political election, a batch of statistics of morality, a trip abroad, the plan of a South German cathedral, or life in a convent in the Electorate, he drew a uniquely vivid word picture. His was no dead sketching in charcoal, no pallidly tinted water-colour; far from it—he squirted the rich oil-colours directly at the canvas, and worked with the palette-knife. His articles were restless, and a cause of restlessness in others. His style departing from every known model, seemed a mixture of letters and exclamation-marks. Besides the *Kirchenblatt* and the *Katholische Reichswarte*, he also had the Catholic Proletarian High-School, and the Academical Library, the S.S.S., the charge of souls among the Berlin Italians. Yet in comparison with Scapinelli, he seemed lacking in organised activity. Scapinelli saw in men only weak and poor creatures, who were to be rigorously and instructively handled; Sonnenschein, on the other hand, "mixed" with men, lunched anywhere uninvited, placidly slipped his shoes off under the table if his feet ached, lent money and never claimed it back, wrote his mendicant appeals in all directions on open postcards, and usually took his collar off in the office.

That particular day was an unusually restless one for Scapinelli also. As he had not slept the night before, fatigue gradually began to make itself noticeable. The popular songs of the public houses still echoed in his ears, too. Every now and then he would find his lips shaping to whistle the tune of "Now You Just Listen To Me"—then he would pull himself up and concentrate on the battle of words that awaited him.

Half an hour later, he was actually addressing angry Nationalists at a party headquarters. "You are mistaken if you think that we should go against your racial ideas! We should be just as filially obedient to a Chinese or Negro Pope as to an Italian one. . . ."

Then he took a taxi again, climbed more stairs, rang at closed doors, explained to a gentleman with a woolly white moustache that the State was a soulless mechanical abstraction; evolution ("but, please, not 'progress'—we have outgrown that fairy-story, long ago!") had abolished the conception of a rigidly demarcated, self-contained, narrowly bounded state. Over a generation ago, Leo XIII was already against compulsory military service. Now, we have gone still farther—a fight against atavisms is a fight for Rome.

The old gentleman sighed. The Jesuit shook his flabby, limp hand, and went. There was no lift in the building. Once more he hurried down the carpeted staircase. He was hungry. He must eat somewhere. In a coffee-shop he ordered two eggs beaten up, and as he consumed them read the *Völkischer Beobachter*. He looked at the time again. He rushed off to the Presbytery of St. Anthony, and then back by the Silesian Railway station. There he spent ten minutes in terse, impressive speech to the priest, and from there went to St. Joseph's Presbytery, thence to St. Aloysius in the Ofenerstrasse, from there again to the Church of St. Clement, the Church of the Rosary, and St. Hedwig's. He dashed from the electric railway to the motor-bus, from motor-bus to taxi, from taxis to stairways, to attics, along corridors, into parlours, into workshops and factories, into presbyteries, into poorhouses. Finally he arrived at the French Embassy, where he was due for tea. He found himself sitting next to Mme de Kergeilhou and a dear old gentleman whom at first glance he took for an Egyptian diplomat.

"That is Councillor Nahabedian Tschichlidze of the Soviet Legation," whispered Mme de Kergeilhou. "He is a prince, and—a Bolshevik!"

Scapinelli looked at him attentively. He was extraordinarily fat, with slightly bulging eyes, and his hair already beginning to show some grey.

"You are a Bretonne, Madame?" asked Scapinelli, between two bites of bread-and-butter.

"Yes," she said, "a Bretonne—and a staunch Catholic. When Pasteur was asked how he could be a believing

Catholic, with all his scientific knowledge—a question which only the nineteenth century could have asked—he replied, 'It is because I know so much that I have the faith of a Breton peasant. If I knew a little more I should have the faith of the Breton peasant's wife!'"

Nahabedian turned round. Clumsily he wheeled his arm-chair about and stared at the speaker.

"The nineteenth century? Why the nineteenth century?" His brow creased into great, fat wrinkles.

"That was the culminating point of the trial period," explained the Jesuit.

"What trial period?" asked the envoy, puzzled.

"Let's get that clear!" said Scapinelli. "First we Catholi-cised Europe and exercised the supreme power here for fifteen hundred years. Then human nature was suddenly seized with an attack of irrational madness, a sudden dementia, and believed, in its megalomania, that it could stand entirely on one foot. Then there followed that unique process, which began with the Humanists and ended with the Liberals of the nineteenth century—the process of disintegration by individualism, secularism, which ended in the Great War. We have now let human nature carry on for four hundred years, and you have—as we perfectly well foresaw—driven the car right into the ditch. Economics, philosophy, art, politics are all in a state of chaos. Matters have by now got into such disorder that we are taking the privileges away from the worthy little fellows, and will now reform them in our own way."

"What sects do you mean?" Mme de Kergeilhou now asked in surprise. "The Protestants?"

"N-no," said the Jesuit, with some hesitation. "The Protestants are a Christian sect, a Christian heresy, who have selected a certain portion of the Gospel for themselves. But to return to what we were discussing before; we have for four hundred years failed to reckon with one factor—the secularised masses had on the one hand been turning away from Christ, but on the other hand, under various cloaks, so that they should not recognise their origin, adopted typically Catholic lines of thought again; the prohibition of usury, trades-unionism, or the idea of the guilds, opposition to the Superman-complex of the individualistic, Nietzschean school—in a word, it amounts to a Catholic heresy, that accepts the circumference of the Faith and denies its centre, seeking to base it instead on an empty materialist 'doctrine'— hence materialist socialism, hence bolshevism!"

"So you consider bolshevism a Catholic heresy?" said the Councillor with the Armenian-Georgian compound name, dubiously.

"Of course!" exclaimed the Jesuit cheerfully.

"And how long will it be before you have taken the reins out of the people's hands again?" asked the other, rousing himself energetically from a gloomy reverie.

"These things are always rapid," said Scapinelli, quietly. "Just a wave of the hand—perhaps a wave of the arms— perhaps, three or four generations. A mere moment to us!"

"You will find that even that is not long enough—in fact, you will find it is never. But tell me, what would follow?"

The Councillor had spoken heatedly, but Scapinelli just emptied his cup.

"I must be going," he said suddenly, turning to the lady. "I haven't a minute to spare. But I am looking forward to meeting you again," he added, turning to the Councillor, "to-morrow. I will come and see you at . . . about six in the evening? Good!" He hurried off again. Outside, the lamp-lit evening life of the streets rushed past. With full lungs he breathed again the petrol-laden air, and strode swiftly over the pavement, head bent forward. He pulled his hat well down over his forehead, and was suddenly glad to be unknown and alone in the midst of many people. All the crowds and noises, bells and hooters, shouts and cries of the streets of the great city he enjoyed. But his thoughts were still busy and undistracted. His enjoyment was simply something external.

When he got home at about eight o'clock he found Eugen sitting on his doorstep.

"Hallo, Düring! What are you doing here?" he called out. "Has the *Reichswarte* already gone into liquidation then?"

"I wanted to speak to you yesterday, Father—but I couldn't get you on the telephone all night."

Scapinelli opened his door, let Eugen go first, and gave him a seat. Without any circumlocution, Eugen began telling him about his sister, and Scapinelli listened attentively.

"The temptation is great—too great," he said finally. "You could have gone straight to Father Sonnenschein, but I shall be only too glad to help. We'll simply send the girl to St. Maria Afra on the Liepnitzsee, with the Grey Nuns. I'll be outside your house with my car about eleven tomorrow evening."

He shook Eugen's hand warmly.

When Düring had gone, Giovanni Battista Scapinelli, the Jesuit, knelt at the *prie-dieu* as rigid and upright as he had been all day long with his fellowmen. At first one word followed another mechanically and it seemed as though he were repeating mere strings of empty phrases. But gradually a great warmth stole over him and, caught up as it were in the prayer, he pressed his head against the hard white-washed wall. He felt at last in the unrestrained communion with God such joy that he forgot all about the struggle for the establishment of the Kingdom of Heaven on earth and like a child gave himself up completely to this Presence which seemed to animate the whole world.

CHAPTER IV

TWO KINDS OF ARGUMENT

WITH a restored sense of peace and calm Eugen Düring took a taxi back home. It seemed to him that the next day would be full of trouble and conflict, and it was only in order to be fresh and strengthened for the clashes he anticipated, that, after a quick supper and a bath, he went straight to bed. Being unused to such early hours he could not sleep, and about ten o'clock he still lay awake on his tumbled pillows, with thoughts and memories of episodes in his life chasing each other through his mind. But this time they were not colourful pictures of lands filled with adventure that thronged before his eyes, but rather fragments of the more distant past, whose vividness had long faded. He saw himself back in the austere provincial secondary school where, for the sake of his people, he had pursued his studies, perfunctory and shallow as they were. When they brought financial pressure to bear on his mother to guarantee his future career, he left the school and went straight into the big college in the neighbouring capital. The restraint, the discipline, the liberal-conservative spirit, almost drove him to desperation. And yet these four years of his life had been a valuable preparation, a period of quest and seeking, of roving from idea to idea. It was here that the spirit of collective co-operation had first cured him, as by the surgeon's knife, of an anti-social individualism; it was there that he first learned to efface self and think of himself as a link in a chain.

It was in the middle of this period that Eugen made his first contact with love. Looking back at it, he saw himself at that time so immensely vain, gauche, and grotesque, that he writhed, and made a determined effort to turn his thoughts in other directions, away from the embarrassing memory of this event. Out of it there had developed later a silent scorn for everyday romance. Later he met other women who simply roused his senses without his being at all carried away in his inner self. He had never yielded to indulgence. There was much in the world around to antagonise him, many warnings, that either took their rise from Catholicism or flowed into Catholicism, and in addition, the clear perception that such an act meant surrendering one's own personality and ego, primevally fixed by God, to another person. The thought that perhaps that other person found in it nothing but sport, whim, or sensual pleasure, pure and simple, would have been anything but attractive to him. The other must absolutely have the most complete intellectual and spiritual and all-round comprehension, and be almost as completely long suffering; and then she must not and could not go to any other man in the world and carry his secret thoughts with her. There came into his thoughts only one solitary person to whom in anticipation he looked forward with pleasurable yearning in this connection—his wife.

This longed-for ideal obsessed him more than was desirable. Even while still at school he had pondered over the same topic, and, like every Catholic who begins to consider the divine laws one-sidedly, he arrived at heretical fallacies. He found himself on the very threshold of Tertullian-Montanist ideas, denying the right of re-marriage after the death of a marriage partner, only to realise at last, after prolonged study, the materialism of such a view. It was this collapse of a laboriously built-up world of ideas that made him look on all other ideologies, by comparison with Catholicism, as on stars blotted out by the sun. Then if one may have two, or even three, women standing by one "up on high," who have risen from death with clear-seeing love, and not see them oneself, in the whirling mutations of life, God and Self, Self and God, then race, national prejudice, law, age, calling, standing, all dissolve in the searchlight of Catholicism.

And yet he felt, apart from all this, that his destiny was bound up with women. There came a time when he was constantly meeting women, near them, becoming their friend, adviser, confidant. He brought to them all his un-bounded sympathy and kindliness, as it were to a distinct nation, a separate race. At first this was a sentiment full of compassion for living beings who seemed to him undeve-loped, childish, awkward, almost grotesque, who were not made for the fight and conflict of the world around them. It was only later that he came to recognise them as fully developed human beings, though without any of the tragic, bitter after-taste of Rudolph Medek, who, with every indication of their developed independence, saw the devil of sex suspending, as it were, a two-edged sword between man and woman.

In the afternoon he went to the *Reichswarte* office at his usual time. Stegelin greeted him at the entrance with the clenched fist and the war-cry, "The Black Front!"

At the same moment, the Jesuit Scapinelli was approach-ing the U.S.S.R. Embassy. The porter stared at the sight of the Jesuit in amazement. They were little accustomed, at that embassy, to be visited by priests wearing the Roman collar. Stealing another side-glance at Scapinelli, he took up the telephone and spoke to the Councillor, enquiring whether it was really correct that a certain Father Scapinelli was to be admitted. On a voice replying in the affirmative, the gate swung inward on its hinges, and an iron grille opened.

Beyond this iron grille Scapinelli was received by a clean-shaven, tall, aquiline-nosed serving-man, who led him up three flights of stairs to a door on which the name of O. Vazetis could be read, leading to the Councillor's apartment. This he opened, and closed again behind the entering guest. Scapinelli was locked in.

Now a snub-nosed, starched-capped maidservant came to Scapinelli and ushered him to Nahabedian's reception-room. The latter at once made his appearance and bowed with much ceremony.

"You make the way of transgressors who steal documents very hard," said Scapinelli, wryly, as he sank into an arm-chair.

"Our land has many enemies," declared the other, proudly, offering Scapinelli a cigar, which he accepted.

"You are—were—of royal rank?" the Jesuit asked, apropos of nothing.

"Yes—perhaps—well, one can't put it like that," replied the Caucasian, placidly casting about for the right word. "My father was a Prince Tchikhlidze. Nahabedian is only my name on my mother's side. My mother was an Armenian. It has very seldom come about before that a Georgian and an Armenian have married. Well, as regards my father's title of Prince—Royal Prince, that is, *Fürst*, not *Prinz* —its authenticity is rather doubtful. In the thirties of the last century the dynastic archives were burned at Mzchet, and for some years it was sufficient for the establishment of a princely title to have the sworn attestation of two kindred, which was naturally not difficult to obtain. My mother's brother, on the other hand, was an Armenian revolutionary, an ardent sympathiser of the Dashnakists. That is why I put my Armenian name first. My mother recently died at a great age in Paris."

"In Paris?"

"Yes, we generally used to live, formerly, half the year in Paris. I was myself to a large extent brought up in Paris," he said, not without pride. "After all, we Caucasians are Europeans."

"And yet you turned Bolshevik? Surely, that is really too primitive!"

"Monsieur," replied the other, with a slight tinge of affectation in his voice, "*La garde se rend, mais elle ne meurt pas!*"

Then he pulled himself up, and added hastily, "That was simply playing with words, of course, a bad habit of mine. In truth, in grim, earnest truth, I am a convinced and confirmed Communist."

He had spoken swiftly and emphatically. Scapinelli stared straight before him with immobile eyes—he believed him implicitly. He felt thoroughly convinced that he was not dealing with a mere cynical time-server. Otherwise he would not have come. But the Councillor was vexed with himself for the phrase he had let fall a moment before. An uncomfortable pause ensued.

Mirhan Nahabedian turned his long head on his thick-set neck, and fixed Scapinelli with a direct, unrelenting gaze.

"Yesterday, at tea, you, also, juggled idly with words. You spoke of bringing back the lost sheep. You are perfectly well aware that, out of your dwindling position, you will never recover world-wide supremacy."

"We are not speaking of a dwindling position," answered Scapinelli, accepting a brandy. "Remember what I said yesterday about Catholic heresies. You forget that the Catholicity of the Middle Ages was geographically and quantitatively limited to the small peninsula of Europe. But at the present day the whole world is impregnated with the seed of Christianity and of its organically kindred offshoots, of Catholicism and of its modes of thought. I spoke yesterday of Socialism and Bolshevism. Look at Europe, and we see that the typically anti-Christian philosophies are obsolete. Where is Pantheism to-day? Where is Spinoza? Where is Nietzsche? Here in Europe, thinking and discerning people feel and realise that the ultimate refuge from all dissensions and perplexities lies in Rome and with the Cross. We are completely certain of being the final and definite eschato-logical hope of all men—all men, from the rabidest Nazi to the most virulent Red-Front Bolshevik. And wherever we look we see Christian ideas, Christian modes of thought, Christian and Catholic heresies—whether we take Ghandi or Pacifism, Sun Yat Sen or Internationalism, Feng Hue Siang, Tchangkaishek, or the Collectivists, at the present day the seed of the doctrine of the Son of Man has been scattered fruitfully, taking practical form, over the whole earth. For-merly, our Church was surrounded by a desert, but to-day it has become the capital centre which has fertilised all the rest —to which all the world's streams of tendency converge. The Catholic Church has become a symmetrically balanced *Summa* of all the truths—outside it, look at the great chaos that prevails; they lean unconsciously towards us. Our task is to bring into this wild welter of Christian ideas gone astray some order, harmony and system, and unify them, *ut omnes unum sint in Christo*—that all may be one in Christ. The technicians have broken down the barriers of distance—they have discovered the radio, telegraph, telephone, teleprinter, airways, and rocket-cars, and in three or four generations we shall have cleared up most of the heresies."

Mirhan Nahabedian had made many awkward gestures while Scapinelli was speaking.

"That is all very fine and large," was the diplomat's retort, "but the suggestion that we Bolsheviks, as you have just said, are a Catholic sect is simply absurd. That cannot be your real opinion."

"I am in absolute earnest," Scapinelli assured him. "In the winter of 1917 I was down in the Capital—in Rome, I mean—and one day I was at dinner at Uccello's, the Secretary of State, with the Prefect of the Eastern Congregation of Rites, Kallikrati. We had just received and read, with great attention and interest, a newly arrived confidential report from Russia. We were feeling very disillusioned and irritated about it. We had expected to read some definite news, but we found nothing except an impressionistic account of an Oriental Manichæan state with gnostic excesses. This was simply fifteen-hundred-year-old stuff. A phenomenon of reaction against the Greek Orthodox primary gnosis. Ever since the Orthodox community, from Photius to Dostoevski, for thirty generations, has been preaching a war against every corporeality, everything concrete and material, all organisation and world-wide unity of the Church, the Bolshevik reaction has been bound to break out, aiming above all at more and more corporeality, materialism, organisation and world-wide unity of the Church or of the Party. The Manichæans, in their insistence on the repudiation of matter, swung suddenly round in the opposite direction, just like the Orthodox community, and revelled in a sort of Bacchanalian orgy. That is also the reason that we cannot leave the sects as they are, but must lay our hand on the wheel. The sects are utterly unfit to be left to themselves. The Orthodox Church, with its absence of any missionary work, is succeeded by Bolshevism with its hysterical passion for far-flung propaganda. Only in Catholicism, with its dual nature, can the proper balance of things, to which it evermore returns, be found."

"And yet it will be Bolshevist monism that will win the day!" exclaimed Mirhan Nahabedian, with curt irritation.

"No," Scapinelli smiled, "that is completely impossible. You have weaknesses in your system, and so must collapse. The Orthodox Church is a thousand years old, almost, and Protestantism almost five hundred—both are already in their death-agonies.   When you remember that East-European Bolshevism is only a reaction from the Orthodox Church, and reactions are always more short-lived than the original forces from which they rebound, because they are based only on the latter's partly spent energy perverted to the opposite direction, it is not too much to predict that the duration of Bolshevism will be under a hundred years——"

"And why must it be Bolshevism in particular that must fade out of the world after a hundred years?   Catholicism has lasted a couple of thousand years," broke in the other incredulously.

"Yes, you see," explained Scapinelli, "we owe that to the circumstance that we are precisely the only sanctifying Church. With regard to this attribute of 'the only sanctifying' one, we have always been constantly attacked by heretics of all shades; but this expression does not imply that everyone of a different belief is *a priori* excluded from eternal happiness—what it implies is not the condemnation of the individual, but of the heresy as a doctrine. For if people take only a single point of doctrine out of our structural unity of teaching, the whole thing caves in, everything crashes to ruin. Protestantism is dying out rapidly; that is the fault of its deficiency in definite moral standards; but Bolshevism is doomed to extinction on account of its foreignness to humanity, its inconsequence, and its optimism."

"What do you mean by foreignness to humanity, and inconsequence?" interrupted Nahabedian, who sat with his head resting on his hand, gazing before him abstractedly.

"Are you convinced that Communism is thoroughly practicable?" asked the Jesuit, before replying.

"Yes!" the word was let fall without hesitation.

"Is it your aim to abolish the family? Yes or no? But I will not put that so uncompromisingly: has the family, the idea of the family, a positive part to play, in any way defined, in the Communist State? Has the family to be done away with?"

"Yes—the family will be done away with."

"And the children will be brought up by the State—will be taken away from their mothers?"

"Yes— at least, that is our programme."

"Birth-control and abortion legalised?"

"Yes, of course."

"Now, just tell me," said the Jesuit, speaking slowly and deliberately, "what woman in the world, who has lost the positive Christian faith, will go through the ordeal of the months preceding childbirth, and the agonies of the birth itself, to bring into the world a child which, after the briefest possible interval, is going to be taken from her again?"

"And yet the Russian birth-rate is higher than—than the German, for instance," retorted the Councillor proudly.

"That is no wonder, since of the population of Russia only two or three per cent are members of a Communist organisation, while in Germany some fifteen per cent are, according to the estimate based on the last elections.* The tendency of the population statistics among those without religious beliefs in Western Europe, is, on the whole, to remain stationary. But nevertheless, that gloomy situation that I have sketched will not actually arise——"

"Ah! You admit that, yourself!"

"Of course. It won't come to that because you would rather be false to your programme. So that you will live, just like Protestantism, by a continual policy of making concessions, and then one day, quite painlessly and quietly,

*This was spoken in 1932.

'return to the primeval slime', as the German phrase has it
—simply fade out!"

Mirhan Nahabedian remained for a while in concentrated
thought, and sought for some escape from the argument,
desperately, but could find none. He poured himself another
liqueur-glass of brandy, and laid his cigar on the edge of the
ash-tray.

"Your view as to the Orthodox Church is very interesting,"
he told the Jesuit, finally.

They had sat talking a long while when Scapinelli was led
back from door to door by successive functionaries; night
had fallen over Berlin, and the busy shops were overflowing
with light that flung vivid yellow beams in great medleys of
rectangular patches across the pavements.

Eugen Düring sat with Stegelin, who had completely
forgotten the Sunday article he should have finished writing
for him. He wanted to lay it aside, unfinished, but Stegelin
would not allow that. He plunged his pen into the ink with
puckered brows, and scribbled furiously over the rough
copy-paper, his face bent till he was almost rubbing it with
his nose. And then Düring's gaze wandered from him to the
picture of the Nuncio Pacelli, which hung on the white-
washed wall above Stegelin's desk. Pacelli, too, had that
open, genial smile always on his lips, like Scapinelli; that
smile tinged with a hint of melancholy; sorrow at the perish-
able frailty of things, at the pitiful paltriness of his own
endeavours, at the meaninglessness of the great whirl of
activity around him. This smile of a world-weary ache, that
comes from experience and is yet free from pessimism,
seemed to Eugen to be the stamp of all his Catholic acquaintances who had passed the climacteric of life. Often there
arose in him a feeling of envy, and he would have gladly
accepted the shortness of their prospective mortal life, to

have had their faculty of soaring above things and gazing down on the world. He was conscious that he himself stood so close to life that he was like Stegelin, there, with his nose down on the paper he was writing on, that he only saw the great coherent whole by odd, glimpsed hints, often caught a momentary sight of a fragmentary scrap, and was none the less lost to the unity of it all.

He waited impatiently till Stegelin had finished his article. In the press-room, the advertisement section had been set up a long time past. He had to think of Helga again now, he was no longer master of his thoughts, and he was obsessed with an anxiety lest there might have been something happening at home to form an obstacle to his plan. These thoughts were broken into by the sound of Scapinelli's car outside. Stegelin had just finished his article.

The Jesuit was sitting in a dark, thin ulster. Eugen marvelled that he was not frozen as he sat down beside him. Scapinelli stepped on the accelerator, and the twelve cylinders hummed—they were off. Eugen looked at the speedometer; he wondered whether his mother was out at Frau Brinck's, the wife of the Councillor of Commerce, to dinner, or whether she was at home? A long dead and buried nervous awe of his mother, belonging to the bygone days of childhood, began to stir again in him. Then his nervousness disappeared again. *He* was the Catholic; it was for *him* to order and arrange. What had years or relative ages to do with that? Obstinate and self-absorbed, he sat in silence by the Jesuit's side. Ah, there they were!

He leaped down from the car and opened the gate. He ran through the hall and found Katharine, the maid. Helga he could not find in her room. Her trunks lay about, open and half-packed. He raced from room to room, switched the lights on and off, called out her name, and searched the attics. A haunting premonition grew within him, becoming

more and more a certainty—Helga had forestalled him and
fled. Obviously that was what must have happened. He
went into a box-room. Light seeped in with him. There
stood, rigid, white, tear-stained and trembling—Helga. He
bit his lips.

Silently she followed him to her room. They exchanged
no word. She did not utter as much as a sigh. He handed
her one article after another. He did not look at the time. It
must be more than half-past. Downstairs, Scapinelli waited
silently. He was entirely free from impatience. The trunks
were full. In the doorway, Katharine stood, with questioning face.

As he went downstairs with her, the Jesuit was already
awaiting them with the door open. A lamp shone nearby,
and Scapinelli used its light to study the girl's face. A few
minutes later the car was humming away northward. The
lights of the capital only sank out of sight behind them as
they neared Weissensee. At last the darkness of night
swallowed up the last of the outlying scattered outposts and
suburbs of the great city, and there was wafted against
their faces the night scent of damp meadows in early spring.
Eugen opened the roof, and the car seemed like a grimly
locked casket of steel that dragged struggling human bodies
pitilessly with it over the harsh highways. Helga drew a deep
breath. The invisible oppressive grip of the city was lifted
and the everlasting romantic sombreness of nature by night
had laid its spell on her.

Weary, helpless, and a little wretched from the sudden
change, she lay back on the leather cushions and stared up
at the pitch-black of the impenetrable sky. As soon as her
eyes had become accustomed to the darkness, she noticed
that the heavens were heavy with bellying, shadowy clouds,
that ran into one another like formless daubs of dim, dusky
water-colours. In front sat the Jesuit with his long, tapering

hands on the wheel, and the diminutive globule of blue light beside the gear lever cast weird shadows around his wrists. The rush of the wind did them all good; the cool draught freshened their faces, brisking the sleep-slackened skin, raced refreshingly over their brows and through their streaming hair. But the Jesuit and Eugen had to battle against the force of the wind—it had begun to drizzle, and the windscreen-wiper was not functioning so they had lowered the windscreen.

Bernau sped past them. In the streets all was still. Only here and there was a solitary light burning behind the blinds; the headlights of the car gleamed in winking cat's-eye rays, picking out lofty walls with ochrous yellow light, and transforming the intermittently bad roads into the light-and-shadow-chequered likeness of a landscape of the moon. Eugen turned round and looked at Helga. Her eyes were closed, and her throat thrown open to the elements. She made no attempt to shelter from them, but let them wreak their will on her. Her eyes were closed, she was trying to be unconscious of all that passed, to slip through everything in a dream, feeling nothing.

A light shone out in the distance: Lanke. Again the headlights wandered over the sleeping walls of houses and the unseeing panes of shuttered windows; again the endless, pitted road lay ahead of them. Uetzdorf, too, slipped past; their destination was not much farther. Their route lay through a forest. Beeches and pines grew up, wanly whitening, by the sides of their road, and their trunks shone in the glare of their headlights with a ghostly eeriness. Not far off sedge rustled in the wind—there lay the Liepnitzsee; but a garage came into the circle of their light, and before them, severe and simple, rose the Grey Sisters' country house—St. Maria Afra.

CHAPTER V

AND TWO DEVELOPMENTS

THE German-Evangelical correspondents of the paper were sending shoals of malignant criticism of Sonnenschein, who continued to be ill; the radiograms about the proceedings of the Eucharistic Congress in Australia were far from pellucid. In addition, Eugen had to edit a short pronouncement of the Jesuit's against the talisman and the superstitious use of "mascots" of St. Christopher on motor cars. So he had not much time to devote to thoughts of Helga and his mother, who behind his back had entrusted a private detective with the discovery of Helga's hiding-place.

On a rather quieter evening about a week later, Rudolph Medek came to his room in the offices again, and, after boring and irritating him for a good long while, suddenly asked, apropos of nothing, "By the way, what has become of Helga lately? Where has the girl got to? We never see her about, nowadays!" And, without waiting for any reply from Eugen, who had interrupted and was biting his lips in confusion, he went on talking. "This Sunday," he remarked, "I happened to be calling on Sister Brigitta and out there at St. Maria Afra I had such a strange experience, that I made up my mind I must certainly tell you about it. When I had said good-bye to Sister Brigitta I went along a long corridor, that led to one of the quadrangles, when whom do you think I saw walking across the quadrangle? No, can't you guess?"

"No," said Eugen, in a dead, expressionless voice. He

dared not look Medek in the face, and was ashamed of his evasiveness and lack of candour.

"It was Helga I saw!" cried Medek, loudly, and struck the table with his waxen hand. "I was utterly flabbergasted to see her there. 'Helga!' I called out, 'Helga! Hi!'—but she had already got to the corner. It was a very long corridor, and I ran after her. She had disappeared as if she had vanished into the ground! Now tell me—was Helga really there, or was that only an hallucination? As she turned the corner, I heard a noise like you'd hear if somebody banged a door. But there were so many doors across on the other side of the quadrangle, that I rather funked knocking at them all and asking the idiotic question, whether Miss Helga Düring had slipped in there."

"Helga," said Eugen, slowly, almost as if the words were forced out of him, and without lifting his eyes from his manuscript, "Helga was really at St. Maria Afra."

"The saint, Maria Afra, was a Greek. Her grandparents came from Cyprus. In *Augusta Vindelicorum*, the Augsburg parchment, she figured as *Grande Cocotte* of a famous house," explained Rudolph Medek, pedantically. "She was visited by two Spaniards, who converted her. Under Diocletian she was put to a martyr's death. But tell me," he broke in, interrupting the flow of his own lecture, "why did Helga so —well, let us say, avoid me? Is she staying there, then?"

These were the questions that Eugen had so been dreading. But it was Rudolph Medek who thus spoke to him, a man who stood side by side with him on the Catholic Front. He would not lie. And sooner or later it must be told.

"Helga," he said, crudely and plainly, so that he shrank back at the tone of his own voice, "is at St. Maria Afra because she is expecting a baby, and my mother at all costs wants to send her into a sanatorium to have her unborn child made away with!"

For a fraction of a second amazement was depicted in Rudolph Medek's eyes. Then, however, his expression changed to one of surprise and pleasure. "And so she will really bring the child into the world at St. Maria Afra?" he said, with forced ease.

Then he jumped up. "She's a great woman, your sister," he cried, enthusiastically. "Man alive!" he exclaimed, dropping into the real Berlin idiom for the moment. "And you didn't tell me a thing like that at once! Making a fuss about it like an old maid! This is good enough for a leading article. I'm going to see Helga first thing to-morrow morning. Here's a woman at last who has some guts."

Just before nine o'clock, the Jesuit came to the office, where he made straight for Eugen. He had had a letter from Sister Brigitta, in which she informed him that Helga was feeling quite well, on the whole, but rather bored. The library at the Sisters' country house was very modest; Helga had read both the novels of Medek's that were to be borrowed there, but had laid them down with reluctance. Could not newspapers and magazines be sent to her? She was also waiting for news from her brother, who had not yet written to her.

Scapinelli asked Eugen what sort of reports had come to hand from Russia.

"All quiet on the Eastern Front," answered Eugen, "only the reception on Saturday at the Soviet Embassy is cancelled owing to the indisposition of a Councillor with an Armenian name!"

"That must be Nahabedian," said Scapinelli. "I will go and see him to-morrow."

And the next day, accordingly, he went to the embassy. Once more the whole tedious procedure of reception and introduction and safe conduct had to be gone through.

Upstairs he went in, to find the Councillor sitting in an arm-chair. His head rested back against a pillow that was soaked in perspiration. He had to keep coughing incessantly. "It is very good of you to have come to see me," he told the Jesuit, holding out his hand. "I feel frightfully lonely here. It is a pity you did not meet the doctor. He only went half an hour ago, fetched X-ray photos, and looked very concerned at them. It is in my chest here, whenever I——"

A fit of coughing racked him. His face became purple and congested, and Scapinelli had to hold him up. "Papal action in support of Moscow!" he said, with a smile. Then he sat down by him, and crossed his feet.

"Have you got over the fright of last week yet?" he asked him, in friendly tones. "I mean, the definite conclusion on my part, that things in Russia must come to such a state as Aage Madelung describes in his 'Circus Man,' the compulsory mating of women by force, the establishment of artificial harems, with compulsory child-bearing. Then you would approximate appreciably close to the plans of the race fanatics, who also want to set up polygamous 'reservations' for the 're-nordification' of the population."

"But we shall retain marriage," groaned the Councillor reluctantly. "There is nothing so hotly discussed——"

"But don't you think," interrupted Scapinelli, "that such compromises with the programme will give the proletariat a narrow-minded bourgeois outlook?"

"No!" replied the Councillor, fiercely. "Our ideal is too heroic for that, too true and vital, too——"

"You see," interrupted Scapinelli again, softly, "that is where our views utterly part company. In Rome, for instance, they think that Bolshevism, as a programme for the world, is the very maximum limit in narrow-mindedness!"

"We have precisely the same view of Rome," retorted

Nahabedian from his armchair. "Just think of the thousands and thousands of old bigots, candle-women, old maids in sodalities, of the Catholic club organisers, the—oh, one grows tired of enumerating them."

"Certainly these people are inclined to be narrow-minded," admitted Scapinelli, "but they are the soil from which really fine things can spring. But your red soil is sterile. The man who prays is no narrow-minded bourgeois at that moment even if he is at all others. But with you there is bound to be an unbroken desert of unrelieved, inevitable, narrowness. Doubtless the citizens of the Soviet Union will all be prosperous; they will all have their lawful spouses—for we're not going to do away with marriage, as we decreed that we were, last week—all have their little houses, or probably their three-roomed suite in a sky-scraper, all have the right of using the collective motor-car, their ticket for the confectioner, the cinema, the masseur, the merry-go-rounds in the amusement-park; and so far they will take their delight in a rosy-tinted atheism. And finally, the counter-revolution will come—a revolution of the dreamers and visionaries, of the mystics, of the occultists, of the superstitious, of the primitive Manichæans surviving secretly, the revolution of the ambitious, of the place-hunters, of the despair-bred nihilists, of the hysterical and the epileptic, unless——"

"Unless what?" asked the Georgian, interestedly.

"Unless the hand of the Church takes hold, and makes an end, once for all, of the chaos."

"Ah, you hope for a union of the churches?"

"I hope for it with my heart, but I do not expect it with my intellect. I do not believe there will be any union. Obstinacy has characterised all heretics from the Monophysites down to the Bolsheviks; there is only the one way now, to leave them to the judgment of God and to let them die out after fulfilling their mission."

"Indeed!" said the Councillor, grimly. "And so we *have* a mission for you, after all."

"A two-fold one, in fact," replied Scapinelli, sarcastically. "On the one hand you purge us of diseased elements, and on the other hand you are forerunners preparing the way for us a little. Thus did the Arians, for example, first infect the Ostrogoths with their Christian-heretical faith, and then we simply catholicised them. You have done genuine preliminary work for us. Believe me, there are ever so many Malays in Java who received their first Christian notions from the mouths of Communist speakers. We could almost be grateful to you for your work. Where once the Agitation Bureaux of the Communist International have sown, the Propaganda of the Faith will soon reap. That is precisely the tragedy of all heretics; that they are for ever doing productive work for the Mother Church from which alone they derive all their ideas after all. As an example of this, we are at present reaping the fruits of the Nestorians' mission in India. In five or six years they will all be petitioning the Holy Father for the Mass, which is celebrated according to the Syrio-Mala-bar rite——"

He was interrupted by a terrible bout of coughing that seized the Councillor. Mirhan Nahabedian lay, exhausted and pallid after he had partially recovered from it, against the sweat-soaked pillow. Scapinelli looked anxiously at his drawn and glistening face. Tiny pearls of sweat stood out on his forehead.

Rudolph Medek had for some days stopped coming to the office. This happened by no means infrequently; it was what he had a perfect right to do, since he had only the literary feature to contribute, had not been assigned any specific room or desk, and had not any personal duties to carry out on any particular day of the week by agreement.

On one of these evenings Eugen had been kept unnecessarily long by a priest who had come from Latvia. The cleric, born in Dünaburg and working in Riga, had brought him an article, and was entertaining him with all the length and breadth of his views on the geographical spread of Catholicism.

Suddenly the telephone rang. Eugen took up the receiver and announced his name. For a while he heard nothing. Then came Helga's voice quite distinctly: "Yes, he is at the telephone," he heard her say to somebody at the other end. Then there spoke a deeper voice. It was Rudolph Medek. "Hallo! Is that you? This is a trunk-call, so I've got to hurry up. I am now with Helga in the Convent, and Sister Brigitta is by my side too, watching me with Argus eyes, on the ground that masculine persons have no right visiting young ladies in the evening in convents. To come to the point: since I've had the chance of staying a good half an hour with your poor bored sister, I've just got engaged to her. Did you get that? *Engaged.* We're getting married on the 25th of the month. Settled. Friends are requested not to send condolences. Honeymoon at Mariazell." Then Helga spoke a few halting words, of which nothing was to be made except every now and then the reaffirmation that she was "so happy." Finally all was silent in the receiver.

When Eugen laid aside the telephone, his eyes were sparkling. "You've no idea what has happened!" he cried to the bewildered priest, who was still sitting there staring. "My sister, who is expecting a child by some blackguard or other, has found a husband—and what a husband! Fine, isn't it?"

"Yes, that is certainly great good fortune," replied the other without seeming specially shocked at Eugen's disclosure. But the latter felt an unexpected sense of relief. The fight with the dragon of Society was to be spared him, and that made him light-hearted beyond all measure.

The priest from Dünaburg could see that he was superfluous here, and soon took his leave. Only the loud echo of his excited words still hung about the corners of the room. Eugen, however, remained leaning over the back of his chair, motionless, in joyous, dazed rapture, as if his lips would unconsciously murmur a mute thanksgiving.

Soon, too, the marriage was to be solemnised. Sonnenschein, who was feeling somewhat better, wanted to officiate. But Scapinelli insisted on being one of the witnesses. The other was to be a taxidermist who was unemployed and whom Sonnenschein, in pursuance of some obscure purpose, had picked out for this wedding function.

CHAPTER VI

A SILLY BUSINESS

Scapinelli was laid up with a broken collar-bone. He was at St. Hedwig's Hospital; Sonnenschein and Eugen, who frequently visited him there, were engaged in a discussion of the slow progress of the tax collections.

"Don't talk to me so dolefully, Düring," said Scapinelli, joking.

"Dr. Lindner can't be in two places at once," remarked Sonnenschein, blowing his nose. "The last time he had to hang round Franz Blei for an hour before he could get the Church tax out of him. The whole thing is so petty. If the person in question doesn't fork out, the executive officer comes and levies a distraint on him. That is a position that from our point of view is utterly intolerable."

"The people must simply pay peaceably," declared Eugen. "In the second category the annual church tax amounts to just four times the cost of a ticket on the city tramcar. Everyone has that—everyone can afford that."

"Only not everyone will pay that," declared Sonnenschein dryly. "For example, in the Old Jakobstrasse there is a certain professor named Knallfinger who obstinately refuses to pay his one-mark-sixty-seven."

"Then I'm going to call and see him," said Düring.

"He will courteously bow you out of the door," said Scapinelli.

"That is precisely what he will not do."

"What then?"

"He will discourteously bow you out of the door."

"I won't go away empty-handed," declared Eugen, "I will stick to him like a leech."

Sonnenschein made a dubious grimace. Scapinelli closed his eyes and went off to sleep again.

Düring pressed the button of the electric bell. Nobody answered. Then he rang again, and again without result. Before he would go away he took the precaution of trying once more, and listened attentively to the silence within. Then he became aware of the sound of footsteps. It must be an elderly woman shuffling over linoleum. Then he was aware of a peep-hole opening, and a red, inflamed eye regarding him hostilely. The peep-hole was closed again, and Eugen heard somebody breathing heavily. Then a wheezy voice enquired, "Who is there?"

Eugen felt irritated. What was he to answer? His name would be unknown. So he answered as shortly as possible. "I am!" he said loudly. Once more there was a pause. Then he heard a key grate in a lock. The noise came from upstairs. Then again there was a second noise of unlocking of doors. This time Eugen heard it lower down. Then the door opened to the extent of a slit. A chain on the door prevented it from opening farther. A scared, nervous woman's face became visible in the opening.

"Who do you want to see?" she asked.

"Professor Knallfinger," said Eugen.

"Who do you want to see?" now asked a harsh, high-pitched, almost shrill voice, in the background. The woman who had opened the door was pushed to one side, the door pulled open, and two ladies approached Eugen. The elder of the two—she was obviously the mother—wore an altogether too antediluvianly elaborate garment with leg-of-mutton sleeves, trailing train, ruchings, and stiffenings; the younger, who had, however, passed at least her thirtieth year, was dressed with an over-done simplicity that did protest too much, and wore rough woollen stockings, a washing print dress, severely combed-back hair and a menacingly stern school-mistress-like expression.

"Yes, to whom *precisely* do you wish to speak?" the elder woman asked him once more. Eugen had the impression that these two had all along been lying motionless, in wait for him, in the background, to fall upon him and frustrate his mission.

"Does Knallfinger live here?" he asked, cautiously.

"Yes, this is the von Knallfinger residence!" said the younger lady.

"I should like to speak to Professor von Knallfinger," said Eugen.

The two ladies now exchanged a long-drawn-out, amazed, almost stupefied look.

"The Professor *never* receives callers," said the elder lady, positively and reproachfully, as if Eugen had offended against one of the rules of propriety. "And I really cannot venture to say that he will receive you. Besides, if I am not mistaken, he is not at home."

"He is not at home," echoed the daughter.

"And of course you must tell us what it is about—people who call here always come about something unpleasant."

"With begging stories and to ask for things," said the daughter, sternly.

"And with bills," added her mother.

"With bills," confirmed the daughter.

"You might as well tell us, at any rate, what you have come about. In any case, you may sit down."

"Come inside," said the daughter.

"Don't sit on this chair—it has only just been repaired," the mother warned him.

"It is only for guests," explained the daughter.

"We never sit on it," the mother added, in confirmation.

Eugen looked round the room. The walls were hung with daguerreotypes.

"You have not told us yet what you have come about," cried the daughter impatiently.

"It must be for somebody else," the mother assured her. "It can't be for us at all."

Eugen pulled himself together.

"I have come with a begging story, and to ask for something, and with a bill," he said.

The mother and daughter exchanged an eloquent glance.

"You are a swindler," cried the mother. "We owe nobody anything—we are honest people."

"We have even paid the piano-tuner."

"Even the piano-tuner."

"People must prove their claims."

"Certainly, people must prove their claims," Eugen interrupted. "You have not paid your Church tax!"

A cry of relief broke from mother and daughter almost simultaneously.

"Ah!" cried Frau von Knallfinger. "So the screed was from you. You are the Church tax collector. The paper has been lying about here for days. We have nothing for you—that is not being paid at all."

"That will certainly not be paid!" said the daughter, mockingly.

Eugen felt the anger that every Catholic feels when he comes in contact with people incapable of great ideas and who bring great ideals into ridicule.

"Very well," he replied, icily, "Then I shall———" Then

he broke off. He did not want to be too severe all at once. "The 'screed' was not actually from *me*," he explained.

"Indeed!" said the mother, sharply. "Indeed! Then why does the clergyman not come himself?"

"The clergyman," retorted Eugen, "is, in the first place, a priest—he is not a tax-collector, to run about after every three-halfpence. He has more important things to do. But you——"

"But I," the professor's wife interrupted him, "but I shall not pay a red cent. We have no use for the clergy. When we had to sell our last Persian rug four years ago, the clergy did not help us——"

"Do you know," Eugen demanded of her, seizing on her words triumphantly, "so long as you have a bed to sleep in and warm clothes to wear, something plain to cook, and a five-roomed house to live in, you are of not the slightest interest to us from the point of view of charitable assistance. Especially as you keep a housemaid——"

"*We* do?" exclaimed the women, indignantly.

"Or you have a cook," he ventured; "she opened the door to me."

"You mean Frau von Kamps, my husband's sister-in-law, who lives with us as a paying guest——"

"A paying guest? That is very interesting. If you have somebody as a paying guest, then you can afford to pay one-mark-sixty-seven!"

"Certainly we could afford to—that is a trifle! But on principle we will not pay. And why should we? We never go to church. When we want music, there is the wireless. If I should feel like praying I read a few pages of the *Stunden der Andacht*, by Zschokke. If I were to die at any time, I should have cremation; and I shall not get married again!"

"The civil marriage will be good enough for me!" said the daughter.

"Yes, if it ever comes to that!" murmured Eugen, succumbing to temptation.

They were interrupted by somebody opening the door of a room, from which issued a cloud of smoke shimmering with electric light, that flooded the parlour. But these exhalations were followed by a man with a dishevelled mop of hair, puckered brow, dirt-smeared spectacles, flying coat-tails, and a high collar whose stiffness had given way under the relaxing influence of much perspiration. Without a glance at those present, he dashed across the room on his way out.

"The Professor?" asked Eugen.

The mother bit her lips.

"The Professor, yes," she confirmed, with the dignity of a governess when the child in her charge has detected her in a pedagogic lie.

"Perhaps it would be best if I went to your husband direct, with my application," ventured Eugen.

"Then you're on the wrong track altogether," boasted the daughter. "You will have no effect with father."

"My husband has no need of religion," said the mother, taking charge of the conversation again, "he has his Greek philosophy. In my opinion, he does not enter into the question at all, as regards the Church tax."

"He has *his* Greek philosophy?" repeated Eugen, puzzled.

"Certainly, my husband has his Greek philosophy. But you can go to my niece Trude, who has money; she has a car, and will very likely give you the amount."

"Yes, she has piles of money," corroborated the daughter. "Whether she is of good life, that, to be sure, we cannot say."

"No, as to that, we are completely uninformed," the daughter again corroborated.

Eugen, who could see that he would get no further with the two women, rose. He made a curt bow, and left. Only at the door did he turn round and ask for the address of the rich niece.

"Brühlau, No. 19b Siebenkräutergasse," the daughter told him.

Then the door closed behind him, and as he thoughtfully descended the steps one by one he continued to hear the protracted noise of the locks and bolts being shot once more in their numerous sockets.

CHAPTER VII

SUBURBAN PRELUDE

THE Jesuit was no longer keeping to his bed. He was sitting up in an armchair with a blanket wrapped round his feet, and looked like a petty tradesman. Sonnenschein, who seemed to be better lately, walked restlessly up and down the sick-room, while Eugen reported the result of his errand.

"He actually has his Greek philosophy," said Sonnenschein, bitterly.

"You can't make anything of those people," replied Scapinelli, dropping into a Viennese idiom.

"Where did the niece live, did you say?" asked Sonnenschein after a while.

"In Brühlau."

"In Brühlau! It *would* be in Brühlau, naturally!" said Sonnenschein, sarcastically, and then, when Scapinelli and Eugen looked questioningly at him, he began an excursus on the subject of Brühlau. "The sodalities," he said, concluding his introductory remarks, "lead a barren, emasculated communal life, and the priest can't be stopped from publishing an anti-semitic Church rag entitled the *Sonntagsglöckle*. He is as fierce as a Jaguar in upholding this, and expresses the view that the Berlin *Kirchenblatt* doesn't go into local affairs sufficiently. I'm just going to publish a standard work under the title, 'Catholicism as a Local Religion.' Tell you what, Düring—you go down to this pestilential little provincial hole and play the part of a pike in a carp-pond, stir up the community's director a bit, buy up the whole plant of the *Sonntagsglöckle*, and make a bit of noise in the world, among the clod-hoppers."

Eugen laughingly promised that he would do so, and took his leave. When the door had closed behind him, Sonnenschein looked after him with sparkling eyes.

"He's coming on, that lad," he remarked.

Scapinelli's face remained serious.

"I am very anxious about him," he said. "He is posted in one of the most dangerously exposed sectors of the Front. One where people look primarily on the aim of Catholicism as if it were a policy, an ethical and æsthetic aspect of philosophy. While they are armed on the outside, they get undermined from within."

For a while they were silent.

Then Scapinelli turned to Sonnenschein.

"You will laugh. Well, don't laugh, all things considered," he said. "But the Councillor Nahabedian comes here for the light—I refer to the sun-ray treatment for a tumour he suffers from. The people at the embassy are naturally not very edified at his visiting such a clerical hospital."

One Sunday afternoon that he had free Eugen actually went out to Brühlau on his motor bicycle. He was in a good humour, and whizzed round the corners, for he found the visits about the Church tax were excellent fun. The people one met, with their scandalised indignation and their conceited vanity, were certainly amusing. In front of a villa in the Siebenkräutergasse he pulled up, and sat still for a while on the saddle, studying the outside. He was reminded against his will of the outside of his own villa, and concluded that the occupant must have about the same means as himself and his mother. Then he rang the bell.

A parlourmaid led him into a drawing-room and took his card upstairs. He had not unduly long to wait, till Gertrude Garrieter came, and offered him her hand. He liked the way she shook hands immensely—her grip was firm, almost masculine. She herself was above the average height, almost as tall as he, with awkward movements, a rather deep voice, eyes set at a feminine slant, dusky fair hair, down to her shoulders, and prominent collar-bones. Her walk, too, was clumsy and hesitant, and her clothes clung tightly about her, of heavy material and English-looking cut.

"Yes, what did you wish to see me about in particular?" she asked with some curiosity, dropping heavily into a chair.

Without any beating about the bush Eugen gave her an account of his ill-starred mission in "the von Knallfinger house," and when she began to laugh—a most un-Society-like, hearty laugh—he began to portray the Knallfingers quite unsparingly, to her inordinate delight.

"Why I really did come here, I actually don't quite know," he said, in conclusion, "for I can't possibly make *you* pay. There is no law on earth that makes a niece liable to pay her uncle's debts. I was simply immensely curious to see whether you were as Knallfingerish as the people in the Old Jakobstrasse!"

She laughed again.

"I understand perfectly well why you came," she said. "You need the money, and I shall be delighted to give it to you. What would become of us, if people refused to pay the Church tax!"

"Are you a practising Catholic?" he asked.

"Practising? That depends what you mean by *practising*. Certainly, I go to church and to the Sacraments. But even so I am not 'righteous overmuch.' But what do *you* do? Only collect taxes?"

"No," he laughed. "I am the maid-of-all-work for

Berlin. I write articles in the *Reichswarte*, take part in the work of the sodalities, officiate as drawing-room poodle in Society, and do odd jobs of instructing converts. At the moment I am specialising in taxes and Bolshevik meetings."

"Bolshevik meetings?" she asked with some curiosity.

"Certainly. Father Redel and I visit the different Communist gatherings, and then in the debate we monopolise the speaking—in this way, we get off very cheaply. *They* pay the hall-rent and the heating, and *we* make the speeches. Often, we feel quite sorry for the organisers, for the K.P.D. is quite poor. But then, we are no richer ourselves."

"Then you aren't frightened at all?"

"No, I'm not."

She leaned back against the cushions somewhat dreamily, which did not particularly suit her, and murmured, "How lovely it all is! If only I could do the same sort of thing! Is it possible?"

"Fancy asking that!" he said. And then he worked out for her almost a complete programme of work; what she was to read, to whom she was to apply, what she was to begin with. He urged her to take her car and drive into Berlin next day, and go with him and Father Redel to a meeting. She cupped her chin in the palm of her hand and listened intently.

CHAPTER VIII

TALKING OF CHAOS

THE meeting of the Communist Workers' association, *Die Flamme*, had not yet begun. Gertrude Garrieter stood excitedly with Eugen and Father Meinrad Redel outside the entrance of the public-house, from which a loud babel of voices echoed out into the ill-lit street. Whenever a fresh arrival passed them on his way in, she would grip Eugen's arm, with an excited cry, "Did you see *him?* He was really one of the underworld!" or "How awful! *He* had on a rowing jersey! And his scars! And his expression! Just like a hold-up man on the films!" Eugen feasted his eyes and ears on her in excitement and wonder.

Meanwhile, inside, the meeting was being opened, and they hurried in to make sure of getting seats. They sat in one of the last rows, and listened patiently. "Aren't we to make any interjections?" whispered Gertrude Garrieter. "Sh!" Meinrad Redel warned her. A member of the audience next to Gertrude reeked drunkenly of crude spirits, and seemed to be nodding. And now, at last, the wearisome speech was over.

"Has anybody any remarks to make?" the chairman asked now, curtly, to get this formality over.

"I have," said Meinrad Redel, and stood up to his full height. The audience at first looked at him with bewilderment, but when they saw that it was a priest, there was an angry, excited murmur. Many, however, seemed to like his courage, and they shut up the others who were inclined to protest angrily. In a moment, Meinrad Redel had reached the platform. On the steps sat some Young Communists who did not seem inclined to move. But that appeared to offer not the least obstacle to Meinrad Redel's advance; with one standing jump he was on the platform, and bowing ironically to the audience.

"My word, you can jump!" said the chairman, with the five-pointed star in his button-hole and the bitten pencil in his hand, taken aback.

"Certainly" said Father Redel. "One must cultivate one's body; for, when all is said and done, we do consist of bodies too, made in the image of God, and which will rise again, in a glorified form, on the last day. I specially advise everybody to cultivate assiduously the gymnastics of the hand—strong hand-muscles are a great deal more useful than swollen biceps. If anybody attacks you from in front, for instance, with a knife—now, this Comrade here with the pencil will let that represent the knife. Now try and stab me —come on, now, it won't hurt me. Aha!—So-o-o-o!—Shall I bend it back any further?—No? Very good then; now you see what good finger-muscles can accomplish? Naturally, there is a class of cases where that would not be enough, or where the muscles of the body must co-operate. Come up here, Mr. Düring! Now, then—this gentleman is struggling with me—now—Ugh!—He's down. Simply grabbing his coat by the lapels, and one quick jerk down over the shoulders, so all the buttons burst off, and he can't use his arms any more. All right, Düring, you can go back!"

The spectators applauded enthusiastically.

"Your time's up!" declared the chairman.

"Shall I go on speaking, or who else will?" he asked the audience, with great presence of mind.

"You! You! You stay up there!" They all shouted back at him, with enthusiasm.

Gertrude sat there with sparkling eyes. She had never seen anything like this in Brühlau.

Redel calmly went on speaking.

The people listened to him, engrossed, and were disappointed when the chairman closed the meeting at eleven o'clock. At the entrance stood a young man with a collecting-plate, but when Redel was about to drop a copper coin in, the youth with the red tie refused to take the money.

"Nope!" he said, "we ain't 'ad nobody 'ere speak so fine as what you did—and we can't take your money off of you!"

In the street outside, the priest left them, and she walked with Eugen as far as the nearest tram-stop. She had garaged her car at a friend's, in the west end of the city. During the journey she did not speak a word. The excitement had left her, and she sat broodingly staring out before her. All that she had heard and seen produced in her a mood of sombre meditation. At the Tiergarten station she jumped up.

"Just a step to the zoo," remarked Eugen.

"No," she said, imperatively. "Come along." And after dragging him out of the tram by his sleeve, she added, as if excusing herself, "Do you know, I couldn't sit still another minute. We'll walk to the Kurfürstendamm."

He nodded. She took his arm, and he liked her uncompromising way of stepping out. They walked through the silent park, where couples sat, interlaced and whispering, on the benches.

"I can't get rid of the impression," she said, "that all that Father Redel is doing, is only like rain-drops on rock. Just think of those faces, those eyes, those barbarous scars, that those people had. To-day all this was something quite new to me. I simply shudder at the idea that these denizens of the underworld want to get possession of our power, that these people, uncultured, primitive and uncivilised as they are, want to live in our houses and sleep in our beds. I am absolutely without any class-prejudice—for instance, I am very fond of our peasants, and I take an interest in all the little sorrows and pains of my maid—but there are certain things that neither I nor, probably, you, can get over."

A policeman's lantern wafted its circle of light over the path.

"And yet our days are already numbered."

She turned, aghast, and tried to read his expression, in the darkness.

"You, then, are a pessimist?"

"No," he said, a little sadly. "But I have already had it all out with myself. However sorry I, personally, the selfish, egotistical, Capitalist Eugen Düring, may feel about it, as a Catholic—as a man, therefore, who can think objectively—I am forced to recognise that there are great economic truths in Socialism——"

"And you say that as a Catholic!" she interrupted him indignantly. She had freed her arm, and stood still. "You want us to have our possessions expropriated, our own inherited property taken away from us, our homes, our roofs——"

"You have landed property?" he said, and when she nodded, he remarked briefly, "Private ownership is not holy."

"Indeed, then what is holy?" she cried, her voice rising. But then she stopped short, aghast—she had just realised the crass paganism of her ideas, and looked away in confusion. Eugen felt her momentary weakening, and pressed his point.

"There will always be private property, but even private property must be considered *sub specie aeternitatis*. That is why a corrective for the position that has become untenable through unearned income and interest has to come eventually."

"Why should not interest be allowed?" she broke in. They were entirely alone now—even the seats around them were empty. He cleared his throat. The night was chilly.

"First because it is unethical, and secondly because it leads to too awful an accumulation of wealth. I will just give you a practical example of what I mean. What do your own means consist of, for instance?"

"How can you ask a question like *that?*" she said, more amazed than offended. She slowed down in her walk.

"This is one Catholic talking to another," he said sternly. "You must never again take such a Brühlau-ish attitude with me."

A cold breeze stirred. A few leaves drifted, rustling, across the path.

"Here we turn to the right," he said, still more sternly than before. He could sense her resistance, and it gave him a silent pleasure to be leading a sulkily refractory person round in a dark park at his own good will; he noticed, too, how she was groping for just the words she wanted, without being able to find them. But after a while, when the cessation of speech had eventually begun to grow up into the semblance of a hostile barrier between them, and the surrounding silence threatened to become unbearable, he began to speak, quietly and impressively.

"Let us suppose you have lodged five hundred thousand marks of your wealth in the bank. Very well, then—you are *rich*, you have half a million marks. On this, your own money, the bank makes you a *gift*—mark that, a *gift*—of twenty-five thousand marks a year. You don't work. You go down to Abbazia or go up to Swinemünde, take your sunbaths, and let those sums that are gifts to you, accumulate. Chapter Two: There is in Berlin, or in Hamburg, whichever you like, a certain labourer who commands a monthly income of one hundred and eighty marks. He works from early morning till night, is poor, and receives no gifts of money. You must always draw the contrast: 'I am rich, I receive gifts of money, I do not work; he is poor, receives no gifts, and works.'

"Chapter Three: Where do you *get* that money? How is it that those five hundred thousand marks of yours become five hundred and twenty-five thousand? Does the money in the bank beget offspring, according to its kind? No! The bank builds factories and pays the labourers not their full hire—that is to say, not the rightful share of the fruits of their labour. But in order not to remain without work, the labourer is compelled to go into a factory where usury, oppressive interest, is extorted from him to be allowed to work for what does not belong to him. There, in crude outline, is the gist of the problem. Every penny you spend is extorted from somebody else. The sinfulness of it is not so much in *your* not working. After all, a man can lead a Christian life as a beggar who lives on alms; the malice lies in this, that their *rightful pay is withheld* from the workers. Do you know what sort of sin it is, if we withhold their rightful hire from labourers, servants, and employees? Don't you remember that, in the religious instruction lessons at Intermediate School, at High School——?"

"I have heard it—'defrauding labourers of their wages'—the words sound so familiar—it must be a great sin——"

"One of those crying to Heaven for vengeance," he exclaimed. "Classed together with murder, oppression of widows and orphans, and sodomy."

After a pause, he went on:

"For every sin, reparation must be made, if it is in our power. . . . One day we must give back our private property in one way or another. That will be very hard for us all——"

From outside they could now see the beginning of the lights in the Budapesterstrasse. She was afraid to return to the turmoil of the capital—she felt too much strained and changed. She looked for a bench. "Let us sit down," she said, somewhat recovering her voice again. He had long ago forgotten his intention of not giving in to her, and did as she wished.

She sat for a long while quiet and motionless, resting her head with her cheeks supported between her closed hands, and gazing straight before her. Then she leaned back. "Terrible," she moaned. "Terrible."

Then she suddenly turned round to Eugen and said, with a girlish, child-like naïveté that Eugen silently delighted in: "I have such a dread of the future. I could never be poor. Where will it all end? And then I have such an irrational terror of the consequences—you must know, I am a coward really—when I get faint-hearted you must rouse me up——"

"It shall be so!" he promised her.

Then there stirred in her the true feminine urge to visualise a concrete picture of the developments the future held in store; and there in the park, in the darkness, with the dew falling, and the distant noises of the streets, whose attenuated sound drifted brokenly to the two on the park bench, she besieged Eugen with: "Do say something. What will it be like? What will it feel like? Utterly comfortless, utterly dismal and drab?"

He so hated talking of it, and it was so unwillingly that he ever brooded on the subject. And yet, there beside him sat someone who insisted on knowing the whole truth, a comrade in arms, towards whom a man must be honest and candid, who could not be put off with fair-sounding words. So he began to speak and to paint the picture asked for; he talked himself into a world of infinite wretchedness, which beckoned them; the world of equality, the world of the levelled down; the world of nothing to wish for; of poverty; of simplicity; of materialism; a world without emotions without colours or high lights, without its great Cæsars, without pomp, or "ornament," or pleasure, or fine subtlety of style.

"And the silver lining?" she broke in to ask him.

"The only beautiful thing about this world will be precisely the fact that there will *be* no silver lining except God and the Church; they alone will be its warmth and its fire, and the burning sun within us which will make life worth living for us in that night, in that chill darkness; God and the Church—these will be the sole why and wherefore, means and end, of our lives—because all '*other gods besides Him*' will have been cast down together into ruin."

"A religious age, then—and yet so gloomy."

"Gloomy for us, who have to make the renunciations."

"I am so terribly fond of the Renaissance," she broke in. "I should like an age of the Conquistadors. My whole library is filled with Burckhardt and Gobineau, Mereshkowski and Pastor. I cling to my property and to ages that knew no bounds—I shall be mortally unhappy. God will be only a solace to me, then—not a *meaning*. Even in the Renaissance, there was a Catholicism. Among men of culture, among women of culture. I don't understand the future —I don't want it. Don't you think that the proportion of those who are happy to those who are unhappy, is pretty well as great among the poor as it is among the rich? Divide a million marks among all the population of Germany—each person will get about a pfennig and a half!"

"That is not the point," he retorted. "Great wealth arouses envy. We shall not go hungry. I shall be an editor at three hundred marks a month—you, probably, a sick-nurse at about two hundred. Certainly we shan't get more. But, now, just look at the envy, the discontent of the proletariat in the state, in the country, in the cities—when he goes for an evening walk in the Kurfürstendamm and sees motor-cars passing with silver-plated mud-guards, while he can do nothing for his own tuberculosis; when he sees Society doings and forms that he can't follow; clothes he can't buy; resorts he can't enter; social circles in which he can't move; when he hears of countries that he can't visit; sees girls he can't marry because of his status, his means, his manners; when he continually sees nothing but the outer walls, the walls of scorn and contempt; and people, just like himself—people with two nostrils and two ears, like his own—who, through a chain of accidental circumstances, from birth to inheritance, have come into possession of all conceivable things—then he is bound to experience a gnawing envy——"

"If the proletariat are envious," she interrupted, bewildered, "that is nothing to do with us—that is *their* sin."

"Certainly that *is* a sin, too," he replied. "But doesn't it say in the 'Our Father,' 'Lead us not into temptation'? Don't we every day lead them into temptation with our parade of luxury? That is why we must practise renunciation!"

"By what authority *must* we?" she exclaimed, vehemently.

"Don't you understand, then?" he cried. "For Christ's sake. We don't want to leave the field clear for the anti-Christ of the Kremlin."

"Let us go," she said, shuddering. "I can't answer you."

They stood up. His limbs were aching with sitting on the hard bench, and his coat, too, was damp. She no longer took his arm, but walked by his side with a strange, worried pucker of the brows. He had thrust his hands back deep into the pockets of his overcoat, and hummed through closed lips a popular melody of the streets. He racked his

brains for some witty remark to make, that would round off
the discussion, for he detested any tone of melodramatic
harangue—but he could think of nothing.

They had reached the Budapesterstrasse, and walked
towards the Kaiser-Wilhelm Memorial Church. The dazzle
of the electric advertising signs and street lamps, the lights
in the cafés, and the head-lamps of the cars, smarted in their
eyes, that had grown acclimatised to the darkness of the
park. But when they had got used to the light they let the
life of the streets work its influence on them, and let their
gaze pick out individual figures among the passing throng.
Gertrude, too, glad to have escaped from the darkness and
Eugen's uncomfortable words, found herself taking at first
an unexpected pleasure in studying all the people who
slipped past her like featureless lay-figures, and involuntarily
she found herself taking refuge in the thought that between
the present day of a refined material culture and the coming
day of a sublimated spiritual world with which men would
try to intoxicate themselves in order to forget the carking
cares of real life, there still seemed to stretch a great expanse
of time. And yet these people did not satisfy her, neither
their expression, nor their perfume—which her nostrils
picked up intermittently—nor their gait, the swinging step
in which they vied with one another. What she sought was
a person, man or woman, whose face, expression, walk,
would show the radiance of a well-rounded, harmonious
personality. Vainly her gaze wandered to the farthest seats
of the cafés on the Kurfürstendamm, in search of somebody
at the first sight of whom she could touch Eugen's arm, and
whisper, "Look! There is a MAN!" Ever and anon there
brushed past her a suit of clothes displayed on some non-
descript body or other; hats beneath which noses just
peeped out; and dead eyes; hysterical little sex-creatures
tripped past her, peering nervously out from their mouse-

like eyes, beneath thick daubs of paint; self-conscious male creatures with chests enlarged by sport, and their jaws quivering with energy; people who let their hair grow down over their ears, and who felt that by this excess growth of the flimsiest form of horny matter they were proclaiming their practice of the fine arts; great burly courtesans with perversely curled carmine lips, smiling sympathetically at cold comrades waiting with crossed feet, with bare shoulders and stumpy fingers; slimy, rolling forms, keeping an anxious look-out through their eye-glasses; figures utterly befuddled, drunk, intoxicated with the value of their existence. This confused throng of drabs, bank directors, gigolos, professional women, homosexuals, gentlemen riders, bar-tenders, courtesans, cocain-addicts, sports instructors, and show-girls, made her mind reel, and the thought that these were destined to destruction was made so familiar to her that she thrust her arm again into Eugen's, and suddenly found herself looking at the unreal eyes of the passing throng with tight-pursed lips. But he was thrusting a passage through the massed crowds, with hunched shoulders, simply going on his way.

They had reached her friend's house, beyond the Uhland underground station, and were guiding the car out of the garage; he was going to take his leave of her, but she asked him to drive a little way with her, and turned into the Tauentzienstrasse. After so much argument and resistance, she felt she must admit that he was right—but the right words would not come, since she absolutely wanted to avoid letting him triumph over her, or expose how her mind had changed. She wanted to make some casual remark at first, to pave the way—but still she could not find the right expressions to use. She drove slowly, and avoided meeting his eyes.

In the side-mirror she saw his face, the features in repose, the eyes lost in reverie. And suddenly she felt herself in an unconventional and strange position—driving alone with a young man through Berlin at night, with a man of whom she knew little but the name, and that he collected taxes, and disturbed Communist meetings—with a man who, a little while before, in a dark park, had questioned her about her means and possessions, and had simply lost his temper when she opposed his opinions. A great curiosity awakened in her; a consuming urge to lead him out more, and hear more of him, would not let her rest.

"And where do you live?" she asked him, as they reached the Wittenbergerplatz.

He gave her his address.

"I will drive you home," she said.

She leaned forward, and turned the car to the left, towards Wilmersdorf. Soon they were at the villa. He jumped out of the car and took her hand.

"Thank you so much," he said. "I am as hungry as a hunter. I shall raid the larder, and no time to lose."

"Very simple for you," said she. "My larder key is in the keeping of the housekeeper, so I shall have to creep into bed with my inner woman clamouring unappeased."

"We can still hold off nightfall a bit longer," he retorted. "Let's go back to the Kurfürstendamm, and find a restaurant——"

"No thanks," she interrupted. "See all those ape-like faces again? I've had more than enough of them for to-day, thank you."

"Right!" he said. "Then you will have supper with me, here."

"With you—here?"

"Yes, here."

"And you think I should, really, as a well-brought-up young lady, visit you now, at a quarter past eleven at night?"

He made a wry face.

"That was really the Knallfinger blood flavoured with Crême de Brühlau, coming to the surface in you!" he said, scornfully.

He took his bunch of keys out of his pocket, and opened the front door without a word.

"Will you please take that back?" she said, raising her voice.

"Not so loud," he said. "My mother is asleep upstairs— we must be quiet."

He went into the hall and lit the light, hung his coat on a hook, and flung his hat on a table. She had continued to follow him, and her whole body was now quivering with anger. But he just went towards the door of a room and opened it, with a friendly smile. Then, for the first time, he turned towards her.

"My dear Gertrude," he said, placidly, "I gladly take back what I said about 'Knallfinger blood.' But I must earnestly beg you, with all the impressiveness of which I am capable, to drop all that stuff. After all, we are two Catholics, who intend to work together, and not a couple of animals who are going to fly at each other as soon as they are un-leashed."

"Yes, but——at night!" she broke in.

"Indeed! Do you think that the night is an indecent time of day?" he countered.

"If I were seen——" she began.

"O Lord," he cried, "afraid of gossip!"

"I am not afraid of anything," she broke in, again, "but if they heard of it in Brühlau I should be done for!"

"If they heard of it in Brühlau," he retorted, with sarcasm, "all you would have to do, would be to give them twice as many sandwiches as usual with their tea, and the thing would be 'arranged.'"

She laughed.

"It can't be done without confidence," he went on. "But now we are going to make our raid on the larder."

In the larder they took possession of a quantity of sweets and cakes, and in the kitchen, of an electric cooker, and then went back to the drawing-room, opened the windows, and made tea. He sat with his feet up on the hearth-kerb, gazing out at the starry skies. Below, in the road, stood her car, with its head-lamps extinguished, looking like a fat, benevolent, slumbering beast of the forest. It was just on midnight—the street lamps went out.

She sat in a comfortable little chair by the fireside, holding her plate of cakes.

"Isn't it fine here?" he asked, cheerfully.

She nodded. She had recovered her good humour.

"I trust you," she said, "but what do you know of me? You have already told me that the Knallfingers will accept no responsibility for me."

He laughed.

"I am very severe with us women on that point," she went on, taking a bite out of a cherry cake. "To a man one can more easily forgive a little—but a woman who has once gone off the rails is an abomination to me."

"An abomination?" he asked her, ironically.

"Yes," she said, in deadly earnest, nodding her head.

"Then you and my sister will agree splendidly," he said slowly, looking at her testingly, full in the face. "The story is a long and sordid one; but I decided at first sight that you had a good heart."

She looked at him in bewilderment. "That can't be true? Surely I have misunderstood you?" she said.

He shook his head, and she sat staring at the cakes, not knowing where to look. But he slipped silently off the window-seat, turned out the light and came back. Now he was standing by the window, and gazing out at the stars. They lay like specks of chrome yellow in the pitchy blackness of their background. The night air blew, cold and damp, in through the window.

"How beautiful the night is—our night," he said. "And the coming era will be night, too—so why despair?"

"I shall be very fond of her, nevertheless—of your sister," she said suddenly; it sounded strangely forced and came strangely late.

He looked at her, and saw only her hair. It was curly, and hung down to the nape of her neck. It gleamed brightly in the darkness of the room. For a long while he had been feeling a deep, inward pleasure and happiness. His life had already been rich in moments of comedy; he had often laughed, found some inexplicable, surreptitious pleasure, some irrepressible delight, some sudden gusts of passionate enjoyment. Yet now he was standing by the window, the night—his night—above him, and another person, a comrade on the battle-front, by his side; one whom he himself had enlisted; one who was to fight shoulder to shoulder by his side, and who, moreover, was a woman; one towards whom he could draw closer than to anybody else in the world.

He lost himself in dreams. He would have liked to sit down by her, take hold of her hands, and gaze long into her eyes. And then, again, he pictured to himself what it would be like to take her head between his hands, and kiss her, on her hair and her firm brow, on her cheeks. Not that he loved her—he merely felt that sweet urge to approach somebody else with loving gestures, to strip himself for a few moments of the trench trappings of the daily fight; to be ordinary, soft, romantic, childlike, playful, human, for once.

Some instinct cried "No!" to all his dreams. This stern, protesting instinct repeated to him his own words, that confidence between those on the battle-front must prevail, that it was unsoldierly to soften on active service, that every slightest action here on earth carried its consequences. With a sigh, he admitted that this instinct was right. All this created a great, tormenting indecision and uncertainty, and, with his eyes fixed on the Milky Way, he let idea wrestle with idea in his mind. He felt a great loneliness, and a wailing of lamentation welled up from the depths of his heart, like bubbles of breath long held, that burst into nothing as they struck the threshold of his consciousness. And suddenly he discovered, he who had thought himself so filled up and overflowing, that there were in him great chill cavities, containing nothing but cold stagnant air, unpenetrated by the warmth of God, because they had been created for what was human and earthly.

He had lost himself so completely in his broodings, had climbed so far away from earth to the peaks of his daydreams, that he was entirely unaware that Gertrude had risen to her feet and was staring out uneasily into the night. It was only her hand, laid lightly on his sleeve, that brought him to his senses. He looked down into the darkness of the street, and perceived a figure busying itself with her car. He took the table-lamp, and threw its light down—the dark shadow vanished. The cone of light shining down from his hand brought him back to earth. He put out the light, but the dream was gone, and he came sadly back into the room.

"They already want to take my car from me," she said, reflectively. He would have turned the light on again, but she signed to him not to. She found her gloves, in the dark, and together they went down the stairs.

He saw her into her car, and she sped away through the shimmering half-light of the early dawn along the side of the Landwehrkanal towards the east. At the Hallesches Tor she crossed the murky water and turned into the Friedrichstrasse and then pursued her way between clattering manure-wagons.

CHAPTER IX

A COUNCILLOR DIES

THE next morning, as usual, he rose late, and drove to St. Hedwig's Hospital. Scapinelli had turned his room into an office. On the table stood a telephone, on the wall there hung a map of Berlin, a typewriter stood on a chair, and across the bed were scattered sheets of manuscript; on the floor, piles of newspapers—the *Weltbühne,*, the *Allgemeine Rundschau,* the *Tat,* and *Hochland,* the *Neue Revue,* and the *Gral.*

"Do you know who is dying here?" he asked Eugen, who was leaning over his bed. "No? The Legation Councillor, Nahabedian. I guessed right—it's a mediastinal tumour. He is lying in a room a few doors away. Apropos of dying, I suppose you didn't know that we have packed Sonnenschein off to Italy?"

"Impossible."

"It's true. And that's a bad sign," he said, drily. "If ever Sonnenschein really leaves his work, it will mean that the shadows of death have already touched him. Kidney trouble. Nothing to be done. His heart is crocking up, too. He used to sit till five or six in the morning, in his overcoat, in the icy cold, in that map-room at the Georgenstrasse, deliberately ruining his health. At the last, he went without sleep altogether. In him we are losing one of our most powerful supports."

"Is it really as grave as all that?"

"I am giving up all hope," he said, even more drily than before. "However, as we have reached the chapter about cases of death, I should like further to report to you, first, that Father Semienski has been shot by the G.P.U., secondly that Father Trevelyan has been put to a martyr's death by the Red troops in Kiang-Si, thirdly that Father Jouhard died of leprosy in Madagascar."

Eugen was silent. Scapinelli looked long and questioningly into his eyes, then he asked, smilingly, "What were you doing with yourself yesterday? I don't like you to-day."

Thereupon Eugen narrated his experiences of the day before—the Socialist meeting, and about Gertrude Garrieter, their quarrel in the Tiergarten, and their romantic hour together at the Villa.

The Jesuit Giovanni Battista Scapinelli leaned back in his chair and laid down his pen.

"Better marry her at once," he suggested, briefly. "I am quite in earnest," he added.

"Yes, but——"

"There are two things for which one should never marry," said Scapinelli: "for love, and for money; they both evaporate in time. Sympathies and views remain. How old are you now?"

"Twenty-five."

"Twenty-five! Then what are you waiting for? But of course I shall not try to influence you—I was only speaking academically. However, I shall be delighted to let Gertrude Garrieter work with you, but, still, I must give you a piece of good advice—on the lines of the Komsomolzians—promise one another to own up immediately if either of you feels any likelihood of falling in love."

"Shall be done!" he said, laughing.

"Good," said the Jesuit, "then everything is in order." He bent low over his papers, began writing, and took most honest pains to conceal his satisfied grin from Eugen. And he succeeded.

When Eugen had gone, and he had finished the page down to the last line, he got up and left the room. In the passage, where the air was heavy with chloroform and the sickly scent of ether, he met Dr. Günther, who, with a hasty greeting, would have passed him by.

"How is our patient in No. 47 getting on?" Scapinelli asked.

"At any moment, he may——" He made a gesture indicative of apology.

The Jesuit bit his lips.

"Is he alone?" he went on to ask.

"No," replied the Doctor, "a nurse is with him, and somebody from the embassy."

"You don't know who it is?"

"I don't know his name. He was here a few days ago. Tall and fair, with a heavy jaw and white spats."

"Indeed," he reflected. "That must be the Secretary of the Legation, Vazetis, a Lett. Perhaps, even a confidential agent of the O.G.P.U. Should he go and see the dying man?"

The doctor was in a hurry, and went off. Hesitantly, Scapinelli walked down the passage. He gave an indecisive rap at the door of No. 47. A nursing sister put her head out.

He went in, and shook hands with the Lett. Then he sat down by the bed and turned to the dying Armenian. Mirhan Nahabedian was scarcely recognisable. Between enormous white pillows, damp with perspiration, lay a head like a baby's but incredibly old, shrivelled up with disease; on it grew grey hair, seeming strange there, living its own life. His cheeks with their brittle skin sagged like paper against the bones of the skull. And on the fresh whiteness of the sheets there trembled a blue-veined, almost transparent hand, with fingers outstretched to the Jesuit, as if groping for help.

"Stay here now," besought the moist famine-like face from the pillows. "Do not go away." It was the dying voice of the friend, the friend made during those long spring nights that had been passed in bitter and unavailing dialectical strife, begging him to stay.

Mirhan Nahabedian tried to turn his head sideways. His eyes, sunk deep into their cavities, became protuberant and staring, gazing evilly and suspiciously at the Lithuanian, who sat motionless. Then he collapsed again, groaning.

"I am so horribly full of the Faith!" he said, his eyes fixed on the ceiling.

"What faith?" asked Scapinelli, bending his head forward. The dying man began to cry.

"You ask me that. *You*, who worked it all out before me for nights on end, with paper and pencil! Now the stuff has got into my head and into my very limbs. Yes, it has got into my head—but not into my heart. My heart won't take any part in it! In my heart, there is just emptiness, chilliness! You should never have started talking to me about it, unless you were certain that you could convert me to it altogether. Listen—make me *warm*—make me *feel* it!"

"God alone can do that—that is the work of His grace," said Scapinelli.

"Where is God's mercy," he screamed, "if he does not let me believe? You attacked me with the quintessence of two thousand years. You have disarmed me and left me helpless without taking me prisoner."

The clammy fingers slackened their hold of the Jesuit's wrist.

"Comrade Vazetis," he demanded, with cracked lips, "speak—say something!"

The diplomat had risen.

"Be composed, Comrade," he said, at a loss, "think of the future! The individual may pass away, but we hold the fate of the world in our hands! *Magnitogorsk! Dnyeprostroy!* We will name a factory after you, and ——"

"Do stop that!" cried the dying man. "Can't you see, that is all phrase-making? I am not a collective body of men, but an individual. I must go out alone, there is nobody to keep me company."

The Lett reached for his hat and whispered to the Jesuit that he was going out for a few minutes, to smoke a cigarette.

"What good to me are the Child-Settlement Homes and the heavy oil motors of the Soviet Union, when I am all upset about my future?" he broke out, when the Secretary of the Legation had gone. "As far as I am concerned, the Piätiletka may not be ready for another two thousand years, but I have a horrible foreboding that all you have been saying about survival after death has a devilish probability about it. I have been in civil war, I have carried weapons in my hands—and used them. You can't ever have experienced that—that feeling you get, when a strong, tall, clever man is dodging before the sight of a rifle. One may simply be a dirty, feeble cad oneself—with nothing but a sharp eye—but *he* is done for. A tiny hole behind his ear is enough, and then it's all over. Then over falls this object of flesh and bones, and begins to decay on the spot, there and then. You can smell that putrid heap of flesh—and if you dig up the ground years later, you only find a few broken bones. Just as when you drink and empty the cup, and leave only dregs. 'Man dies and is no more,' I have always said to myself, 'man dies and decays, disappears.' "

Talking had greatly exhausted the Armenian. His breath became laboured, and his hands strayed over his shirt-buttons. The ward-sister opened a window.

"Now, when I have to die myself, it all seems so different," he began again, after a pause. "Now I refuse to understand how that in me which loves, hates, thinks, hopes and despairs, can ever go out, be extinguished. I can cut my finger off, boil it, and eat it, but that something in me will always exist. But where? And how? If there is something beyond *this*, as you have tried to make out, then I must suffer like the devil. We Bolsheviks have no hereafter, but in *your* heaven, it will be no good my displaying my Red badge, and my certificate of affiliation to the Party. It is all so unjust. How do I come, as a Communist, to be arraigned before your Christian Last Judgment? I am an old man. I am lying on my deathbed. I can't simply give up everything. My heart wouldn't be in it."

His eyes were wet with rage and despair.

"Repent of your sins," said Scapinelli earnestly.

"Repent!" He tried to laugh, but only a dry cough came from his constricted throat. "What use is repenting, when the angelic officers of justice are going to pitch me down into hell simply for the bare fact of my sins? I was at the Tiflis Tshrezvitshaika—and not as an idealist, though there were some there—but out of sheer wickedness, out of sheer sadism, sheer delight in evil. Your most vivid imagination could never picture what I experienced there, with priests, with women, with people I had hated for ages——"

He stared down with glassy eyes at the coverlet of his bed. They were dry eyes again. The sister had gone out as well. His labouring breath no longer sounded through the room. Outside, was the hooting of cars and the noises of the street. Suddenly he turned his head, and with all the force that was left in him, commanded: "Lean closer to me, there is something else I must tell you."

Scapinelli leaned forward, and the grey-haired, dying Armenian suddenly thrust his bony hand about the priest's neck and drew him down more closely till his dank, evil-smelling breath came in Scapinelli's face, and hissing, stumbling words were poured into his ears. Every now and then the hand gripped his coat-collar again, and the roving eyes, in which the last flickering flame was dying—eyes that spoke of despair and of hatred, and yet again of hope—searched his face. At last the damp, bony head sank finally back into the pillows, and the clenched hand fell motionless. The lips ceased to speak. There was a rattle in the chest. Everything was still around the dying Councillor to the Legation. Only one eye peered sideways at him, furtively.

"And do you still dare to say that your God will pardon me?" he scoffed again, with breath that hissed whistlingly through his throat. "And now dare you still maintain that anything that one repents of and does penance for can be forgiven in time?"

"Certainly." The Jesuit's voice was like oil on a troubled sea.

"It is a lie!" The dying flesh reared itself up in the sheets. "Christ only forgave one thief and the second was—was—down with him, into hell with him! Yours is no Church of mercy. You are just as much terrorists as we are. You aren't a shred better——"

"That is unfair," the placid voice broke in. "We know nothing about the other thief, whether he went to eternal damnation or not. We do not know that of anybody, not even of Judas. The mercy of God is infinite. Perhaps hell is almost empty——"

"Ah, now we'll be hearing that it doesn't exist."

"It certainly exists."

"Perhaps heaven is empty," quavered the bloodless lips.

"Of heaven, we *know* that it is populous."

"That is what you are like," croaked the dying man. "You come with that infinite mercy and infinite forgiveness that we have not got. Anyone who hoards silver and gold up in his cellars, or who distributes Czarist writings, is punished with death and torture. But you always come along with this mercy and forgiveness. You are just the 'opium for the people.' You alone, your ghastly magic, can give us the final explanations of our Whither, our Why, our How. While our savants work themselves vainly to death in their laboratories you read your incantations out of the Gospel. You keep the masses happy and contented. You heal their wounds. You give them the opiate. We leave them in the dirt. We have nothing but our accursed machines and our empty phrases. You will have all men on your side in this way. How cunning you are! How cunning!"

His eyes filled with water, and soon the tears ran down over his shrivelled cheeks. He began coughing, and his emaciated, hectic frame was shaken with great shuddering convulsions. The weeping calmed the dying man.

"Give me that crucifix!" he said suddenly, in husky tones. The Jesuit took down the plain wooden crucifix from the white wall, and handed it to him. He took it in one hand, and gripped it so tightly that the white knuckles began to gleam through the brown skin. He had the feeling that he had something definite and palpable to hold in his hand. He felt his fingers gripping something real and concrete, and this concrete reality somehow gave him a sense of support.

"To pray," he said dully. "I should like to pray—I don't believe—but pray—yes, I am willing to do that—it will warm me—I shall be just like a believer—it is only the external appearance, the form—but we all grew up first to put on the appearance——"

"Say the 'Our Father,' " the Jesuit said calmingly.

"Forgotten it."

Then the Jesuit Giovanni Battista Scapinelli sat on the edge of the bed and recited the *Salve Regina* in prayer for him, and the dying man repeated his words after him, haltingly and slowly.

"'. . . Banished children of Eve,'" murmured the lips beneath the sunken cheeks. "That is what we all are—banished, exiled and wretched."

After half an hour's prayer, during which the Councillor's voice had grown ever feebler and more broken, with one hand he made a weary gesture to desist. The other hand gripped ever more fiercely on the wooden crucifix.

"I'm already a lot warmer," he said, gratefully. "I am wholly enwrapped in the faith, and no chill from anywhere can reach me now."

He lifted the wood to his lips. Then he glanced at the Jesuit, with a look that Scapinelli did not at once understand. It was some incredible joy and happiness that the dying man perhaps wanted to express. And his lips moved. On his face there grew an expression of the utmost effort; his forehead dripped with perspiration.

"I——" he stammered, "I——" His eyes had taken on an almost imploring expression, the creases smoothed out on his cheeks, there almost shone a light of happiness in his face, but it only lasted for a second. Then came the reaction, his head sank convulsively back, his lips fell slackly over his teeth, and the expression of his eyes became feeble, spiritless and dull. He seemed to swallow once, convulsively, and then he lay quite still on the white linen.

The Councillor to the Legation of the Union of Socialist Soviet Republics in Berlin was dead, and the Jesuit closed his eyes.

CHAPTER X

TWO HUMAN BEINGS

NEXT day Eugen got on his motor bicycle and rode to Brühlau. It was past seven in the evening, and already beginning to turn dark. Gertrude was not in the hall downstairs, and the parlourmaid led him up to the drawing-room. There, he saw her standing before a mirror, dressed for the evening, and straightening her hair.

"What are you doing there?" he asked.

"As you see, I am getting ready for a dinner," she answered. "By the way—you will think the question very frivolous and silly—but how do you like my frock?"

"There is no question of 'liking,' " he answered, "I loathe these disgustingly feminine rags."

"Am I to put on a dinner-jacket and stick a cigar in my mouth, then?" she asked, out of humour.

"You can dress humanly without dressing mannishly," he retorted. "This get-up exhales an odour of gossamer frailty, fairy-like unapproachability, and positively idiotically dished-up eroticism. What else do you expect to achieve at this dinner?"

"Achieve?" she questioned, and passed her fingers through her hair. "What should I *achieve?* Nothing. I am going to eat, and dance, and play bridge."

"Thanks," he interrupted her. "That is all I wanted to know. Just one more question: Where is this party you are invited to?"

"The Bohlens'. You know, he is the barrister, whose sister married the——"

"The Baroness Bellwitz's nephew," he completed drily. He turned to go. "I'll be back in a minute," he called from the doorway.

When he returned he said: "I have telephoned the people and left word that you are unable to go. You'd better get changed now, and get into human clothes again. I have a number of important things to tell you. I have to go to Münster to-morrow, where I shall be staying a week. I cannot put anything off. I'm sorry!"

She had risen, and was staring at him in indignant amazement.

"You dared to telephone to the people without asking me?" she enquired, icily cold.

"So you would have gone straight to the party, and left the work to look after itself," he replied, just as coolly.

"Certainly not," she said. "But you might have asked me first. You can't go making decisions over my head."

"Why need I have asked you," he replied calmly, "if you were unable to come to any other decision?"

"I might have," she began scathingly.

"I shall go down into the hall now," he interrupted her politely. "Come when you have changed. We have a good bit of work before us."

"I shan't come!" she exclaimed.

"Yes, you will," he said, even more suavely than before, squeezed her hand, and went down.

In the hall below, he lit the fire in the grate, and armed with a newspaper, threw himself into an armchair. Before him on a small table stood a china dish with chocolates, into which he kept dipping. The leading article in the paper he had picked up proved to be a most interesting one. He sank more luxuriously into the deep upholstery of the armchair, and forgot all about Gertrude. The fire crackled and spluttered most pleasantly, the melting chocolate slipped smoothly down between tongue and palate, and the words he was reading grew more and more vividly expressive. At last he was wholly immersed in the pleasures of taste, warmth, and the literary presentation of dry facts, and all the spatial realities around him began to fade out of his consciousness completely. When he laid down the newspaper and roused himself from his dreams it had turned half-past nine, and the fire in the grate had burned low. He kept looking at the clock, which indefatigably went on exerting itself to make the minute hand rotate on its axis. The growing feeling that she would not give in to him, and that she would not shrink from letting things come to a rupture, became a torturing certainty. Then again, this tormenting doubt turned to a calm sorrow; in his depression, he passed his hand through his hair, and then let it fall, and stared at the ruffled head of his image in the mirror facing him. He felt as if a precious treasure had slipped through his fingers, as if he were losing something that had fallen into his hands once and was for ever irreplaceable, but which would now go its own ways and be swallowed up in oblivion. Once he became conscious how fearfully alone he stood—all those who served with him at the "front" stood apart from him at the same, uniform, measured distance—even Scapinelli, although it was from him that he received his orders. Gertrude, however, had been so close to him that he had felt her breath on his cheek, so near that, without having to lean towards her, he could, where he stood, lay his arm about her neck. This nearness of a feminine fellow-creature had something soothingly maternal about it; it was like the foretaste of the long yearned-for ending of an equally long, wearisome, cheerless strife. And now all was to go back and become again as it had been before.

He got up and paced awhile restlessly to and fro, then sat down again quietly in the armchair. He tried to bury himself in the newspaper again, but he could not. He held the paper gripped feverishly in both hands, and stared despairingly at the meaningless print.

A slight sound made him raise his eyes. Gertrude came softly down the stairs. She was stepping cautiously, listening, from stair to stair, and she had put on a different dress, that made her look more youthful and human.

"What are you doing here?" she asked him, more in embarrassment than surprise.

"As you see, I am reading a paper," he said.

"Then you were not afraid of my not coming?" she asked, almost offended.

"Certainly not. I knew you would be changing your dress."

"For an hour and a half?"

"Oh, women——!" He tried to joke it off.

"Please stop!" she ordered him. Then she came up to him, hesitatingly. Many of her steps sounded to him as if she were on the point of turning back. He looked curiously into her eyes—and she did not seem to like it. When she had reached him, she bent down and kissed him.

"Nothing like this must ever happen again," she said in a grimly stern voice. "This hysteria of vain pride is really too silly for words."

He was a little disconcerted.

"You are my brother, and I your sister," she proclaimed, and gave him her hand, which he gripped cordially. "Agreed?"

"Agreed."

She had thrown herself into the armchair opposite his, and laid her folded hands across her knees.

"Scapinelli gave me an amusing order," he now began, "and that was—H'm! how shall I put it? We are to give one another a binding promise that if one of us should begin to fall in love with the other that one is to say so immediately."

"To whom, the Jesuit?"

"No, the other partner."

"Really, that is too stupid," she exclaimed, irritably.

"It is not stupid at all," he broke in. "Just think what a lot of useless bothering can be avoided that way. After all, we live for our work, which must not be interfered with by things of that sort."

"Something stands between us," she said, drawing her brows together. "It is as well that you are drawing my attention to the fact. Between us, there stands—well, sex. Whether it acts as a wall between us or as a magnet between us, is all one—in either case there stands between us a medium, a channel of communication."

He was surprised at the way she spoke, and raised his head.

She was silent for a while. The last remains of the fire were dying down in the grate. In the background the pendulum of a clock was sawing the air. She had rested her chin on her closed hand and was following, with intent gaze, the thin columns of smoke that crept timidly, in serpentine spirals, up the sooty chimney.

He regarded her attentively. Her profile was towards him. He saw again the high, clear forehead, against the background of tapestries, the short, blunt nose, and the energetic, firm chin. She was staring again into the sinking fire, and began to speak again.

"I had once lost all contact with the Church," she said, without warning. "But last year, I went to Mass here at Brühlau. I am quite unmusical. I only like popular tunes, marches, dance-music, jazz—perhaps a few motifs from *Carmen*, *Tiefland*, and *Aïda*. Wagner's operas are simply musical pagodas to me, and Beethoven is utterly incomprehensible—I sat there in one of the back pews, said one 'Our Father,' and then almost went to sleep. But suddenly I awoke from my dreams. The papal hymn was being sung— the feverish martial ardour and wild abandon of the rhythm inspired and delighted me. Suddenly I became madly proud that I was a Catholic in the midst of the governess-like, tepid, respectable Protestantism of this town. All day Sunday I was whistling that tune. I could have embraced the Grand Inquisitor who burned heretics in the Auto-da-fés. I was wild with joy. But it was only joy in the external forms that moved me so. Now you have at last shown me what lies behind them."

"And now you are disappointed!" he finished for her.

"No," she said. "I am not disappointed at all. It is far more beautiful than I had imagined. I am only confused. You must simply give me a little time, and then all will be well."

"I understand you perfectly," he said, reflectively. "You have only seen in Catholicism its outward activities. The heart is Faith and Charity—Love. And actually Love, or Charity, comes first. However active you are, if you do not know and practise Love, you remain a bad Catholic."

He had risen to his feet, and crossed over to the window. Outside, there was the utter blackness of a night in which no object could be picked out by the eye. So he went out, walking slowly, and descended the few steps that led to the garden. The villa was situated at the end of the city, and only in the distance could the street lights be discerned. In front of the garden, the road stretched away into the country. Like a dusky grey river of pallid dough it came out of the darkness and flowed away into the uttermost dark again. Cars with great yellow-gleaming cones of light from their dazzling head-lamps hummed past on the crest of the road, as it changed to a low, moonlight-flooded landscape of little hills.

The night was as cold as in May. He turned up his coat collar and plunged his hands deep into his pockets. And thus he remained, motionless and silent, in meditation, leaning on the chill metal of the garden gate. He looked up at the sky, and saw it filled with stars. That disappointed him. He only liked the night sky hung with clouds, so that one beheld it as a drooping piece of scenery hung above one's head, with curious bulging contours. But as it was now, it seemed lofty, glassy, and the irregular scattering of the twinkling stars made it look like a dome-shaped roof all awry. He turned to go again and, with sunken head, mounted the steps once more. In the doorway of the hall he saw Gertrude; she was sitting in the same place where he had left her, by the grate with its dying fire. How differently she looked now. . . . He understood for the first time the vast responsibility he had to bear for the course and the mission of this fellow-being. The weight of this responsibility made him hesitate so much that he approached her quite humbly and modestly, and asked her, without any of that feeling of superiority and of being the better-informed, whether there was anything that was not clear to her; he would *try his best* to give her an answer in all candour.

She shook her head. He saw only her hair, but he felt that she was still terrified at her task and at the path she believed she had to tread, but which seemed to extend so many miles ahead before her, and seemed to be smiling sorrowfully. But she turned her head unexpectedly towards him, and looked at him. The radiance of her features dazzled him like a search-light, so that he was almost blinded.

"Eugen, do you truly love me?" she asked him. "Can I always depend on your help, in action, in prayer; can I

build upon your counsel?" was what she meant by those
words.

He understood her and nodded.

Then she stood up and looked into his eyes. She was
almost as tall as he. She stretched herself and her shoulders
were on a level with his own. He still had his hands in his
coat-pockets.

Two human beings.

Outside, night. Outside, Europe—the world.

CHAPTER XI

PREAMBLES TO DECISION

SONNENSCHEIN had already returned from Italy; the sisters had put a notice on his door, "No Visitors," but he had secretly removed it. He had even had a telephone brought, and, from his sick-bed, carried on the work of Catholic Charity. A host of people came to see him. In a corner of the room somebody was tapping out on a typewriter his latest article for the *Kirchenblatt*. Presents from visitors accumulated, but Sonnenschein placidly gave everything away again. Visitors often looked with amazement and suspicion at poor men and women whom they met on the staircase with their arms loaded with the presents they themselves had brought that day to the man who was dying of his illness. Sonnenschein gave everything away that he possessed. Even his weather-worn and patched cape—which in the days of his work out of doors had lent him the appearance of a scarecrow—he gave away; he gave away his clean linen from the laundry, his hat, his collars, even the cactus plants which belonged to a sister and which she had kept in the room he was occupying, in which she had formerly lived.

But at night, when all about him was quiet, he lay, open-eyed, counting the strokes of the chapel bell, praying wildly and with passionate ardour, and groping in the grey-blue darkness of the lonely sick-room for the wooden Crucifix that lay upon the bed-table, beside the medicine bottles, the

teaspoons, water-glasses, and thermometers. He would carry
the hard wood to his lips, and not till morning would he
pass over in sleep to the realm of restless dreams. Then the
hospital odours—the smell of white enamel, linoleum, and
sickly decay—slipped through his nostrils to his lungs, and
tremors of anxiety for his successors, for the continuance
of the work he had started, surrounded his thoughts like a
hampering network. Since the imminence of death had
become a certainty in his mind, he was not tormented by
the haunting thought that he might lose his eyesight. He
was so closely encircled now with the shades of God that
the thought of no longer being able to work for His Kingdom
on earth merely filled him with a melancholy sense of leave-
taking, without causing him actual pain.

Gertrude was in love with Eugen. The consciousness of
this fact came to her so suddenly that she was genuinely
frightened by the discovery. He had arranged to come for
a talk, and had arrived very late. She had waited for him
with an impatience to which she was quite unused, had
walked excitedly up and down the room, moved flowers
from one table to another, and kept looking in turns at her
wrist-watch and up and down the street. At last the bell
went, and when she heard from downstairs the sounds of his
footstep and his slightly high-pitched, loud voice, she could
feel the beating of her heart. She looked at herself in the
glass, and noted how a large vein in her full-throated neck
was throbbing visibly beneath the taut skin.

Her excitement disappeared at once when he greeted her
with his cheery, laughing face, took her hand, and shook it
vigorously, dropped into a chair and began, without transi-
tion, to talk about the work. She scolded herself silently
for her state of nerves, and after a time, began to get angry
with that air of mocking, didactic superiority that he always

displayed. Shortly before he left, she asked him about his own plans, and so he told her about the problem of collective guilt, and of Scapinelli, who had told him to travel round the various outposts in the Soviet Union this year, to take over accounts, pass on orders, and call in reports.

"Shall you do that?" she asked him, indifferently. "I should think it must be pretty risky work."

As she was about to go up to her room again, she noticed his gloves, that he had forgotten, lying in the hall. She took the thick, stiff leather, and examined them amusedly. She slipped them on—how huge they seemed, on her hands! Slowly the picture of Eugen rose in its entirety before her mind's eye, and by the time she got back to the drawing-room her heart was beating as noticeably as before his arrival. She could see him now, his hands in his pockets, hatless, his blonde hair a little inclined to droop over his forehead, with a smile that creased long furrows from the corners of his nose down to his chin; that, and his blunt, short nose, gave him a droll air—almost like a clown. She sat down on the arm of the chair in which Eugen had sprawled, and looked wistfully about at the emptiness of the room. She *felt* the emptiness, too, for those few moments—and it was only then that the unexpected suddenly happened. She fell back and spread out her arms, buried her face in the cool leather of the club chair, and was seized with a furious longing to see him again, to embrace him, to kiss him. This surge of emotions rushed over her in broken, irrepressible eddies—like a river in flood that bursts through a broken dam. Now, for the first time, she realised what a hunger for love clamoured to be appeased, behind all the cold mask of her preference for solitude. In every way, now, she saw him as Franz Zechmeister's superior—was he not big and wise and brave, a tempestuous saint of the highways and the pavements, a tramp of the Church, without ties of time, space or thought, a modern Hound of God? He glowed with a great inward warmth, and despite all his inexorability, his severity, his decisive strictness, he radiated such a genial warmth that even the most callous and ill-disposed felt themselves softening under it. And he had, too, that impersonal detachment peculiar to all Catholics on the "fighting front," and gave one the impression that every word he spoke was inspired in him by some heavenly power; that he was a mere unit in the forces engaged in the service of God. On the other hand, unlike Scapinelli, who had already suffered the sanctifying "freezing to death" of human passion, for the greater glory of God and His Church, in Eugen's case personal feeling would break through its barriers every now and then, and then he would feel so curiously uncertain and helpless. Then he would come out with actions and words over which Scapinelli had to smile his sunny, paternal, indulgent smile.

She was still sitting alone in the drawing-room with the gloves on the arm of the club chair, and she lifted the gloves to her lips. Suddenly she started—there came over her all at once, brutal, urgent, the memory of her promise to tell him of her love. She struggled against the thought with all her might, and was almost in despair; for she hated the sense of being bound by any tie or coercion. She crossed the room and sat on a sofa, and strove to persuade herself that these feelings she had for Eugen were infinitely remote from anything that necessarily involved the conclusion that she loved him, in the sense in which love occurs between the sexes. She remembered that once, when she was tormented by doubts of the Faith, she had quickly formed a resolve to tear out of her heart the pallid, problematical, dimmed image of Christ, on the principle that half was worse than nothing, and the attempt had been a failure.

In the same way, now, she deliberately made her imagination play with the thought of what it would be like if Eugen had never come into her life, or if, through any combination of circumstances, he should even now disappear from her horizon; if, for example, he were to go to South America to plant coffee, or to Australia to carry on meteorological research, or if he crossed the boundary-line between White and Red on the Polish frontier, and passed over into the grey realm of the Red Czar, to take part in the organisation of Catholic work, persecuted by the Lubyanskaya Ploshtshad. His words, when speaking about the Jesuit's proposal, and his embarrassed and uncertain answers to her questioning, came back to her mind—and, suddenly, she had the vision of him, with pale face and alabaster-white body, bathed in blood, on his knees in the cellar-dungeon of the "Extraordinary Commission," with his neck shot to bits, with horrible festering wounds, and then, again covered over with quick-lime—buried, simply disposed of like refuse. The thought of not having his eyes shining for her, his mocking mouth reproving her, made her realise to the full how close to her he had become.

She knelt down in front of an image of St. Ignatius, that stern, man's saint, and prayed for the strength to keep her word. And then, in this prayer for strength and almost masculine sincerity, she realised to what a vast extent he had become, during long, long days, separated by dark nights, the central axis of her life, the innermost content of herself, and the typically feminine zeal to do anything, anything, for him, to sacrifice recklessly, give away everything, seized her and filled her with a wild, blind, insensate joy.

But Eugen guessed nothing of all this. In St. Hedwig's Hospital, Sonnenschein lay in his death-agony. In St.

Hedwig's Hospital, too, Helga was lying, dangerously ill with fever, after the birth of her child, and the doctors were shaking their heads over her. How he hated the hospital, with its sickly-sweet smells that seemed to hint of decay, its dreary corridors. This was a time of many grey, sad memories, but with no living, vitally active, experiences—he found himself longing for a drawbridge, for soldiers, tumbling down steep declivities like sacks of flour. He drove out these pictures of satanic paganism, and immersed himself more than ever in the unhappy anxiety that he was always careful to conceal from Gertrude. With her, he was engaged in active service at the Front, and that meant that he must keep his poise. But the gloom and pallor of the working day was, with him, always tinged with a somewhat weary fondness for the opposite sex. At times, he even longed to go away somewhere, into the country, and marry a tall, blonde woman, with high cheek-bones and perhaps a squint, to live with her and have children like the ones in soap advertisements, and to sit with a glowing cigarette in the summer nights, talking softly, in front of the villa, with his wife, and gaze at the stars in the Milky Way. These dreams he kept to himself. His vanity would not let him expose to others the sheer humanity of his personal make-up. It was more than vanity—it was a seed of cowardice, sprouting unsuspected.

Helga died just after her confinement, suddenly and unexpectedly, and they accompanied her to the grave. Gertrude went with him. His mother wept. Eugen had his hands in the pockets of his overcoat. Rudolph Medek sat with dry, parched eyes, looking on staringly at the Mass. *"Requiem aeternam dona eis, Domine!"* They sang in the choir, "Our heart is restless, till it rests in thee, O God." Eugen repeated, in a murmur, the words of St. Augustine, "Rest can be only in eternity, rest can be only, solely, in the hereafter, rest is

death. Here, is only strife, sorrow, rage, sin, commotion."
He kept glancing at Rudolph Medek across the upturned
earth. Rudolph's nose had sharpened to a bird-like point.
He had only just got back from France on the receipt of a
telegram with the news. The misery in his heart was reflected in the grey pallor in his cheeks, the skin that stretched
like faded glove-leather from cheek-bone to jaw.

Two days later, Sonnenschein died. Hour after hour, he
fought with death, in the hospital bed, with clammy brow,
cracked lips, sightless eyes, jerky, painful breath, the
telephone mouthpiece on his pillow, his Crucifix in his hand.
The poison of uræmia was rapidly destroying a physique
worn out with superhuman labours and sleepless nights.
The Nuncio himself, with his rimless glasses and his face of
an inspired philosopher, had come from his palace, which
had formerly served as headquarters of the General Staff,
and brought him the Holy Father's blessing. The Chan-
cellor, his former secretary, with the sharp, thin nose, and
the serene, calm brow, had paid him his last visit. There he
lay now, the "Pope of Berlin," done to death, powerless;
the wings of Death casting their shadow over him as they
hovered ever closer. His heart, so restless and yet so filled
with love, beat clamorously and erratically, forgetful of its
normal rhythm, behind his ribs. He could no longer see the
tearful colleagues who had worked with him on the *Kirchenblatt*, and in the charitable movements; he could no longer
see his cupboard, that hung empty upon the wall since, in
expectation of his approaching end, he had given away all
that he had. He could no longer see anything except that
sector of the Front on which he had driven himself so hard,
even unto death—his Germany, his Berlin. He saw the whole
realm returned to the bosom of Mother Church; his tremulous eyes beheld the Cardinal of Berlin blessing the populace
from the steps of a cathedral built of concrete and steel and

glass, the sovereignty of the banks shattered, the Kurfürsten-damm, the streets of fashion and ostentation and wanton luxury, abandoned; Chorin and Lehnin blossoming afresh; Gregorian chants of praise echoing in the churches on the Baltic coast. Then, however, his vision cleared, and what he beheld was the company of the Saints, the Church Trium-phant, and he knew that he was entering into the Kingdom of God, into the ranks of the Blessed, among whom were St. Francis, St. Vincent, St. Peter Claver, all the great friends of the poor and ailing, all apostles, pioneers, preachers of the word.

Thousands followed his coffin: members of the cabinet, pickpockets, officials, Protestants, burglars, members of sodalities, Bolsheviks, old women, students, newsboys, lawyers, Jews, tramps, business men, canal-dredgers, tailors, typists, actors, pilots, office servants, domestics; all and everyone. On his grave there lay over eleven hundred wreaths. In Berlin, the traffic was held up. An army was being transported to his graveside.

Eugen had attended the funeral with Gertrude and Rudolph Medek. Gertrude wore a mask of inscrutable sorrow. As he parted from her she said, "I have something very important to speak to you about—not to-day—when you come to Brühlau next, but come soon, don't keep me wait-ing."

Eugen went home with Rudolph. Arrived at the house, Rudolph showed him a host of photographs he had taken in French religious houses—in the Haute-Combée, at Lisieux, Chartres, Lille: "Wouldn't you like to bury yourself in one?" Rudolph asked him.

He shook his head.

"No," he said, "once, I should have—in the later years of adolescence—but two years ago I was in Hungary, at the

Pannonhalma monastery, and walked through the corridors. It was deadly quiet, there. And that quarter of an hour there sounded a warning in my mind—I can't stick that. I want a wife, I want children."

"A man of your sort," said Rudolph, "of *your* sort—and you have the absurd yearning to caress a fellow-human with long hair, and to absorb yourself in the question of gas bills—a whitewashed nursery smelling of milk-bottles. A man like you."

Eugen searched through his wallet, till he picked out a photo of a Bulgarian woman with her two laughing children. "There," he said, "that is a mother with her young——"

Rudolph waved the picture aside. "The baby complex!" he said, scornfully. "It's quite true, of course, that marriage is a sacrament, like the others—but a man like you! And in such a terribly critical time, of all things, when every man is wanted. What are you really doing—what does it all come to? Just travelling along obscure roads—and falling by the way."

Eugen sat on a table, and studied Rudolph's face attentively. "You talk," he said slowly, "as if you were about to become a Trappist to-morrow——"

"Bad guess," Rudolph interrupted, "I'm going to be a Discalced Carmelite, and I enter the Lille Carmel next week. It's all fixed up!"

Eugen was thunderstruck. He saw Rudolph laughing at his dismay, and then saw him again, with his soulful eyes, in a dinner-jacket, surrounded by girls, scintillating with wit, boisterous, with mischievously twinkling eyes, alert as a peeping mouse, in the midst of men and women swayed with the heady wine of pleasure, the old Rudolph, the Feuilletonist, the epigrammatic critic of the Kurfürstendamm, in the Roman Café with his pocket-books full of pictures of the saints, the man who had been constantly falling and then

telling, wearily and despairingly, how women pursued him.
And then again he saw him as he would look in a few
weeks' time, his will broken in, his hair shaved off, those
dancing feet encased in sandals, his body in a shapeless
robe. He reflected how secularised the world had become,
when he, the Catholic, was so horrified and incredulous at
Rudolph's decision.   He seemed to himself like a war-
correspondent who had for a year been working on an
assignment on the life of the battle-front, and had penned
all the time only words that had none but an impersonal
and theoretical significance for himself—and who was
now, for the first time, suddenly confronted with a shell
bursting at his feet.

He pulled himself together, however, and said in uncertain tones: "Just when the times are indeed so critical, and
the world filled with heretics, we need every man at the
front.   Your proper place is the drawing-rooms, and you
want to bury yourself. Why not go to the Jesuits?"

Rudolph Medek pursed his lips into a Carmelite smile.

"It comes to the same thing whether I deliver lectures
like Fahsel, or whether I pray in my cell at Lille. The results
on the battle-front are the same—or aren't they? Or have
you already given way to the morbid mechanic-rationalist
complex?"

Eugen bit his lips.

"No!" he said, grimly.

But Rudolph Medek did not let him off.

"You," he said, "you are the one who ought to go to the
Society of Jesus. You are a front-trench man of action, to
whom God has appeared in the heat of skirmishing at the
Front. But apparently you see everything awry, like the
common run of men turned out by mass-production, who
wear out the pavements with their shoddy shoes. To you
the contemplative orders appear like places for those 'half-

wits' to foregather in, who carry out no 'useful' work, and just 'grovel' at the feet of God. But you've always had a terrible inclination towards the spiritual dainties of the cutlets-and-crumbs order, for petty little, cowardly narrow-minded bourgeois notions, and a sensible sort of Catholicism."

"I could, of course, join the Society of Jesus," said Eugen. "I am not too big a coward to do that—but I should become dried up, I should not be perfectly poised and balanced, like Scapinelli, even—and carry a quietly glowing flame within myself. I should get hard, mean, artful, cold, become a great servant of our Church, indeed!" He spoke with a show of emotional sentiment and pathos that was foreign to his usual wont. "But nothing good would come from me, because Charity, Love, would have gone out of me. I should be the terror of the Protestants, the Bolsheviks, the Philistines, a gloomy, un-Catholic, un-Christian creature in a soutane. And after my death, it would be found that I did not even belong, like Ghandi or any Red Indian of the Tierra del Fuego, even to the *soul* of the Church, but. . . . Oh, let's drop the subject."

A week later Rudolph Medek and Eugen Düring were at the railway station. They were meeting Anton Brosig, who was to arrive from Rome. Half an hour after the scheduled time for the arrival of the Rome express another train was to carry Rudolph off from the station to pay a farewell visit to his mother, who was going to Vienna. The Rome-Berlin express came a little late. Anton Brosig jumped out of the train and hurried up to them. The greeting was a hasty one. Brosig was inclined to be talkative, and needed no pressing when asked for a short report.

"Down there one feels that one is at the centre of things. Everything is so quiet, and yet so full of tension; ceremonial, festive, and yet, beneath every unobtrusive word that is

spoken, there lies some far-reaching significance. When you
read the Encyclicals you begin to realise the meaning that
underlies the mask of their mediæval, stiff, colourless formula,
if you realise how they determine our life here at the Front.
Down there, they go about in long soutanes, and are strict in
preserving a becoming dignity. Here all is excitement; here
is a trench full of unbalanced men and women, of un-
reflecting, rushing, uncontemplative zealots in feverish
activity."

"And what do they say about us?"

"The Holy Father's eyes light up when anybody mentions
Germany. But how different things are there, how different
the atmosphere is there, when compared with that at the
Nunciature or the Bishop's Palace. I was at the Russian
College and at the German-Hungarian College; at the
Ethiopian College, where the Abyssinians are lodged; in
the *Propaganda Fide*, where I talked with the newly anointed
Chinese bishop; at the Congregation of Rites and at the
Sacra Rota—wherever you go you meet men who are full
of a calm repose and dignity: courtiers, high dignitaries of
the Church, directors of the great Catholic orchestras,
aristocrats of the altar, officiating in a centralised work of
organisation; and the one worry of them all is—Russia."

Rudolph Medek was on tenterhooks to go—his train was
due in five minutes. Eugen explained Rudolph's resolve to
Anton Brosig in a few words. Rudolph secured his seat in the
train, and then came back. They stood silent and awkward,
on the hard concrete floor of the station. They felt, all of
them, that any word of emotion they uttered now would
release the floodgates. The picture that Brosig had conjured up in their minds, of the supreme command at Rome
was effaced. Eugen and Anton Brosig saw Rudolph now
not in his travelling ulster, but in the great tonsure, the cowl,
and the wooden sandals. They felt like doctors who, through

the screen of the X-ray apparatus, see the skeleton of a patient, a sight not given to other people till after death and decay have exposed it. Rudolph Medek, however, gazed at the station and its structure with wide-open eyes. His gaze wandered over all the notices and advertisements referring to Berlin, and once more he drew in, in great breaths, the coal-dust and sulphur-laden air of the city—a city in which he had done almost two years active service at the Front, that had caused him so much bitterness and sorrow, and yet had brought him so many steps nearer to perfection.

He turned to Eugen with a smile. From his face radiated the serene happiness of the Jesuit Giovanni Battista Scapinelli; and once more they shook hands. It was done quite mechanically. Rudolph Medek got into his train, and then everything passed off according to programme. Guards waved small flags, guards whistled, a station-master looked about, excited; people were waving handkerchiefs; to the agitated snorting of the engine the train drew away from the platform, and streamed over an almost endless ocean of rails, through a forest of signal-posts and signal-boxes, and sped onward, till people's hands waving handkerchiefs dropped to their sides, and the crowds turned, suddenly become indifferent, towards the exits.

Eugen said good-bye to Brosig. He wanted to be alone, not to have his thoughts distracted by his journalistic colleague's chatter, for he was busied with a resolve which was gradually ripening in his mind. He sat down on a bench, and stared at a hoarding, where his eye was caught by the white-yellow-and-white notice to foreign Catholics that is exhibited in every railway station. His gaze roved over words in Lithuanian, Dutch, Ukrainian, French, Polish—and at the end he read, in Russian, that a Catholic service for Russians would be held in Charlottenburg. There was also information as to when and where there were facilities for confessions. All this seemed, somehow, reassuring. Satisfied, he passed on.

He gazed out from the station yard, and looked at the lonely sea of rails. "That is how I would depict the future, in a symbolical painting," he reflected. "A railway station exit with rails and signal-lamps—and the rails glistening a little in the sunlight." He went on. "The great anxiety is still Russia," he mused, almost speaking his thoughts aloud, "is still—Russia! And it afflicts the Holy Father." He went on. The words had been spoken so bluntly and emphatically. He went on, seeking something; his brow was moist. He went up to a telephone kiosk. For a second his hand hesitated on the catch of the door. Then he went in and called up the Jesuit. "Brosig is back," he said. "He will be at the editorial offices this evening. News? Not much. The Holy Father is worried about the sectarianism in Russia. I shall be glad to go. Where? To Russia. It was you who made the suggestion to me. Good-bye."

CHAPTER XII

GOODBYE TO ALL THAT

THAT afternoon Eugen drove out to see Gertrude. He had thought to find her in the garden, but the garden was empty, and the crunch of his shoes on the gravel paths remained unheard. All the doors, however, were open—the garden door, and the front door. So he went up to the drawing-room. The staircase windows were open, too, and so it happened that the sunlight poured in, in bright, wide streams, and the villa, with its great airy rooms, gave the complete illusion of a country summer-house, far remote from all the petty narrowness of a small provincial town.

As he entered the drawing-room he saw her sitting on the wide, bright-hued sofa, reading a book. He stopped whistling and paused, surprised, hesitant. She had not risen as she usually did, had not held out her hand to him, but stayed there, seated, staring at him, her head thrown farther and farther back, with absolutely Slavonic slits of eyes above her high cheek-bones, till he was standing before her like a dark wall. He picked up her unresisting, passive hand from the book on which it lay, and shook it. Then he sat down, next to her, on the divan. "What do you want to see me about?" he asked, brusquely. Then he realised how rough his tone sounded, and added, "you told me that you had something important to tell me."

She looked away, past him, her cheeks slowly colouring.

"You remember our promise," she said softly, "that time —as Scapinelli had insisted on, to you——"

He understood it all now, and for a moment, a small-minded rush of pleasure, the delight of gratified vanity, swept through him. Then, however, such brave honesty touched him, till he wanted to take her in his arms—but she sat so far off, that his finger-tips scarce met behind her neck. "My dear, good comrade!" he whispered to her. His fingers closed, till her body relaxed, yielding to the pressure of his strong hands. They both sank sideways back, leaning their heads in the deep pile of the soft, velvety upholstery, and eyed one another. Their faces were so near that her breath fanned his cheek like a faint breeze. Under his hand, he could feel the throb of the vein in her throat, and a jubilant voice within him cried: "See! There is a being who *loves* you, a body created for you, and a soul clamouring for the warmth of your words!" He felt that he had found a resting-place, somewhere where he could relax and unbend, tired and weary, exhausted even beyond tears.

"I am so happy!" he said, his eyes creasing up into a smile. "So happy! I shall go my way calm and in gladness. It means so much, feeling oneself loved." He became silent, his brow wrinkled, and he looked, thoughtfully, broodingly, wistfully, at her, over the barrier of his arm. Her throat was warm to his touch. He could feel—Life.

"And—am I, too, loved?" It was she who asked the question.

"Of course I am fond of you," he smiled, "*very* fond."

His fingers relaxed, and his right hand slid over her cheek. His voice went from gentleness to utter tenderness.

"I shall use *du* to you.* That will be better, won't it? When I see you lying there like that—perhaps never to see

*The "you" of relatives, lovers, intimates, in most European languages (cf. French "tu"). —Trans.

you again—then I realise how dear you have grown to me——"

"Fine sort of active service for the Front the *Herr Lieutenant* is doing now," she laughed. "He lies on the divan and forgets all about his poise. *Tenue, Monsieur, tenue!*"

"It is 'good-bye,'" he said, gravely; but immediately, tried to laugh again.

With true feminine instinct she had guessed the danger that threatened him.

"'Good-bye'! Why? Where are you going?"

She had jumped up, and stood staring at him.

"To the U.S.S.R. Seccatura with sectaries—a tour of inspection," he said, half raised on his elbows.

"That means to your death," she said, "your death—and you love me, too. To your death—it is madness!"

"Oh, no!" he exclaimed, "I shall be drinking a hefty toast to Scapinelli's health, with dear old Uncle Stalin, in the Kremlin—and I shall nominate you as prefect of the sodality of female employees of the Ogpu."

"Stop!" she interrupted. "If you care for me, even a little——"

"Nice sort of Philistine you are," he said. "If there were anybody listening, he'd think we were a bourgeois married couple, and the wife was trying to stop her husband going to the dance, because she was jealous. After all, we aren't married——"

The last sentence came to her with a blow of disillusionment. He was so near her, and yet so remote. Now for the first time, she felt that he did not belong to her.

She dropped into an armchair and buried her face in her hands. "A Church of frightfulness!" she exclaimed. "Of frightfulness! A man-eating Church! Sonnenschein, Medek, Helga, and now—you!"

"If the Church of Christ does not please you," he said,

his voice hard, "you can select what you like from it, and set yourself up as a heretic. Then you will become 'strict,' 'righteous,' 'simple.' Choose yourself some northern, governess-like religion, where you can interpret the Bible for yourself; and then brush your hair back, put on eye-glasses, and become a Deaconess, and gush about a simplified, 'while-you-wait' Christianity, altogether reactionary—a 'primitive' Christianity built up on a foundation of philological acrobatics, with a deep resentment in your heart against the two-thousand-year-old development. As background, a motherless, washed-out Christ."

She sat up, and looked at him. Her Slav eyes had become dilated and weary; there was no more strength in them now, no more power to resist. But in her face was the reflection of a nameless misery. She felt that her own views had been turned against her, that she had been beaten with them—not only beaten, thrashed. She looked at him: his mobile lips sent a thrill of emotion through her—they were like the smiling lips of one bound to the post, to the stake of martyrdom. She was very close to tears, and her body slumped back.

"Go," she said, "I shall pray for you. And do you pray for me, that I may not fall. You are so brave, and I am so small and petty, and in love. And you are going away. And then, I love you so, and ought to be so proud of you, not hold you back. Oh, the misery of it all! It is——"

Then, for the first time, she felt his lips upon the hair about her temples. She did not look up again. She only heard his step upon the stairs, going down. But downstairs, in the garden, he stood still—breathed once more the perfume of the flowers, and blinked up at the glowing sun. A little sadness for Gertrude's sake weighed like a gossamer cloud upon him. A gentle wind stirred the fabric of the great garden umbrella. In the hedge there were birds, singing. Sunshine upon the garden, sunshine upon his face —and, for the last time, sunshine within his heart.

He closed his eyes, and, turning his face upwards towards the sun, saw the red blood in his eyelids. He laughed up at the glowing, warm light—it was a child's laugh. For the last time.

PART II

INSTRUCTIONS FOR DYING

They were working through the list and near the end Eugen was reading it out, with the Jesuit making a comment on each name, and then he would make a pencil mark against it.

"Mgr. Stoskin, Bishop of Vilnius——"

"Soloki."

"Fr. Richard Suberevo, S.J., Elektrozavod——"

"On duty."

"Fr. Meinrad Flechtner, O.P., Red steelician——"

"Missing."

"Dom Sebastian Deboru, O.S.B., compositor on the Tsentrizdat——"

"Dead."

"Fr. Thaddaeus Kochanowski, D.V.M., Mnspolntzai——"

"Dead."

"Father Georg S. Popov, X.A.I.S——"

"Dead."

"Fr. Lodovico Perruxi, S.J., Dinapostrin——"

"In service."

"That's all."

The Jesuit Count Battista Szapinelli leaned back and began to talk in low tones. This was the way—by dropping his voice—that he made his audience doubly attentive.

"I am perfectly sure," he said, "you understand very clearly just what sort of step you are undertaking. You have

CHAPTER I

INSTRUCTIONS FOR DYING

THEY were working through the list, and near the end. Eugen was reading it out, with the Jesuit making a comment on each name, and then he would make a pencil mark against it.

"Mgr. Sloskan, Bishop of Mohilev——"

"Ssolovki."

"Fr. Richard Suberceau, S.J., Elektrozavod——"

"On duty."

"Fr. Meinrad Flechtner, O.P., Red Mechanician——"

"Missing."

"Dom Sebastian Dobozi, O.S.B., compositor on the Tsentrizdat——"

"Dead."

"Fr. Thaddaeus Kochanovski, O.F.M., Mospoligraf——"

"Dead."

"Father Georg S. Popov, Z.A.G.S.——"

"Dead."

"Fr. Lodovico Peruzzi, S.J., Dnieprostroi——"

"In service."

"That's all."

The Jesuit Giovanni Battista Scapinelli leaned back and began to talk in low tones. This was the way—by dropping his voice—that he made his audience doubly attentive.

"I am perfectly sure," he said, "you understand very clearly just what sort of step you are undertaking. You have neither to break down bridges, nor to set fire to factories, nor to derail trains; you have simply to watch and observe—fruitfully and objectively—to travel from place to place, and to collate the reports from the different observation posts and working centres.

"You will learn the language fluently within seven months, starting to-morrow. At Charlottenburg you will get a room in a suitable neighbourhood, and I will guarantee you a pronunciation that will not involve you in any embarrassing difficulties.

"Your pass you will, as it happens, be able to get from me —we got it from a fugitive from the Soviet, who died in St. Hedwig's hospital. This good fellow was born in Kraslava that is to say, in Latvia. And that is a very important fact to realise, for it means that if you are located there, it will be difficult to establish your identity in your birthplace. Of course you will have no foreign passport, simply the papers and a document that amounts to the equivalent of the French *carte d'identité*.

"That already contains mention of St. Hedwig's Hospital. Have you your appendix? Yes? That is a pity—it will have to be removed, as in the case of the missionaries. Last year, one of the fathers at Sverdlovsk, where he worked in the disguise of an iron-founder, fell ill with acute appendicitis—he was operated on, talked while under the anæsthetic, and was carried off from his sick-bed to the prison cell. The outcome can be imagined."

There was silence in the room. When the Jesuit became aware of this silence, he began to speak again.

"You must clearly understand," he said, "that you are not going to Central Africa, among simple-minded, brave, kindly, thorough-going pagans, to Bantus or Zulus—but among heretics. These people are pitiless. Of the Fathers sent to Russia from the Collegium Russicum at Rome, over ten per cent go to their death the moment they cross the frontiers. The loss is ghastly. Often, it is our best material. A Jesuit pursues his studies and training at least till he is thirty-two. I knew one who was sent there as soon as he had completed his second noviciate, and was riddled with shots by the heretical guards on the Dniestr—the Dniestr ran red.

"Of the men who are engaged in the work there, nearly a quarter are detected and brought to trial. On the way back, another ten per cent or more meet catastrophe. You must make no mistake about it—less than half come back again.

"Now we still have to consider the way in. The Dniestr is ruled out altogether—that is no longer a route to be thought of at all. The Esthonian frontier is guarded with barbed wire, and rigorously watched. The Polish frontier is now very unsafe—and I advise you to keep away from the Lettish frontier, since you were—on paper, at least— born at Kraslava. The Finnish frontier? The part from the mouth of the Systerbäck to the lake of Ladoga is out of the question. It is covered inch by inch by the Ogpu. Through Asia is rather too long a route, but apparently the only one left. Turkey swarms with spies, but on the other hand the Manchurian-Russian frontier and the Mongolian-Russian frontier offer an unguarded opening——"

"And the Caucasus?" suggested Eugen.

"Can you climb? You can? Well, that's not a bad idea. Only be careful, because the authorities in Ankara and in Moscow are rather too closely in touch. We should find at least one thousand marks for travelling expenses! You wish to do it? But, I repeat, the heretics are pitiless—once you find yourself brought to your knees in the Lubianka you can amuse yourself with Thomas More in a detailed discussion of this topic! Believe me, the 'Orthodox' heretics were not by any means soft—but now it is a case of one heresy devouring the other—not a pretty spectacle, by any means!"

The Jesuit sighed.

"But to get back to the question of your way in. Perhaps you would do best to take one of the *Compagnie de Navigation Paquebots* from Marseilles or Stamboul to Trebizond. From there you can go up—but quite unobtrusively, please —to Rizeh by boat, and walk from there on to Adsharistan; and once you get to Batum you'll find some way of getting on."

He was silent again. When he resumed, his voice had become much lower.

"Another point to bear in mind is the way to die. If you are being martyred, you can then becomingly say everything openly that you know is no news to the people there. Offer your sufferings for Russia. Pray to St. Laurence if you are in their power—he is the patron Saint of travellers to Russia. And, above all, don't pose! Don't protest, don't bawl, don't display any cynicism, and don't kill any prison-guards. We are the advance guard of the Church of Christ in Russia, and so you will not take up any weapons against either the agents of the oil magnates, or the tooth-brush factories. The Franciscans of Bosnia, fifty years ago, certainly went about with guns and many a Muslim had his Kaftan riddled— but we've got far beyond that nowadays.

"And listen—don't disgrace me—especially if it comes to a matter of negotiations. And never beseech any State to intervene! It is of very little help—the fall of Cieplak and Budkiewicz showed that—and it only does harm to us.

"It is really very hard on one," said the Jesuit, after a reflective pause, "when one is being tortured, and has no evidence to give them, except the names of the working priests, which one must not under any circumstances disclose. I warn you not to let yourself be seduced by the Evil One in that hour—in such circumstances, the prisoner often becomes a prey to the deepest depression and is capable of anything. It's an undertaking—yours, I mean—that really only a *man*, in the fullest sense of the word, is fit for."

Once more Scapinelli was silent. Outside, it seemed already to be growing dark. The Jesuit's face gleamed whitely through the dusky twilight of the room.

"Have you anything else to ask?" he enquired. His voice sounded broken and hoarse.

Eugen made no reply. He looked over the papers, the lists, the maps, the documents, which lay strewn indiscriminately before him. With difficulty he raised his eyes from these, and lifted his head. He saw the picture of St. Ignatius of Loyola on the white-washed wall. He felt that he was standing very close to him. He was no longer up there in the picture hanging on the wall—Saint Iñigo, the Basque, the ascetic, the warrior, the mystic and the thinker. He felt the radiance of his lofty, serene brow, the pressure of his veined, parched hand on his shoulder, and the sense of utter devotion in the service of the Cause gripped hold of him; shut out his view of everything else. He could see only the path that lay before him, and there was nothing of pain in the recognition of it.

He stood up, and held out his hand to the Jesuit.

Out in the street Berlin was buzzing, Berlin in her youth, in her light-hearted aimlessness, in her joy—but here, inside, were Eugen and the picture of a saint, smiling. It was a smile such as is no longer seen in the streets of the metropolis. No longer; but in the future, perhaps, it will return.

CHAPTER II

THE EDUCATION OF A RUSSIAN

THE next day Eugen was taken to the psycho-technical examination clinic, where pistols loaded with blank cartridge were fired behind his ear, and innumerable other experiments carried out with him. Here he had the sensation of being a piece of merchandise, a great sample of inanimate flesh. From the psycho-technical institute, he came to St. Hedwig's hospital, where, in a sick ward, his abdominal wall was shaven and then, when he had been anæsthetised, in the operating theatre, his appendix was removed. He could not get rid of that sense of being an article of trade. He did not like being dispatched up and down stairs at eleven o'clock in the morning, on a stretcher, in his night-shirt. When he was first laid, in a creaking iron bedstead, in the company of four strangers, helpless with the pain of his wound, stiff, and angry, he was thoroughly out of humour.

Out of doors it had continued to be sunny now for some days. A bright golden sun it was, that blazed into every corner unmercifully, and cast sharply-outlined black shadows. And through all the blazing sunshine Berlin roared with a raucous medley of motor-horns, tram-car bells, lorry-wheels, and news-boys' cries. But through the hospital the sisters sped indefatigably, night and day. It was so bewildering—the heat, the chloroform smell, sickly-sweet, that crept into the most sheltered corners, it seemed powerless to affect these veiled figures. He, however, was tied up in bed, instead of hurrying to and fro, and in the night—his night—his light was turned out, and he lay there alone, open-eyed, the crisp linen sheets up to his chin, and strove to make out the forms of things or people around him. He was ashamed before those women, to be lying so idly in bed, so helpless, and be waited on by them.

He remained a week in St. Hedwig's hospital, then said good-bye to his mother, who did not realise the seriousness of his undertaking, and warned him when in Russia, to "just be very careful." Meanwhile, his room had already been got ready for him in a Russian-Catholic home at Charlottenburg; here the dullest monotony awaited him— he must not even take his German-Latin missal with him. He was immediately given a text-book of the East-Slavonic rite. In the morning a Russian servant woke him, and brought him his breakfast. At nine o'clock a Russian emigrant came, and gave him conversation lessons. At twelve o'clock a little hunch-backed, ugly, Moscow woman replaced this teacher, and at three o'clock in walked a former Bolshevik departmental chief, who had been one of Trotzki's party and had recently been converted, and then at five o'clock, at tea, there was dictation, followed during the evening, by exercises and reading; Radio Moscow and Radio Leningrad, Russian newspapers, Russian books, Russian maps, Russian fairy-tales, Russian gramophone records, and Russian prayer-books. Even the tear-off calendar was Russian, the house-keeping routine—every-thing.

German-speaking visitors were not admitted, and he was not even allowed to peep out into the street. The chief emphasis was laid on the importance of a correct accent and pronunciation, in which of course they concentrated on giving Eugen, not the pure accent of Russia proper, but the slightly Latvian accent of Kraslava. He was, too, strictly warned against thinking in German; every morning he was asked whether he had dreamed, and if so, in which language. At first, they often laboured for half an hour over the pronunciation of a single word, and the compulsory thinking in Russian caused him an intolerable effort; he felt himself thrown back years in mental development, and crippled in expression. In a couple of months he had already made enormous strides, and still they did not relax their efforts with him. The Jesuit once visited him—and he already noticed how imperfect was Scapinelli's mastery of Russian. He was never allowed to see the letters that came for him— they were translated to him, that was all.

At the end of the fourth month, he was introduced to fresh Russians, who still noticed the slight trace of German accent in his speech. From that time on he laid aside his ordered *curriculum vitae* and concentrated exclusively on his pronunciation. He often remained with his teachers till late in the night and toiled torturingly with them at the acquirement of a correct accent. He was often tired out and exhausted with work, but the dangerous moment of crisis, as it comes in the case of young Carmelites and Carthusians, had already passed—not for the least moment of time did he find himself brooding. He was engrossed in work and prayer. At the beginning of the sixth month he had already become thoroughly contented; the nerve-straining flickering strings of Russian verbs in their various "aspects" or forms of conjugation no longer pursued him in his meditations, he no longer cried out in Russian in his sleep for help against the Tchecka, he no longer woke up at night, cowering in his bed, fighting off the oppressive weight of torturing thoughts, to awaken again in the dim hours of the morning bathed in perspiration—even those moods, in which he would have liked to weep over his helplessness, in nascent cowardice, had left him—he was completely broken in, he seemed to himself to be no longer the same person as of old, work and devotional exercises had made somebody new of him. He felt light and buoyant, he thought coolly and soberly, human love with its warmth gradually came back to him. Time had come to seem something measurable to him; what seemed strangest to himself, was his lack of any longing for freedom, and his fearlessness of anything that was to come.

By the beginning of his seventh month Advent was at hand, then came Christmas, then the Feast of Wise Men, and Ash Wednesday; Easter was upon them. One morning, Scapinelli called to take him out, accompanied by an unprepossessing young man. They drove through Berlin in a taxi; the streets struck Eugen as comical. There was so much needless haste there, so much absurd self-assertion in the airs and graces men and women put on. You could read it in their faces—the extraordinary value each one set upon himself or herself, and their utter contempt for others. From every countenance alike there shone forth the mystical sky-sign, "Look what a fine fellow I am!" or "What tragedy is embodied in me!" or, in the case of the women, "Who is more femininely alluring than I am?" It all tickled him immensely.

Scapinelli's companion turned towards Eugen, and the latter noticed from his accent that he was a Russian.

"You are an *émigré?*" he asked.

Scapinelli, however, himself answered, instead of his companion.

"This young friend of mine is Dutch. He is your deputy. If you had failed, he would have stepped into the breach in your place!"

"In my place?" asked Eugen, amazed. He was displeased to find that his staying-power had not been believed in.

"In yours," declared the Jesuit. "It has often happened that really reliable men have begun to brood in the loneliness of their abnormally forced grind at the study of the language, and then given it up in advance. Half a year is too long for thinking it over, and too short for a language, Nikalai Sergeyevitch!"

The Jesuit had spoken in Russian again.

"It was only the accent that took me by surprise," Eugen apologised, "but he is Dutch, and speaks German like a Russian!"

"Don't you run away with the idea," chimed in the Jesuit, a little mockingly, "that you speak with a Berlin accent, in the very least. Your German is like a secondary schoolboy's French!"

"I am not I any more," said Eugen gloomily. "Eugen Düring is slain—he committed Harakiri with a Russian grammar. And in his place lives Nikalai Sergeyevitch Kisseleff."

They had arrived at the station; there was the sun again glinting on the rails. Like masts at a harbour, the signal posts loomed up, and the train was already standing by the platform. Old Stegelin, too, was waiting for him, with a pile of literature—Russian newspapers and periodicals.

"Be cautious, and talk to nobody on the journey about your mission," Scapinelli said. "And now I have one more surprise for you that will please you. I wrote to Rome about you, and the General—with the approval of the Holy Father—extended to you all the spiritual privileges and indulgences of the Society of Jesus. Besides which, the Holy Father sends you his Apostolic Blessing."

There were tears of emotion in Eugen's eyes. He knelt down in the midst of all the people on the hard concrete flooring of the station, and received the blessing that Scapinelli pronounced over him, and a furious Philistine, with a fat neck, eye-glasses and an attaché case, watched them with indignant annoyance, and was almost on the point of asking them whether they were in their right senses. He went off, hesitantly, his knowledge enriched with the dubious item that those papists had the brazen cheek even to desecrate the cities of German progress and modern technical enlightenment, with their scandalous mediæval goings on.

Till the departure of the train, not another word was spoken. They stood in a silent group, satisfied to know that they were, if it were for the last time, in bodily contact with one another. Before the final departure, they shook hands mutely.

When the train began to move, Eugen was alone in his compartment. He would not look out at the window again. Even Rudolph Medek had not done so when he had set off on his journey to the cloister. He took out the Old Slavonic psalter from his pocket and began to pray. "*Vladyko Gospodi Issuse Christe, Ty essi pomoshtchnik moi, v rukakh tvoich essm as, pomosi mi, ne osstavi mene———*"

But the train rushed on with ever gathering speed, the tireless wheels of the carriage rattled on over the joints in the rails, but in one of those steel boxes Eugen Düring was praying, seeing before himself a grey, hostile prospect. He knew full well that he was destined to travel over the "points" where the lines of the Church Suffering and of the Church Militant intersect here on earth.

CHAPTER III
DROPPING THE PAST

Across Brandenburg, across Saxony, the train rushed on. As night fell over central Europe, it was passing through the land of the Czechs. Eugen's fellow-passengers were constantly changing. More and more new faces appeared, and then disappeared as noisily as they had come. Again and again the door of the compartment was wrenched open—uncertain, nervously contracting eyes would peer in, and blink enquiringly and apologetically at the seats and racks, and then a heavy body would slump down on the cushions, and a low snort of satisfaction would be heard at a feat well accomplished. Once the frontier was crossed, the first foreign noises began to strike the ear. Words with a poverty of vowels, and with a distant relation, as Eugen noted, to Russian, buzzed about here and there; finally, with the approach of dark, to fade away into faint whispers. The compartment was full, and towards midnight, his fellow-passengers were trying to settle their heads comfortably back into the cushions, some snuggled their noses into the coats that hung down from the luggage-racks, and snored into the lining. Eugen, seated by the window of the carriage, leaned his head on his forearm and tried to sleep. Prague had long ago been passed—Prague, with Hradshin, the city of St. Nepomuk, the martyr of the confessional, the city of revolutionary Protestant tradition, the city of the Chalice and of Master Huss, of St. Wensel and the fall from the window, of the free-thinkers, and of Durych, Masaryk, and Kordac.

By early morning he was in Vienna, and then they went on, eastwards and southwards; it was a journey through lands so near and yet so strangely unknown. First, through a land of Europeanised Mongolians, and then through a land of Slavonicised Tartars; factory chimneys became rarer and rarer, railway workers' uniforms greasier and greasier, the self-determination and individuality, the will to power, of the separate states became more and more clearly perceptible. Prohibitions and notices were everywhere, and the people Eugen met had no vision of distant things—their eyes saw only as far as the next frontier stone, they understood only their own callings, their own tasks. All else was through its strangeness to them, meaningless and senseless in their sight. And yet it was a strange experience for Eugen to meet a race of men who worked extensively on the land and had an intensive mental culture. The Hungarian "*Regnum Marianum*" had been left far behind—he was in the heart of the Balkans, the early home of the darkest and most dangerous sectaries, the Manichæans and Bogumil, the Monophysites and the Arians, the Monothelites and the Nationalists.

The journey he was making was without stop or halt. He heard different accents, saw notices in stations—sometimes in this country, sometimes in that, the language would sound more like Russian. He felt he was riding round the gigantic land, creeping round and up to its Achilles-like heel—carefully, surreptitiously, calculatingly. He became dirty, his hair greasy and matted; he tried to wash in the toilet-compartment, but the dirt would not budge from the folds of his skin. His shirt adhered to his flesh, like the skin of a plum adhering to the palate. His feet were chilled, and he could not eat. At the different stations he bought sausages and tinned foods, cheese and chocolate, acid-drops and mineral waters; all the currencies were new and strange, and each time he returned to his carriage he would reckon up how much he had been cheated of. He reckoned in marks, then in pengös, and then he brought it all down to levas. And thus he passed the time till; in Yugoslavia, a notice instructed him to report to the conductor every bug that he found, but the bites of these dusky red insects did not cause him any particular disturbance. "A preparation for Russia," he thought, and carefully counted the little pink swellings on his hands and chest. Beneath his seat the collection of stoppers, cheese-rind, and sausage-skins continued to accumulate. It was only of the night that he was afraid. Every now and then would come a brief, fleeting thought of Gertrude that was gone as quickly as it came. "She is so dear, so dear!" a fellow-passenger heard him murmur, on the red hills between Nish and the frontier. And that was all.

He could hardly sleep. As he squeezed his way through the narrow corridors he would glance enviously in at the sleeping-car, his eyes caressing the snowy linen sheets on which lay a litter of untidily strewn slippers, pyjamas, night-shirts, and illustrated magazines. He seemed a prey to a longing, with difficulty banished, for ease and luxury, good living, and feminine company. He had not been able to book a berth in the sleeping-car—Scapinelli had made his decision too late—and the Paquet company's steamship, the *Imeréthie II*, was leaving Stamboul in three days. So the nights were a painful striving after some scrap of sleep. Often he would wake up somewhere in the night and stare out at an arc-lamp glaring in at the carriage window, yellowish-white and idiotic. Then he would rise to his feet, stretch his cramped limbs painfully and stagger out a yard or two, away from the muggy warmth, into the fresh coolness of the spring night.

The daze of the short sleep of exhaustion usually persisted

a while, so that he would stumble and trip over rails and wires and steps and rotting wooden sleepers, till he stood in the canteen of some forgotten station, and drank down hot coffee under the suspicious gaze of railwaymen and gendarmes. The black wetness went like a glowing sword down his gullet, and moistened his parched mouth. The man enjoyed it. It was simply that slavish habit of eating and drinking that seizes everybody on a long journey. Finally a whistle sounded somewhere outside, and then he would hurry back. Signals were changed, doors slammed open and shut again, guards waved their lamps.

Suddenly the Balkans were passed, and with the Balkans, the wild sternness and roughness, the deep-seated discontent with all European culture, and that choking of the life of Faith under the tangled wild growth of natural instincts and popular notions. Those strips of land, with their obvious possibilities, their queer sectarian one-sidedness, had slid away beneath the wheels of the train. The train rolled on cautiously, as if pleasantly fatigued by the strain it had undergone, proceeding under a bright blue Mediterranean sky with a gentle gait, as though anxious to go carefully and conserve the remains of a gradually spent vigour. Then one afternoon he arrived at Sekirdshi, the Stamboul station. By now his passport had been decorated with a vast number of stampings of many colours and of many shapes—circles, squares, oblongs—his cheeks were bristly, his clothes crumpled, and his heart filled with an unrest and emptiness it had never before known.

He stopped at the Hotel Bristol in Beyoglu, avoiding the noise and commotion of the large hotels. He shaved, changed his clothes, and went, whistling and swinging his stick, down through the dense crowds in the Street of the Golden Horn. He enjoyed being alone among the many, and it pleased him to pass unnoticed, merged in the throng. The soldiery he met attracted his attention—fair-haired infantrymen walking arm-in-arm with Semitic-visaged Arab comrades; negroes, in similar uniform, thick-lipped and with a blueish tinge in the whites of their eyes, were controlling the traffic; smooth-haired, Mongol-like artillery-men strolled side by side with woolly-pated Levantines. It was a picture such as he had seen nowhere else but in Paris. In the one place Catholicism, in the other Islam, had broken down the untenable popular conception of nation-ality; in the light of a faith that sorted all things according to their relative values, the arrogant prejudice of racial distinction had died out.

Down below, he leaned over the side of the bridge and looked into the sky. A sparkling riot of colour bathed the city and people, and the high-pitched shriek of the motor-boat signals cut through the monotone of noise into which the murmur and movement of the people merged. Above it all there glowed a sun which was not so much an orb as a circular hole cut away in the picture-postcard blue of the sky, and through which could be glimpsed that disc-like view of a miraculously bright background. On this bridge of Beyoglu to Istanbul, over the Golden Horn, life pulsed in all the vital fire of its uttermost reality; on this bridge people from five continents laughed, chattered, and smoked in the sunlight of the Second Rome. It was, indeed, a focus and meeting-point of all nations, like Paris, Shanghai, Cairo, or New York. He could scarcely tear himself away from it all, and would almost have stayed till evening had not the sun begun to shine with a tinge of reddish orange. As he went the first red beams were shining over Scutari and Haidarpasha, and the mists began to bring back the trip-pers from the Princes' Island. He crossed over to Stamboul, dined in a little Turkish estaminet, drank a glass of a wine that was too sweet, and walked slowly back towards Pera. At the very top of the hill, not far from the British Embassy, he sat down in a garden restaurant and stayed alone, with a glass of lemonade, till the dew began to settle on his hair and all the stars had come out one by one in the once dark sky that was dark no longer. He would have felt inclined to speak to one of the many cocottes who sat, like himself, doing nothing, at the tables, but his courage and enterprise failed him even for that. At last the fatigue of his sleepless nights on the railway made itself felt, and he took his way through the rows of seats homewards. Weary eyes set above slightly pallid cheeks and incredibly red lips looked at him with sorrowful curiosity as he passed.

In the middle of the night he was awakened by a savage blare of music. He jumped up and looked out of the window. Exactly beneath his window he saw a jazz-band in a roof-garden, and couples dancing. The band burst into a song that struck Eugen's ear with all the force of something familiarly known: "Oh, you, Oh, you will play me false, you'll——" It was all so utterly *banale* and commonplace, and simple—and yet it set a whole chain of memories stirring in him. It was Gertrude who had been always humming this tune—Gertrude in her car, Gertrude walking along the pavement with him arm-in-arm, Gertrude in the Grünwald and in the fields at Brühlau. He closed the window and drew the bedclothes up over his ears. But all at once the same notes found their way to his ears again and awakened in him a hitherto unknown torment. He experienced an almost physical pain, which still hung about him in his restless broken dreams in the morning.

He awoke next morning with a heavy head. On this day the *Imeréthie II* was to take him to Lazistan. He was not, however, as he usually was before a great undertaking, intoxicated with a sense of enthusiasm, self-confidence, and that great, brave contempt for everything small and trivial. The first time he had gone to Morocco, when the alarum clock had shrilled him out of his bed at seven in the morning in Berlin West, he had leaped out yodelling and singing, flung bolster and quilt to the floor, and stormed into the bathroom and splashed, tied up his shoe-laces with one hand while he stuffed bread-and-butter into his mouth with the other. But now he sat there with ruffled hair, staring across at the bare wall. Suddenly a fit of cowardice such as had never touched him before seized on him, and painted seductive pictures before his eyes. He saw the warm, pleasant editorial offices of the *Reichswarte*, on a winter's day, with gossiping, chattering men talking politics and busy with important work, the sea of lights in Berlin by night, Gertrude's villa with the sunlight rippling over it at Brühlau, and everything that stood for comfort and amenities and friendliness. And now he must leave it all, say good-bye to what was dear and familiar, and concentrate on how he was to behave under the rack of the Tcheka's first, second, and third degrees—what he was to do in order to avoid becoming melancholiac in the darkness, how to grit his teeth if they should start hurting him, which way to turn if they should be hard on his tracks. He could hear the voice of the Jesuit warning him to look for no mercy from the heretics; he could hear the shrieks of the priest whom they had dragged from the operating theatre in Sverdlovsk to the dungeon.

Eventually he got up, dressed, and began to pack his trunk. On the floor lay a little pile of ragged clothing, two pairs of shabby factory shoes, Russian goloshes, Rubashkas, a pocket-knife—also of Russian pattern—a few articles of washing; and when he had finished he fell to his knees and prayed, wildly and desperately, for strength and for trust in God.

The *Iméréthie II* weighed anchor and steered through the Straits of the Bosphorus towards the north and the Black Sea. He stood by the rail, a little disheartened and humbled, caressing with his gaze the receding coast of Europe, the towns, Therapia, Büjükdere, and the little clouds of dust that rolled up over the roads, and the birds that came from the coast of Anatolia and flew westwards. At the sight of these pictures displaying themselves before his eyes, he almost made a solemn vow that if he returned safely he would buy a little farmhouse either here or on the Riviera, or else in the Grunewald, and read rustic novels, or flutter the pages of old bound volumes of Protestant family journals, and live contentedly upon the revenues from his fortune and not meddle with affairs in which he had not been brought up. Then there came a thought that cut right across the others—Gertrude. It hurt him to think of her. He wondered why he had not drawn closer to her all the time they had been together. The tunes of the popular songs, which had already haunted his broken restless slumbers, came back to torment him. He began to murmur against the fate that had let him discover the true nature of his feelings so belatedly. "How different it would have been," he thought, "if I had—if I had——" He was himself none too certain what he wanted.

On the boat he met nobody beyond the ship's surgeon, Dr. Lenoir, and an American engineer from Tiflis who was returning with his wife from an extravagant shopping expedition to Stamboul.

For the most part he avoided people, and passed his time in solitude and privacy. The American woman smiled very alluringly at him if he, restless and distracted, crept out of his cabin to savour the fresh air on deck, yet the flash of her white teeth between her thin but shapely lips had no effect on him at all.

Throughout the night the steamer's bows cut through the waves of the sea, but in the morning anchor was cast, and the few passengers went ashore to open a quick fire with their Kodaks on the minarets and the harem-windows. Meanwhile the ship's hold was fully loaded up—great, clumsy boats brought eggs for the French biscuit factories, and manganese ores. The crane worked and groaned and the windlasses creaked without cease, and not till morning did the siren shriek.

On the third day the friendly vessel's voyage was over. They had called at Samsun and Ordu, and the port of Trebizond was in sight. Not far from the harbour-bar a wreck stood out above the water. "That is what I shall look like on my return," he told himself. He bade Dr. Lenoir a cordial good-bye, and received from him the *Chant du Berger*, by Marguerite, with a high-flown dedication. He shook hands with the stewardess, almost embraced Mr. White, and got into the motor boat. Those people had suddenly become so close to him, the ship had become a home, the humanistic doctor was his best friend. After all they were human— living beings who meant him well, who neither hated nor persecuted him, with whom he could speak quietly, whose healths he drank, for whom he picked up articles they had dropped, returning them with a smile.

He took lunch at a large eating-house belonging to a Mohammedan convert. A bazaar dealer accompanied him to the kitchen, and their host removed the lid of every saucepan and let him taste and smell the food. The realm of gloomy heretics loomed before him like a menacing grey wall, and there flamed up in him once more the yearning to eat well, sleep in a soft bed, read a witty book, pray in a church.

But when he sat at table and bent over his steaming plate, he lowered his spoon pensively into the soup, observing how the liquid gradually ran into the spoon and engulfed it, then said to himself, bitterly, broodingly, "Gallows meat!"

Next day, early in the morning, Holy Communion and the blessing of the Lazarist prior. Then he threw a small bundle of clothes over his shoulder, put the papers into an inner pocket of his coat together with the tchervontses, printed on tissue paper and liberally adorned with watermarks, dropped his rosary into his pocket, and went off to the steamer that brought him to Rizeh. Then he got out his special map and set off on his journey on foot. He was often held up by damp fogs, and often, owing to the utter inadequacy of the map, he went wrong, and had to resort to endless conversations with the inhabitants of the villages, where he tried to use the few scraps of Turkish he had picked up in the Balkans. Gradually the rhododendrons and the bilberries were left behind, and the summit of the Vatchenbeg loomed into view. The path became an interminable switchback, up and down over slate-grey barren land and crumbling rocks. The landscape became mortally desolate. For a time he followed the course of the River Tchorokh, then he crossed it in the neighbourhood of Artvin, and one bitterly cold night slipped across the boundary, still directing his route of march towards Kartchal, then bending off to the north-west. The morning sun, in all its resplendent glory, rising from the Caspian and coming over Azerbaidjan and Armenia, surprised him in a sleeping-bag, not far from Khertvis. He saw the Adsharian valley far beneath him, with its long, flat houses, their roofs seeming almost to press them down into the grey earth. Higher and higher rose the sun. He took out his rosary, once more fingered the cross with its figure of the Saviour, and laid it under a stone. Then he rolled his bundle of clothes into his sleeping-bag, and kneeled down beside it. "*Vladyko Gospodi Issuse Christe, Ty essi pomoshtchnik moi, v rukakh tvoich essm az, pomosi mi, ne osstavi mene. . . .*" ("Lord and Saviour Jesus Christ, thou art my help, in thy hands am I wholly, help me, and leave me not. . . .")

Then he arose and, with slow, hesitant steps, went down to the valley. By evening he had arrived at Batum. The grey realm of dismal heretics had swallowed up Nikalai Sergeyevitch Kisseleff, of Kraslava.

CHAPTER IV

THE PROMISED LAND

It was difficult to find shelter for the night. It was only the end of April, and yet, in Batum, it was still so hot that the perspiration rolled from his forehead in greasy, glassy beads. In the bar of the Hotel International there sat American engineers and petroleum experts, in their shirt-sleeves, drinking whisky and cocktails and discussing naphtha rates and women, polishing their horn-rimmed glasses with check handkerchiefs. Shy and suspicious, he looked in at the noisy men, but at a sign from the bar-tender, a hotel-servant in a grey-blue hospital overall came hurrying in and threw him out with a stream of curses. It happened to be a hotel that was only open to foreigners and high officials of the Soviet. The latter slept all together in an open conservatory on the second floor, in unaired beds.

Weary and dispirited, Nikalai Sergeyevitch dragged his sleeping-bag from alley to alley. A Greek tailor advised him to tip the hotel porter a few roubles. A photographer, after declaring his willingness to take his picture in a Tcherkeska for three roubles, gave him the name of a lady in whose room he could spend the night, combining convenience with pleasure. A Ukrainian-Jewish intellectual, with a confident manner and a white Palm Beach suit, whom he met in the public park, advised him to look in at the inn for tourists. It was already very late, and he shouldered his sleeping-bag once more and trudged off towards the station. On his way there he passed the Catholic Church. He was

seized with a fierce longing to go inside and see whether the
Body of Christ still rested in the Tabernacle, or whether a
yawning emptiness would await him beyond the door of the
church—museum rooms, or school benches, or hospital
beds, or stored goods. He restrained himself, went on,
stumbled, went on again. At the inn a fierce, excitable man,
with a white blouse and a fat neck, ordered him to fill in four
printed forms.

Nikalai Sergeyevitch sat down at a wobbly table over
which an electric lamp threw a bright cone of light, took up
the scratchy pen, and began to write.

"Look here, young man!" interrupted the manager of the
hostel, "write properly, not like a cockerel on the dung-
heap! That's a State Document you're filling up there. A
document, d'you hear? And, by the way, you'd better show
me your papers."

He passed him the whole pocket-book at once. The
manager pushed his cap back over the back of his neck,
scratched his head, and kept looking down at Nikalai, who
quietly went on scratching with the pen, and kept grunting
crossly. The buttons of his blouse, embossed with the
hammer-and-scythe, sparkled in the gleam of the electric
light.

"They're old, these papers, very old," the hostel-manager
resumed. "You won't swizzle me, my son. Show me those
forms. H'm—are you sure you spell 'Rodilsia' with an 'o' and
not an 'a'? Very well, then—but there's a full-stop missing,
a full-stop, I tell you! It must all be accurate—without
accuracy the socialistic uplift of the socialistic state will never
be accomplished!"

Still muttering, the hostel-manager glanced through the
remaining forms. "There are stamps to pay for," the man in
uniform went on. "Stamps—four at ten kopeks, and to stop
here you must put the serial number of your membership-

book of the Profssoyoozi. Show me your membership-book."

Sleepily and crossly he gave him the membership card of the Newspaper Correspondents' Union. Hardly had the hostel-manager turned to the first page, than he suddenly looked as if he had difficulty in restraining himself from bowing to Nikalai. "Ah, Comrade, Comrade! So the comrade is a journalist! I might have known! I wonder if the comrade might mention our tourists' home in his reports to the Moscow papers—and your humble servant, an old-standing party-member, the acting president of the local Militant Atheists' Group, the treasurer of the Ossoavia-khim, the Secretary of the Red Crescent, the——"

Nikalai Sergeyevitch was dead tired. He stopped listening. He followed passively as he was led through a large hall, where half-naked men slept on mattresses, beds, sacks of straw, and blankets piled up in a heap, and up a staircase, which he mounted with his mind a blank, simply staring stupidly at the boots treading the steps ahead of him, did not at first notice the meaning of the thumb that pointed into a small, malodorous room, and then flung himself onto a creaking camp-bed.

"Good-night," he heard the voice continue. "You ought, by rights, to have shown me your railway ticket, but still that won't make any difficulties for you, Comrade Kisseleff. And I should have liked to see your certificate of vaccination —and the bed is only two roubles for the night—but, never mind, Comrade Kisseleff——"

He sank deeper and deeper into his sleepy stupor. The door closed on him. He was too tired to pray: "*Gospodi v tvoich rukakh essm az*——" and no more. And then he saw stamps, and applications, and printed forms, and—ink. The ink was bloody. Or was there some sort of blood that was inky? Somewhere was written up in giant letters, "THE

SUNDAY BELL: THE JOURNAL OF THE MILITANT ATHEISTS." Between them stood Turkish villagers from Lazistan, and stared at him stupidly, without understanding, till everything faded into the singing of an alto voice that he knew so well: "Oh, you, Oh, you will play me false, you'll——" And so it went on all through the night.

The next morning heavy, wet clouds lay over Batum. He got up and went into the street and strolled towards the port. When he saw the Americans standing around the Hotel International he felt no envy of their well-pressed clothes; with an almost impudent air of self-assurance he walked past them. The port lay deserted. Only across there by the naphtha wharves were two Italian vessels tanking. On their bows fluttered the red, white and green flag with the Savoy arms, but on the mainmast the Red Flag, with the five-pointed star, flapped in the mild breeze. The dairy-cafés were still empty, and the restaurant built out over the water seemed to be still without visitors, too.

Now, for the first time, he saw the people by daylight, and he could easily distinguish the people of Batum from the tourists of the R.S.F.S.R. The former were conspicuous by the simple, badly made white linen clothes that hung about their bodies. Everything they wore was cheap, bad and dirty. Their shoes were trodden down at heel; their tennis shoes, their plimsolls, their sandals, their flat caps or tartar hats, their belts. Women were to be seen in filthy, ragged slippers, and piquet hats, with blouses showing the remains of their last meals, and woollen stockings that failed to disguise their ugly legs. The most terrible thing, however, was the expression on these people's faces—it betrayed the complete paralysis of any sort of soul-life, with a crude cynicism, and an insanely aggravated self-importance. Withal, everything about these people was hard and inflexible, final, and without sense of the past or ideals for the future. There was nothing Catholic about them, nothing—except poverty, which was not voluntarily chosen nor humbly borne, but endured with a gnashing of teeth.

As he walked down from the port to the sea front he was engrossed with the question of how far these men and women might belong to the *anima Christi*—incorporated with Christ as members of the "soul" of His Church, as being of good will and in good faith and in some mysterious way in the grace of God, even though, through inculpable ignorance of the truth of the Faith, they might be outside the "body" of the Church. He passed on through the public park, and then turned aside to the shore.

And a long, far-stretching shore was all that the "sea-front" was, with the waves of the sea beating in all their force on the strand. Hundreds of men and women were lying about naked on little piles of their clothing, or letting the salt water toss them hither and thither. While the men lay huddled together, talking, playing cards, or sound asleep with their heads pillowed on their bundles of clothes, and newspapers spread over their faces, the women and girls walked about, craving attention, or dashed, shrieking and shouting, into the water.

Through a blue hole in the wall of lowering clouds, the sun beat down unmercifully, scorching his shoulders. His clothes became drenched, and he undressed. Near him was a one-eyed man playing cards with a man with one arm—there were many cripples to be seen here. Then he lay down on his clothes and stared up at the sky. A rather cooler breeze wafted from the sea played across his half-closed eyelids. He was still tired with the day before, and went to sleep again.

When he woke up, the beach supervisor, a man with a flat cap, bathing shorts, and a signalling bugle suspended on a bandolier, was quarrelling with a gipsy woman who was trying, with her children there on the shingle, to show off and "throw her weight about." His body was wet with perspiration. He leaped into the salt waves, which played on his reddened skin, smarting. He felt thoroughly happy. It was quite pleasant here. One was poor, dirty, and care-free; one had no cause to envy anybody; one could lie down anywhere, and sleep, wherever one went; there were no dividing walls between people. "The *anima Christi* is not dead in these heretics," he said to himself.

Meanwhile his clothes had dried again, and when he had dressed and was going to the station he was in a good humour. He whistled the Internationale, and got two pounds of pears from a street-vendor. But at the station his efforts to obtain a ticket to Tiflis did not meet with much comprehension. They shrugged their shoulders; held out hopes for the following weeks, questioned him as to who he was, asking for a ticket, like that, without notice—why did he think of leaving just on that particular day? And so on.

He did not want to make himself too conspicuous, and abandoned his efforts. He was hungry, and went back to the port. In the restaurant many tables were already occupied. The food was certainly not cheap, and it was not good either. But hunger made him indifferent to both facts. For his portion of butter he paid two marks—still, it was butter. While he was sipping a glass of milk he heard a familiar voice at a table behind him. It was the hostel-manager, who had met a friend.

"Any news, Vassili Petrovitch?" the stranger asked, in rather haughty tones.

"Not much," said the man addressed, assuming a very confidential manner, "a journalist has come to our place—one of those young cheeky ruffians from Moscow. If I had my way I should deal very different with these whippersnappers, with the milk still wet on their lips. But there you are! A journalist! Writes articles! A quill-driver, an ink-slinger! Dangerous fellows!"

"Jug of beer!" cried the other; then, turning to the hostel-manager, "On the whole, I don't like the younger generation. Look at that young Issatchenko in the customs office. He's not a serious, reliable young man now."

"You're right there, Grigori Andreyevitch. Not reliable, especially from a political point of view—far from reliable!"

Meanwhile the waiter had brought the beer, and the white sparkling froth showed on the stranger's moustache. "Here's to you, Vassili Petrovitch!" he said in a hoarse voice, raising the glass again to his lips.

"I don't like that Issatchenko at all," resumed the manager, lowering his voice this time, impressively and mysteriously. "My wife saw him passing a cordial greeting with the 'pope'* in the street!"

"Suspicious, very suspicious!" murmured Grigori Andreyevitch. And he passed a handkerchief over his forehead. "It must be true, what they say about him in the Rezino-trust. They say—h'm—lean this way, Vassili Petrovitch—that he is supposed to read Masses to himself in his room!"

"Outrageous!" spluttered Vassili Petrovitch. "And a creature like that is employed in the State Service. The State Service mind you. Well, I am very intimate pals with Veislovitch of the T.O.U.G.P.U.—they ought to watch him."

"Certainly not!" Grigori Andreyevitch contradicted him, with a dignified gesture, for he did not like the hostel manager's boasting of his connections with the Ogpu. "My brother-in-law is Vice-General Secretary in the purification department, and at the next Tchistka Issatchenko will be sent flying."

*Russian parish priest.

"Good!" said Vassili Petrovitch, with malicious glee. "But, as you are so well connected, Grigori Andreyevitch, I have a nephew in the Tchakva at the 'Tchaitrust,' a very industrious man, a convinced Communist, a party-member of many years' standing, an eager member of the Workers' Union. How would it be if he got a small post at the customs—through your connections, ha-ha! I'd be much obliged to you——"

"What do you know about Socialist official service, Vassili Petrovitch?" said Grigori Andreyevitch mockingly. "Your father—everybody in the Tsentrosoyus knows that—was a librarian, a librarian and Social Revolutionary. Revolutionary! Well, I ask you! Revolutionaries are never reliable people. This Issatchenko is a revolutionary too, I shouldn't wonder. That's the Trotzki brand. Lev Davidovitch is done for—we don't want Jews and Freemasons. But *my* father, dearest," his voice rose, shrilly, "was a working man, and my grandfather, too, was a working man. I come of a very old working-class family. Good health, Vassili Petrovitch!"

"Bring me a jug of beer, comrade waiter!" cried Vassili Petrovitch to one of the figures lounging about. He had expected that attack from Grigori Andreyevitch; this thunderstorm had periodically been breaking over him for two years past, and he could do nothing about it. He simply had to take it lying down. Grigori Andreyevitch was closely connected with Tskhakaya and Eliava, rode every month to Tiflis—and one could not prove his irregularities. All one could do was keep quiet and put up with his Napoleonic moods.

The humble silence of Vassili Petrovitch seemed to put Grigori Andreyevitch into a better humour.

"Have you heard," he asked, after a while, lighting a long-stemmed cigarette, "that our salaries are to be raised fifteen per cent? Both the salaries of those who are registered party-members and those of the Bezpartinny's as well."

"Koba's a great fellow!" cried Vassili Petrovitch, in a tone calculated to suggest that he went to breakfast every morning with "Koba"—as Stalin was called in his intimate circle. This arrogance of tone annoyed Grigori Andreyevitch very much indeed.

From the sea blew a light breeze, cooling the brows of those who sat now close-packed about the tables.

"Phew!" said a fat woman, sitting at Nikalai's table. "What a heat—and this only the beginning of May too! You see what temperatures we shall get in July and August! And what rain! Rain, I tell you! Phew!"

"They say there's some linen come!" said the other woman, eagerly. "Fifty metres—at ten roubles. And that you can get it at Communar 12. Don't you know anybody there?"

"Pah!" said the fat one. "Linen—nonsense! Silk! My son-in-law can get it for you at fifty roubles a yard—unrationed, of course."

"Oh, lucky you! But we, in Moscow—my Fedya had to queue up in the Teatralnaya Ploshtchad for a day and a half before he could get three metres of cloth. He had a folding-chair with him, and bread, and a water-bottle, and I gave him the blanket, the large red one, off our bed too. But when he got back he was quite ill, quite ill."

She had spoken in a thin, broken, miserable voice, this woman with the comical feather-trimmed hat on her wobbling head.

"And what's Fedya doing now?"

"My God—he's working in the factory," sighed the broken voice.

Then the other:

"I thought he was an official."

"No—he's not an official," whispered the broken voice, ashamedly.

"Pity!" said the fat one. And that was that.

CHAPTER V

INCIDENTAL ETHICS

At last he had the map, the connections, the information. At last he had picked up the threads that ran out from the centre to the circumference. He held the ends of those Ariadne-like threads that alone would help him to penetrate into the interior of the vast country with the feeling of assured security.

Once more he sat in the train, shaken up in the steel boxes. The evening began to darken. Hot and humid, the air drifted from the tea-plantations of Tchakva in through the open windows, and, in the distance, the lights of Kobuleti already twinkled. But now he sat dirty, unshaven, and worn out, his feet not crossed but placed awkwardly, ankles pressed together, and talked softly with two young men and a girl who sat beside and facing him. Like himself they came from Batum, had bathed and swum, and walked in the Botanical Gardens, and visited the Turkish Frontier.

"What do you do, actually?" he asked of the older lad.

"I am a student—a proper student, not at the Rabfak like Yegor Yegoritch, but in the real Polytechnik."

"And what do you mean to be?" asked Nikalai.

"An engineer. I have influential connections in the industry."

"Why didn't you become an ordinary worker?" asked Nikalai, watching him closely.

"There'd have been no sense in that," said the youth, astonished at Nikalai's question.

"But is an engineer any better than a worker? Aren't all men equal?" asked Nikalai again.

"Are you an agitator from the Politprosvet? Then you must know Myshkin!" cried the girl.

"No," cried Nikalai. "I have nothing to do with the Politprosvet—I am a journalist. But are you a member of the Kompart?"

"Yes," said the future engineer. "I am a member. I used to belong to the Komsomol."

"And you—if you could do anything you liked, what would you do?" Nikalai asked the younger lad, the one who went to the Rabfak to study.

"I should like to own a villa in Yalta or Livadia, or Suchum—it would be too hot for me in Batum—out there by the sea. And I should live all alone. There would have to be a big library in the villa. And there, in the villa, I should work out a plan in a big scale for collectivising the U.S.S.R.!"

"That is to say, work out a collectivist plan in individualistic solitude!" said Nikalai mischievously, but the other did not hear the remark, so he went on: "So you would never want to go amongst people?"

"Oh, yes I should," retorted the youngster. "Near the villa there would have to be an inn where one could get a really good wine—Kachetian, of course—and there I should meet like-minded comrades of an evening, and then for amusement gamble a little at cards. Like that, life would be jolly!"

" 'Like-minded comrades!' " thought Nikalai. "So a renaissance of the regular club table—where everybody who thinks differently is to be knocked out with the tankard! A club table with Skat cards! And that is what the massacres of the G.P.U. have been for!"

Then he remembered the words of Scapinelli, who had

always pictured Bolshevism to him as the evolution of Philistinism.

"Won't you get married?" he went on, feeling his way carefully.

"Married?" the other reflected. "Oh, yes. I shall get married. But my wife will not have to interfere with my liberty!"

"And won't you be jealous of your wife?" asked Nikalai, a little surprised. "Will you let her have her liberty, too?"

"The younger generation have given up being jealous!" said the Polytechnik student proudly.

It was already dark. The lamps in the train were lit. Most of the passengers had put down their sleeping-boards, and had settled themselves down on these with their clothes bundled under their heads. Nikalai and his new acquaintances were talking very loud, so that a few people began to "Sh!" and cry "Quiet!"

"But if you were in love—in love with your own wife," said Nikalai, now lowering his voice but speaking insistently to the technician, "and you were deceived by her, if you found her with another man when you came home, so that there could be no question of doubt about it——?"

"That is impossible," said the technician.

"But just suppose," Nikalai insisted again.

"Nobody will deceive me," declared the other.

"But if——" Nikalai tried to press, once more.

"There is no 'if,' " asserted the technician.

The sea had disappeared from sight. The train lumbered heavily inland, snorting as it went.

"What sense is there in getting married if one can have love without even registering it?" began Nikalai again.

He spoke the words as though talking to himself.

"In prison only the registered wife can visit you," said the younger, surprised at the question.

"You are very unworldly," said the girl, combing her hair with the aid of a hand-mirror.

"Merely because of prison?" asked Nikalai, in surprise.

"Why do you say 'merely'? Haven't you ever been in quod?" asked the Rabfak student, with some irritation.

"Let him alone," said the girl, "he is a journalist, and probably belongs to the 'extraordinary' crowd. That's why he puts on airs and pretends not to know what a prison is!"

"Of course!" said the Rabfak student bitterly.

Their eyes all looked tired by now, and they settled down to sleep, opening down the sleeping-boards and taking their bundles from the window. The students climbed to the upper boards, while Nikalai and the girl lay down below, stretched out on the seats.

"We ought to have travelled by day—the scenery is lovely," said the technician, upon which the Rabfak student replied, "You could have got us a ticket for the day journey."

There was a smell of onion and garlic, and above the clatter of the wheels could be heard the snoring of an Armenian shepherd, who slept in his stinking sheepskin. Nikalai lay there with his eyes open, unable to sleep. He rubbed his eyes, watched the sparks that blew past the carriage window, and scratched his neck where vindictive fleas were biting him.

"You are not asleep yet?" a voice asked him softly.

It was the girl, who was lying next to him.

"We shall soon be coming to the highest point on the route," she whispered. "Last year I was here, too, that's how I know. They have to put the brakes on terribly. In the tunnel you'll be hearing the queer bell-signals."

And the train actually passed through a tunnel in which ghostly bells were ringing, bells that rang hollowly.

"Vsevolod Pavlovitch is very conceited," she said, after a

long pause, in lower tones even than before. "I have known him much longer than I have Yegor Yegoritch, his friend. He treats Yegor like a small child because Yegor goes to the Rabfak. But whenever I am alone with Yegor he comes at me, and I offer no resistance. Why should I?"

"Why should you?" said Nikalai pensively.

"Why should I, eh?" she whispered excitedly, and turned to Nikalai. "Life is short—and it is only for about twenty-five years that you can get any kick out of *that*. And there is nothing else but that—and vodka. But then I'd sooner have *that*. With vodka you get thrown out of the factory, and peg out in the end. Also, you can't learn anything—not a thing. Still, abortions hurt, hurt horribly."

He could see in the dimness the face she made.

"I've had two abortions," she went on. "It was only the second time, that I was able to get it done through the State. The first time they refused my application, and I thought it was going to be too late. And they dragged it out a deuce of a long while the second time, too."

"Why didn't the State authorities want to do it the second time?" he asked, curious.

"You must ask Vsevolod that when he wakes," she said softly. "You may ask him that, but don't tell him about Yegor and me. You mustn't breathe a word."

He promised.

"Vsevolod said they were afraid that the bourgeois states would become too well populated, and we should be laid waste," she tried to remember, "but I haven't got it right."

The train stopped. An arc-lamp glared in at the window. He leaned on one elbow, and gazed out, his lips parted.

"What lovely teeth you have," she said. "Last summer I had forgotten to take my membership card of the Profs-soyoozi with me, and I was in Perm, staying with some distant relations. I couldn't bear the pain any longer, and they had to break out the teeth with a pair of pliers. The dentist wasn't supposed to treat me without the authorisation."

"In the bourgeois countries one doesn't need an authorisation," said Nikalai.

"But that's anarchy again," she said. "One mustn't go from one extreme to the other."

"Certainly not!" he said, and, after a while, "Wouldn't you like to marry?"

"You ask so comically," she said, "as if you had lived years on the moon! You talk altogether like a Social Revolutionary! But you're not—you're working for the 'extraordinaries.' Well, it's all the same to me—what does it matter whether I want to marry? So far as I care, yes."

"And children?" he went on asking. He asked questions like Scapinelli.

"No."

"And why not?"

"What does one know of the future?" she said. "They say the children are to be taken away from us. We shall nurse them for three weeks. Whether I have an abortion or a baby, it's all the same. Perhaps if I were an Adsharian or a Grusinian—their children are so nice. But our Russian children—noise-machines, dirty, ungrateful. There's no sense in it!"

For a while they lay quiet. Then she said, "What were you before the revolution?"

"I was still quite a youngster, almost a child. I was studying," he said.

"And your parents?"

"My father was a secondary school teacher, in Kraslava in Latvia. My mother was from the Latgal, too, from Dvinsk," he said, quietly.

"Oh," she said, "now I understand everything—you are

from Latvia, and therefore with the 'extraordinaries.' I once had a boy friend who was in Latvia in the year 1905, when the peasant rising was raging. He told me how the Letts not only murdered the German barons, but also tortured their cattle to death in the sheds. Are you brutal like that, too?"

He made no answer.

"Why don't you come over here; I am quite healthy," she whispered to him, and felt for him. When she saw his lack of interest she said, annoyed, "I haven't any vodka to give you."

The train stumbled over "points." In between these was heard the foaming of the Kura.

"Am I bad?" she asked him, suddenly.

"Perhaps not," he said.

She sighed.

In a little while, they both went to sleep.

At Tiflis they separated. With considerable difficulty, he managed to get a seat on the motor-bus to Vladikavkas. On the Boulevarde Rustaveli he met a Catholic priest of the Armenian Uniat Church. He must not speak to him. He must not make himself known to him. Sadly he gazed after him. Nikolai worked in the Second Class—he was not allowed to come in contact with "officials." He must not have anything to do with them; he, Nikolai Sergeyevitch Kisseleff, the correspondent of the *Vechernaya Moskva*.

CHAPTER VI

DISCUSSIONS IN DISGUISE

In the Caucasus Nikalai found all his beautiful memories of Russia compressed into one: he felt it as a mixture of Macedonia, Spain, the Riffland, Corsica, the people as a cross between Jews, Armenians, Mongols, Kabylians, and Wallachians. His days in Tiflis were brightened by a hot, dry sun. He had strolled at random through the dusty streets of the city, had prowled around the bazaar, and had stood often before the Hotel Orient to admire all the Englishmen and Americans who, confident and superior, went in and out of the hall, sat about smoking pipes of shag and staring into the bright blue sky. People were great Nationalists and great Bolsheviks at the same time. They all felt in their hearts a boundless veneration for the son of a shoe factory hand from the village of Didi-Lilo, near Gori, for Joseph Visarianovitch Dshugashvili, known as Stalin. Moscow is the heart, but Tiflis the head, of the U.S.S.R., a carpetmaker had said to him. He would have liked to stay for ever in Tiflis; one seemed able to live so freely, so unconstrainedly and unfettered. If he got tired while walking he would just lie down in the street and sleep. A mad beggar walked about naked in front of the Hotel Orient. For a few roubles you could get something to eat anywhere and so the land of ease and plenty seemed trying to make him forget his task. Then at night the city was bathed in the dazzling radiance of arc-lights. Outside, on the Kura, in the direction of Mtskhet, they had built an enormous power-station, the superfluous current of which was conducted to the nearby city. In front of the water-dam stood a statue of Lenin, pointing up at the mountains with a hand raised menacingly. "We have abolished night!" a jolly colleague kept assuring him, a *rabkor* who worked for a Ukrainian paper.

The day came when he must leave this city of boulevards and bazaars, of dust, of good living, of idleness and leisure and sunshine. On the Boulevarde Rustaveli he got into a motor-bus, sat in the seat by the driver, and off they went through poisonous green valleys, up steep, serpentine roads, through picturesquely tumble-down villages, and along gaily tinted river-banks. At a village they made a halt and ate, then went on, further up the giddily steep acclivities, winding through a number of tunnels. Next to Nikalai sat a high officer of the Soviet army, with many rank-badges on his collar, and a stern, fixed look. He pumped him cautiously. "What had your profession been before the war?" "Officer, also," the other answered, without turning his face towards him. The bear-like head on the stumpy neck remained immobile. Nikalai understood. There was one who had sacrificed much—or else cast it aside easily—to be able to remain in the sumptuously uniformed class, to be able to shout stentorian orders with his barrack-yard voice, and wear squeaky boots. What did it matter to him whether he served the White Czar or the Red? *Nitchevo!* The service went on!

For quite a short time the snow-covered peak and glacier of the Kasbek might be seen, then it was blotted out again by other mountains. The trees became more and more rare, and a rich carpet of green covered the ground. In the early afternoon a solitary cross and an obelisk announced the height of the Krestovi pass.

Then there happened something incredible. Immediately beyond the pass the motor-bus passed into muddy, dirty snow and a great number of tunnels. Between these there were dreary valleys that looked as if they had been designed by Gustav Doré, with their black, naked rocks and gurgling, dark rivers. On the sides and in the bottoms of the valleys, in these melancholy crevasses, were perched the hamlets of the mountain, Grusinians and Chevsurians, townships of grey stone, with black, square towers, that looked like extinguished and forgotten factory chimneys. Deep and deeper they went, down into the cold valleys of the northern Caucasus. The Kasbek glacier became visible again, and the motor-bus had frequently to stop to let the passengers taste the carbonic acid springs. "Narzan!" the travellers cried whenever they saw water running out of the rocks.

In the Kasbek valley Nikalai decided to stay a day. In the "hotel" he was given a room whose door could be fastened only with a chain. The windows opened on to a verandah on which strangers were eating. The dreary-looking, tumble-down grey stone houses, were not calculated to raise his spirits. Tourists from the north, with worn-out shoes, torn clothing, and sullen, toil-worn, starved faces slept in herds in communal shelters, and, in the early morning, armed with sticks, they streamed into the valleys, hungry for life. For five roubles he hired a mountain horse, with a festering sore on its neck, and rode up to the Stepan Tsminda Ssamebanda Church. Over the stone-heaps of the Gergeti village old women with greasy, brown, unwashed faces peered out curiously, and called unintelligible Grusinian words after him with their toothless mouths. Then he went on, in the wooden saddle, towards Sion or Zno. The Chevsurians watched him suspiciously as he rode along the narrow stony alleys of their village. He had ceased to find life enjoyable in the melancholy northern slopes of the Caucasus. Only the nights were filled with arguments and talk. He sat there hour after hour with Mitusha Shaduri, the young manager of the "hotel," in the co-operatives' guest-room, among armed Chevsurians with dirty forage-caps, and discussed God and the State and politics and economics (political and individual) till late into the night. At such times Nikalai became bolder and more careless in his words, and it was only due to the excitement of the young Tiflis student who was minding the "hotel" for the State that he did not get suspicious of Nikalai.

The next time there was a vacant seat available on the motor-omnibus that went from the Krestovi pass to Vladikavkas he tied up his bundle and rode through the narrow ravines into the plain. The driver went recklessly ahead, and, when his cigarette went out, steered the car by guiding the wheel with his elbow while he relighted the "gasper," with the utmost coolness, on the sharpest bend of the Darial ravine. This indifference to danger was a thing that he often met with in those grey lands.

Just about evening they reached Vladikavkas, now called Ordjonikidze. He just caught the train on the local line to Besslan, and there he had to wait for the connection by express train to Rostov and Moscow. Luckily he got a seat in the most difficult class, but a nervous little oil-engineer from Baku kept asking him where he came from, what news there was in Tiflis, the price of butter in Baku, and whether the mail-cars were still being robbed as much as they used to be by the Tchetchentses.

"Are you a worker, or in the service?"

"In the service," asserted Nikalai boldly.

"Is that all?" said the oil-engineer, contemptuously. "What profession do you actually follow?"

"I am a journalist."

"Journalist?" exclaimed the other. "Then you belong to

Group I! Why, man, where do you live? You're a worker like myself!"

He warmed up visibly, and became a lot more cordial, that little oil-engineer from Baku.

"My son is still a student in Group II, but soon he'll be through, and then he comes into Group I too."

A Swabian colonist's wife could not sleep because of the incessant chatter of the man from Baku. She went to find the conductor, and brought him back with her.

"Now it is night, decent citizens sleep!" he barked at the little oil-engineer. "Open out your sleeping-board and keep quiet!"

"You!" retorted the oil-man angrily, with a loud voice for which one would not have given the little man credit. "You! You want to dictate to us! This citizen and myself belong to the First Group—you are a Slushashtchi, a servant. That is Group III. My son is a student. Quick march! Hop it!"

The conductor fetched reinforcements; he fetched the two men of the T.O.G.P.U. who ride with every train, with fixed bayonets. And then a third man, too, came, without a bayonet, armed only with a revolver slung in a holster attached to a long leather belt. This one was Viennese. The officer, with glasses, Comrade Plesar from the sixteenth district in Vienna, proposed a compromise; the citizens might talk quietly for another hour and a half. Then they, too, must go to sleep. Meanwhile the whole carriage had awakened, and the windows rattled with excited Turkish, Yiddish, Russian, Swabian, and Viennese dialect. Two parties were formed. Women threatened one another with Narzan bottles, and men clenched their fists. Comrade Plesar roared like a famished lion. Not till the G.P.U. men went off was anything like peace restored.

In Armavir it was already morning. Nikalai was hungry,

and got out to buy himself a dried fish. When he came back to the train he saw the men of the Railway G.P.U. digging away with their bayonets under the bars of the waggons. Curious, he stopped and watched them. Suddenly, a few places in front of the spot where they were, a bent form jumped up from under the wheels. He looked back for the merest moment, showing his face. Cold shivers ran down Nikalai's spine. What he saw could no longer be called a human face. In place of the nose there was a dark hole in the skull, and the upper lip, too, was eaten away, so that the teeth could be seen, as in a ghastly grin, in the dark red background. With a single leap, this unhuman-looking creature had disappeared behind a hedge. The soldiers laughed, and went on digging with their bayonets.

"Did you see it?" Nikalai asked the oil-engineer, seated in the carriage again, and described what he had seen. "Some Bezprizorni or other," he said; "what are left of the Wild Children. What would you? It used to be a heap worse. If any of the Cossacks were to catch him here, they'd stick him."

The train rushed on. They had long ago passed into the flat country. Kossack villages and haymakers were to be seen. In Tikharetskaya he saw at the station railway carriages belonging to a local line bearing the inscription, "For Workers Only" and "For Servants Only." It reminded Nikalai of the "Jim Crow" carriages "For Coloured Men Only" on the railways of the U.S.A.

The train sped on across a flat steppe. Here and there was a clattering agricultural machine at work. The sun climbed higher and higher and blazed and scorched over the fields. Then they saw a military camp, with camels grazing before it. In the distance, the sea beckoned to them. In the late forenoon, the train drove over the European frontier, arriving soon after at the main station of Rostov. "Rostiv," announced the Ukrainian boards on the station, "Rostiv! Rostiv!"

He made his way towards the tobacco factory. There was still half an hour for him to wait, and then a thin-toned siren announced noon. He pushed his way into the yard, past a gigantic notice-board. "Hi!" he called to somebody. "Where does Worker Solovenko work here?"

He stopped a young woman worker.

"Gate two, third staircase," she replied sullenly.

There, too, nothing but strange faces. He caught hold of the coat of a passing worker. "Where is the worker Solovenko here?" he asked him. "Speak no Russian!" the man answered maliciously, in Ukrainian. But another worker called out to him, "Over there, he is walking along by the wall!"

He looked over towards the wall, and knew at once which of the men walking there was the one meant. It could only be the pale, worn-out-looking workman with the face of a St. Sebastian.

With one bound, he was by his side.

"Hullo, Solovenko!" he cried. The other stared round in amazement. Nikalai stepped up close, and whispered, "*Vivat Christus Rex!*"

Solovenko started.

"Come on!" he whispered hoarsely.

They went into a quiet corner of the factory yard, and sat down on a packing-case. Solovenko took a piece of bread from his pocket, and let Nikalai break a piece off.

"I am the *commis voyageur*," said Nikalai softly. "No. 6 sends his greetings—he is down with malaria, and I am taking his place. He is in Belgium at present Your report?"

The worker's lower lip trembled.

"I can't stand it any longer!" he said. "This dreary desolation—this ghastly desolation! This spying about! My job means a row every month with the Ogpu, with the Factory Soviet, with the Komsomol of the factory. My nerves simply won't stand it any longer. Simply won't stand it!" He was nearly crying.

"Steady, Father, steady!" Nikalai whispered to him. "You will be relieved in 1934, and then you will go to the Black Forest, or to Bavaria, and then everything will be all right. Where is your report?"

The priest-workman groaned.

"The food is filthy. I am dyspeptic into the bargain. My stomach's upset, and everything. It's all so sordid and disgusting. I want to read a book, for once—a real book, and not propagandist muck. I'd like to hear Gregorian music once more——"

"Your report," Nikalai pressed. "We haven't much time."

"All right," he said brokenly. "Well—my report—my report—well, my work goes on the prescribed lines. I don't carry on open religious propaganda, of course; I try to spread, within the ranks of the Communists, ideas that rest on the foundations of Catholicism or the *anima naturaliter Christiana*. I make friends especially with the leading men of the party, and with the Komsomol, and feed them continuously with Catholic ideas. And at the same time, I pump the teachers and the intellectuals of the Kompart and try to teach them that scientific materialism broke down ages ago. Then I heckle and obstruct at the lectures and meetings of the 'Voinstvuyushtchi Bezboshniki,' take part in the discussions, and embitter the lives of the speakers. My name's always being put up outside, on the Ilitchevka. Owing to my activity against the Bezboshniki I am continuously being locked up in the remand-prison of the G.P.U.; there it rains blows on the ear and kicks, and I have to sign the famous protocol agreeing to supply information. When two or three months have passed and I don't know of anything to say, there comes the terrible temptation to indict some innocent man. I am constantly spied on to see if I am committing sabotage. Loathsome this life of mine is, loathsome! The *taedium vitae* gets hold of one to such an extent that I'd like to commit suicide! But we are getting conspicuous—we—we'd better go."

"We have no factory canteen here for meals," said Solovenko—who was called something else, perhaps Tschurschenthaler, or Speneder, or Oberkofler—"we always have to go to a Stolovaya."

"And what else is happening here?" asked Nikalai Sergeyevitch.

"Crawling, bureaucracy and spying!" said Solovenko, his Russian tinged with a strong Ukrainian accent, as they entered the Stolovaya and queued up at the cash-desk.

"Do you know yet what you want to eat, comrade?"

One had to add up the price of one's viands in advance, and get a receipt for the amount.

When they were finally seated at a table, bent over tea-glasses, a tomato salad, and pieces of sticky bread, Solovenko began talking again.

"You see, everything here is a complete fraud. Officially they say that in the Union of Socialist Soviet Republics the practice and propagation of all religions is permitted, and that it is simply the Communist party, which, quite by chance, happens to be the strongest party in the U.S.S.R., carries on Communist propaganda, entirely off its own bat and independently. Stuff and nonsense! All the Orthodox priests—those that were not put in 'cold storage'—are in the service of the 'extraordinary' police, and a good eighty per cent of all believers that go to Catholic churches as well. You mustn't imagine that the confessional is still a sacrament here. Now it is simply an institution for trapping people into giving information. Pah! The whole nation isn't worth *that*. The townsman is a perfect swine, the countryman a mere animal, and the only variety of the human species worth anything at all is the worker, the proletarian. In 1905 the really religious proletarians of Russia, with church banners, icons, and prayer-books in their hands, fell beneath the fire of the Guards. In 1929 the workers in various factories scraped their last farthings together to add chapels to their new factories. But in 1931 a philistine, bourgeois bureaucracy conducted religious persecution—the same people who, twenty years ago, would go off into a faint if they heard the word 'Jesuit,' and were firmly convinced that the Holy Father was the 'Anti-Christ.' And these little vermin, slavishly addicted to their 'State Religion,' cowardly, without convictions, lick-spittles that they were, became the greatest atheists, the most merciless religious persecutors, wagging their tails every day to the G.P.U. to demonstrate the practical application of the unquotable 'Götz' quotation from Goethe. This spiritless scrapping of convictions. Simply sickening! But, thank God, everything is already fossilised and gone to seed. Little do our German revolutionaries know—those writers in the *Weltbühne*, in *Simplicissimus*, in the *Tagebuch*, for the Piscator Theatre, all the 'Young Guard!'—all their work will be forbidden one of these days, when what is there gets over. In their place, the *Daheim* and the *Gartenlaube* will be brought out in red covers, and Gross the illustrator, as an 'undesirable element,' will eventually be murdered by the infuriated Philistines.

Solovenko's eyes were shining.

With the flat of his hand Nikalai struck a piece of bread on which at least a dozen flies had settled. Then he tried with his finger-nails to scrape off the bread that stuck to the table like a moist, black dough.

Solovenko seized Nikalai's hand and pressed it warmly.

"I just open up like a flower bursting into blossom," he said, "when I meet a man from the outside world. I wouldn't mind the dog's food here, the herding together four in a room—but the atmosphere, the atmosphere of a Godless catechism-morality, the slimy idolatry of work, the parading of technical and scientific snobberies! Ghastly! And these people are doing their stunt—they are completing their five-year plan, they're grinding themselves to death to squeeze us against the wall."

The room was filled with the smell of decayed food refuse. On the walls were hung innumerable red pennons with mottoes inscribed on them. Above the picture of Lenin was a notice that read: "Remember, Worker, that you, as a Collective Eater, in a Collective Eating-house, are a Collective Brick in the structure of the Collective Future!"

"And the young people?" asked Nikalai.

"The young people?" laughed Solovenko. "What do you expect? The children are cheeky little brats, miniature Terrorists—you can't tame them. At fourteen or fifteen they get a little more sense—and then comes the great enthusiasm of adolescence for Bolshevism. And after that the volcano gradually burns itself out, slowly but surely. At thirty the dulled, compulsorily collectivised human Robot is finished—only the cynicism and the parvenu-like impudence remain. Then eventually the monster, 'State,' devours them. You can never really know how I hate it and everything that belongs to it—the police, the Ogpu-men, the officials, the soldiers, the stamps, the forms, the permits—everything. My only fear is that—if God lets me go back—I shall go over to the Anarchists. Everything that is mean and vile comes from the State, it almost paralyses one's free will. It is a great, terrible monster that executes men, hunts them into war, moulds individual destinies and hammers them to shattered ruins. And here, for the first time, one sees the State in its full meanness: one can deal in bloodshed, fraud, lies, blaspheme God, mock one's parents, commit adultery, withhold the wage of one's hired servants, and not be punished—but just you wave a white, blue, and red flag and sing '*Boshe Chrani Tsaria!*' and you'll be shot in a cellar! And what have they made of our concept of collectivism—saint-like, self-denying collectivism, as it lives in our monastic orders? They have forced everybody into this shape. Do you realise the horror of this atmosphere? Don't you get the feeling of it—that the U.S.S.R. is a forcible, obligatorily imposed cloister, with godless, evil-minded monks, and a Terrorist Abbot? Therefore it is a land of bastards, of crawlers, of the gnashing of teeth—of mean vileness. They are monks who have been locked up in cells without being asked—simply convicts!"

They had managed to swallow down the food, and went out into the street. An electric tram stormed past, with a furious clang of bells, and grazed Solovenko's coat.

Again Nikalai was amazed at the people's indifference to death. And when he looked at Solovenko's face again it was once more expressionless and haggard. There was nothing about it to suggest that it was the face of a Premonstratensian priest. Before the gate they shook hands again, and the tobacco worker Solovenko walked past the Ilitchevka with weary, sad, proletarian steps, back into the factory.

The next morning Nikalai was seated in the early train that ran out to the Kolkhoz "Verbliud." He walked from the station all the considerable distance to the buildings of the Administration. Arrived there he inquired for the Agraronom Kolyushkin. A girl with hairy arms and a powdered face assured him, as they walked, that the Agraronom Kolyushkin had now become the manager of the traffic bureau. At the traffic bureau he found a little, Jewish-looking man with rimmed pince-nez and a grey woollen sweater.

"I am looking for the Agraronom Kolyushkin," said Nikalai.

"That is me," said the other in an unpleasant, rasping voice.

"I am looking for the Agraronom Ivan Mikhailovitch Kolyushkin, from Pinsk," said Nikalai.

"That's me," repeated the little man. "And by the way, you might take your cap off when you're talking to me."

Nikalai whispered a few words to him, but he remained unmoved.

"I see you are interested in the Kolkhoz," he said out loud. "Come out in front of the house, then I can explain it all better."

Nikalai followed him. He knew that this man was past his first youth, had belonged to an old line of Czech nobility, had had to resign from the Austrian army owing to his refusal to fight a duel, and had joined the Redemptorists. Outside on the sparsely vegetated, grassy sand, Kolyushkin leaned against the concrete wall that, smooth and window-less, overlooked the fields, and put his hands in his pockets. His probing, half-closed eyes ran over Nikalai's figure with a somewhat arrogant appraisal.

"Your impressions?" he commanded, shortly.

Nikalai told him, in brief, of his meeting with Solovenko, whose name he did not mention.

"Pah!" said Kolyushkin. "An hysterical weakling! When I came here, with my forged papers, I was a nobody—but to-day I am the manager of the traffic department, and I am also on the Tchistka commission. If I don't like a man, he's fired!"

"But if you make a name for yourself, the attention of the

'extraordinaries' is concentrated on you more than need be!"

"Well, and what of it?" laughed the other man scornfully.

"You're dancing on a volcano!" exclaimed Nikalai, almost out loud.

"And they over there, on the other side of the electric barbed wires," he said mockingly, and pointing behind him with his thumb, towards the west, "perhaps you don't think they are dancing on a volcano, too?"

Nikalai bit his lips.

"What do you think of our man's views in Rostov?"

"Not bad," he said patronisingly. "The man has a good nose for things—and Roman finger-tips. But he's overlooked the part played by the peasants. As a matter of fact, the Russian peasant never was religious—simply a weather suppliant, and a statue fetishist. Dunin Borkovski wrote the same thing as long back as '27, in *Stimmen der Zeit*. You know Dunin Borkovski is an S.J. on the one hand—and a Pole on the other. And the national view-point is something that leaves its mark even on the Jesuit. To-day has taught me that Dunin Borkovski was terribly accurate. The Russian, in fact every primitive Eastern peasant, is 'geocentrically' adjusted—his property is measured in acres and square yards. Any enlargement of his property can only happen at the expense of somebody else. So he is covetous and mean. All peasants are a prey to jealousy and greed. Why, the Russian peasant is so miserly, that, to save the second piece of sugar in his tea, he holds a lump squeezed between his tongue and palate, and lets the tea gurgle through. His religion was nothing but prayer for the blessing of the harvest, and gradually, with him, the Liturgical eclipsed the Divine central meaning. I don't know if you've read Dostoevski's *The Possessed*, but at Charlottenburg that is one of the books one must read, isn't it? Somewhere or other,

Stavrogin asks Shatov 'Do you believe in God, or not?'
He answers, 'I believe in Orthodoxy—I believe in Russia—I
believe in the Sacred Body of Christ—I believe, I believe!'
Then Stavrogin, 'But in God—in God!' and Shatov's reply, 'I—
shall—also believe—in God!' *Voilà, c'est la Russie!* When, in
1917, the Bolsheviks promised the peasants *land*, they
shrugged their shoulders at their 'popes' and feudal lords,
and joined the Red Army. Wrangel and Denikin had only
to fight regiments that by then consisted solely of officers.
Then the churches were blown up—and at the same instant
that the Church vanished, the icons, altars, statues disappeared—and the Faith was gone. The 'popes,' or parish
priests, had to be maintained from the gifts of the villagers,
so they perished miserably. Government pressure ceased,
and the 'pope' did not get another farthing. Some of them
went into the factories, and some of them joined the G.P.U.
The Orthodox Church here is a church of the G.P.U.,—
every confessional is a risky chance."

The sun made Nikalai's shaven neck smart. He moved
into the shade. "And what is the position of the peasants
now?" he asked.

"After the civil wars the property held in large estates
was divided up. The peasants, of course, did not have the
means to cultivate the land. It all lay waste. The little they
produced they sent into the towns at profiteering prices.
The peasant always hates the towns. For him they are
concentrated hordes of idlers. Thereupon, of course, the
'extraordinaries' came to conquer them. So, out of spite, the
peasants only cultivated enough to be able to live on the
produce themselves. The reply to that was the 'Piätiletka,'
and enforced collectivism. Now they have been swept in
by the machinery of the callous and omnipotent *petit bourgeois*, who, in their convert's zeal, take a diabolical pleasure
in leading them a dance of arbitrary tyranny. The peasants

are furious with the Soviet, but they cannot even communicate their hatred of the system to their children, because it is precisely the pioneers and the Komsomol that breed the laying of informations and accusations—and so there's nothing left but an impotent rage, and, in one generation, the peasant has become a mere agricultural proletarian."

"And their religious feeling?"

"Gone to the dogs!" declared Kolyushkin, curtly. "Show an illiterate, who has never seen a railway train, a tractor-engine—for a man like that a tractor, with its working efficiency, is a sheer Divine miracle! With the most primitive propagation of technical products that are trumpeted forth as miracles of the Soviets, the land is conquered—with safety-razors, gramophones, cameras, tractors, opera-glasses, wireless receivers, telephones, motor-lorries, cinemas and rupture-appliances. The factory proletarian of the towns is above these things—he is not to be had so cheaply."

A laden camel-caravan trailed past them towards the sheds.

"Last summer," resumed Kolyushkin, "one of our Innospiets, the German Emil Langkammer, was near Kasan among the Tartars. In a village he was solemnly led into a house where a concert programme of gramophone records was performed for him. 'Look'ee there, lad!' the people said to him, 'Ye'll have nought like that back home, eh?' They simply took him for a liar when he said that at home he had the same sort of apparatus that they had. On the other hand, another man, a Mr. McCoy, had brought with him a portable gramophone and Hawaiian dance records, the Revellers, nigger minstrels, and Argentine tangoes. He invited the young people to his room, played to them, and the upshot was, that the club-room of the Komsomoltsi, with its wall-maps and newspapers, was deserted. When the heretics overrun this absurd European peninsula they simply perish with the virus of transatlantic pseudo-culture; the same sort of débâcle as when the Goths overthrew the Roman Empire. The Goths were victorious, and they—were Romanised! But here the case is different. Myself, I think a new Catholic culture should be created. I don't really know what Rome thinks about it! A new God's state ought to be built up, as in Paraguay. The people are primitive, like the Gran-Chaco Indians. The basis there would be, 'Who loves, Conquers!' "

Nikalai disagreed with him. He was against isolation.

"How did you get in here?" Kolyushkin asked Nikalai suddenly, to change the subject.

"A big gap in the hedge," replied Nikalai jovially. "Lachistan and Adsharia."

"I am only asking for myself," said Kolyushkin. "Do you think one can get back easily without getting popped off?"

"A wide gap," Nikalai assured him again. "When do you take off?"

Kolyushkin puckered his brows. He peered out gloomily from behind his eye-glasses. "1937," he said, "1937! Rather remote, that date, isn't it? A good many things might happen by then!" And, after a pause, "Have you any idea what Prince Löwenstein is doing?"

Nikalai told him in a few words.

"Where are you going next?" Kolyushkin asked him finally.

"You have no right to ask me that," replied Nikalai sternly. "We have strict orders to treat you like G.P.U. spies. But I'll make an exception and answer you: to the tractor-works in Stalingrad!"

"You can save yourself the trouble," said Kolyushkin gloomily. "Griboyedov has been shot!"

"First of all, it is no business of yours to know who Griboyedov was, and secondly the service there is in the hands of

American Catholic Innospietses and engine-fitters. How did you get to know of Griboyedov's part?"

There was something of the Prussian barrack-square about Nikalai's voice.

"The Tchekist Martinchook from Rostov told me about him," replied Kolyushkin shortly.

"We cannot allow one post to know anything about another," said Nikalai. "What happens when you are tortured? The flesh is weak—you are liable to squeal everything!"

"And what about you?" sneered Kolyushkin. "You know *all* the posts—if you get into the hands of the 'extraordinaries' there'll be nothing but suicide, madness, or repentant confession into the microphone."

"That is my business!" said Nikalai, heatedly. For a while they stared into one another's eyes, rigid and hostile. Then Nikalai said: "Were you able to say a Mass for Griboyedov?"

Kolyushkin shook his head.

"We'll pray for him!" said Nikalai.

"Pray!" said Kolyushkin, reflectively. "Where should we be without prayer? The last warming fire in this wilderness!"

Silently he gazed up into the sky. It was cloudless and distant. But despite its remoteness, it formed a roof over everything. Then they shook hands and parted. Kolyushkin stared after him with a fixed gaze, hands in pockets. When Nikalai had gone some distance, he turned round, and saw Kolyushkin still standing there, a black smudge against the concrete wall.

Suddenly, it seemed to him that he was waving to him. A waving hand across the Kolkhoz "Verblyud," a waving hand of a man drowning, in the grey work-a-day of the most dismal of all heresies!

CHAPTER VII

MOSCOW

At the beginning of August Nikalai made a longer sojourn in Moscow, in order to set off from there for Leningrad.

He had been going about in the Soviet Union for almost three months; now he was starved, down-and-out, verminous, exhausted, and broken down. He had visited almost all the outposts, and got to know the most diversified types of men; the abysmally despairing, the joyously swift-living, the cautious, the brazen; in Magnitogorsk, in the Southern Urals, he had spoken to a young man posted there belonging to the *Societas Verbi Divini*, on the dizzy height of a smelting-furnace chimney.

"I feel as fit as a horse here," he said laughing, with the chalky patches all over his face. "I used to be at Gabun, where I couldn't stand it without getting ill. It broke my heart, but I had to leave there, although I love primitive people. Here, it is just as interesting—the natives here are every bit as primitive as the Nyam-Nyams or Shillucks. Every Fifth-day I just take it easy and gossip in the company about here, then I pretty well laugh myself ill at the moss-grown fudge that they all babble! You'd have no idea! I should be sorry to leave here. What are the others doing? Have you ever heard of the Wild Men? Yes? Well, you see, here they are the Udarniki, the Storm Troops. They keep their noses to the grindstone, work from dawn to set of sun, to fill up their quotas of Piätiletka to x per cent—

swotting like the most perfect specimen of star pupil of the Faculty of Arts—and, with it all, they haven't gone the very least bit of the way towards solving the problem of proportion as between the individual and the machine, in an economic manner. I say Mass alone every Sunday in the forest. Can't you just hear my confession?"

He was disappointed to learn that Nikalai was not a priest.

Yet another man, in the "Red October" wood factory, a melancholy, consumptive-looking priest, seemed from his expression to be broken and downcast. "It's the end of things for me," said he, "I shall never win back my peace. If I celebrate Mass back in my own sunny Italy the altar will suddenly vanish from before my eyes, and I shall see nothing but numbers, numbers, smelting furnaces, red flags, demonstrations, factories, shrieking placards. Here God has been erased from the face of the land; that is why I am broken up. It is better for me never to return home, to meet my end here. And it will be the same with you. You are a journalist. You will sit in the editorial offices and have visions of the Soviet. You will be dancing at a ball and see the headquarters of the Azneft suspended before you. It is not good to visit the Devil in his own Kingdom."

Then he had gone on to Siberia, and gone down to the Kuzbass, to the cities, had been right into Turkestan, then back to the lower Volga, to Ukrania, to the Donbass, to the Dnieprostroy, to Charkov, to Kieff, Tula, Kaluga, Oyel. And always there was the complete picture—new, sober, plaster-white factory buildings, but already dirty with surly, underfed workers, men and women, and everything new and swiftly soiled, machines first-class but neglected, everywhere reckless, wasteful exploitation of men and material, everywhere spying, tale-bearing, the struggle for advancement, envy, bureaucracy, strife and snobbery. The children were

ill-mannered, neglected, furtive and impudent. The nearest
to him were the youths from fourteen to fifteen; they became
completely serious and zealous, had reached the wild period,
formed bands, held conferences, made speeches, agitated,
yelled for justice and amusement, and still hoped for something from life. But they soon grew hardened, the Udarniki
took that air of supreme self-importance that had so often
made Nikalai smile, and they became stiff, conceited,
men of the talented chauffeur type, with shirt-sleeves and
cuffs turned up and caps set at a perky angle, and their necks
scrupulously shaved at the back. From among these men
came the Union leaders, the Tchistka commissions, the
club merchants, the medal hunters, the factory poten-
tates with the puckered brows, sweeping gestures, and
impelling passion for dictatorial power—run after by the
painted and powdered women workers with their squat-
nosed faces, worn-out plimsolls, red kerchiefs, broad hips,
and sumptuous bosoms. Nikalai was always hearing the
same words on the lips of the workers: "Quota—Party—
Union—Collective—Udarnik—Promfinplan."

The men of the "minus six," who had belonged to the
former stiff-necked "intelligentzia" and had not been quick
enough to turn their coats at the opportune moment, nor
had useful connections among the new men in power, were
often forced to live outside the six principal cities. They
were lodged outside in the suburbs, more miserably starved
than the emigrants, herded six in a room, with steaming
samovars, unaired beds, air heavy with cigarette smoke
and unemptied slops, and whined in hushed voices over
world-events. They often gave their last farthing towards
supporting the "pope," and then paid tribute to the head
of the Tcheka so as to be allowed to live in safety. The
children fell away—their sons went to the Bolshevik schools
and their daughters went wrong, one after another. Mean-

while they read theological treatises in manuscript, on abstract questions of the past, and secretly cursed Alexander II, who had abolished serfdom, as the spiritual father of Lenin and Stalin.

By the time Nikalai reached Moscow he was heartily sick of his travels. When he arrived at the Brest Station, with the bundle of clothes from White Russia, tired out with loss of sleep, and suffering from dyspepsia, he was the richer by the knowledge, gained from much experience, that these State-made heretics certainly were masters of their trade. The population was constantly kept occupied. Every week a fresh spasmodic wave of hysteria and zeal for activity shot through the country, and caught the people up and shook them. Now, an Aviation and Gas-Defence Union week; then, for a change, a week devoted to arousing popular enthusiasm for the destruction of insects with cyanide; then a week of the "Mopr"—i.e. of the Red-aid—filled with talks, collections, films, and theatrical performances, for the benefit of Bolsheviks in the prisons of foreign countries. A month was dedicated to the Red Crescent, the Bezboshniki, the Destitute Children, the Piätiletka. Already everybody was connected with some sort of organisation: was president, treasurer, secretary, honorary chairman or section-leader of some club or other, and felt himself to be an important and well-known personage, and a corner-stone in the Socialist future. Hence the neurotically feverish air of the active Communist, the reflective pose with puckered brows, the stereotyped beginning of sentences with the word "I," the contemptuous gesture when the conversation turned on the "beloved neighbour," the telegraphically abbreviated manner of speech. If they got on in the world they blossomed out into the Central-European, Philistine, Bourgeois Official type. In the alternative case they dried up into dull beasts of burden. In any case the members of the Communist Party were a coterie of the elect, but only from a secular-ethical bourgeois point of view. When it was a matter of confidence Nikalai always turned to Compart-members, who did not steal, did not go with prostitutes, and were seldom to be bribed, and who kept their promises more frequently than the others.

He had to fight hard for his place in the tram. He stood there, wedged tight among rather alcoholic-smelling prole-tarians, and could move neither backwards nor forwards. Passengers were only permitted to get on at the back and get off in front. A screaming woman with a red kerchief, a greasy dark-blue jacket, and muscular forearms, pushed her way through the close-packed crowds and sold the tickets. He who had no change had to buy ten tickets at a time. At every stopping-place there were some who could not get out, and these would start cursing miserably. On the boulevards the electric car shot along as swift as an arrow, amid furious bell-ringing, and the passengers were thrown together in a heap. More screams, more curses, and laughter. At the Arbat he got out and tramped through quiet streets. No. 27, in the Afanasievski Pereulok, had a porter's lodge and a neglected front garden, with two trees. On the first floor, he looked for Apartment No. 4. It was situated at the end of a long and musty-smelling passage. He knocked, and went in. Near the window, a slim young man, with ill-shaven face, and blonde, ill-cut hair, rose to his feet. A wireless loud-speaker blared tinnily in the confined space of the room.

"What do you want?" the fair man asked, with an un-mistakable Polish accent.

Nikalai lowered his voice.

"Number Seven demands quarters."

The Pole nodded, and said in a toneless voice: "You will live here, in this room; during the day, however, you must not enter the house. You will sleep here from ten at night till five in the morning."

Now Nikalai nodded. The conversation was finished. The Pole took the bundle from him, and threw it behind a sofa. Then he pushed back the catch of the door, and turned again to his newspaper.

The Third Rome is a large grey, sad-looking village, with a proud museum, the Kremlin. For half a generation, the Soviets had money for anything that promised immediate profit or utility. In the main streets there was often an asphalt road, for the State motors and lorries had to convey goods and passengers along them. The footways, however, had been torn up in 1927 when the giant village was newly canalised, and had only scantily been thrown together again. It would often happen, that, after some rain, one might step into what looked like a puddle, and break one's leg in a hole a yard deep. In the suburbs, cars often sank up to the axle in water.

Over the crumbling, broken pavements, three million dull-eyed people dragged their feet in tennis-shoes. Clothes and shoes earned no profits—the State did not trouble about their production. But the proletarians of Moscow were vain—and so the shabby elegance of this Metropolis of Anti-Christ was all the more conspicuous. The streets were filled with people: Negroes, listening to the atheist lecture-courses with cigarettes that had gone out dropping from their fleshy lips; sullen, crushed workmen, with patched coats, and Tartar caps set at a rakish angle; Chinese coolies in dull green uniform and blue caps; Tartars with gay, gipsy-coloured wraps, that bellied out in the wind and English caps; old women with weather-beaten, crushed hats and faces brutalised with suffering.

The houses presented a varied appearance—many had

only a ground-floor, others again shot up high and projected with blind window-panes into the grey sky. Over every roof stood a forest of dishevelled aerials, in which the wind from the Sarmatian plain whistled monotonous tunes.

Advertising was unknown. Often the shop windows were broken and provisionally patched up with boards. In the book shops an infinite number of books was on sale—books of technical, pseudo-scientific, or propagandist tenor. They were printed on bad paper, and broke when they were opened. There were long queues of men standing in front of the spirit shops, and of women in front of the chocolate shops. Everywhere notices thrust themselves on the eye, in the service of the never-ending, monotonously devastating propaganda.

Lost in thought, Nikalai had traversed the whole of the Ochotny Ryäd. In front of the Hotel Metropole he saw some Americans standing about, and regarded them with almost proletarian hatred. Then he went on, up to the Lubyanskaya Ploshtchad. Standing on the pavement, he gazed in at the headquarters of the Ogpu. But a Tchekist with a very long rifle, who was standing guard there, at once drove him away. "Pass on, there! Pass along!" he shouted.

Evening and the dusk came late. As he was walking back through the Nikitskaya a young worker, with big acid-stains visible on his coat, stopped him to ask the time. He drew out his silver watch.

"Incredible!" said the young workman, at the sight of it. "You have the identical watch, citizen, that my uncle Vanya has. Did you buy yours at the Tverskaya, too?"

"No," said Nikalai, "I bought it down in Ukrainia, in Zinovievsk."

"Oh! You work in Zinovievsk?" the young man exclaimed delightedly.

"No," lied Nikalai, "in Zaporoshie, in the agricultural machine factory Communard."

"But you're not a Ukrainian—nor even a Cossack?" the young worker asked, now slightly suspicious.

"No fear!" laughed Nikalai, "I am half a Lett."

"H'm," said the young worker, "and where are you going now? I can see you're not a Moscow man. I'll go along with you."

They went together across the Red Square, back to the Ochotny Ryäd.

"I'm in a deuce of a fix," the young workman began, without any preliminaries. "I'm in love with a girl employee of the Mosselprom. It's true, I'm a worker myself, and my father was a worker too. She's a pretty girl. Last week a van of lipstick reached Moscow. And she had to try and get a lipstick too. Wouldn't you think the same? You can't help noticing it, being in the town. To-day I went to the Narko-mindyel for my factory—the women there have the greater part of the delivery. Oh, and some shirts arrived too—but the people belonging to the Gossplan have claimed them all. They say that in the Gossplan they are all sitting in their shirt-sleeves, so that people can admire their shirts. Well, we'll let that pass. Katya is very pretty, and brainy—and she likes me too. But Sadkov's courting her. I don't expect you know Sadkov. That swine has a brother with the Soyuskino, and he lends Sadkov bourgeois clothes. He puts on these bourgeois clothes—just imagine it: puts them on, and dares to go out in the street in them. In broad daylight! He goes into the 'Inturist' of the Hotel Metropole, has lunch there, and then goes down and buys soap. When I wanted to buy soap there, they nearly called the Tchresvitchaika. But Sadkov goes there as bold as brass, sticks his nose up in the air, takes off his hat, unbuttons his coat to show his check breeches off, and says in English: 'Give me

some soap, sir!' I ask you! He says 'sir!' And all the
foreigners standing round him are terribly nice to him.
They smile all over their faces. How does he know English?
He's been learning it from an old general's wife—he gives her
bug-powder in exchange. Then he gives the soap to Katya.
I'm a respectable worker—I don't go putting on bourgeois
clothes to swindle soap out of them. Katya's a good girl,
but all the same she has a perverse leaning for bourgeois
clothes and manners. Sadkov often comes to see her of an
evening, all dressed up. And that makes a big impression on
her. So once I went and borrowed a monocle from an
optician. Just to show her, don't you see, I could make a
show too, if I had a mind to, but the monocle wouldn't stay
put. It kept falling out of my eye. And then Katya and
Sadkov both started laughing at me. What's a chap to do?
Of course, I might have him run in by the Ogpu—but
where's the use of that? His uncle Parfion has a brother-in-
law that's with the Tchresvitchaika. It's enough to make
a fellow cry——"

A long demonstration procession blocked their way in
front of the Rumiantsev Museum. Banners were being carried
—women and men marching, factory-wise, in groups—
leaders unintelligibly shouting, "Doloi. . . . Doloi!" Somewhere in front, a band was playing. Suddenly the procession stopped. There seemed to be a jam.

"What demonstration's that?" Nikalai asked an elderly
worker, who, with an air of boredom, was lighting a cigarette.

"A demonstration for the Pope of Rome!"

"What do you mean?" said the young worker with Nikalai,
in amazement. "Why, this afternoon they announced a
demonstration of the Bezboshniki! That's *against* the Pope of
Rome, not for him!"

The elderly worker was not to be put off.

"Just now," he said, "a young comrade from our factory

gave a speech against the Parish 'popes'—if this demonstration is against the parish 'popes,' it can't be against the Pope of Rome at the same time!"

"Yes, it can," insisted the young worker. "It's against the popes and against the Pope, against the Rabbis, and the Mohammedan priests—all at the same time!"

"That's nonsense!" replied the elderly worker, just as stolidly as ever, puffing at his cigarette. "Must be either the one or the other!"

At the head of the procession, the music recommenced, and the line moved on.

Nikalai and the young worker went into the "Park Kultury i Otdykha," the "Park of Culture and Recreation." They wandered through the whole Pretchistenskaya, marched on to the Krimski Bridge, and queued up in front of the pay-box at the entrance of the park. Often there were only three or four people waiting at the ticket-window, but automatically, from force of habit, they took up their positions in single file. Nikalai had once, even, seen two people buying apples from a street-vendor; one had stood himself behind the other.

"Do you know," the young worker began again, "I have another bit of cursed luck, too—my girl always has her time off two days later than I have. Since they've brought in the Piätidniovka I hardly see her—and I'm going mad with jealousy. Sadkov has influence, of course—he's managed to get his rest-day every Thursday. Naturally I did all I could to get the Thursday off too, but then I had to work on the night-shift, and I was so tired I could hardly keep my eyes open for want of sleep. So I had to give it up."

At last they had paid their ten kopeks and got into the Park. At first they shot at figures of the Capitalist, of Trotzki; and of the Pope, with air-guns; then, past the Gosstsirk they came to a shed in which were displayed skeletons of

human beings and of apes, an electrical machine gave off
sparks, diagrams and pictures were on the walls, and a frog's
heart was pulsing under a plate of glass. In the background
there was a desk, and behind this desk sat a gloomy-visaged
man who looked like a slightly demented German apostle of
education, nervously fingering the pages of some book of
propaganda. Above the desk was to be read the legend,
"Enquiries—Astronomical Matters."

One could walk up to this desk, drag this creature out of
his neurotic preoccupation, and ask off-hand how many
English miles apart the earth was from the moon, or Uranus
from Neptune at the moment of their closest proximity.

Close at hand was a club-house, in which innumerable
people were playing chess or reading propaganda pamphlets and spitting on the floor. Above, on the roof, others,
lying in deck chairs, were gazing at the ships, boats, and
trawlers on the river, and reading the *Vechernyaya Moskva*, or
Krokodil, the *Bezbozhnik*, or smiling insipidly at the jokes in the
Vechernyaya Moskva.

Nikalai began talking with the young worker about the
west and the bourgeois states. "Well, what on earth do you
imagine it is like in the bourgeois states?" he cried, in dismay.

Then the other man began to talk, and unfolded a picture
at which Nikalai felt disturbed and by no means unmoved.

In the bourgeois states, said the young worker, there were
innumerable factories; industrialism was carried into force a
hundred per cent. The one and only yearning of the factory
proletarians was to strike. When they went on strike, they
would all stream out of the factories. But lo! around each
factory was drawn up a cordon of policemen, gendarmes,
and soldiers. Automatically they fired on the crowds of
workers. The workers would tear open their blouses and
shirts, crying, "Comrades, do not shoot at your own flesh
and blood!" The soldiers would begin to waver—and then

the priests would step up to them with raised crucifixes and threaten them with hell if they did not go on shooting. And the blue-teethed capitalists, with the tiger-fangs, dressed day and night in tail-coats with top-hats, would press fantastic sums of money into the mercenary, grasping hands of the priests.   During the fighting these would sneak in where the women workers were and violate them.   Finally the workers, their heads streaming with blood, were forced back into the factories, to go on working at the vice, amid the glint of bayonets. Till one day——

Meanwhile it was already evening, and they strolled back to the State Circus. In front of the State Circus a number of young people stood in a large ring, holding hands. In the middle was a table, and on the table a lad was sitting, and another lad was playing the concertina. The lad stood up and waved little flags, and, in time to the rhythm of the concertina, howling to the night air, in fanatical frenzy, sentences that got shorter and shorter: *"Poidyom, poidyom, poidyom tovarishtchi—mooi vypolnim piatiletku v tchetire goda, mooi boodyem unitchtozhat bourjoaziyoo i papy rimskavo—poidyom!"* Quicker and quicker the concertina squealed, the solo-singer and the chorus howled, while feet tripped in an ever-growing acceleration of excitement.

At last the tousled hair of the dancing and screaming throng hung down over their moist foreheads, and an ecstatic fire flamed in their usually dull eyes. Nikalai never knew what force it was that impelled him to join in— suddenly, he had stepped forward; two powerful, perspiring girls' fists gripped his wrists, and his throat was mechanically yelling, joining in their chorus: "Come—come—come— Comrades!—We'll fulfill the five-year plan in four years! We'll destroy the world-bourgeoisie and the Pope of Rome!"

The young worker had long ago disappeared.

Nikalai's toes were skipping in the sand, his eyes glowed,

his arm-joints cracked. It was night, the stars came out, and Nikalai Sergeyevitch was still dancing and shouting, leaping about and howling, before the State Circus in the "Park of Culture and Recreation."

He did not go straight home. He strolled about for another half-hour in the night life of Moscow. The electric trams were still tearing round indefatigably with their furious clamour of bells. In the sky, heavy and awkward-looking bombing planes were droning in the glare of search-lights. The Vassily Blashenyi Cathedral, on the Red Square, with its ghostly contours and alarmingly ugly towers, was bathed in a cone of electric light, and the Z.I.K. building, with its illumined windows, looked out over the high wall of the Kremlin. People hovered hither and thither in the half-light, street car brakes creaked, luxury cars with sombre-looking State officials whirred past over the asphalt, guards, with fixed bayonets, were changed. Restlessness and the tenseness of anxious care lay like a pall over the Third Rome.

It was late when he got home. The Pole was already in bed, but not yet asleep, reading the leading article of the *Ekonomitcheskaya Zhisn*, and holding between his lips a cigarette that had gone out. From the toned-down wireless loud-speaker could be heard muted balalaika music.

Silently Nikalai began to undress on the sofa. Suddenly he stopped, "Have you ever been imprisoned in the Lubyanka, Ludovik Kasimirovitch Sawicki?" he asked the Pole. The latter dropped his paper, and shook his head.

"What sort of people are working here for the 'extra-ordinary'? " Nikalai went on asking persistently.

"All sorts!" said the Pole quietly. "In particular, Chinese as hangmen; Letts as warders; Magyars as examining magistrates; Jews as officials; and Poles as directors!"

"Haven't some Catholic views crept into the ideology of

the Lubyanka, through Dzerzynski and Menszynski?" he asked again.

The Pole nodded.

"Felix Edmundovitch is dead. He was a good man. Of an evening, he used to sing songs to the children in the hospitals. He could refuse nothing to any who wept. But he signed death sentences—to him, that was merely pen-work. He was no sadist—he could not have watched an execution. I have seen him myself sitting by the little ones' cots, holding their hands. He had a countenance of sorrowful pathos. Then he became People's Commissioner for the Traffic Organisation, and led a restless nomadic life on the railways. He died on his wanderings—he may have returned to the church. We say Masses for his soul. Savicki, the Director of Prison Management, was also a Catholic."

Ludovik Kasimirovitch Sawicki gazed up reflectively at the ceiling with his blue eyes. The balalaikas had stopped on the wireless. A dreary voice was delivering a lecture.

It had become deadly quiet in the room. Only the dreary voice in the loud-speaker went on. Mechanically Nikalai continued undressing and slipped under the bed-clothes. Supported on one elbow, he tried to tune in another station by rotating the control on the wireless panel. Suddenly a Prussian twang sounded in the bug-ridden "Apartment 4" of No. 27, the Afanasievski Pereulok. Nikalai almost shouted for joy—the Announcer of Königswusterhausen!

Then a stern hand touched his own—the Pole switched off the wireless. The valves in the box went out. The electric light went out too. Outside a motor-car drove past with dim head-lights. He folded his hands. He prayed. His prayers remained on the surface—in his subconscious mind he was still howling, shouting, dancing, leaping, foam on his lips and sweat on his brow, in the Culture Park, before the State Circus, as a possessed dervish of the strange heretics of the Third Rome.

CHAPTER VIII

LENINGRAD

A few days later Nikalai was en route for Leningrad. His work in Moscow had soon been finished. He had gone once or twice to the swimming baths, and let the sun shine down on his back. The bath was on the Moskva, situated opposite the Culture Park, and frequented by a typically Tchekist public—greasy, brown-baked, semi-prostitutes, with flat feet, brassiers, bathing trunks, and scarlet-painted lips; screaming, noisy Chinamen; ash-blond Lett women with antediluvian bathing costumes; squat-nosed Hungarians with flapping cotton shorts down to their knees; a few young Rabfakovtsi; and brown-skinned, black-haired men who might equally well have been mountain Jews, Grusinians, Armenians, or Nogaïc Cossacks. Above, near the entrance, was a restaurant, in which quite European fare was to be had for ten or fifteen roubles. Nikalai could not understand how the people managed it—they sat there, in close-packed crowds, eating and drinking to their hearts' content. It was well known that a member of the Kompart was not allowed to receive more than 250 roubles per month, and in the south a shepherd did not get more than $1\frac{1}{2}$ roubles per day.

It amused him to gather young people round him on the steeply rising steps of the swimming bath, and gradually instil into their heads growing doubts of the non-existence of God. This was a very bold undertaking, but it was just the very audacity of fighting Satan here, in the *buen-retiro* of the G.P.U. devils, that seemed to him so attractive.

"God does not exist," said a Komsomoletz. "I can't see him."

"Does Australia exist?" asked Nikalai.

"Certainly."

"Have you seen it?"

"No—but I can read about it in books."

"You can read about God in books, too."

"All right—but I can go to Australia, and set my feet on the land."

"If the Ogpu give you a foreign passport," mocked another lad.

"Tell me, Comrade, do mourning, sorrow, joy, exist?" began Nikalai again.

"Certainly, but——"

"But what?"

"Well, go on."

"Well, sorrow, joy and mourning cannot be touched, and yet they exist, don't they?" went on Nikalai carefully.

The Komsomoletz did not answer. Gloomily he stared before him.

"Can one see something that does not exist?" Nikalai went on searchingly.

"No," said several, half aloud, not knowing what he was driving at.

"Can one love something that does not exist?"

Again sounded that uncertain, "N-no."

"Yet there are millions of people who love God."

For a while a sullen silence prevailed.

Then one of the boys said, "Perhaps there is really a God —I'll go so far as to believe he exists. But I hate him. He's a god of the bourgeois. He's an enemy of the proletariat."

A few dissented. Most of them went away. Two disputed together excitedly. The sun glistened in the water of the Moskva.

A Caucasian who had listened to Nikalai's talk, and who had been standing in the background, came forward and said in an undertone:

"I am a teacher from Daghestan. I consider it my duty to point out to you that you are deliberately corrupting these boys. I don't know who you are, nor what your business is, but you must know that in our instructional textbooks, approved by the Narkompross for elementary and secondary and advanced education, every kind of religiosity and belief in God is regarded as injurious and inimical to the Party. To hear you talk one can tell at once that you've read far more books than those boys—you're taking advantage of your superior instruction to pervert them. Remember that, once for all!"

"I completely share the view taken by the People's Commission for Instruction," said Nikalai disingenuously, now no longer easily to be taken aback. "We should, however, stimulate the young people to think, and strengthen them in their views by means of discussion and debate."

"Oh, I see," the teacher apologised. "You are, so to speak, an agitator for the young, an *agent provocateur* in a good cause—perhaps, Comrade, you belong to the 'extraordinaries'? " his voice sank to an unintelligible whisper. "You must know that I have an immense respect for the honourable institution of the Ogpu. I once wrote an epic on the Ogpu in the *Daq'stân*, and I was proposed for the Order of the Red Flag. Mustafimov is my name—perhaps you would be good enough to remember me? Mustafimov of Makhatchkalah.

Not far from the Ogpu's house in the Lubyanskaya Ploshtchad were the French and Polish Catholic churches. In front of the French church he once heard two old women talking French together—they were Russians who had once belonged to "Society." One was wearing a window-blind, that looked like a bed-mat, made up into a cloak; he stopped, and pretended to be studying the posters on the scaffolding-boards of a new building, and listened to their conversation.

"Are you coming to the church now, chère Sophie?" asked the one with the window-blind cloak, wagging her head—the tassels on her cloak waggled with it.

"Of course," said the other. She had an ill-favoured, pinched, old-maid's face, and helped herself along with a walking-stick.

"There's to be Benediction with Sermon to-day—with Sermon!" cried the one with the window-blind cloak. Her shrunken, unshapely mouth was encircled with a sparse growth of hairs.

"With Sermon! you don't say so, chère Cathérine!" exclaimed Sophie, in high glee. "Sermon! Who's preaching, then? Père Carnot?"

"Quite right—Père Carnot. The one with the black beard. What fiery dark eyes he has!" enthused Katerina. "I dreamt about him yesterday. A handsome man. And strong. Pity he doesn't wear long hair like a 'pope.' But really I don't care at all about having had to be converted."

"Indeed," asked Sophie, "who got you to do that, chère Cathérine? Szegedi? Or Balindis?"

"Balindis," said Katerina. "I went down on my knees to him, and said I would rather be burned alive than forsake the faith of my mother. But Balindis, 'c'est un homme avec une bouche mal lavée—un letton sans éducation—mais ce qui lui manque, c'est des manières,' he said, 'Lie down, you old witch!' To me, a Repinskoi, he said, 'Lie down, you old witch! If you don't obey me straight away, I'll give you a pair of thick ears!' So when it came to absolute force I had to give way, didn't I? I couldn't draw back again, for fear of his beating me! So I got up and went to Père Bontard and told him I wanted to be a Roman, and to believe in the Papa-Rimsky. But it is not so bad here."

"Our old Orthodox Church is aristocratic," declared Sophia. "When I went into the Lubyanka with Princess Globukov she took me in with one glance from top to toe—with one glance I tell you, chère Cathérine. It was heart-breaking. Then I went out to see her at the Serpukhovskaya—she lives right at the end of the Shabolovskaya Street. I came to tea, and I gave her my bread and sugar cards, and 'Perhaps I am supposed to stand in a queue myself!' she said icily. I began to weep and kiss her hands, but she never forgave me. 'Isn't it all the same to you whether I spy in the Orthodox Church or in the Roman Church? What does it matter to an old woman like me if I get the 'minus 6' '"? I stammered. But the Princess Globukov pulled a whalebone out of her corset and said, more icily than before, 'A Romish Sofia Nikolayevna is nothing to me!' I went away and slammed the door—and now, well, now I am beginning to be a good Catholic! You will laugh, but now I do almost firmly believe——"

The conversation did not seem to strike Katerina as particularly interesting. "But say, chère Sophie, one doesn't notice particularly that you go so very often to confession? And yet one must go to confession. That is the best opportunity for trapping the priest."

"No, not at all," declared Sophia, "only I have a poor memory for the sermons, but a good memory for faces. And by the way, what has happened to that young girl who always sat in the second row, the brown haired youngster? She was a Pole."

Katerina whispered something into Sofia's ear, at which the latter screwed up her face into a grimace that was a mixture of gruesome gloating and enjoyable horror. "Then she won't come to church any more," said Sofia. "Let the fool come a cropper too; and who knows whether Balindis won't have his fun with her too——he-he!—he'll want a bit of stolen sweets from her too, he-he!—*cela me donne un frisson d'une volupté inconnue.* Has he locked her up in the dark?"

"She will just have to sign," said the other broadly.

"Of course, she'll have to sign. Who doesn't have to sign?" retorted the woman in the window-blind cloak. "I certainly had to sign. Well, anyhow—didn't you notice the fellow who often used to come and stand at the back? A fine handsome fellow, young too. That's suspicious, isn't it?"

"Very suspicious," murmured Katerina.

"Well, I'm going to denounce him," announced Sofia heatedly. "But first, I shall go to him and tell him that unless he comes to see me and——" her voice sank to an indistinguishable murmur, and then, loud again, could be heard the words, "—but then I shall denounce him just the same."

"Of course," said Katerina. "Of course, of course——"

Then the two women giggled, and hurried through the gate, in among the low, weed-covered walls. Nikalai turned and stared after them incredulously. "Poor Saviour," he said to himself. "Poor, crucified Saviour, to have to dwell here in this church! Poor, poor Saviour!" From the new building opposite somebody hummed the song of Stenieka Rasin.

In the evening he was at a cinema in the neighbourhood of the Nikitskiya Pforte. An instructional film, "Female Hygiene," was being shown. There was less of the erotic in it than in certain operettas of Western Europe. At first Nikalai was disconcerted when he saw hundreds of feet of film of distorted women's faces not only undergoing abortional treatment by the old crones who practised it surrepti-

tiously, but also in the official State clinic for the elimination
of unborn children. The agonised faces were transformed
into flowering meadows, in which naked babes by their
thousands were toddling about like little gipsy Cupids.
They gradually developed into robust, virile-looking women,
who rose up and trained Red Army recruits in marksman-
ship and the use of hand-grenades. This was not Rome in her
Divine teaching office, but the plump beast, the State,
demanding that the people "increase and multiply" to
provide it with subjects and warriors. Nikalai saw clearly
there was no question here of good or evil, but only of the
welfare of the Beast, which, once created by men for their
service, had become a living creature and had begun to
enslave men.

After the show he went to the refreshment-room. There,
too, was the heavy odour of sweat and dirty linen. The
people stood, close-packed, listening to the music of a
squeaky gramophone, drinking warm kvass and lukewarm
narsan, looking at the display of photos of the Meshrab-
promruss, and keeping their hands in their pockets. Nikalai
went out into the street, strolled down the Nikitski Boulevard, and finally sat down on one of the seats. From his
pocket he drew a sticky piece of bread, and took a bite.
The sky was not yet quite dark. The twilight sank slowly
down into night. A cold breeze was blowing over the
tangled aerials and the dreary pools of light round the
Arbatskaya and the Tverskaya. The electric trams rushed
past, dark and over-crowded with people, making an
unearthly din with their everlasting clamour of bells, all
along the steeply descending boulevarde. The trees rustled;
a lecture on the world-revolution went feebly forth on the
loud-speakers over the silent, weary people on the seats;
paint was peeling off the walls of the houses, and drifting
down in flakes; dark figures, whose faces could no longer be

made out, walked past in their rubber-soled plimsolls, talking quietly, between the rows of trees, their cigarettes glowing like red points in the dimness. It was all the while growing colder, and Nikalai turned up his coat collar. He thrust his hands deep into his ragged pockets. Night took possession of the city more and more. In the School of Arms the dry rattle of weapons was silenced. Street lamps glittered afar off on the square in the yellow chill, but restlessness spread ever more widely over the city like a pall. Night-work was going on in the factories around the periphery, wizened women set up their camp-stools to sit in the queue for the necessities of life, and throughout the night, the sirens shrieked unceasingly, on high notes and low, whistling, singing, or moaning. Even in the railway stations late trains were drawing in, croaking in the bass tone peculiar to the locomotives of the Soviet Union. *"Poidyom tovarishtchi-poidyom-piätiletka v tchetire goda!"* the noises kept hammering out in his head. Close-packed hordes of night-workers thronged the electric cars, the blaring of the loud-speakers never paused, the hammering in his head became frantic.

When the unrepose in him had reached its culminating peak, he got up, and walked, with stumbling, erratic steps, across the Arbatskaya Ploshtchad to his desolate, friendless abode.

Then, next day, he got to Leningrad. How different this city was from Moscow! Moscow was a drearily dismal, heretical State village, with the Kremlin as a museum, a veritable Third Rome and the metropolis of the Third International, a place of that puritanical sobriety which is common to all sectarian towns—the old Boston, Amsterdam, Victoria, Salt Lake City, or Aberdeen. The people there all had the same characteristics as the Puritans, Mormons, Calvinists, and all the other fossilized sectarians—they were fatalistic, dressed ridiculously, were hard-hearted and schoolmasterish, had governess-like mannerisms, and were devoted to an insipid faith in the written word. But in Leningrad one breathed a different atmosphere. Here, the "extraordinary" police ruled unchecked, and one saw, instead of Chinese and Caucasians, innumerable Jewish intellectuals. The era of grey state Bolshevism seemed not yet to have dawned. Here, in the late domain of Zinoviev, they went on busily defrauding, forging, debating, drinking, murdering, loving, and grumbling. In the evenings women in long dresses were to be seen hovering in the streets; in the Oktiabrski Prospekt, provided one was not stingy with the tchervontses, one could eat roast chickens and ducks; in the Kammyonni island innumerable amorous couples were to be seen entwined in each other's arms; in the buffets and Stalovayas, men with long, unkempt hair and incongruously mingled philosophies of the universe, strode about excitedly. But over all there brooded the memory of the accomplishment of an important revolutionary act—Kronstadt, the Winter Palace, the Smolny Monastery, the Fortress of Peter and Paul with the Trubetskoi bastion.

But Leningrad, with its comparative air of prosperous well-being, its plastered street steps, its helmeted police, had not become a peril nor a problem, nor a "writing on the wall" for Europe. Over Leningrad—which, on the lips of the people, was still "Pieter," Petrograd, the City of Peter —there lay an anarchic restlessness. The Bolshevik Petrograd was a metropolis of neurasthenics, sadists, nihilists, Jews and maniacal zealots. Here it was that Meyerhold, Eisenstein, and Mayakovski began their work, men of the theatre, of the film, of the pen. It was here that Dora Kaplan shot at Ulyanov-Lenin, the petty noble of Tartar descent; here it was that the student Kannegiesser killed the head of the "Extraordinary Commission," Uritzki—the

Jew slaying the Jew because of the everlasting shame that the other had brought on his people. It was here, in front of the Winter Palace, that the people were routed by the forces led by the priest and police-agent, Gapon. Here stood —with wings now decaying—the former Imperial Ministry of War, where the accounts of Redl, the treacherous Austrian General Staff Officer, were being examined.

Moscow is the hard, dirty capital of the world's sectarianism in its Asiatic form. Moscow is the city of the Piätiletka, of the people's tenements, of night-work, of restlessness— the city of steep street declivities and droning lorries, of the fantastic wireless tower, and the frenzied Church of the Vassili Blashnny, with negroes, Malays, Chinese, Englishmen, Tadshiks, and Germans in the streets; the city of fugitives, gaol-birds, the whipped, the wretched, the envious and embittered. "Pieter," on the other hand, is the city of the idealists, the Liberals, the Æsthetes and degenerates. Moscow is the front, "Pieter" is a halt en route; Moscow a dreadful glimpse of the future, Petrograd a reminiscence. Moscow is an arsenal, and Petrograd a museum.

In the train he had already made the acquaintance of a certain Shatzkin, a garrulous, black-haired official, who entertained Nikalai all through the night with his accounts of the wonders of Leningrad.

"You must put up at the Hotel Europe," he urged him. "Nowhere but the Hotel Europe! Actually, one is supposed only to pay in foreign currencies there, but I'll fix it for you, as you are a newspaper correspondent. And the women there *are* there! Umph! *What* women! And all for the foreigners. But there's always something left over for us."

Little Comrade Shatzkin painted their future prospects in glowing colours, with great glee.

They came to the Oktober-station, and immediately were in the thick of a tussle of words with the Izvostchik. From three tchervontses, the driver gradually abated his price to eight roubles. In the hotel hall were standing people of various nationalities and types: Americans with bored expressions; a few Innospiets, who treated the Russians with careless arrogance, and bullied the porters; girls who murdered the English language, and wore whole kitchen-gardens and floral plantations on their fashionable hats; and powdered Ogpu-courtesans, with dead-looking mouse-like eyes under their plucked eyebrows. Comrade Shatzkin talked in excited whispers to a micro-cephalic man who was standing behind the unending janitor's bar. They got their rooms right away, and, after a long wait, went up in the lift to the upper stories.

During the morning he went to the nearby Catholic Church of St. Catherine, in the Oktober-prospekt, to inspect the baptismal certificate of a Moscow observer. In the sacristy he learned that the church books had been seized by the authorities, and taken to the magistrature at the Ploshtchad Uritzkavo. For hours he ran up and down stairs n that building, found his way into obscure offices, into the "Central Bureau of the Board of Control for the Inspection of Population Statistics in the Leningrad Area," into the "Accountancy Office, Pensions Department," "Public Assistance Fund for Widows and Orphans of Red Sailors fallen in the Second Baltic Flotilla," and other offices that belonged to even less comprehensible services. He wandered about from door to door with his "propusk," a docket given him in the ground-floor lobby, which declared the object, time, and date of his visit, and the name of the bearer. Everywhere the same scene—in a cramped, fly-ridden hole, men or women with greasy necks or kerchiefs, gripping chewed pencils between their fingers, making up for the way their pay had been cut down to the level of the workers' wages, by an overbearing insolence, to try and re-establish their lost social superiority; they would receive Nikalai with suspicious looks, and forthwith begin to question and cross-examine him, to examine his papers, and enquire where he lived. Everywhere, gloomy mistrust, inquisitorial questioning, the air of petty authority and bourgeois arrogance; everywhere, the smell of ink, bread, beetles, mildew, and dirty linen. After three hours wandering he was advised to go to the Z.A.G.S.—the Central Bureau for Registration—in the Smolny Monastery.

From there he went back to the Oktober-prospekt, to the Departmental Inspectorate. There, again, no success. Meanwhile, it was past midday, and he called for Shatzkin at the Hotel Europe. They first went to the Anti-Religious Museum at the Isaaks Cathedral, where two mummified Yakut corpses were intended to teach them that it is not the bodies of Saints only that are incorruptible after death; then came the Holy Father, riding astride on the barrels of big guns; then Catholic priests walking arm-in-arm, for pleasure, with frock-coated bourgeois Capitalists. But the most space was given up to the sects—the Chlists, the Scopts, the Molocans, the Duchoborzians, the Stundists, the Maliovanzians. "Where are the Bolsheviks?" he asked himself. "The sects are not complete—the Bolsheviks are missing!" Then, audaciously, he turned to Shatzkin and said, "Not bad—the idea of arranging an Anti-Religious Museum—certainly the Anti-Religious movement has great museum value!" But Shatzkin seemed not to hear. He was studying, with attentive, lack-lustre eyes, the pendulum that swung from the great dome.

They went up the steep stairs into the dome. There were people sitting, often on the extreme edge of the parapets, with their feet dangling over the yawning abyss. They were all people from the plains, and yet the height did not make them giddy. They just took their chance of danger indifferently, with careless, weary, stony faces. High up on the dome, Shatzkin explained the view to Nikalai. Far beneath them they saw a burned-down house, and then what had formerly been the German Embassy, robbed and plundered by the patriotic mob in 1914, the same mob which helped to make the unpatriotic barricades in 1917. Then they saw the military training college, bulbous church spires, the Winterplatz by the Uritzkiplatz, with the Victory Column, and absolutely cannibal-like primitive statues of black-painted wood; the Peter and Paul Fortress in the background; and, on the horizon, half hidden by a veil of mist, a seaside place.

"What is that?" Nikalai asked his guide.

"Sestoretsk-Kurort," he said shortly. "And beyond there lies Finland," he added, after a pause.

"The gap in the hedge!" thought Nikalai. "The gap—the way out! Only need go down to the beach in the evening, go into the water, and swim five hundred metres—and I'm safe!" His eyes strove to pierce the mist. "Only twenty kilometres from here," he thought, "two thirds of the distance from Berlin to Brühlau. Freedom is so near!"

He did not know Finland and could form no mental image of the people there, but in his imagination, there lived there none but angels, seraphical, fair angels, soaring and hovering over flashing blue woodland-fringed lakes. He became conscious, for the first time, that he was obsessed by the same longing to be back among his fellowmen that drives to melancholia the heroes of those Utopian romances that imaginative authors have set in some hopelessly inaccessible primitive forest, or on some planet peopled by intelligent semi-animals. A hitherto unknown longing to be among good and beautiful women, who were neither in the pay of the secret police nor yet boasting of their fifth miscarriage, took possession of him. Descending the steps, he felt oppressed, restless, rebellious—so that he did not notice that he had passed across the nave and had gone half-way round the dome again, but went on past the exit to the Square, and round the whole circumference of the dome again. Behind him walked Shatzkin, and behind Shatzkin three other men—nobody noticed it. Six times he had made the round of the dome before the last man in the line realised it, and pointed out the exit, with a grin. His chuckling laugh infected the others, and soon the whole party were guffawing, tittering, and giggling, Nikalai included. To such an extent had they become mere dried-up robots.

Then they dined—not in a cheap eating-house of the "Lenpishtchepromsoyuz," but at the Oktober-prospekt, in a real restaurant, where one could have almost anything for about fifteen roubles.

After their meal Shatzkin went to sleep, but Nikalai went to look up the Guarantors. One of them was sitting in the State Bank, surrounded by a hundred other inky slaves of the pen; the second was composing canons at Putilov; the third was employed in the Polsi Dom Oswiatowy; the fourth was translating the novels of Kurt Landsberger into Russian for the "Myssl" Press; the fifth was a tramp, and was sleeping in an electric automobile that, wholly unmovable and rusted, lay abandoned ever since the October Revolution not far from the State Publishing warehouse on the bank of the Yekaterinski Canal.

Then he went along by the canal towards the Moika, and gazed at the house that had formerly been the abode of the Ochrana, and, in the Square of the Revolution, made the acquaintance of a worker from the Vyborg district, who showed him the sights of the town and strolled through the streets with him. From the Ogpu Headquarters in the Prospekt Rashalia there came women workers with the expression of ravening tigers, and lined up at the exit with permits

adorned with photographs; in front of the Yenukidze
Institute lounged students from the East; but the Red Fleets'
Quay, and the Boulevard of Unions was empty. Nikalai
made himself out a great Bezboshnik, and asked a number
of questions about the work of the "Militant Atheists" in this
town. The worker gave calm, business-like answers: In the
Lesnoi-prospekt fine, new workmen's dwellings had been
built, and care was taken to see that only genuine, reliable
people, people devoted to the Party, the State, the Piatiletka,
and the Socialist movement, were assigned dwellings there.
And what had happened? Hadn't he read the last number
of the *Bezboshnik?* Those new dwellings were soon chock-
ful of icons. The people brought Bibles and crucifixes into
the lovely new Soviet dwellings. In the fourteenth year of
the Revolution!

Meanwhile, they had reached the Kasan Cathedral,
and the worker urged him to visit it. On the door was an
ecclesiastical calendar, which a child had illuminated in
water-colours. A child painting ecclesiastical calendars,
among the atheist heretics, with flowers and garlands and
festoons—a child that goes to the Soviet school, and at
Easter probably has to dance along in clowns' costume with
a wooden cross in the No-God Carnival! What sort of an end
will that child come to? Starve with the third Piatiletka?
Go down, bathed in the blood of his fellow-men, in the
death-house on the Prospekt Rashalia? How will this child
be able to keep his faith in the Crucified One of Golgotha
amid the paralysing chill of this scepticism, this cynicism,
this stupefying insensibility?

The worker knelt at the entrance, clumsily and solemnly
made the sign of the Cross, removed his cap and only spoke
in whispers. Outside in the Square, after they had left,
Nikalai asked, laughing, "Then you're no Militant
Bezboshnik, comrade?"

The other silently drew from his pocket his membership card of the Militant Atheists, and held it up before Nikalai's eyes.

"But you kneel down in church, and make the sign of the Cross!" said Nikalai, in surprise.

"Of course I don't believe in God!" said the worker. "If one sees the monkey's skeleton side by side with the human skeleton—and look in the microscope—and so on—you understand all that a lot better. He doesn't exist now, through all that—I think it has something to do with the fall of the Czars!"

"Yes, that certainly has something to do with the fall of the Czars!" thought Nikalai to himself. "The Czar and the Orthodox Church lived in a sort of morganatic marriage. When the Czar was killed, the Orthodox Church was left a widow—but we're in Asia, here, and the widow has to be burned. A tragedy of the Throne-and-Altar complex!"

Nikalai was not satisfied with the worker's answer.

"But why that crossing yourself?" he asked again.

"Well, the church is a sacred place, anyhow," said the worker calmly.

"How is it sacred, if God doesn't exist?"

"What about the saints?"

"Radi Boga! What saints?"

"The saints in the statues, in the icons——"

Nikalai stared at him in amazement.

"Iconodoulists and iconoclasts!" he said out loud—"worshippers of images and destroyers of images." The problem of Byzantium, that great mother of the heretics, the Second Rome, was here celebrating a ghastly renaissance. Nikalai clasped his forehead.

In the late afternoon he went round the churches and chapels. In the Oktober-prospekt, in the Kovenski Pereulok,

in the Ushakovskaya. There were still two official priests in
Leningrad—a Lithuanian and a French priest. All the other
bishops and priests were in Solovki, in Siberia, or buried in
quicklime. The Bishops of Magilev, of Kiev, of Leningrad—
they were shot, exiled, expelled. Nikalai went to an afternoon Benediction at which only old, weazened women kneeled,
crossing themselves sanctimoniously. When he heard the
priest, with his stony, hard countenance, reciting the
gloriously pathetic Sorrowful Mysteries of the Rosary before
the Holy of Holies, and then looked again at the whispering,
muttering women in the prie-dieux, he thought of the story
of the destruction of Sodom and Gomorrah, and he pictured
that priest fighting it out with himself, as Abraham had with
God, how long he would suffer them—if ten, if five, if only
one per cent believed in Him, whether he must still stay
there and serve. For if once he departed there could be no
return to the city on the shore of the Neva.

When he was on his way back the first batch of "drunks"
were already lying about on the pavements. People stepped
over them indifferently and passed on. The sky had turned
to a slatey blue-grey, and a few clouds were gathering.
Two mongrel dogs were scampering round each other in the
Simeonovkaya. A peasant in a Russian cap gave one of the
curs a kick, and sent it flying under an electric tram. Red
viscid splashes were all that was left on the rails. In St.
Simeon's Church a couple were being married. A "pope"
with long hair and finely chiselled, Christ-like features sang
a psalm. How often, how many times a month did he make
his way to the Prospekt Rashalia? The bridegroom wore a
shabby, threadbare dark suit, and the bride herself wept
with melancholy, dark-ringed eyes, blood-shot with cook-
ing. But behind the bridal pair two boys stood, with trembling arms holding the crowns, bound with cloths, over their
heads. His road took Nikalai past the circus and menagerie

buildings to the Engineers' Square. In this square, there is a shooting-range, where he saw what is so significantly typical of Leningrad—male and female creatures playing hand-ball. The males were thin, feeble, anxious and nervous in their movements; the females, small, broad-hipped, powdered and painted. It was this peasant-drab type of morbid, sex-ridden stable-girl that invariably irritated and repelled him so. Meanwhile, however, the game of ball went on. The sun had long since set. Between the thin patches of grass the muddy ground was kicked up. Many of the players got the leather ball in their faces, and had their painted lips smeared with dirt. Half-way to the hotel Nikalai turned round and looked back at the half-naked, silent players, with their muddy bodies, still hysterically jumping about in the vacant shooting range.

At the hotel Shatzkin was impatiently awaiting him. In the hall below a group of people were waiting to be assigned a room. They were the same stamp of men who are to be seen in Berlin in the "Society of Friends of the Soviet," or in Moscow in the Foreign Club in the Mala Spiridonovka. White-clad women, who, with angelically bovine faces, wanted to lead a life of "beauty and purity"; long-haired, simple-minded, credulous Englishmen; gloomy coffee-shop Berliners, who regarded everything as problematical, from their own existence onwards, and hysterical, elderly, American women, whose eyes began to sparkle whenever they saw dirty children being washed in Louis XVI drawing-rooms.

Shatzkin was so impatient that he dragged Nikalai into the lift, and took him up to the roof-garden. It was quite cool up there. One could see the silhouettes of the dreary forest of aerials, and towards the north, the Peter and Paul Fortress beckoned, with its two-headed eagle set jauntily askew. A few drops of rain were falling. Inside, in the

dining-room, the tables were laid, and a jazz band was
playing. The musicians looked like bagno convicts on leave
—wearing black fabric-shoes in imitation of patent leather,
and white paper fronts in imitation of starched linen shirts,
stiff wing-collars, and dinner-jackets covered with scurf.
In the smaller dining-room Nikalai saw a statue, probably
"manufactured" before the war, embodying a conception
whose coarseness revolted him—the figure of a drunken
woman in long lace pantaloons, with long cork-screw curls
cascading down over where a chemise of the 'eighties exposed
half her naked bosom. In her right hand she held a wine-
bottle, and over her lips played a sweet, dreamy smile, like a
little girl's. It was this combination of crude sensuality and
that fraudulent childishness of the senilely perverse, *fin-de-
siècle* mood of a society that was now swiftly dropping down
into the shadow of the anti-Christ, that stirred and appalled
Nikalai.

They sat down at a table, and Comrade Shatzkin ordered
a bottle of Jardin des Jésuites, off the ice. Nikalai felt ill at
ease here. Somehow he had become "proletarian-conscious,"
and he began to hate this atmosphere, from the proletarian
point of view.

At the next table were seated some Hungarian Bolsheviks,
who must have come into the world not far from Munkács,
drinking champagne and talking in incisive tones to a hunch-
back who was chuckling maliciously to himself, and eating
caviare with a soup-spoon.

Eventually, la Gorskaya sat down at their table. She had
obtained European clothes from a Soviet diplomat on leave,
and Shatzkin whispered to Nikalai that she was once a
countess. Shatzkin was in a good humour, clicking his
tongue, and laughing idiotically. Then, conveying his vege-
tables to his mouth on the end of his knife, he asked the
Gorskaya woman whether la Boimenblit would care to join

them; upon which Gorskaya contemptuously drooped her deep blue-shaded eyelids and remarked that Boimenblit only entertained the hotel guests for a dollar fee. Gorskaya, who was over five foot six in height, was continually stroking Shatzkin's hand, while he whispered quite unambiguous things in her ear. Meanwhile another G.P.U. prostitute sat down by Nikalai, and hummed the tune that the band was playing, in a hoarse, beery voice. Nikalai looked at her, out of the side of his eyes. Only an Innospiets who was absolutely insanely amorous, and had lost his glasses, and suffered with deafness, could find any pleasure in her. She laid an arm about his neck, and breathed a reek of alcohol in his face.

Meanwhile the life of the place had reached the acme of activity. The waiters tripped across the carpets, with white aprons and freshly whitened tennis shoes. The perspiration streamed down the jazz musicians' animal-like faces. A *maître d'hotel* mumblingly translated the menu card for nervous Germans. An American married couple splashed about indifferently in their soup-plates, and watched, bored, the Russian at the next table, who had removed his collar, to snort the better. At the table near the exit on to the terrace one couple had risen and begun to dance. Shatzkin knew those two—it was Popov, of the Town Soviet, and the Shuslova woman. Shuslova was dressed after the European style, but her clothes were made from Soviet materials, and she wore thin cotton stockings.

Shuslova had a round, tubular mouth that looked like a blood-sausage in longitudinal section. Her hair all ended in little curls. Popov wore long pointed side-whiskers, and gave the impression of a morpho-maniac. He was hugging Shuslova to him, executing tango figures with complicated steps that only provincial Don Juans in little places far from the big cities ever master, fixing his mouth by suction to the tubular mouth of his partner, and making movements with his knees meaning of which was unmistakable.

Meanwhile the night outside had grown dark. The tram-car bells were heard more and more infrequently; only in the west was there still a bright streak in the sky. The moon had risen, unnoticed, and shone down over Leningrad, the Baltic port of the Collectivist State, the metropolis of Love meted out by Tariff.

CHAPTER IX

UNDER ARREST

NIKALAI SERGEYEVITCH KISSELEFF, Citizen of the Union of Socialist Soviet Republics, subject of the Russian Socialistic Federative Soviet Republic, correspondent of the *Vechernyaya Moskva*, member of the Union of Militant Atheists, got back to Moscow on August 18th in a very melancholy mood of depression. When he saw once more those streets, those people, those squat houses, smelled that smell of squashed vermin, mouldy bread, and spilled petroleum, he had an ashamed sense of guilt at having, for days, lived inexcusably in a city of Western bourgeois pleasure-seeking, in the appreciable vicinity of the Esthonian and Finnish frontiers, a vicious life of excess and idleness that he was not entitled to. He did not even get rid of this "morning-after" feeling when he faced the Pole in his room in the Afanasievski Pereulok, who, with a slightly contemptuous smile, listened to Nikalai's account of his impressions of Leningrad. This Polish Catholic felt, just as did Nikalai and every other proletarian of Moscow, a deep-seated disgust for that unfinished city of compromises and of simulated cheery geniality. Here, in the proletarian metropolis, Nikalai felt much more sure of his behaviour, and the basic mood of this environment, in its entire freedom from any ambiguity, was much more to his taste than the atmosphere of the city of the Czar Peter and the Tartar Lenin, on the edge of the sea of Finland.

He had still only to visit Ivano-Vosnesensk and Troitzko-

Sergeyevsk, in order to finish his work there also. Then he returned to Moscow. The next day he meant to leave for the Caucasus, in order to return to Turkey by the same route by which he had come. He still had numerous purchases to make, and was in a great hurry. On the Theatre Square he would not wait for the signal of the policeman on traffic-duty, who, when Nikalai was nearly knocked down by a Rolls-Royce, stopped him and took his name and address. Nikalai attached no particular importance to this incident.

The next day, he tied up his bundle, locked the door of his room and hid the key in the place agreed on, and turned to leave. But on the staircase he was surprised to meet two militiamen. They were young, fair, enterprising-looking lads, with red tabs on their collars.

"Are you, by any chance, the Correspondent Kisseleff, Citizen?" asked the younger of the two, pulling from his tunic the same photograph which Nikalai had on his pass-port.

Nikalai did not speak—he was tortured by a premonition of evil. He had paled. He nodded affirmatively.

"Then you will accompany us," said the elder of the two coolly. And he took a revolver from his pocket and pulled back the safety-catch, then let the weapon dangle in his hand, swinging it backwards and forwards by the plaited leather strap.

Nikalai turned sick with fear. His feet were trembling, and he was forced to close his eyes a moment and lean back against the wall. No quick prayer came from his lips—he felt so ill with misery that he could almost have vomited in the militiamen's faces.

"Quick march!" they commanded, as with one voice.

"Quick march!" he himself repeated, mechanically copying them. Then he picked up his bundle and staggered down the stairs.

In the front garden the elder put a pipe in his mouth and went on in front. Nikalai had to walk behind him. Almost unconscious with the paralysis of fear, he stumbled on like a madman over everything that lay in his way on the ground. Behind Nikalai followed the younger man, with his first finger cocked round the trigger of the revolver. In this order the procession crossed the Starokonyusheni-Pereulok and the Miortvy-Pereulok, or "Dead Men's Alley." People just stepped out of their way indifferently. Again and again the little whistle sounded—but Nikalai saw and heard, thought and felt nothing. He hardly noticed even, that he was being led into an unprepossessing grey building, where his papers were taken from him, his skull measured, his braces removed, and he was then led down into a cell with the smell of a grave.

In the cell a number of men were sitting round, smoking, mumbling, playing and snoring. Nikalai dropped on to a seat. From without a sunbeam penetrated. His lips quivered. He had not been able to complete his mission. Nothing was finished. And the suffering had already begun. But what hurt most was the suddenness and unexpectedness with which everything had happened—the cruel unexpectedness.

Night fell on the Third Rome, a night that, for Nikalai, was not essentially different from day. The sunbeam that at first had penetrated the window set high in the wall, slanting downward, glistening whitely on his shoes, had crept up the wall slowly, and vanished. Imperceptibly the activities and talk of the other occupants of the cell had diminished with fatigue, and the chatter had died away within those four walls. Before they lay down on their palliasses to sleep, they had all come up to him, one at a time, and stared, like animals, into his face. One asked him in a low voice what his offence was, but he did not reply.

It grew darker and darker in Nikalai's cell, but he was still incapable of concentrating on any sort of thought. The unexpected shock and the fright had paralysed his powers of thought. His hands and feet were icy-cold, and his heart was beating faintly and uncertainly, while his whole circulation seemed to be stagnating. He felt that he was already slowly dying and decaying. His mouth was so parched that his tongue felt to himself like a piece of wood between two sheets of sand-paper. On his forehead, like a thin icing, there lay a cold layer of dense, greasy perspiration, and his dry, cracked lips were twisted into a distorted grimace. His life of prayer he had neglected of late, and so it happened that he sat there on that bench empty, burned out, paralysed in thought, without sensation, and devoid of any emotion, staring out into the darkness with lustreless eyes, and only now and then caught by some memory that, without stirring him in the least, left him as soon as it had come. Thus, he heard Scapinelli warning him to expect no mercy from offended heretics. Then, vacancy again—again, the rush of blood in his ears. Then, out of the darkness, Gertrude laid her arms about his neck, screamed, implored, whispered, and vanished. Then again, nothingness. Only the snoring of the sleeping men. Outside, sirens. Outside and inside, the ghastly melancholy of the Third Rome. When morning came, the militiamen found, among the sleepy, groaning, yawning men in the cell, one figure who was the embodiment of human misery, pain, and disgust with life. Beside him the mugs of food and the blankets lay untouched.

CHAPTER X

THE BIRTH OF A MURDERER

THEY had not tried him yet. But the more consciousness came back to him, the more the paralysing shock changed to a desperate horror in which his mind conjured up gruesome visions of his imminent end taking shape and form. When he had succeeded, for the first time, in fighting down his torturing anxiety, and absorbing himself for a while in prayer and meditation, the hardness and coldness that had been weighing on him for weeks, a mountainous load of oppression, dissolved, and it seemed to himself as if his soul had begun to breathe more freely. Nevertheless, death was beckoning to him—farewell to the body and to the world.

He spoke little, scarcely at all, to the men in his cell. Between his prayers he began, confusedly and without any real planning, to think about ways of escape, and the possibilities of a defence, without arriving at anything definite. More and more it became clear to him that he could not now escape from death. To enter the service of the heretics—even only ostensibly—was forbidden for him. Therefore, sitting in a quiet corner of the big cell, rigid and motionless, he began to prepare for death. At first the men laughed at him because of his retiring manner. A man who had committed outrages on children would, he declared, get off with two years. A good-natured looking highway robber estimated his own sentence at three years in the Butyaka. And a genial tramp, who had snatched an attaché case

containing 200 tchervontses from a government departmental
chief, counted with certainty on being sent to the convict
settlement of Bolshevo. This man delivered a speech in the
cell, on how pleasant life was in the G.P.U. camp at Bolshevo;
his brother was there and had married there, and had children who were going to school. One was free to come and
go, and could work either in the shoe factory or the ski-
factory. Besides, one had always the chance of eventually
becoming a Party-member. Nikalai, however, had ceased to
listen to any of these talks. He had, so to speak, crept away
inside himself, praying, conscientiously refusing to let himself
think of the Third Degree questioning he would be subjected
to, and, in his moments of relaxation, taking refuge in the
realm of bitter-sweet memories. German words came, half-
aloud, to his lips, and the realisation that, along with
Nikalai Sergeyevitch Kisseleff, there must also perish the
cheerful Berlin Catholic, Eugen Düring, confused his
thoughts.

The next night he fell asleep from sheer exhaustion.
Joyless dreams tortured him beyond all endurance. He
would often awake with a start and stare into the darkness
with tingling hair and straining eyes, and see nothing but a
lifeless black void. At one o'clock in the morning he saw a
light gleaming over him, heard a voice, and felt a hand on his
chest. This time it was not a dream, but a militiaman.
Drunk with sleep, and trembling, he followed him through a
dimly lit passage. Then a door opened, and he saw he was
in a room.

"Saditess—sit down," said a voice.

Now Nikalai perceived a man reading under a green china
lamp-shade. Like an automaton, Nikalai dropped into a
chair. The man pushed cigarettes towards him—he did not
see them. He kept staring at the face of the reading man, an
expressionless, mongoloid face, that seemed to belong to a

realm outside the domain of good and evil, heavy-lidded, squat-nosed, and with thick, dry lips, and thin eye-brows. In his toil-worn hands the reading man held a gnawed pencil, and from time to time he made a mark in the book. Nikalai's eyes drifted from the reader to a map of Moscow, marked out with the police districts, then to the Menszynski picture, and the corner-statuette of Lenin; from that, to an empty narzan bottle, and thence to an almost black fly-paper that hung from the low ceiling. The arrangement of the room was utterly without any hint of personality—as devoid of personality as the figure of that man reading his book and making marginal notes.

"Proletarians are playing at running a state," thought Nikalai—and, oddly enough, his thoughts drifted right away from himself.

"So you are Kisseleff?" said the reader, suddenly, closing his book.

Nikalai was startled out of his thoughts; a ghastly spasm shook him—his body became clammy with perspiration.

"I pictured you as a harmless-looking fellow, like that," said the other, and seemed to be groping for words. In Nikalai's face not a muscle stirred.

"Confess!" said the militia-officer, sharply, just then. He had suddenly decided to adopt a stern, martinet-like pose.

"What do you want me to confess?" asked Nikalai, quietly.

The militia officer struck the table with his limp hand.

"Don't try to make yourself out such a fool!" he shouted, excitedly. "We know all—all!" His breath became laboured. It was then that Nikalai first realised that the man must have passed his fortieth year.

The militia officer directed his mad-bull-like gaze at Nikalai—like the muzzle of a big gun, the bear-like head had rotated, heavily and awkwardly, on its bull-like neck.

"You need only say 'Yes' or 'No,' " growled the harsh

voice. "I will reconstruct the whole case to you, it is as clear as noonday. I only hope you're reasonable enough not to make my work unnecessarily difficult, trying to take refuge in any idiotic lies."

Nikalai made no answer. Once more he could feel the blood pounding in the hollow behind his ears. It was only now that he realised that he had already begun dying, from the moment of his arrest. He was dying bit by bit, all the time. He could feel now that he was nothing but a pile of bones—what was hung upon them was simply so many kilogrammes of flesh that might be sold by weight—decaying flesh wrapped in mouldering cloth. The end was not coming all at once—it was a state, or rather, a process.

"Even the directors of the G.P.U. are very much interested in your case!" said the officer. "And now confess, before anything else, whereabouts did you get across the frontier? And"—his voice dropped to a low tone—"did you have accomplices among the frontier troops?"

Nikalai looked straight before him, like a mummy. The upper part of his body sagged forward.

"So you won't speak!" exclaimed the officer violently. His anger was genuine. His eyes protruded from their sockets; he half raised himself from his chair, then let himself fall back, and looked suspiciously, appraisingly, at Nikalai, from under his brows, as if he were trying to weigh up the effect of the words he meant to address to him. Then he folded his hands on his lap, twirled his thumbs, and began his recital in a sing-song, monotonous, matter-of-fact, business-like speech.

"In the year 1927," he said, "you were in Verny—in Alma-Ata, I mean—as a member of the staff of the *Vechernyaya Moskva*, in order to write articles on the building of the 'Turkssib'—the Turko-Siberian trunk railway line—and the woman Serpuchova was working there as engine-driver on a tender. As an Udarnitsa she played a prominent part in the Kompart. She was a great 'activist,' and at Alma-Ata, at the head of a brigade of storm-troops, she had sought out the homes of the Mohammedans and ripped off the veils from their women's faces, and burned them in the market-place. At that time she was the mistress of the engineer Gertsin, a regular weakling, whom she is said to have bullied and often boxed his ears. But Gertsin was only a hanger-on, not a Communist.

"You came to Alma-Ata on the 27th April, and got to know Serpuchova the same day at the City Soviet—she was introduced to you by Akhun Babaiev himself—and she began an affair with you the same day. You drove out into the open country with her, and did not come back till late at night. Serpuchova was as violent as a beast. When Gertsin reproached her she hammered him with her fists till she drew blood, and Gertsin deliberately threw himself under the rock in some blasting operations; he had been her slave, absolutely infatuated.

"On 1st May you married Serpuchova, who dropped her work on the Turkssib, and followed you here. You lived with her on the Tchistoprudnuy Boulevard. Serpuchova entered the 'Tchubar' armament factory as a heavy labourer; you were not happy with her; she seduced the fifteen-year-old son of a lodger in your house, or rather half seduced and half forced him. She also had an affair with Shikhin, who was turned out of the Kompart for having gone with prostitutes. She had also the chief of the 'Tchubar' completely under her thumb. On the 12th of March, 1929, there was a breach between you and Serpuchova. You learned of her intrigues through young Plechinski's father, whose son she had ruined, and who complained to you. This was in the morning. Your room had thin walls, and the neighbours could hear all that passed. In the evening, when Serpuchova came back from the factory, you began accusing her—and the woman thereupon cynically retorted that she was also carrying on with three other men. Then there was a big scene. But that night you slept with Serpuchova—you had made it up with her, and made use of her influential connections to secure promotion. You came to the Don district, and Serpuchova got two months' leave from the 'Tchubar.' On the 2nd of April, 1929, you removed with your wife to Nakhitchevan, on the Don."

The officer extinguished his cigarette on the bottom of a sardine tin that stood by the inkwell on his desk. His expression was one of complacency; Nikalai had not interrupted him. He kept his eyes turned towards the floor, to disguise his surprise. He was still a prey to a torturing uncertainty; he only knew that he was to do penance for his former life as Nikalai Sergeyevitch Kisseleff, for a transgression of Kisseleff that he neither knew, nor probably approved, nor could imagine. But the delight of not having been recognised as an imposter stifled even his indignation at being brought to book for the offence of some stranger. The sensation of death had disappeared. In its place there had come the dread of a wearisome, endlessly long-drawn-out imprisonment—gaol, penal servitude, exile, chains. He looked at the officer, who was engaged in the attempt to light a second cigarette with his stumpy fingers; and at the sombre office, through bars cunningly designed to shut him off from the outer world.

"In Nakhitchevan you discovered that Serpuchova was expecting a child," proceeded the officer, absent-mindedly blowing smoke-rings from his lips and gazing up at the sloping wall, as if he were striving to project the scene visually on its whitewashed surface. "You were very pleased about this, because you knew it could only be your own child. But Serpuchova did not like the idea at all, because it meant her getting unwieldy, helpless, and defenceless. So she pestered and nagged you to let her have the unborn child done away with. But you wouldn't hear of it. After the lapse of two months, you took your wife back to Moscow. It was only when Serpuchova began undressing at your home, that you learned that, behind your back, she had procured an abortion. 'Murderess!' you yelled at her, 'You murderess!' and raised your fist. Then Serpuchova got frightened of you, and ran away. Mad with rage, you chased her down the staircase. In the street, she got a lorry between herself and you, and escaped from there through the women's lavatory."

The official knitted his brows, and made a great effort to link his thoughts into a coherent picture. Then he went on with his narrative:

"You saw red. You wouldn't go out—you just waited for Serpuchova. It was cold in Moscow, and you hadn't a coat on. You lay in wait for her behind the door of the room. When Serpuchova came back you fell upon the woman. She struggled and fought with the strength of a giant, but in the heat of the fight you broke the leg off a table, and beat her with it till she was dead. Then you flung the body on to the bed, pocketed all the money there was, and fled. The whole house was upside-down. Drenched with blood, you ran down the steps like a madman—nobody dared to stop you.

"You fled across the Polish frontier. That was on the 11th of June, 1929. The frontier troops shot at you—you were wounded. You left a part of your property behind—but they couldn't catch you. You were in the 'Strana Panov,' in the country of the Poles."

These last words, he had pronounced with infinite contempt. It sounded to Nikalai as if he were trying to taunt him with cowardice.

"And now you come back, and go placidly strolling about

the streets of Moscow as if nothing had happened. What I can't understand about you is that mixture of cowardice, brutality, and impudent audacity. After you had escaped—you come back. If you hadn't come to live here under your own name I should have sworn you had been corrupted by the Capitalists and came into the country as a saboteur, as a spy. And, anyhow, how *did* you get in?"

Once more there was something peculiar about the officer's tone. He spoke of Nikalai as if it were the Singer of the Wartburg speaking of Tannhäuser, who had sojourned in the Hörselsberg, and had there led a life of unheard-of luxury and earthly pleasure. Somehow Nikalai was unclean in his eyes, because he had lived among the bourgeois, among those handsome, clean-washed, well-groomed, but suavely, refinedly tricky, bloated, cunning men. He had certainly thrown the dust in their eyes; they had not seen through him.

But Nikalai was thinking neither of the officer's emotions nor of the wonderful turn events had taken for him. The vision of death by Chinese tortures had disappeared—he was gazing down the vistas of his own past life, the life of the journalist Kisseleff. The fact that a strange destiny had led to his getting, through another's words, a glimpse into his own past, did not particularly affect him—he was trying to picture the Serpuchova woman, that brutal, sensual man-woman, who handled locomotives in Turkestan, fought with men, and forcibly seduced boys. Kisseleff had been infatuated with that soulless, hard creature, till the moment when he had realised that there was nothing left that was sacred to her, that this lustful female flesh was utterly selfish throughout. With that disappointment came a mad rage and with that murder.

Kisseleff had fled across the Pripet marshes to Poland. On the frontier he was wounded. In the hospital at Brest he was discharged as healed. But in Berlin the injury took a turn for the worse—and he entered St. Hedwig's Hospital. His mother had secretly had him baptised as a Catholic, which, even under the Czars, was no light matter. But here, at the very centre of activity of Catholic Berlin, bitter-sweet memories of childhood revived in the dying man: of the days when there was no Serpuchova in his life, no teams of Red speakers, no hunger, no unrest. Restful, sunny days he remembered—at Dvinsk and Pskov, at Kraslava and Vitebsk. His heart brought him back to Mother Church: he made his confession, and received Extreme Unction. And a few days later he lay in the cemetery, the "garden of peace," and Scapinelli was examining his papers. Things would have happened very differently if their were no seal to confession and Scapinelli had been able to consult the dead man's confessor.

"Tell me, once for all, how did you get here?" muttered the officer, impatiently.

Nikalai looked up at him like a whipped dog. In the eyes of the questioner he was a murderer. He was Kisseleff, and Kisseleff was a murderer. The memory of Eugen Düring was completely extinct in him. The knowledge of having murdered his wife lay heavy on his conscience. He had been so blithely confident here, so enthusiastic; and then those endless hours after his arrest had come—hours of growing chill, of going through death; hours in the shadow of the grave, and of annihilation; and then, finally, had ensued the awakening, the awakening as a murderer.

"I came over the Turkish frontier," said Nikalai, and then recounted in a few tired words his apparently aimless wanderings in the Soviet Union. "I was homesick—it broke me down altogether," he said finally. He no longer felt it as a lie what he told the officer then. That was just what the dead Kisseleff would probably have felt, he thought.

The officer made notes on paper of some of what Nikalai said. A few greasy flies buzzed around the lamp. Nikalai's words were at first hesitant, cautious, and spoken below his breath—but later he began to talk fluently and coherently, confessing and accusing himself, until at last the pencil racing across the paper could not keep up with him. The officer wrote with knitted brows, and Nikalai's eyes were humid.

The night before Nikalai Sergeyevitch's trial, Rudolph Medek lay with his forehead on the stone flags of his cell, wakened out of a restless sleep by a sudden impulsion to be near to God and to be moved by His Spirit. The sky above Lille was bright with stars, and seemed as hard and clear as glass. No street noises, no hooting of strident klaxons, penetrated the sombre cell from the Rue de la Gare, and yet Rudolph Medek's heart was oppressed by an inexplicable, obscure fear for the weal and woe of the whole orb of earth, of all men near and far, for the inner peace of mankind beyond those walls, in the hard, glassy, expressionless night.

The State Prosecutor, Antoni Trophimovitch Shvernik, however, was still sitting in the lamplight at his desk in the former headquarters of the "Phœnix Insurance Company," working at the "Nikalai Sergeyevitch Kisseleff" brief. The case seemed to him simple, straightforward, trivial. He did not give it any close attention. Absent-mindedly, he lay aside sheet after sheet, till suddenly there lay before him nothing but the hard wooden surface of the desk, on which lay his nervously drumming fingers. That brought his thoughts back. The image of the wife-murderer, who had taken refuge for two years among the "bourgeois," had dwindled and faded out. What he saw was only himself, reflected in the mirror on the wall before him—himself, with knitted brows, great pendulous pouches under his eyes, grey pointed beard, and greasy, thin hair. And as he gazed at himself in the glass, his eyes suspiciously narrowed, dark-circled, and slightly bloodshot, there returned the memory of that afternoon when he, trembling and panting, had enquired for Zinaïda Pavlovna in the "Yevropeiskaya Gastinnitsa," only to learn that she had gone away to Yalta with Krashenninikov. Then he had wandered hours, till late in the evening, about dusty boulevards and unsavoury back-streets, and turned into the bar of the Hotel Metropole, where he had planked down his last few dollars. Absolutely oblivious to all around him, he had sat there, and with staring, glazed eyes, had gaped at shrill-voiced cocottes and untidy American women with bare arms. Through the monotonous pounding of the jazz-band, however, the pictures conjured up by torturing thought had thrust themselves, so that he had leaped up in a mad frenzy from the table where he had been sitting in raging and despairing solitude, had flung aside the paper streamers and confetti, and had rushed back, like a wound:d beast to its lair, across the Nikolskaya, to the house in the Lubyanskaya-Ploshtchad.

Now, when he found himself forced to think of Zinaïda Pavlovna once more, his heart began throbbing again—at first beating wildly in his breast, and then in great, staccato pulsings, that sent the blood surging heavily through his veins and throbbing in his throat, in his temples, in his aching, decaying teeth. Only his hands seemed to remain cool and undisturbed, only his hands, with which he illustrated his speeches for the prosecution in vivid, conductor-like gestures. Nobody could excel Antoni Trophimovitch in theatrical and rhetorical eloquence. True, he had not the exterior presence of the hard, callous, typical Public Prosecutor, like Krylenkos; but Antoni Trophimovitch understood his stage-management better. He liked to speak out of the shadow, with a soft, menacing voice, and satanically raised eyebrows. And if it was his speech in the first place that was not without its effect, yet it was to his hands that he attached the greater importance. And now, up there in that lonely room, in the yellow lamp-light, with a fly droning round him, it seemed to him that his hands were the only things that had remained true and faithful to him throughout his life. He let his manicured fingers play now, on the top of his desk, and admired the expansion and contraction of the veins and ligaments in the back of his hand. He was so intoxicated with his hands, that he closed his eyes and lifted his right hand up to his lips. He kissed the flesh of that hand passionately—it was *his* flesh, beneath the crinkly skin; warm, blood-filled flesh, soft flesh.

He scratched the back of his hand, and rubbed the flesh with his fingers—it was soft as bread, pliable as rubber. But suddenly a terrible picture shot through his mind—he saw himself dead, his flesh putrefied. He saw, in the mirror, the desk empty, himself erased from the surface of the earth. And then he saw himself at the desk again—but without his flesh, a skeleton. And, as a skeleton, he was no longer *he*. As a skeleton he was neither man nor woman, neither Bolshevik nor Bourgeois, neither Russian nor English-man. He was only the heap of calcined bone left behind by the process of death. There was, then, no difference between himself and the prelates Cieplak and Budkievicz, whom he had had shot; between him, the atheist, and those two Catholic priests, who had said Masses and prayed with breviaries—and, with the memory of Cieplak and Budkie-wicz, there came to him also the memory of the Metropoli-tan Avxenti, who before a cluster of students had declared, with wagging beard, and macabre voice: "As a punishment for man's original sin, God has condemned man's body to the uncleanness of decay!"

Oh, how the "enlightened" young students had laughed at him! And he, Antoni, among them. But now the laugh had faded from his bloodless lips. His hands were faithful and obedient, but his heart was rebellious, old, used up, and weary of toil. His heart longed to be dissolved, his lungs longed to be dissolved, only his brain would not have it—his brain and his hands. And while the jazz-tune of "The Little House on the Michigan Lake," that he had first heard not long before at the Hotel Metropole came back to his mind, a fury of sheer misery came over him. They had invented God —it was clearly stated so in the Proclamation—God, for them, existed as little as did a Rumanian Bessarabian, but the "uncleanness of decay" was still there. What they did with the body of Vladimir Ilitch was mere senseless self-deception — they had abolished God, and yet He carried on His activity unchecked. "This is satanical!" he cried, "satanical!"

He switched off the electric light, sat himself on the window-seat, and stared up at the sky, twinkling with the pallid, faint stars of the northern night. Beneath him spread the tangled forest of aerials over the lodging-houses, with their dead, dirty windows. But above him arched the sky, like a lofty, infinite domed roof, a roof that spread away to infinity before it closed. He saw the stars—and knew them to be often thousands of light-years distant, often ten thousand times bigger than the earth or even the sun.

But here he was, creeping about in a little corner of this earth, and he was vain, and delighted, if somebody was condemned to the Chinese death on the strength of *his* eloquence and the movements of *his* hands—and almost wept because he could not put his arms round another mortal just as insignificant as himself. *O vanitas vanitatum!* But then pride returned, and he reminded himself that he could play the piano and play Tarock, but the mighty planets were compelled to move in their orbits according to the laws of nature which they must obey. "The whole system of materialism is a mad delusion!" something in him shrieked, "I am no jelly-fish, I am no mineral! I'm not a bacillus, I'm not a louse! I am a man, a man, a man!"

Despairingly he stared up at the dark, impenetrable skies. "What is in me, there, cannot die," something sobbed, within him. "What loves and hopes, there—what hates and desires—that will always be, always be!"

"Wish-complex!" mocked the party dogmatist in him, by way of retort. The realisation that everything earthly is merely relative, and finite in time, overwhelmed him, broke over him like a great wave over a flimsy canoe; the realisation that in a thousand years Bolshevism would exist as little as an Eastern Roman Empire does to-day, the Russians then as little as the Avarians to-day, a dialectical materialism be as obsolete as, at the present day, a Pythagorean school, was too powerful for him. All his striving, all his labour, was in vain, the mere activity-neurosis of a megalomaniac, since with every stride by which he helped Bolshevism on to completion he was lessening the distance from that ending. Even the training of children, the building of houses, was provisional and frivolous—the mere idiotic manufacture of things that were already doomed to destruction in virtue of their origin.

A profound, morbid fatalism took possession of him, there on the hard window-seat of the Tcheka headquarters, under the brightly lit-up night sky of Moscow. "All births must be prevented," he declared, seriously, "all life must be abolished!" He completely failed to realise that he was already taking up the ideas of audacious, self-exterminating Christian sects. And he kept saying over and over again to himself: "The way is wrong—wrong—wrong! I will write to Stalin to-morrow—the way is unrighteous, the way leads to madness!"

Then he thought of Cieplak and Budkiewicz again. They had, both, always been happy, always placid. They held the "absurd" belief in the soul, with which they soared over every chasm as if it were a gliding plane. He could see, quite clearly, that these two black-coats possessed the key to earthly happiness.

And now it suddenly seemed to him as if the world were about to stand still, silent, as if the whole cosmos, the insane cosmos that to him it appeared, were about to halt its irrational, breath-taking commotion. Even so do locomotives still the din of their loud, clamouring sirens when they have reached their station. And with the silence, which lay over Moscow like a pall, there came to him the sensation of solitude, and in that loneliness he began to grow chilled; he could see that the whole scheme of collectivism was nothing but a great loneliness among many, a destiny of anonymity, an orphan existence, a very pinnacle of loneliness. And if he loved Zinaïda Pavlovna, then it was he, himself, who loved her—it was not some part of the Permanent Executive of the Old Bolsheviks' Club, it was not the Purchasing Co-operative Department of the O.G.P.U. organisation that loved her. If he died, then he must die alone, he, not the whole organisation of officials of the U.S.S.R. He told himself that from the beginning he had always been alone. Most utterly alone. When, on his last night, Bishop Cieplak had been put in solitary confinement, he had written on a wall: "O sola beatitudo, O beata solitudo!—Oh, sole happiness? Oh, happy solitude!" But in reality the Bishop could never be alone—God stood, ever and everywhere, by his side. God was with him, before and after death, in an eternal synousia. And then there came to him the terrifying thought that perhaps God really did exist, but was not with him. Cieplak and Budkiewicz knew God by His continual presence—but he, Antoni Trophimovitch Shvernik, Public Prosecutor of the Soviet Union, knew God by His absence. In the same moment in which he became aware that he was in darkness, he ceased to doubt whether there was any such thing as light—he simply despaired because it did not shine for *him*.

But now, when he thought of death, which for him meant the extinction of personality, the passing away into the anonymity of the graveyard, collectivism seemed to him a barbarous, insane delusion. How right Budkiewicz had been, when he had visited him in his cell, a week before his death. In reply to a laudation of Bolshevism, Budkiewicz, weak with hunger, lying on a pallet-bed, had said to him: "In adolescence, Bolshevism is all very well, for some individuals; but you are no longer young, and there is nothing more miserable than ageing courtesans and ageing Bolsheviks—they both grow old in hopelessness. . . ."

And while he was thinking of Budkiewicz, something happened in the sky that filled Antoni Trophimovitch with a panic of fear—a star fell. A little, tiny star, that till then he had not noticed at all, had suddenly shot down through space, and flared up as it fell. His weary Bolshevik heart pounded in his throat again. He knew: a whole world had gone to destruction there—a whole solar system, perhaps, with countless planets and countless moons, perhaps with countless, thinking, human-like beings, with States and Officials, with defence systems and industries, with Chief Inspectors of Police, and Assize Courts—and all suddenly fused and melted up and shattered, blown to nothing, annihilated. And perhaps, on that planet, there were Soviet Republics set up, with rubber stamps, and Central Executive Offices, with laboratories and universities. And perhaps their science had simply been able to predict the coming disaster, without being able to do anything to prevent it. Vain would have been all the edicts of the Central Executive, vain all the Demonstration Meetings in the parks, vain all the petitions and newspaper articles, vain all the threats of revolution and the strikes, the proclamations and the protests. A shriek, a conflagration, a blaze of light, and the end.

But now the silence brooding over Moscow seemed to be broken. A wind began to blow and bluster, singing and whistling through the wires and the aerials, and a strange life flowed back into the streets. Out there in the railway stations, locomotives again rumbled in a deep bass, factory sirens hooted wailingly in the suburbs, and, through the midst of all the chaos of turbulent noise, there sounded as it were a hollow, grimly chuckling laughter. And this laughter—so it seemed to Antoni Trophimovitch—this laughter was at him; at him, the busy and assiduous one, him the imaginative and theatrical, him the party dogmatist and the short-sighted.

He was conscious now neither of the reality of the Soviet State around him, nor of the Tcheka, of Zinaïda Pavlovna, of Kisseleff nor of the Kremlin—only conscious of that warm wind on his forehead and cheeks; and that wind was nothing else but a breath—the breath of God, the Spirit of God. And what rose now before his eyes, there, brooding like a shadow over Moscow, without bodily form, without face or features, merely a mighty influence looming high over the city, was God—but not the Son of Man, born of a tender Virgin, the Brother of us all, not the Crucified Christ or the Man of Sorrows sweating blood on the Mount of Olives, but only God as He revealed Himself at the beginning to mankind—the LORD, who had demanded of Israel only obedience and fear, the Infinite, Great, Almighty, Vengeful God; not the Saviour, but the Judge. What Antoni Trophimovitch experienced now was only dread and abasement, he was crushed and irrationally, mortally afraid. He clasped his hands over his face—as Moses had done once before the Burning Bush.

And, meanwhile, Rudolph Medek was praying, on the eotsn flags of his cell, in a happy solitude, to God, with God.

CHAPTER XI

THE LEFORTOVA PRISON

NIKALAI had now become aware for some time, in his cell, that the worst danger of all was not yet past. Prison was certain for him, but how easily it might happen that he should be confronted with somebody who knew the dead Kisseleff. Nikalai must certainly bear a strong resemblance to the dead man, but if somebody who knew the real murderer well were to see him it would be all up with him.

But the bureaucratic machine worked on, lumbering and mechanical. He was transferred to another gaol, questioned again, photographed, forced to sign protocols; the food was in no respect worse than outside in the city; the warders were stupid, indifferent and friendly; and the officials inexperienced, awkward, and self-important.

The trial took place in a small room. An armed militia-man with fixed bayonet stood by the door. Behind a barrier sat sad, unmoved proletarians, among them a woman with a perpetually running nose. Nikalai replied to a few questions. When the presiding magistrate heard that Nikalai had lived not only abroad but also in Leningrad, he puckered his brow. Then he threw a significant look at the woman with the running nose. A few minutes later Nikalai stood up—he had been sentenced to three years' imprisonment. The Butürka was spared him. The next day, he was transferred to the Lefortova.

Antoni Trophimovitch had made only a brief and colourless speech. The listeners were disappointed with him.

And when he ended, he did not specify any particular sentence that he claimed. And yet this was contrary to his custom.

The Lefortova is a prison in the east end of Moscow, not far from the terminus of an electrical railway. The principal part of the Lefortova consists of the gaol itself, a rectangular building with three spreading wings of equal extent and converging towards the middle.

Within these wings were to be seen the galleries, steel-barred corridors, and truck-rails, behind which were the prisoners' cells. On the truck-rails, at meal-times, were the trolleys of food. In these headquarters, it smelled like the den of captive, badly-tended, monster cats.

Behind the gaol is a small garden. That little park might equally well have been attached to a secondary school in Central Germany, or an Austrian hospital, had it not been enclosed by a high, turreted wall. In those watch-towers on the wall, sharp-eyed soldiers, armed and with fixed bayonets, kept constant watch day and night.

In front of the prison stood the carpet factory. This factory was connected with the prisoners' dwelling by a courtyard. The inmates had to work there seven or eight hours a day.

Outside this courtyard, was the Governor's house, with the offices connected with it. The ruler of the Lefortova was, of course, a Lett; a stern, Prussian-looking official, of soldierly stamp, who was one of the oldest adherents of the Communist Party, and had been an inmate of almost all the prisons in Russia under the Czars. He was a typical Lett, a man of little genius but the highest intelligence, who understood the art of combining the soldierly with the democratic.

Nikalai was brought in after working hours. First he was

taken before the Governor, who was knitting his brows over the dossier of papers accompanying the prisoner. His little, gingery moustache seemed as if it were trying to creep away and hide in his nostrils. "Lett Russian?" he asked, curtly.

"Mother Latgalian!" replied Nikalai, in the same tone.

Thereupon the Governor addressed him in Lettish, and Nikalai replied with the few broken words of that language which he had learned in Charlottenburg. This pleased the Governor. He got up, walked up and down the room, and treated Nikalai to a benevolent lecture; "a worthy citizen, a useful member of human society, a brick in the fabric of the Socialist state, a peaceful party-member, and a respectable man," were repeated with amazing reiteration. The governor of a British prison could not have done it better.

Then Nikalai was led back to his cell. He had to share the apartment with a man of the Red Army who had been given eight years for urging his father, a Kulak from the Kostroma district, in a letter, to oppose collectivism with all the means at his disposal. He at once confided his troubles to Nikalai.

"I never get a single leave, because I'm a political prisoner, pure and simple—a respectable counter-revolutionary."

"Leave?" asked Nikalai, in surprise.

The prisoner nodded.

"All the non-politicals," he explained, "get a month's leave every year."

Nikalai leaned forward on his pallet-bed.

"And if the leave-men don't come back?" he asked significantly.

The former Red Army man smiled sarcastically.

"Then the Ogpu would get them within twenty-four hours. If a man hasn't got influential friends and plenty of money he's done for. Everybody's glad to have the opportunity of supplying any information—nobody would dare to harbour a fugitive. He wouldn't get ration-cards for necessi-

ties, nor clothes, and in a while he'd perish like a Bez-
prizorny."

Nikalai was silent.

"Besides, they do you well here!" the Red Army man
added. "Only the politicals don't get any leave. Do you
know what a deuce of a life it is, without any women?
You'll find out for yourself. The eleven months' waiting will
be more like thirty years to you. Devilish!"

"What are you going to do when you come out?" asked
Nikalai, to change the subject.

"I shall go back to the army," said the prisoner, lighting
himself a cigarette.

"Will you get back to that after your prison term here?"
asked Nikalai, in surprise.

"I should say so," replied the other, with emphasis. "I'm
not going to give up my four years' service as easily as all
that."

A bell resounded through the gaol. Upstairs, in the former
chapel, a cinematograph show began.

After the entertainment the men streamed downstairs in
groups and crowds, to smoke a cigarette in the garden.
On reaching the ground floor, Nikalai felt a hand on his
shoulder. He turned, and recognised the Governor, who
took his arm and led him aside to a corner. "You mustn't
have it in for us," he said, "for putting you in with an enemy
of the proletariat. Don't deny it. To you, as an active member of the party, it must be intolerable to be forced to live
with a Kulak's son who has agitated against the working
classes. But at the moment we have so little room that there
was nothing else we could do. Till we get the medical report
on Balakirieff, the Ripper murderer, I dare not put you in
with him——"

Then Nikalai went into the court, and sat down by some

unknown prisoners on a bench. "Who are you?" "What's
your name?" "What are you in for?" they asked him. "My
name's Nikalai," he replied, "I'm a journalist. I'm in for
murdering my wife." They saw, from the brevity of his words,
that he wanted nothing to do with them at the moment.

Nikalai put a cigarette between his lips and lighted it.
The sun had already set, and only its last dying rays illumined the orange-tinged clouds on the western horizon.
From his cigarette a thin, bluish spiral of tobacco-smoke
drifted up into the evening air. Outside, in the far distance,
could be heard the furious clamour of bells on the electric
railway. The shadow-silhouette of the soldier on sentry duty
on the wall was outlined, clear-cut and sharp, against the
magically shimmering clouds in the west. The men's voices
were hushed. In their dark blue tunics the prisoners looked
like hospital patients. In Nikalai's hand, resting on his right
knee, the cigarette gradually burned away. It was a tired,
hospital-like mood that had fallen upon this twilit prison
garden.

A brief autumn was followed by an icy-cold, Russian
winter. In the Lefortova an enforced warmth reigned, and
the wild-animals'-lair smell grew more intense. The treatment was better than in the prisons of Western Europe.
The Red Army man, Trifunov, fell out with the Governor
once a month—called him a "blasted Bolshevik," whereupon
the Lett stormed back at him, and the inmates gathered
round them with malicious enjoyment. Nikalai worked by
the side of a housebreaker, who had a bald head and a
clown-like face, sallow, and outlined with a few furrows,
adorned with pimples, and a protruding chin. But his
eyes were expressionless and dim. His movements were
timid and terrified, and when anybody threatened him, he
would cry out shrilly and pusillanimously, like a rat.

Nikalai's monotonous life was only broken by one incident: he received a letter from a stranger, who wrote to ask if he might see him, and whether he remembered the pleasant days at Alma-Ata? Nikalai wrote back to him with a beating heart. Then the everyday life closed round him again. In the morning, the work; in the evening, the cinema or concert; the wearisome time in the courtyard; garden, radio, card-games, smoking, propaganda lectures. Thus the whole winter passed. Once a party of foreign ladies came, with a guide from the W.O.K.S. There were brazenly inquisitive women among them, in horn-rimmed glasses, who invaded the cells, forced their way into the shops, photographed the barber's shop on the ground floor, examined the material in the factory and cut off samples for themselves. Nikalai happened to be sitting with the old engineer Barvitch in his cell, and trying to give him a clearer notion of some principles of Catholic doctrine, when the door suddenly opened and the grinning face of a woman of the "bourgeois," with gleaming teeth exposed, was thrust in, and stared at them with stupid cordiality. The old, white-bearded engineer turned round in sullen silence and looked out of the window, while Nikalai shouted, hostilely, "Get to hell out of here!" in English. That produced amazement and dismay. The door was slammed to.

When Nikalai had come, he had resolved, from the first day, to begin the work of enlightenment without any looking back. It had been, for him, something of an adventure, the joy of activity, like that experienced by people who roll up their sleeves and, singing, throw themselves into some unaccustomed and (to them) hard form of bodily labour. The mechanical, monotonous life in the Lefortova, however, had resulted in his getting more and more slack, so that after a while, at an evening science course, while he was still wearing the head-phones, he made the discovery that his faith was undeniably beginning to become rigid and to fade. Life among the atheists, in a country where the Church had atrophied to an unnatural, dismembered shapelessness, had distorted the image of God within his heart, till, from a picture of warm, rich colour of passionate reality, it had become a pale, improbable, out-of-date figment of artificiality. The bitter battle, in the dark, that he conscientiously waged on behalf of his Church, remained a dead, futureless, piece of cold, calculating work by a clever linguist, dialectician, and intellectual—but, for himself, it was the last, the very last flicker of the hearth-fire at whose dying glow he could still warm his faith. A whole year had passed since he had last heard a Mass or made his confession. Now, for the first time, he understood, with a painfully belated insight, why we are commanded to be physically present at the Sacrifice of the Mass; only it was not enough to kneel once a week before the Altar, or at home before the loud-speaker, to listen to the Prefaces—the Church was an "ecclesia," a meeting of human beings who recognised God in His true being. In memory, he experienced once more the sensation of being together with the congregation in the Church in Berlin, standing shoulder to shoulder with his fellow-believers, placing his hands, in spirit, on their shoulders, with the feeling; "I love you all, you love me, we love God, God loves us!" It was this synousia, this organic, collective feeling of being together with the Church, the Mystical Body of Jesus Christ, that he so bitterly missed, and that tore a great gaping hole in him. He went, psychically, to pieces, because, in spite of all allowances that one might make, he was robbed of his freedom, and, like some animals in captivity which, however well cared-for and treated, perish miserably, refusing to breed, refusing food, and going mad, so in time his true being crumbled away like the broken side of a cliff.

This state of deprivation of God, to which he was slowly succumbing, brought him closer and closer to the people here, who, apart from the crude, animal, wilful laughter on their lips, carry about with them a dreary melancholia. This was a melancholia utterly different from the short-lived unhappiness, shot through with fear, of the men of the jungle, tortured by a belief in demons, which has about it nothing horrible, or oppressive, or seriously affecting fundamentals. It is rather that condition of the soul, grounded on problems that extend into the sphere of intellect, which, in history, has lasted over periods of decades; that appallingly un-Catholic episode in history that began with the debased dance of animalised women round the guillotine, and ended with the cunningly artificial decadence of a warfare of poison-gas, newspapers, air-machines and submarines; the war was ruled by this particular type of melancholia. This epoch, that had begotten, involuntarily, ideas far removed from God—ideas of nationalism, of materialism, of imperialism, of communism, the superman, and class-hatred, ideas in conflict with one another, but agreeing in their hostility to the Rock of Peter—this epoch was sunk in melancholy and the tedium of life; Gustave Doré created landscapes; Mann, families; Huysmans, men and women; Strindberg, Ibsen, Dostoevski, Tolstoy, Van Gogh, Kubin—they were all melancholy, or, if they were not among the sad ones, then they were decadent and malicious. There was no joyousness smiling on the metal cacti, red plush furniture, brown daguereotypes, patricide-collars, cul-de-Paris and sinister, evil, mattress beards, of this period.

As to the empty, mechanical nature of his faith, Nikalai was soon fully enlightened. When he realised that he was far from living in the consciousness of God that was his in his Berlin days—that he no longer even felt himself to be a servant of the Church, but merely an acrobatic juggler with theological truths—then he began to think things out with a desperate intentness. Between whiles he was tortured with the realisation that in many respects there was more sin in the Christian West than here in the official domains of Anti-Christ. How well he, the murderer, was treated here—how little they made him feel his guilt—how magnanimous, how truly Christ-like, was their mode of thinking about sinners, outside the prison walls. Then, again, there would come times when he would look at everything with eyes merci-lessly Western; when he himself, gradually coming to believe the newspaper stories, foresaw the early downfall of the Occident. Then he would curse his powerlessness, his inability to leave the place, and would fall into gloomy brooding.

What kept him up in the Lefortova was the thought of the dead Kisseleff. His suffering, his dejection, his bloodless, ineffectual wrestling for the Faith, he offered up for this man. This notion of "offering" stimulated his courage, strengthened his endurance, kept him from rebellious murmurings, from giving way to despair and letting that point the way of "escape" from the grey, day-by-day monotony of youthful days uselessly spent.

Most of the prisoners were a prey to a deep-seated unrest when the time of their month's leave drew near, but Nikalai watched without excitement and without joy the approach of his temporary liberty.

All the Moscow observers had been changed over during the winter. The Pole Sawicki, however, must still be living in the Afanasievski Pereulok. Calmly, he considered what lay before him. Here, there was nothing to hold him back; his work had borne no fruits, he had only been able to talk, talk, talk. After all, what results could he have expected to show? What miracles could he have performed? He was a convict just like the others; he was tied as to place, and time, and routine. He was as little a free man as were they—and the spoken word, by itself, is always fruitless. In the Lefortova everybody talked, and it was the custom to listen very quietly and attentively to the views expounded by the other man, in order to be in a position to claim, legitimately, the same attention for oneself when it was one's own turn to speak. Discussions very seldom occurred—one did not usually bother to go into the other man's ideas. But if an argument did arise, it was threshed out with the utmost acrimony, and each party defended his case desperately, resorting to the most obvious quibbles if his fallacy was in any danger of being exposed. This sterility and egotistical superficiality of the men in the Lefortova had got Nikalai thoroughly annoyed and irritated.

For a while they did their best to do something with Nikalai. They knew he had been a Party-member for years, and wanted him to direct the Propaganda section of the V.K.P. in the Lefortova. In the country outside, admission to the Party was very difficult to secure—but here in prison they were much broader-minded. They knew that the criminal (who, unlike what happens in the West, often leaves prison a better man after years in this communistically-minded enforced collectivism) would be a better, and a better-schooled, Party-member than anybody from the outer world. Nikalai, however, refused the offer crossly. This he did at a moment when his second life, as Kisseleff, seemed by a strange sequence of varied impressions and moods, to be a loathsome lie. Such a view was not at all usual with him—it was only now and again that his earlier life as Eugen Düring emerged from his subconsciousness and came to the surface of his imagination, undimmed, and clear-cut. At such rare moments the past tortured him with a wild fury —all resistance seemed so vain.

So one night he awoke from restless, strange dreams, and stared into the darkness. He had not had that so-frequently-repeated dream of the murder of Serpuchova that disturbed and excited him at intervals of a month regularly, but he had seen Scapinelli, Scapinelli and his mother, Gertrude and Rudolph Medek. He had not only seen them—he had heard them speak. They had been quite tangibly close to him. But now he could hear nothing but his cell-mate's snores, and footsteps in the far distance.

"I never killed Serpuchova at all!" a voice within him cried. "Madness, madness, madness! I am Düring, a German! I am a Catholic! *Credo in unum Deum omnipotentem, factorem cœli et terræ!* What business have I got in this building —why am I weaving carpets? My youth is passing away— My youth, not Kisseleff's. He's dead—dead ages ago. I am living at the expense of Eugen Düring!"

A wild despair seized him. The reminder that a thousand kilometres away there lived, still lived, a number of people with whom he had been associated of old was like a new discovery for him. He was ready to burst into sobs. His thoughts became absolutely banal: "Mother, mother!" he sobbed inwardly, "Look what they're doing to your son!"

Then he saw before him the brightly lit editorial office of the *Reichswarte*—Brühlau, Gertrude Garrieter ("Oh, you, Oh, you will play me false, you'll——," she sang)—the station, that wonderful station with the ocean of rails and the cleared forest of signals. It all went on, alive, creative. The whole world went on without him. All knew that he was a prisoner.

And yet—who was bothering about him?

No, they did *not* imagine him a prisoner. To them he was dead. And Gertrude was in love, engaged, married—had children.

That last idea tormented him most, gave him a sense of

sorrow and dismay. Before his departure he had been
indifferent to her, but now, here in the Lefortova, she represented in his memory the world of women; and when the
other men there, hour after hour, would talk of women,
either sentimentally, basely, cynically, or passionately, it was
Gertrude who appeared again and again before his inner eye.
It was just this uncertainty of his feelings for her, this
enslavement to women through sex, that was so hard to
describe. It bred suspicion, and jealousy, without constitut-
ing love; produced a trifling enthusiasm, a petty, meaningless warmth in the emotions, without establishing any claim
to acknowledgment by the intellect.

The next morning it was all over. The ghastly, devastating
sense of being bound and powerless was gone, had given
way to a peculiar apathy and the dull feeling of guilt of the
wife-murderer Nikalai Sergeyevitch Kisseleff.

One fine day in June he was called into the office to see the
Governor, who began by telling him that his leave would
commence on the next day.

"Where will you live?" he asked.

"At the place where I used to live—in the Pretchistenskaya," said Nikalai, hesitantly, and added, "if I find I
can."

"You can live here, if you like, and be free to go in and
out," said the Lett.

Nikalai nodded.

The next day it rained, and Nikalai was allowed to leave
the Lefortova at eight o'clock. Without looking about him
at all, he made straight for the stopping-place of the electric
trams, and swung himself on to a car. In his pocket were his
savings—thirty tchervontses. Next to him sat a young
woman worker smelling of untanned furs. The rain
thrummed on the window-panes. The conductress had no

small change. Wouldn't he like to take fifty tickets at once? She could give him five roubles. It was all the same to him—he was profoundly disappointed. He had the definite feeling that this leave, far from being a beginning towards liberty, would only be an interruption in the humdrum of prison life.

Arrived at the Arbat gate, he got off and proceeded on foot. Nonchalantly he went up to the first floor, and knocked at the door. A strange voice answered. Did the Citizen Sawicki still live here? No. Did they know where he had moved to? No, the speaker didn't know that either. The caretaker of the house did not know. Did he remember Sawicki? Remember? Sure. The fair citizen with the Polish accent. Who could help remembering him? But where he had moved to? Nobody was likely to know that. Had the citizen admired the new plate on the house? Please have a look at it.

On the door-plate was a five-pointed star, an anchor, cannon-balls, swords, a rope, rifles, a bottle of poison. Beneath it the inscription, "Krepim Oboronu, S.S.S.R.— We strengthen the defences of the U.S.S.R."

Nikalai nodded, and left. In the street, a group of German Communists was passing. "Red Front!" they shouted, by way of greeting. They went along the Krapotkina, and stumbled over the holes in the road. Sadly the ruined Church of St. Saviour gazed out over the Moskva. On the opposite bank of the river stood, almost completed, the palace of the Soviets. Much had altered here. Surely, the world, in its movement, would not stop to wait for Nikalai Kisseleff.

He was hungry. He put his hands in his pockets, and knit his brows. There was nothing for him to seek in this city. A Grusinian, in a small private shop built of wood, sold sausages at an iniquitous price. He stood in a queue and waited. When he had the sausage in his hand, he bit into it hungrily—it tasted of soap. He spat out the mouthful.

He would gladly have spat out the whole city.

He felt a slight yearning to go back to the Lefortova. Lonely and motionless, he stood in the midst of the street's turmoil, staring before him with the expression of an unhappy dog. Disappointed.

CHAPTER XII

A TRANSFER

AFTER a few days Nikalai began to muse whether flight was really impossible. But he realised that, the very first evening that he was missing, his description would be circulated everywhere, and would frustrate any attempt at flight. Then he began again, considering other possibilities of flight; made friends with a military air-pilot, boasted of his savings, and told fairy-tale-like stories of the marvellous life to be had in the lands of the bourgeois. He had already, quite deliberately and obstinately, begun working towards his new aim, with all the concentrated artfulness of the Westerner, and made the simple, mistrustful man waver. Then he dropped that plan.

One evening, as he reported at the prison office, and was about to go into his cell, a clerk called him back.

"A parcel has been brought for you, Citizen."

"From whom?" he asked—he was rather disquieted.

"From the Militia," said the clerk, "things they found in your room belonging to you. Please sign this."

Nikalai scrawled his name at the foot of the receipt, and took the parcel. It rustled inside the paper wrappings, under his arm, as he went off into the main building. In his cell he undid the strings and unwrapped the paper covering. Within, he found a thick, short winter coat, with a fur collar, a fur cap, gloves, a pair of stockings, a bundle of expired food-tickets, and a photograph. He was alone in his

cell; and, sitting down by the bedside lamp, he looked long
and intently at the portrait. It was Nikalai Kisseleff, the dead
Kisseleff, the murderer. It was not the same photo that
Nikalai had in his passport, which bore a striking likeness
to the living Nikalai also. This picture that Nikalai, trembling,
frightened, and strangely stirred, held in his hands, did
indeed show him the face of a murderer. Hard, evil, secre-
tive this Kisseleff in the picture looked. Involuntarily
Nikalai recalled the Komsomolka's unbelievable story, told
in the railway carriage between Batum and Tiflis. She had
told of the bestial fury of the Lettish peasants, who had not
only murdered the German barons but had also tortured
their cattle to death in the sheds. Nikalai now could see the
dead man's relations with Serpuchova quite differently—
her crude strength and ungainliness must simply have
excited his senses, her disobedience excited his rage; thus it
was that he had come to batter her to death. He set the
photo on the bedside table, sat down on the bed, dug his
fists into his cheeks, and sat staring at the picture with
glassy eyes. Not till the return of his cell-mate who, with the
others, came trooping noisily down the stairs after the
cinema show and burst open the door of the cell, did he
grab hastily at the picture and conceal it against his body,
hurrying past the other convict, like one haunted, out into
the passage.

An hour later, when he was lying on his bed, the other
man still asleep, and the light still burning on his bedside
table, he cautiously pulled forth the picture again, and
stared at it desperately. Now it was pity that moved him,
now fear, helplessness, and sadness. In the dead Kisseleff all
Nikalai's bad traits seemed to have been embodied. "My
other self, my brother," said Nikalai to himself. Then,
sorrowfully, he tore the picture up into small fragments.

Hard days came for Nikalai. There came hours during

which he was firmly determined on flight, and others in which nothing but his surroundings prevented him from falling on his knees to beg God for the strength to do penance for his dead brother. He could not, and did not try to, account to himself for his wanting to suffer for the dead murderer Kisseleff; it was certainly, for the most part, the monotonous sojourn in the Lefortova that had given him the leisure, and his own fate that had given him the initial impetus, to reflect on the spirit and meaning of "collective guilt." Then, again, there was the feeling that he must suffer utterly, in Christ-like patience, the consequences of the great lie of his existence in Russia. His misfortune, too, had made him thoughtful—the retrospect into his life up to the date of his journey into Russia had brought him the gnawing consciousness of sin.

These doubts as to the rightness of the course he was taking increased towards the end of his month's leave. Indecision destroyed his rest and his equilibrium. Often he would decide to seek out the air-pilot—and, every time, he would turn back half-way. Impatient, excited, confused he would let the time pass, constantly counting how many days were left, looking needlessly often at his watch. Awkwardly, planlessly, he would kill time with senseless and inappropriate things. Buy books that he never finished; start conversations with strangers in the parks, that bored him horribly; stand about in the markets, nervously sucking at his cigarette; or remain sitting at his table in the Stolovaya with a vacant look on his face, and work out meaningless sums with his pencil on the table-top.

At last numbers came to be, apart from prayer, the only things that distracted him. He would put long rows of figures together—stamp-values, arithmetical and geometrical series, roots, squares, cubes, progressions, and probability-calculations. Then again he would thrust his figures and calculations aside, and bury himself once more in the pictures in his memory—pictures that wore ever more and more threadbare—of Berlin, Brandenburg, Germany, the West; their succession interrupted only by the crude, plastically transparent evil features of the dead Kisseleff.

On his last day of freedom he was seized, with satanic force, by a ghastly regret at not having fled, not having thrown to the winds all other considerations, and fled. That day he went about like a torn, embittered beast. Outside, in the "Dinamo" Park, he could stand it no longer—the activities of the sportsmen seemed to him futile and ostentatious. He rode back to the town, passing through the Culture Park, and walked towards the Lenin Hills. Walking tired him, and he sat down on the damp grass growing on the steep, red clay bank of the Moskva, and let his feet dangle in the water. The river was alive with boats, and on the opposite bank naked people were laughing, and skipping and jumping about. A few words were wafted across, distinct and intelligible; the rest, carried away by the cool evening wind. The sun inclined more and more to the west, on the point of disappearing, in a red glow, behind the Lenin Heights. When this shimmering, metallic globe of fire was completely hidden by the black silhouette of the hills, far-spreading, windmill-like beams forked out in truly Biblical magnificence as a final leave-taking, and bathed the irregular masses of clouds looming over Moscow in a tinge of sulphurous yellow. The rest of the sky began to shimmer greenishly—and the whole city, with its church spires and factory chimneys, took on the rustic, peaceful look of a "mood"-painting. Nikalai, resting on his elbows, looked at this picture as through a window, peering further and further into its depths, the depths of that milky symphony of colours, drinking in every detail of its harmony, like one dying of thirst, and finally seeming to become the central point of the sleepy landscape. The cries and laughter of the bathers became clearer and louder, enriching and enlivening the scene like a crescendo of sound. Nikalai found all this painful—the treasures of life suddenly sprang into his conscious mind with such an unexpected force that he could easily have howled like a chained-up dog, as he thought of his own fate. "Life, life, life!" wept a voice within him. But now he "ran down," as Scapinelli used to put it—he "ran down." The clock's hands rotated, the calendar-leaves were torn off, the ledgers in the counting-house were replaced with new volumes, the schoolboys dated their exercise-books with the number of a new year, his flesh ran down—his skin, his eyes, his ears, his teeth, "ran down," were used up, used up ceaselessly. What bitter irony! *Deus qui laetificat juventutem meam!* "God who giveth joy in my youth!" What sort of youth was that here—against his will—tied to the place, tied to time, and outside, unbelievably far outside, was—life!

Travelling back to the Lefortova, he clung for support to the hand-rail of the electric car, his knuckles gleaming white. The picture of the landscape, fading out in the reddening dusk, clung in his memory. A little uncertain, and reeling like a ship in a heavy storm, he staggered into the office of the Lefortova. With a military carriage, of unaccustomed smartness, he drew himself up and stepped forward before the Governor, saying:

"I have come back."

"Right," said the latter, and turned again to his work.

"I've come back—I've actually come back!" exclaimed Nikalai. The Governor looked up in surprise. His eyes met Nikalai's. He was on the point of addressing a few cordial words to the prisoner, then he thought better of it, and bent lower over his papers, murmuring unintelligibly to himself, and waiting till the tall, black shadow before him had gone, mutely and sadly.

Two days later, Nikalai was again called into the office. The noise of the weaving machines still buzzed in his ears, but the Governor was in a good humour, asked him to sit down, passed him a cigarette, and folded his arms.

"Well, your time with us is about up, Citizen," he said. "To-day you will be taken to Bolshevo."

"To Bolshevo?" Nikalai queried, at first—but, then, he remembered all that that place stood for. It came suddenly back to him—of course, the convict-settlement of the G.P.U., where the prisoner was allowed to go in and out freely, could talk to the girls in the village, and now and then, on the off-day of the five-day week, ride into Moscow. Bolshevo! Among the prisoners, the name had the effect of a magic spell. It was the yearning of all who were serving long sentences. Even the most hardened atheists made the sign of the Cross over their application forms before handing them into the prison Governor.

"Well, aren't you pleased?" asked the Governor, cross at such long reflection.

"Yes—very," said Nikalai, in a low voice. But hardly had the words left his lips, when he realised the enormity of the lie. He did not want to leave this place—he had not wrestled, groaning, with the devil in order to be dragged away again, almost the moment he returned. The resolution he had taken was to return here, to the Lefortova, to hold endless discussions with the old, white-haired engineer, Barvitch, stretched out on his bed; to doze off and have restless dreams, sitting at the concert in one of the back rows of seats in the former prison chapel; to have the scanty, but perfumed foam rubbed into his cheeks in the barber's shop on the ground floor—that shop so marvellously fitted up to impress foreign visitors—and in the mornings to stand by the side of the squirrel-faced Ripper murderer, at the carpet-weaving machines. He knew that being sent to Bolshevo meant being given back to *life*, and he did not want to go back to it; he simply wanted to stay in the monastic, sanatorium-like Lefortova, suffer there a little for the dead Kisseleff, withdraw into himself, and follow world events as if silently and sorrowfully eyeing them through a high, narrow peep-hole.

Nikalai made no further reply, but looked indecisively at the floor. The Governor patted his back reassuringly and complacently.

In the afternoon a man of the G.P.U., with an expressionless, yellow face, a cigarette that had gone out, and a greasy cap pulled low down over his brows, escorted him to the Kasan station, and thence, by the electrified railway, to Bolshevo. Mutely sitting beside a number of other silent workers, whose tired, gnarled hands rested on their laps, they were carried to Bolshevo. An absurdly weazened, thin, shrivelled parish pope went begging from carriage to carriage, and the Tchekist coolly turned his unspectacled, amber eyes and thick wrinkled lips towards him—to the Soviet policeman the parish pope was nothing but an out-of-work clown. The train rolled on, hopping over the joints in the rails, to the forests.

From the station another ten minutes walking through the wood led to the prison settlement. The Governor paid no attention to Nikalai's nationality. The Tchekist had suddenly disappeared. Past a row of wooden barracks, summer-houses, recreation grounds and scraps of forest, he was led to his own barrack-quarters. There were an iron bedstead, a cupboard, and a small piece of wall that he might call his own. With hands in pockets, the men stood around, and smiled derisively at the Chief's explanations

In the Lenin corner a few men went on, undisturbedly, playing chess, draughts, and cards.

When the Chief had gone, one of the onlookers came up to Nikalai and shook his hand.

"Foma Efremovitch Katz-Tenteleyeff is my name," he said. And after a pause, "Here it is customary to call one another 'thou'—but I attach no importance to that; I leave it entirely to you to use whatever mode of address you prefer!"

"What have you committed?" asked a lanky, pale man, with an unusually long neck and a sanctimonious expression of suffering.

"My name is Nikalai Sergeyevitch Kisseleff, I am a wife-murderer, and I come from the Lefortova," said Nikalai, rather surlily. He did not quite like the surroundings. Bright sunshine streamed through the mean, poverty-stricken barrack-room. The buildings here were all incomplete, constructed of flimsy, light material; nothing seemed permanent or solid—everything seemed to have been lightly sketched, dashed off in charcoal, splashed in with water-colours. He marvelled that the whole lot did not fall to pieces, or was not carried off by the wind. This, Nikalai reflected, was the end of being a link in the chain—what beckoned to him was the fight for position, for power, for life. From the incubator he had reached the poultry-yard.

"Wife-murderer!" exclaimed Katz-Tenteleyeff, and his glasses sparkled delightedly beneath his black head of hair. "Why, that is what I am in for, too—you must tell me all about it."

Nikalai did not glance up, but continued unpacking his things and putting them away in the cupboard.

CHAPTER XIII

CONVERSATIONS OF A CONVICT

THE first time Nikalai was shaving in Bolshevo, Khrapov, Katz-Tenteleyeff, and the fat Bezdushnov stood about him, telling him, all over again, about the woman Bludova. Nikalai was only half attending to them. The room was bright, and where he stood at the mirror the daylight was full upon him. Now, for the first time, he noticed how slack and colourless his face was. But it was not dry—oilily moist rather. "Like corpse-fat," he thought, and felt an unexpected sense of satisfaction at having escaped from the Lefortova. It was an unpleasant feeling, this standing on one's own feet—a balancing exercise that made one feel unsure of oneself—but at least it was wholesome. As wholesome as eating spinach, or sunbathing.

He had already been here two days, and not yet seen the Bludova woman. But he could already clearly imagine her, for she was on everybody's lips. Everything she had ever said, demanded, discussed, done, forbidden, ordered, was turned over and over and argued about in every aspect. Some of the men seemed to be in love with her, others found her a problem. The fat Bezdushnov imitated her voice. Only Katz-Tenteleyeff could find nothing specially remarkable about her. Bludova was the wife of the Prisstav, the Governor of the State Factory. He was a quiet, steady man, some twenty years older than she, a pipe-smoking, hard-working man with slow movements; she seemed scarcely to have reached her thirtieth year, and filled no public office except that of Inspector of Family Houses. Instead, she worked (with the craving for activity so common among Russian women) in all the clubs of the settlement. She arranged excursions, delivered lectures for the "Militant Atheists," taught the young lads how to shoot, officiated as judge at sporting events, advised the Governor of the settlement, and acted in the theatrical performances. With it all, she was never to be found in the company of the other women. Not that she was a mannish woman; on the contrary, it was a sign of her intense femininity that she only wanted to be among men. Also, she did not smoke, drink, nor play chess or cards, while in her dress she developed that poverty-stricken, tawdry vanity—so absurd in the eyes of Europeans—of the Russian woman under the Soviets.

Katz-Tenteleyeff seemed unable to take any pleasure in the women here. For two years he had been secretary to the Legation, under Joffe, in Vienna, and when the other men talked about Bludova he would shrug his shoulders contemptuously and tell of the Viennese women, of their marvellous lingerie, of their heavenly perfume, of their "divine legs." He had been suddenly recalled from Vienna and put into the "Narkomindel,"[1] thence called to the "Profssoyoozi"[2] and sent to the provinces, and finally employed as schoolmaster in the Syrianian People's Republic. In the U.S.S.R. one was liable, for no reason, to be cast into a career that progressed not upwards, but downwards. Many in their apathy, were indifferent to this, but Katz-Tenteleyeff had suffered keenly under the system. With this slow but constant deterioration in his public position was connected the crime he was expiating here in Bolshevo. His wife was a German-Baltic woman whom, in the bloody days of the Red Leninist militant Bolshevism, he had married straight out of the abode of misery on the Lubyanskaya

[1] Commissariat for Foreign Affairs.   [2] Trades-Unions.

Square. He cared for her, but—he had saved her life.
And for that reason he claimed *gratitude*. After the merry
life of debauchery in Vienna came descent into the grey
monotony of the workaday world. The new Soviet culture
aroused a profound malaise in Katz-Tenteleyeff.   Lev
Davidovitch Trotzki, whom he had worshipped—brilliantly
intellectual, and with all his gifts brought out by the sparkling life of the Viennese cafés—was exiled to Turkestan, and
all the great theoreticians were silenced. At the same time,
he himself became poorer and poorer, more and more
powerless. At the universities reigned the gloomiest Tchekist-
Terrorist brand of psycho-analysis; his own Freudian psycho-
analysis had to make way for still sillier materialist systems;
and, finally, the whole great U.S.S.R. had become one vast
cemetery of intellects, a sad storehouse of mental coffins.
And it was all up with the golden, glowing promise of
Freedom that had illumined the vista in 1917.

Meanwhile Emma Klausovna, his wife, went all to bits.
She was still young, but she already had an ugly corpulence,
crow's-feet about her eyes, grey hair, and loose gums. And
he, the schoolmaster of Kotlass, plunged wildly and desperately into marital infidelities at every opportunity, with
the mothers of his pupils, the wife of the principal, the
daughter of the District Commissioner. He was acting in a
mental and psychological condition of complete confusion, a
somersault of ideas. In this grey country he felt he must
"enjoy" life relentlessly.

She, however, heard of his strayings, conferred with a
peasant woman whom he frequently visited, and hid herself,
fully dressed, in the young widow's bed when he next
announced that he was coming to see her. When he walked
into the dark room he felt a sudden, inexplicable suspicion,
and struck a match—for a moment she saw his distorted face.
Then the smouldering stick of wood fell to the ground, and

the fingers of Foma Efremovitch were encircling her throat. They did not relax till the convulsed, quivering, woman's body had ceased to utter those strangling groans choked into the death-rattle, and her hands had ceased their plaintive, feeble clutching at his forearms.

"A trauma, a powerful trauma," murmured Katz-Tente-leyeff, when he told Nikalai his life story for the first time. "You will understand, if you have heard anything of Freud. The mutilation-and-impotence fear—of course the people of Kotlass knew nothing about that, nothing at all. The land is full of ignorant barbarians! Nothing is done to assist in working off the libido, apart from the Soldiers' Caps. But, there—give me the West!"

While Nikalai cleaned his razor, he had to tell them all about the West in which he was supposed to have spent little more than a year of his life. The eyes of Foma Effremo-vitch glistened; the fat Bezdushnov looked dense and imbecile; Chrapov, the sectarian with the unshaven chin, his head tilted to one side, and his Adam's-apple protruding, cast nervous, lascivious looks round him, whenever Foma Efremovitch interrupted Nikalai with the oft-repeated exclamation, "A witch's cauldron of eroticism, the West!" Khrapov had spent almost two years in a Trudtchast called Lessokhim, a workers' settlement for sectarians who refused military service. Instead of sniping or throwing hand-grenades, he was forced to fell trees. But, by an endless series of lectures and courses, the sectarians were induced to give up their obstinate belief and show their willingness to practise the use of lethal weapons. As often as a sectarian recanted his faith, a photograph of him was taken, showing him with a gun, and frequently these photographs were published. The governors of the various Trudtchast camps vied with one another in keen competition to raise the number of apostates. Chrapov, who was not equal to the constant pressure of instruction, contempt, and ridicule, at last brought himself to handle a rifle. He did not, however, take it in his hands, but took it in his arms, and with a malicious smile, rocked it like an infant, hugged against his chest, and made himself look like an idiot. With half-closed eyes, and head on one side, he squinted furtively at the instructor. And suddenly, as though he had been familiar with the use of firearms since childhood, he pressed the rifle to his cheek, and shot the instructor down.

The fat Bezdushnov, on the other hand, was a provincial citizen of a petty town, who had squandered State money; he emphatically denied being a Bolshevik, but gave the government unqualified praise. He assured everybody he was a devout believer in the doctrines of the Holy Orthodox Church, but thought it was perfectly right that the government should forbid the ringing of church bells, because that would "only offend the atheistic susceptibilities of an honourable section of the population." In other respects he was just the average typical neo-Russian.

Foma Efremovitch had already asked Nikalai, on the first day of his arrival, whether he were a convinced Bolshevik. Nikalai said "No." Had he heard anything of psycho-analysis? Certainly. Was he convinced of the truth of its theses? No, he did not think so. To Foma Efremovitch that appeared suspicious. Was he, perhaps, religious?—that often occurred here and would not surprise him; the repressed libido also made itself manifest in religious obsessions. Nikalai laughed—he said he was a modern, it was only his mother who believed in Freud—he himself believed in God. Had he an inclination towards ecclesiastical creeds, or would he rather "go out into the woods to pray"? Here, it was all woods—the churches had broken down and closed, said Foma Efremovitch, contemptuously. He was a Catholic, said Nikalai, if Foma Efremovitch wanted it more explicitly;

a Roman Catholic, a practising Roman Catholic. Foma
Efremovitch shook his head, and in the background, a
voice was heard muttering that this must be reported to
Bludova at once.

Nikalai was in a good humour. Gradually, he was beginning to breathe more freely again here. He was beginning,
too, to rid himself of the habit of excessive smoking. That
had been a Lefortova habit—having a cigarette for ever
in the corner of one's mouth, spitting about, and going round
with a perpetual hoarseness. Nikalai was glad, too, that he
had told the men outright of his faith, at the beginning.
He was resolved not to be so cautious in his expressions as
he had been at the Lefortova, to emerge from that repulsive
network of lies, to strike boldly and to begin at once with his
work. The oppression and lack of liberty were much less
pronounced here than in the Lefortova, and that augured
well for success.

He dried his razor on a towel, and folded it up.

"Let's go for a stroll," said Foma Efremovitch, snuffling
and wiping his nose on his coat-cuff.

They closed the barrack door, and went through a clearing
of the forest. Beyond a lawn there gleamed the white walls
of a house, and as they drew nearer Nikalai saw a seat. On it
sat a woman, sewing, and apparently unaware of the
approaching men.

"Anna Andreyevna!" cried the sectarian, turning to
Nikalai.

"The Bludova woman!" explained Foma Efremovitch.

At last Bludova looked up, and puckered her nose,
because the sun in her face was dazzling her. Her eyes
widened, and she gazed enquiringly at Nikalai.

"So that is what Kisseleff looks like!" she said, and laughed.

She had an unusually wide mouth, and her lips stretched
over her teeth when she laughed. Her forehead, her eyes,

her cheeks, reminded him uncertainly of somebody he
knew in Germany or somewhere else in the West.

"Perhaps I don't please you, comrade?" asked Nikalai,
with some warmth, but keeping his eyes fixed on her. He
already felt who it was that she resembled—but, for some
obscure reason, would not admit it to himself yet.

The men laughed.

"We all say 'thou' to Anna Andreyevna!" said the provincial Bezdushnov, impressively. "What on earth put it into
your head to call her 'you'? "

"He couldn't be expected to know that yet!" she pacified
the man from the small town, laughing, and looked at
Nikalai with an almost maternal irony. "Could you, my
little murderer?"

That "my little murderer" was not altogether to Nikalai's
liking. Gertrude would never have expressed herself with
such cynicism. Gertrude had now undeniably stepped over
the threshold of his conscious mind—Bludova certainly
resembled Gertrude in appearance; she had the same eyes
and forehead, the same cheeks and hair. Only the mouth,
that old-looking, cynical, wide, womanly mouth, was entirely
different.

To get even with her, and retaliate in her own manner of
speech, he said:

"So you know that I did in my little wife—aren't you
frightened of me, that one day I might get hold of your
throat?"

Bludova laughed. But Nikalai would have liked to bite
back his whole speech—he realised, with annoyance, that he
had used the familiar "thou," that he had copied her
flippant tone, and had boasted of the dead Kisseleff's
deed.

"I am frightened of nothing—nothing at all!" said Bludova.

"Not even of your husband?"   Again a familiarity!
Couldn't he control his tongue?

Bludova laughed again—a wide-mouthed laugh, with lips
stretched over her big teeth.

"He sits and reads Gorki. From morn to night he just
reads Gorki and mutters!"

"Nor of God?" Once more his vocal chords had func-
tioned in his throat without his consent.

Bludova laughed again—this time, open-mouthed and
staring.

Now, for the first time, he became fully conscious that
there were here countless unbelieving women, absolutely
and completely unbelieving women and girls, women with
the same bodies, cast in the same moulds, as any woman of
the West; there were women who bore children without
having them baptised, who had their marriages celebrated
by a civil registration functionary of the state. For a few
moments he had forgotten the fact of the *anima Christi*, and
looked on Bludova as nothing more than a satanic phantom,
a Gertrude unsouled, deprived of grace, mechanised, and
made void. A meyrink-like fantasm, a living corpse.

"Nikalai Sergeyevitch is a Catholic!" the Sectarian
informed her. "He is really a Catholic, believes in the
Papa-Rimsky, and the Madonna—and he's very likely a
Jesuit!"

"That'll be worked out of his system here!" said Bludova.
"We'll give him Osstrovski's book on the Catholic Tertiaries
to read, and Lozinski's *History of the Roman Popes*. He'll be
converted before you can say 'knife!'"

"What things you do say, Anna Andeyevna!"

"Certainly!" said Bludova, "Nikalai Sergeyevitch is un-
educated, and has no idea of the scandalous doings of the
Papa-Rimsky! At the last Atheist Course lesson we heard
all about Alexander VI. Nikalai Sergeyevitch can't know

anything about him! Can you read and write, by the way?"

"Just a bit," said Nikalai, "but, if I may make so bold, I do already know about Alexander VI!"

"Bravo!" said Chrapov, clapping his hands. "A good shot! And what have you got to say abou him, as a Catholic?"

"I think it is a great and wonderful thing that such a great sinner as Pope Alexander VI, once our Holy Father, should have been able to decide infallibly on questions belonging to the Church," replied Nikalai, without heat.

Bludova stared open-mouthed.

"An intellectual!" exclaimed Foma Efremovitch enthusiastically. "At long last, at last, we've got an intellectual. You'll see, Anna Andreyevna, he won't let himself be 'reformed' by you so easily as you think. Ha! You've bitten off more than you can chew, now!"

"What are you sewing?" asked Nikalai, to give the conversation a different turn.

"A brassière," said she. "You'll wonder, perhaps, where I got the material; it's a remnant of curtain that we found in an old mansion."

"That is what you are all doing," thought Nikalai to himself. "You are living on the curtain-remnants from the philistine culture of the West—and that's not going to take you very far——"

An hour later all three were in a large hut, adorned with poster-covered boarding. Within were seats from which the adjacent pool could be gazed at. The "Atheist Hour" was about to begin, which was conducted by Bludova herself. With much clamour and ostentation Foma Efremovitch secured Nikalai the best place to sit, since he foresaw something coming out of this encounter between Nikalai and

Anna Andreyevna. "You'll see—you'll see!" he whispered in the ears of the others present.

Then came Bludova; the convicts stood up and sang the Internationale and sat down again, and spread out their scribbled and re-scribbled scraps of note-paper, which only here and there showed a blank space or two to write on.

Bludova spoke—and Nikalai grinned unabashed.

"You seem to be enjoying yourself at my expense!" she stormed at him.

"He won't enjoy himself—he's a thinking man," threw in Foma Efremovitch impudently.

"You are simply dishing up half-truths and hoary historical lies," said Nikalai. "However, I am accustomed to that—it doesn't bother me now. You carry on."

"How do you mean 'lies'? " demanded Bludova coolly, without showing her rage. And, suddenly, she took a step backwards, stooped down, and swiftly rose again, displaying an object which on closer inspection proved to be a book.

"Published by the 'Gossizdat,' by the State Press, in 1929!" she exclaimed. "You can have a look at it and see for yourself. What more proof do you want? State Press, 1929! State Press, 1929!"

The audience murmured approvingly—Nikalai seemed worsted. "These animals," whispered Foma Efremovitch. The "Atheist Hour" continued without further clashes to its end. When the Governor asked her for her report that evening, she replied briefly: "A new man, a Catholic or something of the sort, made himself awkward at the beginning of the Hour, but I stopped his mouth properly. He won't interfere with the Uplift Work any more."

It turned out, however, in the succeeding days, that it was not Anna Andreyevna, but Foma Efremovitch (who had said people would find that with Nikalai they had bitten off more than they could chew) who proved to be right.

Nikalai himself, however, dreamed the next night of Gertrude; it was one of those terribly "living" dreams, in which people appear, not like one-dimensional silhouetted shadow-figures projected on a screen, but as tangible, audible living beings.

With this night and this dream a new epoch began in Nikalai's life, which left its mark on the whole course of his life in the prison settlement of Bolshevo.

He awoke early, sat up in bed, and stared at the opposite wall—but when he noticed that doing so caused the memory of the faces seen in the night to fade, he closed his eyes again, and lost himself in reverie. Meanwhile, his comrades awoke, scratched themselves, washed, spat on the floor, swore, laughed, giggled, splashed their washing water about, and endeavoured with much shouting, to catch their fleas. But he sat there with closed eyes, his hair hanging down over his forehead. A few of the men looked his way, tapped their foreheads, and called him by name. Nothing brought him out of his abstracted reverie. Foma Efremovitch shook him by the shoulders.

"Up, up, my good sir!" he cried, "we are to be given some more schooling. We are to be made into useful citizens. Into Collective models. We are the Sacred Apes of Stalin! Awake, awake!"

"Let him be," growled Khrapov, "can't you see he's praying?"

Nikalai was not praying. He jumped up, plunged his head into cold water, washed, dressed, hurried down into the factory, and sat down at the machine. He had shoe-uppers to sew; tiresome, monotonous work, only requiring care. Soon, however, he looked up from the needle, leaping up and down in the leather in frenzied haste, to gaze at a large, red tablet with white lettering: "Up with the banners

of Socialistic Uplift!" That tickled him. "Up with the
banners!" The expression delighted him—he kept repeating
it idiotically. Then the dream-picture returned taking him
unawares. Between two shoe-uppers, he paused a moment.
Then he noticed an overseer eyeing him sharply, and hastily
took hold of the leather again.

And thus the autumn drew on.

Nikalai, meanwhile, was changing. After the death-like
sleep, the petty despondency, and the shrinking with-
drawal into himself of the Lefortova days, he caught a wild
passion for action. There was much he might have achieved
and accomplished, during that period spent on the shoe-
uppers, had he not been tormented and distracted by a great
longing, whose fulfilment seemed invisibly remote. Ever
since that night that he told himself was the night on which
Gertrude had appeared to him, he had been obsessed with
an enigmatically belated love for the companion of his
Berlin days. He had the definite sensation that it was not
her image, merely, that had been made visible to him in a
dream, but herself who had come to him. This was a feeling
that had nothing to do with any logical process of the intellect—for the intellect, that analytical and synthetical
apparatus of his brain—told him clearly and unmistakably
that this living dream-picture would never have been
begotten, had he not, the preceding evening, gazed so
intently and unwisely into the face of Anna Andreyevna.
Thus Anna Andreyevna had come to stand between him
and Gertrude.

All this—the strange coincidence of circumstances, the
terribly belated love, and the conflict of feelings in him—
thwarted and diminished his force for his work. On the
occasion of the third Atheist Hour, however, Bludova was
already thrown into confusion, like a turtle turned over

n to its back, and his influence increased surprisingly among
he men. He did not make sufficient use of his triumph. He
:t his zeal for attack fail too soon. He was living for Gertrude
ow. The daily encounter with Bludova gave him an in-
xplicable sense of infinite union, of bridging the gulf of
istance that separated him from Gertrude by the breadth
f whole countries.

But Anna Andreyevna hated him. She lived for her
vork, prompted by an insatiable lust of power. Fate had
een so gracious to her, and had given her the opportunity,
a this camp, to be in command of so many men. From
arly morning she set herself at the head of those men who
ad the day off from work, led them out into the woods,
ecided what songs they should sing, sang with them,
rdered which way they should march, at what pace, where
hey should rest. But in the afternoons she instructed, taught,
rained, the men. Her influence was assured by her always
eing a "good fellow," never starting love-affairs with the
nen, and being free with her cigarettes. Children she had
one. Her mentality was feminine, superficial, and as
sual among the people of the Soviet Union, filled with a
w small branches of science, and withal, with a destructive
redulity, simple-mindedness, and utter lack of critical
udgment.

When Nikalai had, after the first failure, rendered her
Atheist Hours impossible, she used all her influence with the
Camp Soviet, and secured Nikalai's exclusion from the
Atheist Circle. But it was at this point that she really began
o hate him in earnest. He was no longer present in the
lesh, but his spirit—his ideas—were still all too evident in
he men's interjections. From the background, mockingly,
e was stultifying her work of a twelve-month—*her* work!
n her eyes, he became the evil genius of Bolshevo.

Nikalai's love for Gertrude was an autumn love—the love

of a man who has been through bitter sufferings and bitterer disappointments. The love of a young man who was yet old. His very powerlessness to see her, to write to her, to exchange news with her, even to let her know that he was alive, that he lived for her, and that she must regard his existence as the dominant fact in the shaping of her future, awakened in him with that quivering unrest, that impulsive, over-whelming longing of ageing men, to give to the beloved all they are and have, and to declare themselves before grizzled age enwraps them with the veils of egoism and shrinking coldness, that they may retain for themselves, till the end, the last remnants of that genial warmth that once glowed through the whole world around them. This unrest, this often morbid-seeming longing, to give his feelings expression for a moment in word and gesture, had seized him also, and thus it came about that whenever he was left alone with Anna Andreyevna, he would adopt towards her a manner of appealing warmth and tenderness which she took for sarcastic mockery.

This vernal awakening in the autumn of the natural year made him irresolute and divided against himself. At first it was only his physical cravings that were directed towards Bludova, and it was to be ascribed solely to the powerful, animal upheaval of the senses, that he overlooked the physical unloveliness and the commonness of Anna Andre-yevna and followed her everywhere like her shadow. In reality, however, it was Gertrude he loved. But the longing that he had for Gertrude was actually confused with his desire for Bludova. And he wanted to be physically near to Gertrude, to touch her with his hands, to touch her hair, her skin, her limbs; he wanted to take her in his arms, and kiss her; but all that would be only the symbolical expression of his feelings, nothing more. Anna Andreyevna, on the other hand, was to him a Bolshevik soul possessed of a body, as if it were an implement or machine that could be used for love-making.

It was in the clear brightness of the northern nights, in the prison settlement of Bolshevo, that he first consciously realised what a tremendous part woman plays in man's life. The love of Gertrude, if he could have given it visible expression, would have meant for him the end of that terrible physical solitude; but, as it was, his heart was tortured, and it was vainly that he groped in the night by his bedside. His hands grasped only the intangible air. The deep, inward longing for his former companion, haunted him more than ever. With the world he was utterly at war, for the world here wanted him not, it had made him a prisoner, paralysed him, put him in chains. But Gertrude's embrace would have meant his reconciliation with the world. What he missed here was the fellow-being who would stand by his side and be drawn to him in bonds of companionship. Foma Efremo-vitch, Khrapov, or Bezdushnov—these were men with whom he lived in community, with whom he somehow "got on," with whom he "associated" in a communal life, but that was all; and that was not sufficient for him. Before, he had still been young, very young; he had suppressed himself by means of adventure and work, but now that the time had suddenly begun to pass terribly "slowly" for him, and his everyday life was dull and wearisome and beset with a thousand and one little irritations, an everyday life without the Sacraments, or the Mass, cut off from the life of the visible Church, the torturing longing for his companion, for the "person very near," which God has put in every one of us, became ever more and more intense. And thus it came about that the longing to issue forth from his self-centred ego and eventually consciously to lose himself in a loving and self-surrendering fellow-being, took complete possession of him.

One afternoon Nikalai went with Foma Efremovitch t[...]
the married quarters. Foma, despite his bitter hatred [...]
everything Catholic, had become Nikalai's best friend i[...]
Bolshevo. For hours on end they would argue—but thei[...]
arguments and talk were like the interplay of cog-wheels
and if one let fall a fragment of a phrase, the other woul[...]
grasp the whole drift of his thought and aim, with its rami[...]
fications and implications. While Bolshevo was to Nikala[...]
a breath of awakening from a long winter sleep, to Fom[...]
Efremovitch it was simply prison. The weight of the herd
and the didactic atmosphere, were against him—he wa[...]
racked with homesickness for the liberalism and freedom
of thought of the West. He was an utterly devoted fanatic fo[...]
psycho-analysis, but he despised any organically concret[...]
body of philosophical or political doctrine. He detested
Stalin and his following, suffered grimly from the dis[...]
illusionment he had experienced under the government o[...]
the Soviets, and waxed enthusiastic over the conceptio[...]
of an anarchical republic of savants. The terrorisn[...]
practised against science filled him with a silently seething
rage.

"Take the Marr case," he said, on the way from the mess
room to the married quarters. "Marr was a nobody. Unde[...]
Lenin or Trotzki he would have been a canal-dredger or [...]
manure-porter. But he was a Georgian, and a friend of th[...]
idiot Stalin. So he became a philologist and wrote a book—
a book, I say—that would turn one's stomach. He wrote, i[...]
this book—Ugh! Excuse me—it is that canned fish, it neve[...]
agrees with me—he wrote in this book that all the language[...]
in the world were derived from four words. He knows thos[...]
four words. Comrade Marr knows them. How? That, o[...]
course, he does not explain. But he knows them, and thi[...]
cretinistic abortion, through his friend, the idiot Stalin
becomes the most important professor in the University o[...]

Moscow! Or at the University of Tiflis. I ask you! Since
only *one* philological system can be the 'true, authentic,
Marxian, materialist, dialectic, Summa of Philology'
therefore all other philologists in the whole U.S.S.R., who
refused to propagate Marr's lunacy from their professorial
chairs, and so put themselves out of reach of danger, must
go into exile to Cholmogori, or Kem, or Solovki, as 'scientific counter-revolutionaries!' What has the West to say to
that? I will soon show you! A man in our Trade Delega-
tion at Prague who amused himself with philology in his
spare time, came to the editor of a review of Slavonic
Studies there, and happened to see a manuscript lying on the
table there. He looked at it—it was by a pupil of Marr.
'Great stuff!' he cried. 'At last, something really humorous.
Can you lend it me, Dr. So-and-so?' The editor had to
refuse. 'I must have it myself,' he said, 'the manuscript goes
to press to-day.' 'But it's raving insanity!' cried my friend.
The other nodded, unhappily. 'But we might be accused of
party prejudice.' And the article was actually printed.
Isn't it enough to make you cry, to see how the whole of
Europe is made a fool of by these pedagogues?"

In the married quarters they looked for the skate-worker,
Garyashnikov, but could not find him. In their bright,
cheery room his wife was sitting by herself, nursing a baby.
Nikalai was passionately fond of children. He took the
shrinking little creature into his arms, and sang, and tried
to play with it, till the youngster began sobbing and crying
and could scarcely be comforted by Garyashnikov's wife.
Katz-Tenteleyeff had lent Garyashnikov five tchervontses,
and was now demanding it back with excited gestures.
The woman promised to pay back something on account
till the first of the following month, but Foma Efremovitch
would not be put off. Finally, Garyashnikova called him a
crocodile, and Foma Efremovitch threatened, with blazing

eyes, to report the matter to the Governor. And at that point a strident voice from the door cut through the room like a knife:

"Is there to be any peace here, once for all?" It was Anna Andreyevna, standing in the doorway, hands on hips. Foma and Garyashnikova were silent. They slipped quietly out. But Nikalai stuck his hands in his pockets and smiled warmly at Bludova.

"What do you want here?" she asked him, sternly.

"I came with Foma Efremovitch," he said.

She came right into the room, sat down on the table, and folded her arms. A pause of some seconds followed. She was looking him full in the eyes, with knitted brows and tight-pursed, thin lips, and an expression of hatred and of close-questioning examination. At first, he smiled; then, beneath her stabbing gaze his smile shrivelled up into a cramp-like contortion of the features.

"Why are you continually obstructing my work?" she demanded fiercely.

"You know perfectly well why I do so," said he, placidly. "I am a Catholic, and wish to give men faith in God; you are an atheist and wish to take faith in God away from them. We have contradictory aims. On your side you are backed by the State, the 'Bezboshnik,' and the 'Antireligioznik'; on my side, I have the support of God himself, of the Bible, and the Papa-Rimski's encyclicals; and naturally you get the worst of it. It would be surprising if it were the other way about!"

"It is quite obvious, in you, that you've spent a year among the bourgeois," she retorted, scornfully, "for you're great at lying. It is simply out of malice that you stultify my work—malice and meanness and baseness. Do you think I don't notice your sarcastic friendly ways?"

"They have never once been meant sarcastically."

"Then am I to understand you're in love with me?" she asked, dryly, with an incredulous laugh.

"If you really insist on knowing—it might perhaps be called being in love. I really love a German Burshuanka,* whom you are very much like, to look at. That is why I try to be near you."

He did not lose his coolness. He was now merely curious to know how Bludova would react to his confession. She was looking down at the floor, searching for words.

"That sort of thing ought not to be taken seriously," she began, in her pedagogic manner. "Love is simply a bodily process of cerebro-spinal nature, which is determined by the nervous system, propinquity, and internal secretions. You must obtain sexual satisfaction. How, is immaterial——"

"A very intelligent man, Menszyński, wasn't he?" he broke in, pointing up at the picture of the head of the G.P.U., which hung in every room in Bolshevo. "He, by the way, was a Catholic, when he was young."

But she returned to the matter at issue.

"So you wanted to have me?" She laughed brazenly.

"That is not putting it correctly. It is unconsciously that I have always been drawn towards you. In my thoughts, I have often wanted to have you. But in reality I should never have done so, because it is forbidden to me."

"So the Papa-Rimski forbids you that—and you are fool enough to allow such a thing to be forbidden to you. But that is beside the point—the opportunity depends on me, not on the Papa-Rimski."

"Indeed?"

"What are you going to do now?" she asked.

"Do now? In the winter, work hard at the Bezboshniki and then—work in the camp soviet. Or do you think you'll be able to prevent my election? Outside, you would have

* Girl of the bourgeois.

found me easier to deal with—then I should just have been denounced to the 'Extraordinary' Police Department, and pulled in. But here in the G.P.U. sanatorium, self-determination reigns. Out there you have the ægis of your bureaucracy—but in here I'm free!"

Anna Andreyevna looked darkly at him.

"Gertrude when she puts on her darkling kitten-look!" he thought.

"Listen to me," said Bludova. "Are you very much in love with this Burshuanka?"

Nikalai said a stumbling word, then another, and finally began pouring out the story of his love for Gertrude in ever more ready speech. At first he experienced an unaccustomed pleasure in being able to tell Bludova all that, to her face; for it was as if he were telling his love to Gertrude herself. And then, with growing surprise, he realised what a powerful hold over him this love for Gertrude had, the love that his mind and his tastes had at first fought down, that had gradually taken root in him nevertheless, that the life in Lefortova had not been able to kill, and that, after a lapse of many seasons, had put forth mighty blossoms. What a woman Gertrude must be, for her picture, implanted like a grain of corn in his memory, to have grown up, without his tending or encouraging it, to such a mighty plant, filling his whole being, to overflowing, with love.

As he spoke to Bludova now, trying to be harsh and insulting, he could not prevent the torment of uncertainty as to the future, and the pain of longing, that he tried vainly to conceal beneath the roughness of his speech, from appearing ever and again as if glimpsed through a flimsy curtain. But the by-play of his knuckles and fingers told Bludova much more than his words.

Anna Andreyevna waited till he had definitely said the last word he had to say.

"You must be very deeply in love with her indeed," she said. "And that must distract you in your work, doesn't it?"

He could not make out what she was driving at.

"You want to work for the Papa-Rimski, the enemy of the creative proletariat—very well, then!" she said, with studied, hard directness. "I work for the enlightenment of the workers —very well then, once more. Now, then—I will get rid of my inhibitions, and you, of yours! Eh?"

Nikalai made no sign—he was watching her, closely and expectantly, through narrowed lids.

"If you promise me not to attempt to oppose my election in the Camp Soviet, and if you'll leave me, say, the workers in the ski-factory, you can keep the shoe and skate workers. If you will promise that, I will give in to you, you monster. You make me shudder—I loathe you. But leave me my work. My work—leave me that!"

She blazed into a fury of excitement—Bludova, who had never been known before to lose her self-possession. She snatched off her scarf, so that her hair tumbled down over her face—then held out her hand to him.

"In what way will you 'give in to me'? " he asked, ignoring her hand.

"Once a month," she said, and her nostrils were quivering.

" 'Once a month' what?" he asked, perplexed.

"Where you like," she cried, in still wilder excitement, "in the woods, indoors, behind a hedge, in the barracks— you know I'm not in the habit of giving myself to men, but if uplift work is upset, then I'm done for!"

"Out of the question," he said.

"Twice—three times a month—every week!" she cried.

He shrugged his shoulders. His face was haggardly white.

"Dog!" she yelled. "Then what *do* you want?" Her eyes filled with tears, she utterly lost all control of herself. "Bourgeois!" she shrieked, "whining bourgeois!"

Nikalai left the storming woman to herself. He was, him self, inwardly, deeply moved and excited. Fallen, miserably fallen—God and His Mystical Body betrayed, Christ pu up to auction in the market-place of sin—it was the Devil setting up his satanic phantoms in the prison community Bludova was probably good, a mere pawn, an unwitting tool in the hand of the Evil One, of whose existence she refused to be aware. Black clouds piled before his eyes— even though the light nights were over, he still could not sleep. In prayer, in waking, in yearning longings, and despairing indecision, he lay there, in the barren darkness of the barrack-room, with open eyes, groaning into the crackling straw.

"Up with the banners, up!" his bloodless lips murmured. Outside, the autumn winds blustered, feebly, wearied and spent by its struggle through the pine-woods when it reached the window-panes of the G.P.U. prison settlement of Bolshevo.

CHAPTER XIV

DEATH, AN INDIVIDUALIST

A FEW days more, and the phantom had disappeared. All his feelings, without reservation, he had confessed to Bludova—he even experienced the sensation of being, for the first time in a long while, free, clean, sane, and wholly absorbed in his faith. The desperate begging for a miserable remnant of religious conviction was a thing of the past—he had entered into an Ignatian mood of soldierly asceticism, accompanied by a quiet but intensely ardent joy in life. Only his attitude towards Gertrude or rather to the picture of Gertrude lodged in his memory, had remained unchanged. Except that it had become the main *point-d'appui*, the central rallying-point, in the battle; and, not only that, but an essential factor in his development. Often when he thought himself alone and unobserved, he was discovered speaking soft, tender words, smiling, stretching out his hands towards some invisible being. While at work, while the jogging needle was piercing its holes in the leather, his eyes would gaze, gladly and ecstatically, at the white lettering on a red ground: "Up with the banner—up with the banner!"

He was now living a two-fold life—working from morning till evening in the factory with his hands, and then among the men with his words. But, meanwhile, his thoughts dwelt elsewhere. These people around him seemed to be receding ever further from him, in a spatial sense. They seemed to him mere lifeless "supers" whose rôle it was simply to throw in occasional interjections in his monologue. The only exception was Foma Efremovitch. Foma was, as it were, the wall that he would bounce his ball against in order to catch it again—everybody else seemed remote, invisible, shadowy; Bludova, Khrapov, Garyashnikova, the Governor, Bezdushnov, all of them. He seemed to be isolated within an enormous glass case.

In the midst of his period of regeneration, there occurred an incident that at first annoyed him, then amused him, and finally filled him with pensive sadness. On one of his free days he was called in to see the Governor, who gazed searchingly into his eyes.

"Sit down," he said sternly. "Reports have been made against you—or, rather—er—various parties have directed my attention to you. You probably know what it is about. You have been carrying on religious propaganda!"

Nikalai understood the sharp look.

"Have reports also been passed in to the effect that I make anti-communistic speeches?"

"No—not so far."

"Then what do you want with me? The law says that all religious views are permitted in the U.S.S.R.," said Nikalai.

"I see you are an intelligent man," replied the Governor, and nodded his bald-shaven head. "You will understand that your conduct, though not a punishable offence, at any rate amounts to an extremely mischief-making course. Are you doing it out of malice?"

Nikalai did not reply.

"Did Bludova report me?" he asked suddenly.

"If you want to know definitely, no!" replied the Governor, tapping on the table-top with a pencil. "It was Bludova himself who complained bitterly that his wife gives him no peace, on account of your having turned the men against her. I can quite see what he means. I know what it is, when a

woman is nagging a man all day long. But now answer me—
are you acting from malice or idiocy?"

"From conviction," replied Nikalai, crossing one leg over
the other.

"So you are mad, after all," said the Governor, gravely.
"You do really believe in all the junk that is printed in the
Bible?"

"I believe," said Nikalai. Those two words contained the
whole weight of his creed.

"So you actually believe that Christ lived, you believe in
the Virgin Birth, in the Resurrection, in the teaching of the
Last Supper, in——but it is all simply too silly," cried the
Governor, "you cannot make a fool of me."

The Governor pressed a bell-push. A militiaman entered
the room.

"Take him across to Dr. Rovinsky," he said, without
looking at Nikalai, and bent sullenly over some papers.
"And then bring back the report, at once. I'll ring up the
doctor directly."

Nikalai silently walked with the soldier across the dirty
lawn, towards the "hospital." This "hospital" was a large,
airy, wooden barrack. Dr. Rovinsky was a medical official
of flesh and blood, who smiled contemptuously at his patients,
considering everybody a malingerer, and who, when making
out prescriptions, regarded a certain monotony as called for
in them.

"Stand up straight!" he bawled at Nikalai. "Don't pull
such a miserable long face! Good God, I'm not going to
eat you! Undress!"

Whistling coolly, Nikalai began to undress. The doctor
tore backwards and forwards excitedly, up and down the
room, then suddenly halted before a desk, ran through a
report, dashed his hand through his close, curly hair,
drummed with his fingers on the table-top, and shifting his

weight from one foot to another, started staring out of the window.

It was cold in the room. Nikalai had undressed and felt chilly, but not till he cleared his throat did the doctor turn round towards him.

"Show me your tongue," he barked.

Then he asked him about various diseases, receiving in reply Nikalai's assurance that he had never suffered from them. Suspiciously the doctor examined him.

"There you are!" he said venomously. "There you are! Hasn't the most elementary disease—not the most elementary. In my opinion you're not a man at all; and that's the root of the matter. My dear sir!"

He took a breath, then asked, unpleasantly curtly, in a deep, would-be soldierly voice, "What did your father die of?"

"Pneumonia," Nikalai guessed, at random.

"Interesting. And your mother?" he thundered, next.

"Puerperal fever after child-birth."

"We shan't get anywhere like this!" he said, with nervous irritation. "Tell me something of your visions. How and when do they occur and what do you see?" His tone had now come to sound exactly like that of the barrack-square.

"What visions?" asked Nikalai.

"Don't waste my time!" cried the doctor, shrilly. "Don't put me off. I earn my bread dearly enough. Stand up. Answer me, do you hear!"

"I've no symptoms at all," said Nikalai dryly. "If the Governor telephoned that I had, the beast is lying like a book. Incidentally, I'm a candidate for the Camp Soviet."

"You're a candidate! Aha! Oho! I'll soon put a stop to that. You, a lunatic! Suffering from religious mania. Grotesque. A grotesque case. How can one tell? You may

)e a pyromaniac. However—we'll let that be. You believe
n God. Probably you believe in ghosts, too, and mermaids,
and Russalkas! Why don't you sit down?"

He tested the reflexes of Nikalai's patella; lit a candle,
and examined the pupils of Nikalai's eyes, with his own
scintillating nervously; then he blew out the candle and sat
down at his desk. Nikalai gazed at the wall, on which hung
a card with rows of different-sized letters of the alphabet.

He felt frightfully cold. His body was all goose-flesh. He
had difficulty in not letting his teeth chatter. Outside, on the
dirty scrub near the edge of the forest, a damp mist was
settling.

He turned his head towards the doctor, who was writing
a report, he thought—but the doctor was no longer writing.
He was simply leaning over the writing-table, cowering
like a beast of prey, and squinting with one eye at Nikalai.
Nikalai caught the look—and, suddenly, he understood.
That insane, glittering eye seemed to say: "Sheer play-
acting! Everything I am doing is acting! Do you think I
don't know? Do you think I don't understand you? I
only wanted to curse the One Above, to curse him because I
hate him! Hate him with gall and malice, as becomes a
Bolshevik!" Fascinated, Nikalai stared at the satanic eye
glaring at him beneath the bushy brow.

He turned his head aside, and stared expressionlessly, in
his excitement, at the card with the letters on it. That
Komsomolets from the Dinamo Bath at Moscow returned to
his mind—the man who had no doubt of God's existence,
but hated and persecuted him as an inimical being. It was
the real Antichrist that was raging here.

The doctor startled him back from his brooding.

"Pray, pray to that dear God of yours—tell him to keep
the typhus away from us, if that will do any good!" he cried
hoarsely.

The satanic eye was extinguished; all that was left was—
fear. Wretched, animal fear. And the phantom had disappeared.

They let him off with a caution. Foma Efremovitch
made fun of Nikalai's experience, but knitted his brows
when he heard of the doctor's last words. The next day
Garyashnikov was in a position to report that a man in
hospital had a high fever and a curious rash. Moreover, a
special ward had now been arranged, and the hospital
orderlies refused to work in it. These rumours grew ever
more numerous. Other men claimed to have heard that the
pestilence had broken out in Kharkov. Others, again, had
definite news that for some days past cholera had been rife
in Moscow. In the midst of these times of commotion and
excitement, the Governor ordered the camp gates to be
closed, and all free egress and ingress was indefinitely suspended. The factories went on working for one more day—
and then the snow came. And, with the snow, the
epidemic. And despair settled down on the population of
Bolshevo.

Nikalai now had more leisure than ever, and the men
poured in to hear him, in troops. New, unknown, suspicious,
and yet hopeful countenances were those that he now began
to see for the first time. Of his old audience, many a man was
already missing. They were lying in hospital. Or, perhaps,
soaked in carbolic, lying under the earth. The newcomers
stood around, disappointed, with hungry, flashing eyes,
wanting to see miracles, and contradicting, cursing, clapping,
interjecting cynical jokes in Nikalai's speech. A joyless
anxiety and impatience, a nervous curiosity, and a laborious
pretence of composure prevailed in Bolshevo.

In the evening the barracks were closed up. Before bed-
time Dr. Rovinsky, with an assistant doctor, made the round

of the beds, with bent back and dishevelled hair, asked apparently irrelevant question, felt the men's pulses, and with nervous, trembling hands, unbuttoned their shirts. And it once happened, in Nikalai's barrack-room, that the assistant doctor said to one of the ski-workers, in a low voice, that it would be as well for him to go along with them, whereupon the man's face turned sallow-white, and he fell on his knees, and, with tears, begged the doctor not to let him die. This was the keennest of the atheists, and Anna Andreyevna's right-hand man. Foma Efremovitch, on the other hand, once planted himself in the doctor's way, and demanded, on behalf of the whole barracks, to be told the whole truth—what manner of disease it was that was raging there, whether it was Asiatic cholera, abdominal typhus, spotted typhus, or the plague. The doctor, thus confronted, replied that it was none of the man's business—whereupon Foma Efremovitch, like a flash, turned round and called out to the whole room that it was either the plague or cholera. "It's a dirty shame," roared Foma, "that the camp is not immediately disbanded. It is all on a par with the custom on board the imperialist bourgeois' sinking battle ships—the stokers are locked up in the engine-room, and left there to perish miserably!" The doctor protested indignantly, but the whole room began echoing to such cries of "Daloi!" that his words were lost in that roar of hatred. That same week, Foma Efremovitch received a notice from the Camp Soviet informing him that, as punishment for his unpolitical conduct injurious to the communal spirit, he was to write out the text of the "Internationale" ten times, and hand it, within the ensuing twenty-four hours, to Bludova. This punishment, which was not a customary one in the camp, had been devised by Garyashnikov, who knew exactly in which spot he could best hit "the crocodile"—in his pride. Foma Efremovitch's face turned white with rage, when he read the notice. "They can force me, these swine—they can force me!" he snarled. "The humiliation of it—having to knuckle under to these brainless animals!"

But nobody, by this time, was troubling any longer as to the judgments of the Camp Soviet. For death had entered into Bolshevo. More and more spotted typhus suspects disappeared into the hospital, nearly all ashen grey, feverish, and indifferent; but a few of them whining, screaming, or weeping. In the barrack-room adjoining Nikalai's there was one man who had even kept his illness secret. To him, a peasant's son, going into hospital seemed equivalent to dying. But his dormitory-mates had noticed his quiet, uneasy manner, and the glitter of his eyes; they came to his sleeping-place, and found him squatting there, his pendulous nether lip drooping, cowed like a squirrel. He asked what they wanted with him. "Are you sick?" they asked him roughly. "My little pigeons, my little pigeons!" he whimpered. So they dragged him out of bed. His shirt got pulled out of place, and they saw his skin already covered with red spots. Like cattle mortally terrified, running out of a blazing forest, they stampeded into the snow-covered winter landscape, and did not pull up till the cold wind had brought them to their senses.

It was now obviously spotted typhus that was rife in the convict settlement. Nikalai shrugged his shoulders, but Foma Efremovitch drew him aside to enlighten him. "For us Soviet swine, this is no infantile malady," he said ponderously. "You'll see—a fourth of the cases will die. They've all got lice, and the lice spread the infection, and the men's constitutions are not fit to withstand the disease. Weakened by the dog's food they give us, we shall all peg out, like the Red Indians did with measles."

Foma Efremovitch was right again. The sick died off like flies. They were no longer conveyed to Moscow to be

:remated, but thrown naked, by night, into open graves, and
heir clothes put under gas. The "Ossoaviakhim," the civil
;as and aircraft union, belonging to the camp announced a
;reat Cyanide Week, and, amid much shouting, Bludova
aad the barrack-rooms cleansed, to destroy the fleas, lice,
and bugs. Foma Efremovitch and Nikalai made loud,
malicious remarks about the way she showed herself off,
playing the busybody all over the place. Whilst she, shouting
and giving orders, waddled about in her plimsolls among the
morose-eyed and now silent men, the great, sad dying had
set in among the atheists in the hospital. Amidst fever,
delirium, and groans they passed out, despairing, joyless,
like old, tired, worn-out beasts of burden.

While the provincial Bezdushnov exhibited an overdone,
forced gaiety, and boasted of once having recovered from the
same disease and therefore being now immune from it,
Nikalai talked with the sectarian Chrapov about death, and
about nothing but death. Right into the dormitory spread
the smell of carbolic. One bed after another was becoming
empty. The topic had thus a ghastly appropriateness.
Foma Efremovitch, at first, was always taciturn, listening
attentively to the two men arguing, rolling his eyes first to
one side then to the other, as if watching a tennis-match;
but, later on, he began interjecting more and more remarks
into the heated discussion. And, finally, in his excitement,
thrusting Khrapov aside and fighting Nikalai independently
on entirely different lines. On the day when Foma Efremovitch received the notice from the Camp Soviet, he sat all
the afternoon at the big common table, writing. "Doing
your imposition?" asked Bezdushnov, rather sarcastically.
Foma Efremovitch had not deemed him worthy of a reply.
Meanwhile, he did not appear to have done his "lines," for
he put the papers—they were the backs of propaganda
posters, for no proper writing-paper was to be had either in

Bolshevo or in Moscow—into envelopes, addressed these, and placed them in his drawer.

That evening Khrapov narrated an experience in the Valley of the Don. He had worked there as an electrician, in one of those disconsolate factory villages, in whose streets every footfall makes a scrunching noise on the clinker-covered, black earth, over whose fields grows scanty, sooty grass, and damp fogs settle. There was nothing to break the dreary monotony of the landscape except factory-shafts, chimneys, plaster huts, and rotting wooden barracks. The food was wretched, the pay low, and the daily routine only broken by the constantly changing hysterics of propaganda inculcating dreary forms. Early in the morning he used to stagger into the factory, along with hundreds of other utterly neglected labouring animals, and then back in the evening, or dozed, with half-closed eyes, at some meeting or other, and now and then carried some information to the G.P.U. Then in this putrid factory hole, in this famine village with its prison, its hospital, its coal-waste, and its police for "beating-up" the population, there happened something that was quite an everyday occurrence in the U.S.S.R.: a new sect arose. Chiliastic, fatalistic, orgiastic, Manichean, they would eat no fish, would not call God by his Name, and declared that both Lenin and the Pope of Rome were the Antichrist. Seeds of the teaching of Jesus, sown in marshy soil, shot up to a strangely blossoming plant. One day, after their first general meeting, a fourth part of the members were arrested. All the rest were confidential spies of the "extraordinary" police. The prisoners were kicked, their ears were boxed, they were tortured in the "Dynamo," but they confessed nothing. They screamed shrilly, but betrayed nothing. At the trial, to every question asked them, they replied, tonelessly and expressionlessly, with the words, *"Christos voskress"* ("Christ is risen!") The judge blus-

tered and threatened—but all to no purpose. For years
they had starved, worked, seen plaster huts and coal-waste.
They stood in the dock like unreal shadows, dirty and bloody,
their throats creaking mechanically, and fidgeted with
their fingers. They were the Joyless Ones, who had found
God in their own way, and would not let him go. Monotonously their voices screeched in the dusk: "*Christos voskress*" In the dim light of electric lamps of miserly candle-
power, their death-sentence was read out.

They were led out into the yard, men and women together.
They were set against the wall. They stood there, mixed
indiscriminately. "*Christos voskress*—Christ is risen! He is
verily risen!" There is a crunching of the clinkers. The
soldiers, with their strong, animal faces, feel horror penetrating to the innermost recesses of their hearts. A warm
evening wind is blowing, and the factory sirens begin, one
after another, shrieking in staccato, musical bursts. Sullenly
the prisoners murmur in chorus, "Christ is risen! Christ is
risen!" But nobody gives the signal—and the torturing pause
of uncertainty stretches out, while the sirens hoot, from these
men and women into the machine-fouled landscape. One
man fires, and then another; with eyes showing white, the
victims crumble up at the knees, stumble forward, support
themselves on the palms of their hands, and in their greenish,
corpse-faces their eyes are like those of dying dogs, but their
lips are not stilled. Thus fall those "Possessed of the Cross
of the Spirit"; there was only one man still living—and
describing whirling arcs with his feet, like a shot rabbit. A
few seconds later he, too, lay still.

Then they came with unslaked lime, thrust their fingers
between the lips of the corpses and wrenched their jaws open,
in search of gold teeth, but had no luck except with a
woman. Her teeth they broke out of her mouth. A few
hours later, all that remained to tell of the abolition of

the sect were splashes of blood and lime on the crunching
soil.

"A very significant symbol, that breaking out of their
teeth," interjected Foma Efremovitch. "It is connected with
the puberty-rites of the Bantus, who have the boys' incisors
broken or extracted——"

"But that was not always the case," broke in Khrapov,
who could not fully follow Foma Efremovitch's line of
thought. "Very often people's whole jaws were wrenched
off—quite apart from the fact that this was a woman——"

"All the same thing, all the same thing," chuckled Foma
Efremovitch, "it's all the same thing. The perversion of
the Negro symbolism. The female corpse subjected as passive
partner to a masochistic action by State functionaries.
Then people are surprised at neurotic cases. They're surprised at them. Was this in winter?"

Khrapov said it was not.

"A pity!" said Foma Efremovitch. "A pity! For if it had
been they would certainly have had high, pointed phallic-
shaped cloth hats. Of course, the woman was bleeding, as
well. That, of course, is all perfectly fitting. And the dying
people were shouting, '*Christos voskress!*' You can see how
similar that sounds to the word, '*Vosmushaen*'—'*Vosmushaen*,'
'become male!' There can't be any doubt about it. Anybody with a smattering, the merest elementary smattering, of
psycho-analysis, must know that—— You're laughing
again, Nikalai Sergeyevitch!"

Foma Efremovitch had worked himself up into a
crescendo of enthusiasm, and when he looked at Nikalai's
hungry, delighted face, his concluding words were filled with
reproach.

"And yet you're usually such a fine, keen-minded,
educated man," Foma Efremovitch began again, in tones
that were half plaintive and half pedagogic. "You've been

away from these—what am I to call them—imbecile educational dens here. You've been in Germany (I like Germany), and in Austria (I don't mean that as a taunt—I like Austria). You've seen things. But the utter lack of comprehension with which you oppose psycho-analysis is utterly incomprehensible to *me*. If I had a fortune the first thing I'd do with it is erect a memorial to Freud—a marble statue!"

"Psycho-analysis," replied Nikalai, adopting Foma's didactic manner, "is a possible view of life. I can quite understand that there *are* people who actually see and experience things as the Vienna school of psycho-analysts would dogmatically insist on having them. That much I concede. Psycho-analysis's perspective was guided by, obtained from, the experiences of sick men. To the psycho-analyst go none but the sick, and it is only the sick who are successfully studied by psycho-analysts. Their sayings, their feelings, their writings, their art. The healthy man has nothing of any significance to the psycho-analyst. On the other hand, there are all the books and paintings by paranoiacs, utterances of the insanity of a veritable El Dorado for people of your school. Of course, it is the symptom of an enormous arrogance, only excusable on the ground of an ecstatic science-mania, to reconstruct a common norm, and prescribe it to wholesome people, out of a *summa* of the conceptions of the world that are formed by the sick in soul and mind——"

"Children and fools speak the truth!" interjected Foma.

"Very well, then," said Nikalai, a little more excited this evening than he usually was. "We'll stick to your axiom. It is a very ill-chosen one, for between the 'fools' of the proverb, and the lunatic asylum, there is an immense, though a somewhat graduated, distinction. However, let that be as it may. However, if it is seriously your purpose to maintain that the majority of men's conception of the

world is that of 'fools and children,' then this is tantamount
to a confession of reversion to the primitive, undeveloped,
irrational, and barbarian, and a fatal contradiction to your
implicit faith in progress. From my Catholic point of view,
all the heresies go wrong because they lack the Catholic,
or Universal, outlook—the *kat'holon*. One-sidedness——"

"I'm glad you've brought up the subject of Catholicism
again," Foma Efremovitch broke in, impatiently. "For,
from your Catholic point of view, it must be quite immaterial who is the bringer of truth. All souls are of equal
value. The child's soul, the fool's soul, the madman's soul,
the soul of the 'normal man'—yours is a really amazing
democracy. But if this democracy is carried to its logical
conclusion, it ends in the recognition of the lunatic asylums
as——"

"From the purely divine point of view—if we're only
talking of the Church Triumphant, in Heaven—that's *true*!
But here, on earth, men have been endowed with understanding, that same faculty of understanding that, under
favourable circumstances, can lead to God. If Catholicism
were to act on your prescription, we ought to put a stop to
all the work in England, because, in ninety-nine cases out of
a hundred, the English convert, with the help of Grace,
comes to the true faith along a road of pure reason. But you
are still flirting with the regime of the insane—you, here in
the Soviet Union, yourself under the rule of insane, maniacally possessed heretics. But you yourself are not much better
than those heretics. For (as I was just going to explain, when
you interrupted me) you carry within yourself the principal
characteristic of the heretic—one-sidedness. Just as the
Bolsheviks are state-maniacs, so you are a sex-monomaniac.
Both lack universality. Both are hopelessly 'cranks'—the
Bolsheviks with their State psychosis, their 'good-state-
citizen' complex, their G.P.U. hysteria, and you with your

sexuality-scenting. Imagine for a moment what the future state of society would be under a psycho-analyst system: everything pointed or long would be declared male, everything hollow or concave, female. Fountain-pens would be male, and door-knobs, and electric plugs, water-pipes, sugar-canes——"

Foma Efremovitch made an excited protest. But Nikalai would not let him get a word in.

"You would make life deteriorate into stinking obscenities!" said Nikalai, with emphasis. "All heretics have their particular obsessions—and psycho-analysis, in its normalising philosophy, has all the traits of a heresy: one-sidedness, fixedness, obsession——"

Foma Efremovitch interrupted him again. "We have done no evil," he said. "We have tortured no one to death in the Lubyanka, we have brought the freedom that you always praise so much—freedom and truth!"

"Freedom?" Nikalai laughed. "Freedom? Yes—if you conceive of elephants, woodpeckers, and crocodiles as the models of freedom. Your freedom is no human freedom—it is the most intolerable terrorism. You won't even leave men freedom of conscience—to choose between good and evil, to fall or to conquer. We should be the mere slaves of nature—of nature. We should simply be nothing but a *piece* of nature. Like the cattle in the forest, that tremble when the lightning flashes. No, thank you!"

Foma Efremovitch did not give in. Obstinately and persistently he talked at Nikalai, tapped his chest with his finger, and spat while he talked.

"Listen to me, Foma Efremovitch," said Nikalai. "Just suppose for a moment that psycho-analysis were really correct, mathematically accurate, yet it need not by any means have any reality-value. I'll ask you a riddle, may I? Well: Somewhere, somehow, there is a spherical ball. This ball is remarkable for the fact that there exist on it innumerable creatures each of which bears a lumpy excrescence on a short stem. This excrescence has a large orifice that can be opened or closed voluntarily, and is the beginning of a tubular passage which runs through the whole body. In addition to this opening, which is surrounded with mucous membrane, there is a thin, horny material hanging in strands from the hard excrescence, crinkly slabs of flesh are attached at the sides, there are parti-coloured, jelly-like balls imbedded in moist hollows, and at various places there are holes, mucous membrane, and secretions——"

"Cuttle-fish, or torpedo-fish," Foma Efremovitch guessed, unthinkingly.

"No," said Nikalai. "Not cuttle-fish, not torpedo-fish, but part of a creature that here and there devours cooked and cut-up animal corpses with the help of metal implements."

"You mean a man's head? Surely not——"

Then Foma Efremovitch saw that it was true.

"Don't you see?" Nikalai resumed, when the other had got over it. "That was a perfectly unbiassed, objective description, that entirely abandoned all claim to the homocentric standpoint. But it takes us no further. It was simply the report of the eyes. And the eyes' report is one-sided. Equally one-sided, just as one-sided, is the report of sex alone. The secret of Catholicism is its universality—Catholicism is the *Whole*. Hence we probe with our intellect for the things that are of this world; hence there is a Catholic anthropology and ethnology, sexual ethics, and economics, morality and history, sociology, biology, natural history, and literature; hence the Vatican has libraries, astronomical observatories, diplomats, theologians, museums, and cartographers. Outside, in the layman's world, there is nothing but independent science. Independent, unrelated, self-

sufficient. But if so independent, then how can it be science
at all? Such a science is made horribly difficult—in fact,
meaningless. Do you understand? Meaningless, purposeless
science. A science that is like a road running out of a solid,
illuminated, white-washed square, into a dark, unlit, maze
of side-streets, back-streets, nocturnal suburbs——"

Foma Efremovitch passed the back of his hand over his
forehead, and breathed on his glasses.

"You Catholics are simply imperialistic terrorists, too—
but much more cunning ones than the men of the hammer
and the scythe. And no wonder. You've had two thousand
years' start of them. In those two thousand years you have
so perfected yourselves, gained such an uncanny skill, that
every effort to combat you with success must remain episodic.
By means of the celibacy of the priest, you have frustrated the
effects of heredity, by means of the confessional you have
anticipated and usurped the most important discovery of
psycho-analysis—incidentally realising its most daring and
Utopian visions. For instance, the variety of your orders is a
psychological miracle: Jesuits, Benedictines, Trappists,
Franciscans, Lazarists—all harmonising antitheses. In
harmony, in collusion. Thus you have avoided any stereotyped types. Bolshevism, Protestantism, the Orthodox
Eastern Churches, they all produce stereotyped characters
of their own. Rome, however, brings all men under one hat
—all men, all. And without—that is the paradox of it!—
without being liberal at all. Uncompromising, inflexible,
fantastic, even frequently paradoxical-seeming men—
anglers who pursue their mission successfully. I, personally,
believe that you will yet ruin everything—put all men into
darkness, bring the world under the Roman tiara."

Now Khrapov began contradicting. Nikalai lay, staring
with amused eyes up at the ceiling. Foma Efremovitch
mercilessly cut short the sectarian's words.

"What would you, Grigori Petrovitch? A Church that has the impudent audacity to burn Joan of Orleans alive, in order to make a saint of her four hundred years later, cannot go under. Savonarola is to be glorified, too—and, at Rome, attempts are being made to have him beatified. Nikalai Sergeyevitch told me that himself. But believe me, I'd rather be condemned by a court of the Inquisition—by a Dominican court of the Inquisition—to death by fire, than be sentenced by a Soviet court to six months' detention in Bolshevo. Read through the Galileo trials Grigori Petrovitch—you'll see, those were Intellectuals. They did know how to debate. They grasped the problem with real profundity, with deep insight. And therefore, in the final upshot, Catholic science will conquer. For those Popes and monks, free from family, and with their libido unsatisfied, can work very differently from the way we can. Freud stands like a rock in the ocean, but his disciples—well, look at Jung, in Zurich, simply sending his Roman patients to church. It's a hopeless fight, against the 'blacks.' Loyola's corpses. And another thing—these pedagogising, infantile primitive moralists never get away from money and material things. But Rome, in the end, will always be able to pay with promises of the next world. Yes, yes, Rome will survive the fight with the Kremlin. What's the good of paper money and gold, if you can hand out promises of the next world in absolutely unlimited profusion? No treasury-note printing press could keep up with that. So the whole material, real world is hopelessly handicapped by the Papa-Rimski!"

And Foma Efremovitch screwed up his eyes, and looked through his sparkling glasses at Nikalai.

"You Catholics have found out the secret!" he exclaimed. "You have laid bare the meaning of the Universe. You are not innovators at all—your success is due to the fact that you have inscribed as the programme on your banners what is simply the essence of the world. Never in the history of the world has a body of men so perfectly fulfilled everything in the human soul as you have with your mixture of superstition, diplomacy, big-heartedness, sense of order, rationalism, and psychology; your cynicism, your naïveté, enthusiasm, unscrupulousness, ecstatic obsession, puerility, wickedness, love for humanity; with your terrorism, and your rule of life; your generosity, worldly wisdom, and fanatical boldness. You are the living encyclopædia of the planet, Earth. But God exists for you just as little as for me. God is simply the sum-total of your pretence. 'God'—that is the name of your dishonesty, your ever-repeated excuse, the magic word, the 'Open Sesame,' the explanation of everything inexplicable. For, if God *did* exist, he would long since have swept away your supermen, with your materialism, your earth-mania, your realism, and your scientific mentality——"

Nikalai leaped up from his bed.

."You're on the wrong tack—on the wrong tack!" he shouted him down. "God is not what you fancy him. God is among us, with us. God who sent his Only Begotten Son on to this third planet, reckoning from the sun; who created us in his image; who lets us participate, by procreation, in his work of creation; he has given us this marvellous earth to rule, with all that is on it, with its continents, its seas, its lands, its mountains and rivers, the animals, death, joy, love, language. God, the dear God, is the 'God of Love' in very truth—he watches over us while we bore mines in the earth's crust, while we print books, while we build railways, practise politics, put up wires, bear children. Yes, he stands in our very midst, dispenses mercies, intervenes in the course of events, and fills the whole universe with the breath of his love. You alone are not conscious of him—you, you alone, go about with doubts and a dried-up, shrivelled, 'intellectual,' psycho-analyst's heart. Yes, we comprehend the meaning of this world. We understand it. We are not Manichæans, nor Puritans, nor Waldensians, nor Cathari, nor Protestants, putting faith before good works—for matter came from God, and he is the ultimate cause, the origin, the Creator, and eternity. And, to work out this marvellous *Matter*, through him, and for him, is the purpose of this world, this glorious world, which only represents a pale reflection of his glory. For he is a most glorious, infinite God, who permits all that is most frightful and terrible— and pardons; who lets man be born in sin, lets death go about ravening freely, and permits criminals, crucified with his Son, to enter into heaven; who lets courtesans like Mary Magdalen become saints, and lets the visible head of his Son's Mystical Body, like Alexander VI, become a great sinner—for this body, this flesh that is on us, is buried with solemn rites when it is dead, since it was not merely a garment, but was our mission. Oh, Foma Efremovitch, you seem to feel nothing—with you the prostate gland is the axis on which the whole world turns, a loveless, sad, gloomy world; to repress, to satisfy—to repress, to satisfy. Poor Foma Efremovitch!"

Foma Efremovitch nodded gloomily.

"You, too, want to 'educate' me!" he murmured between clenched teeth.

But Nikalai was no longer listening. He was gazing up at the ceiling again.

"Let it melt the coldness of his scepticism, dear Father, Father of us all!" was the semi-articulate cry of his heart. His face was all aglow with a flowing ardour—his eyes were moist.

When the light went out, and a few men near him had already begun to snore, a figure crept, in the dark, towards Nikalai's bed. He propped himself up on his elbows and stared into the darkness.

"It is I!" a hoarse voice whispered. It was Foma Efremovitch.

"Have you come to write your lines?" asked Nikalai, in surprise.

"Drop all that nonsense," panted the other. "Pedagogics —copying, spotted typhus, the programme for Bolshevo and its humanitarian Bolshevism!"

He kneeled down by Nikalai's bed, on the hard floor, and poured excited, jerky words into his ear. Nikalai felt the man's warm breath on his temple.

"I only need *one* assurance," said the shivering Foma, "so listen, Nikalai Sergeyevitch; you are a Catholic, I know; you are courageous, you are a lover of the truth, and I— I am a sad 'complex,' as you once said, yourself. And now I stand on the threshold of a very big, a very critical, decision. Listen, Nikalai Sergeyevitch, you must tell me, just for this once, the whole truth, for everything depends upon it—everything. My whole—future. Yes, let us say, 'future.' I implore you, Nikalai Sergeyevitch, tell me the truth; be brave, no one will hear you."

Foma Efremovitch's teeth were chattering. Without, there was the moaning of a weary snowstorm, and the room was beginning to grow cooler. In Nikalai there glimmered a tiny flame of hope.

"Go on," he encouraged him.

"Listen to me, Nikalai Sergeyevitch. Listen to me!" Foma began again. "I might be a member of the 'extraordinary' police—but, in the name of Science, I swear to you that I am not. And you are a Catholic, that is to say, a brave man, who is not afraid of the 'Dynamo' and the 'Chinese Death.' Be open with me. I have thought about it myself, about you, have weighed everything up, considered everything. You are no ordinary newspaper reporter; perhaps you are not even Nikalai Sergeyevitch Kisseleff;

probably you have not even killed your wife; you bear within you a terrible secret, coolly and fearlessly!"

The speaker's teeth chattered again. Nikalai felt his heart pounding in his throat. His face paled in the chilly darkness.

"A Kisseleff fled from Russia," the voice in the darkness went on. "A Kisseleff fled, and—someone else returned! I no longer quite know how to talk to you. I only know that you are an intellectual, and that gives me courage. And that ought to give you courage, too—for you must realise that when two white men meet among the savages in Africa they will unite against the savages, if they are threatened. But I only want to know, to know for certain: Are you a man from Rome, an emissary, a spy, a daring man who has found his way into the very heart of the domain of the 'extraordinary' police—as an advance-guard, a reconnoitring outpost? Speak! You *must* speak! You are saving me!"

Nikalai turned his face towards Foma Efremovitch. In the darkness, scarcely pierced by a struggling glint of white mist that filtered inward from the window, there sparkled two famished eyes.

"Yes," he said simply, and with surprising calm. "I come from outside."

His fear was almost swamped by his pride.

"The beginning of the end of the Bolsheviks," murmured Foma Efremovitch. "The beginning of the end." Then he felt for Nikalai's hand. "Thanks," he whispered, hoarsely, "a thousand thanks. I am reassured. But you will have no need to be afraid of my gossiping—no need at all, in another twenty-four hours!"

And he vanished in the darkness. There was the sound of a bed creaking. The wind made a clumsy onslaught on the small rattling panes in the double windows. The room smelled of sweat that has dried cold. For a long time Nikalai could not sleep. He tossed restlessly to and fro in his bed—

repentance; a sense of being God-forsaken; cold; foreign pasts——

Not twenty paces from the barracks they found the dead body of Foma Efremovitch hanging from the branch of a low fir-tree. He had hanged himself with his braces a short time before he was due to hand in his imposition. In his pocket they found a farewell letter: "You will never school-master me again, you collectivist swine!" That was what he had written. It was not much.

Foma Efremovitch's end moved Nikalai almost to tears. Among the general dying, his passing went almost unheeded by the others. Only Bludova, who was now seen more and more often in the vicinity of Nikalai, said contemptuously: "An unsocial element!"

CHAPTER XV

DELIRIUM

Two days after Foma Efremovitch was buried, Nikalai complained to Bludova of violent headaches, and a great lassitude of the limbs. In this grey land where the boundaries of personal individuality were so largely obliterated, it was no rare thing for people who had, just the day before, been fighting one against the other, full of hate and fury, to be clasped in one another's arms; for friends to denounce one another to the authorities; relations to rob one another; for deadly enemies, from some enigmatical and ever mysterious remote cause, to seal a compact of undying friendship. A skate-worker, who was supposed to be a friend of the convict family Ilitcheff, started a liaison with the wife, which the husband discovered. The skate-worker had actually been a "bourgeois," and Ilitcheff an officer in a Siberian regiment. One day he caught his friend and his wife together, and began to revile the man furiously; with foul oaths, spittings, blows, and curses, he thrust him out of the house. Then they began to fight, kicking one another, tearing each other's hair out, rolling over and over in the mud, spitting in one another's faces, and ripping one another's clothing off. Finally, they were both bleeding from lips, nose, scalp, and forehead. With curses, they separated. In the evening, however, they sat together once more, with their swollen lips and noses, their foreheads daubed with congealed blood, side by side, in the canteen, drinking kvass and digging bony fishes out of a tin with their oily fingers.

In the same way, that dispute with Bludova had failed to prevent Nikalai and her from meeting. On the very day after their open exchange of words, they met on the edge of the forest, and greeted each other as if nothing had occurred. In time, they had for each other the mutual affection of people who are of similar station, such as often exists between millionaires opposed in financial contest, the leaders of armies, monarchs of rival countries, or high priests of the most diverse cults, and even if Nikalai was not to be restrained from making slighting remarks about Bludova in the presence of others, yet in their faces, when they met, there was to be seen a certain expression of pride which gave the convicts the impression that they both were engaged in the discussion of the welfare and destiny of the camp as if it had been a dead thing, and were proposing cynically Diocletian-like partitions between themselves of their spheres of influence and control.

The abrupt end to which Foma Efremovitch had come— a man who had, for months, lived with him in the fullness of life and reality, brought him to a sense of oppressive dejection. The picture that he had carried within himself of Foma Efremovitch was forcibly deleted and effaced from his recollection. When he thought of Foma now he had to turn his mind's eye forcibly away from the ghastly picture that, in its plastic reality, haunted him disturbingly by day and night—the hanged man, with distorted, livid face, coat that hung with a horribly suggestive ill-fittingness upon the body, dangling fingers, an unnaturally elongated neck, and rigidly fixed calf's eyes. That was all of Foma Efremovitch that was left for him. But Bludova was, in this camp of death, where the population was being smothered out by suicide and sickness, a veritable piece of pulsing vitality. Thus it came about that he renewed contact with her, and, with a small cloud of steam rising before his face, walked with her, wearing a ragged fur coat, through the snow-covered landscape, in eager conversation. On these walks they often sang, but never together. She, with her high-pitched, tinny but assured voice; he, a little out of tune in his untrained baritone; it was warming, and, after so much talking, an agreeable change. His unshaven jaws would open, against the chill wind, and he would sing the song of Mary Star of the Sea:

> *"Ave Maris Stella,*
> *Dei Mater alma,*
> *Atque semper virgo*
> *Felix coeli Porta——"*

It was probably the first time that this hymn had echoed through the sparse woodland, broken with fields of snow. The soft, dreamy melody of the air displeased Bludova, and so she began, defiantly, to sing the air of Kostya the Udarnik.

Bludova had finished her song, and so Nikalai resumed:

> *"Dies irae, dies illa,*
> *Solvet saeclum in favilla:*
> *Teste David cum Sybilla.*
> *Quantus tremor est futurus,*
> *Quando Judex est venturus,*
> *Cuncta stricte discussurus!"*

"Lettish love-songs?" asked Anna Andreyevna, on the way home.

"No," said he, "Catholic hymns."

"You made faces like a love-sick bourgeois on the films, while you were singing," she said. "You were probably thinking of your Burshuanka again? But, apart from that, they're sad songs, and whatever is sad is superfluous and stupid. That's why we've no use for religion—it makes people sad and stupid!" And after a pause, she added, "I find you

so depressed, lately. I suppose you have realised that they'll
never give you a passport, and so you'll never see your
Burshuanka again?   Or could it be this silly business of
Foma Efremovitch?"

"I do not feel well," he said again. "I have no appetite—
I can't get this reptile-feed down at all now. And then, too,
my head hurts. If this damned epidemic were not falling off,
I should fancy the lice had given me the spotted typhus.
But, as it is——" He shrugged.

"Have you seen Dr. Rovinsky?" she asked him, awakening
him suddenly from his train of reverie.

"That swine?   He can go to hell!" he said, angrily.   "I
would rather infect the whole barracks over again!"

"Christian love for your neighbour!" she said.

But he was ashamed of his words, and tried to tone them
down with excuses.

Near the canteen they parted.

"My husband," she said, "is going to Kursk for a couple
of weeks. So won't you spend a night with me? I've got
quite fond of you now——"

Actually, he was a little touched by the warmth that
emanated from this woman's seemingly indifferent words.
He stroked her cheek lightly, and stared away into vacancy.

"That is sweet of you," he said, tonelessly.

Then she thought he was going to shake his head. She
was waiting for some sort of reply. But he turned slowly
around and went away, with a heavy, throbbing head, and
with no word of leave-taking, across the crunching layer of
snow, back to his barracks.

The next evening—a Saturday, by Christian reckoning—
he was suddenly seized with a fit of shivering.

Bezdushnov was the first to discover Nikalai's condition,
and to call the attention of those in the barrack-room with

his reedy, falsetto voice, to the way Nikalai lay, pale and red-nosed, on his bed.

"*Krassnaya lichoradka!*" they screamed, when they saw him, and huddled away together in one corner.

A quarter of an hour later Nikalai was in the "hospital." It was only now that the fever-stricken man realised to what a fateful pass he had come. The vision of the Father from Magnitogorsk whom they had shot in the cellar of the Sverdlovsk hospital came before his eyes. Perhaps he was never to see anything again—not Gertrude, nor his Germany, nor Scapinelli, nor St. Hedwig's Church. Once more death was as close to him as it had been that day a year and a half ago in the militia commissariat in Moscow. He could already see himself killed and buried. He was in the "beginners' room," and could hear the screaming and the cries of the delirious sick. When they had "put him away," not even Bludova, who had found words of warmth to give him, would weep for him. In her eyes, he would seem simply a spy—a creeping, capitalist hireling in disguise. And so he began with all his might, with all the strength that was in him, to fight and battle against the malady. He bit his lips, clenched his fists till his nails dug deep into his flesh, and with all the force of his will, resisted the encroaching exhaustion and undermining of mind and consciousness wrought by the fever. His temperature-curve rose steeply, and he felt like a drowning man whose face is being thrust down beneath the surface of the water by a phantom hand that mercilessly gains more strength and more—until at last all life is quenched in deadly suffocation, until his beating hands, thrashing desperately around, have fallen limply, sinking in the last flicker of their struggle, worn out, exhausted, quivering.

Finally, the searing flame of the fever enwrapped him like a deadly, hot glaze, and beneath the humid, burning

lesh, covered with its red-spotted skin, there hammered
a heart working frenziedly, and a hideously concrete demon
of fear found itself a retired lurking-place.

Sunday dawned, but Nikalai grasped no more than that
of the day's significance. During the night he had vomited
frequently, and the fever was now burning up his exhausted
body with demoniacal relentlessness. Step by step the venom
of the malady was befogging his spirit, his reason, his consciousness of sight and hearing. The decision, long since
paralysed, to resist the onslaught of the fever with all the
resources of his will-power, had paled and faded away in
the fierce fire of the fever itself, leaving not a trace behind.
He was now simply a plaything in the enemy's taloned hands
—a lifeless wooden thing that is tossed about by the waves
of the sea. But the loss of consciousness came quite suddenly
—like an unexpected breaking billow, house-high, unconsciousness crashed down over him and flung him along and
down into its trough. In his ears he could hear a monstrous,
monotonous roaring, that seemed to come, at first, from a far
distance, and that then came rolling over him, a filmy-mass.
And then—the whole barrack-room sank away, the delirious
patients, the smell of carbolic, the corner shrine of Lenin,
and the harassed orderlies, sank away into nothingness.
Hearing, sight, taste, touch, smell—all ceased to function.
His suffering in the world of reality had ceased. All was
ready for the delirium to begin. . . .

He saw the cell in which Fr. Miguel Pro-Juarez, S.J., his
brother Humberto, the engineer Luis Segura, and the worker
Antonio Tirado, sat on their beds on the morning of 23rd
November, 1927. Breakfast still stood untouched on the
window-ledge. Beneath, in the yard, the gendarmes collected round the shooting-range in the glaring sunshine, and
General Cruz spoke with a few officers of police.

Up to two weeks before, four days after the unsuccessful

attempt to assassinate the former president, Obregon.
Miguel Agostino Pro-Juarez S.J., disguised as a mechanic.
had delivered addresses on religion to fifty taxi-drivers
In the previous month he had trained eighty female teachers
employed by the State, and female officials, in Apologetics

Now, however, all four men were lying motionless, after
making their confessions, with hands folded on their breasts
How gaily this morning had started, when Humberto had
laughed blithely and lightsomely over the inanity of their
condemnations by a secret military court! And then,
suddenly, the news had come that now, immediately, that
very morning, the sentence would be carried out. Thus
Luis Segura, the engineer, who during his lifetime had
always been a cool calculator, had been correct when he
bade farewell to his relatives with the words, "In Heaven
we shall meet again!"

Luis Segura had gone to the window, yawned, and with
the bright rays of the sun on his cheeks, had heaved his
mighty chest. Segura was a handsome, tall man, full of life
and energy, and the joy and zest of life, and now he was
pleased, that creole with his bushy eyebrows, his pale white
skin, and his silky black hair, to think that God called him
to himself now, in the midst of his work with the firm of
Luz y Fuerzo, and for Catholic Action, while still young
enough for life not to have become too completely a habit.
With a vigorous, vaulting bound of triumph, he wanted to
spring from this drab life, up—up to Him.

Antonio Tirado had made his confession, buried his head
in the Jesuit's lap, and sobbed. His fate was the worker's
fate—to be credulous and careless, to be torn out of the
crowd, crushed, destroyed, forgotten, punished for things
he never thought of or comprehended. Miguel Pro-Juarez
had stroked his head, and talked to him kindly, calmly.
The whole misery of the deserted, disinherited worker-

class stood before his eyes—and the fight for possession of their souls that was raging through Europe came vividly to his mind. . . .

A lackey tears open the door of the huge and magnificent hall of the Archiepiscopal palace in Paris. A pale young priest enters. Cardinal Verdier is bending over a map of Paris.

"*Mon cher ami*," he says, without looking up, "*Je vous ai fait mander pour vous dire que vous êtes nommé administrateur à— La Maltournée——*"

"*La Maltournée——?*"

"*Charmant présage, du ministère! Où est donc ce pays là?*"

The cardinal's ring-finger is pointing out a spot on the edge of the map.

"*Vous voyez? La porte de Vincennes, Vincennes, Fontenaye-sous-Bois—La Maltournée—il y a un tramway!*"

"*Ah! Et une église?*"

"*Pas encore!*"

"*Un presbytère?*"

"*Vous le bâtirez.*"

"*Un terrain?*"

"*Magnifique!*"

"*Des bienfaiteurs?*"

"*La Providence——*"

"*Des ressources?*"

"*Ma bénédiction!*" . . .

Now there is a deadly silence in the cell. Humberto Pro-Juarez prays—wildly, passionately, with an abandon of fervour. Tensely he turns his gaze away from the food-stuffs, for they are to him, a symbol of the body, from which he has to part. For, with the body, he leaves the perceptible and tangible universe, the scents of flowers, the view of the snowy summit of Popocatepetl, the softness of maidens' tender cheeks, and of caressing music evoked on warm

summer evenings, in lonely haciendas, by mandolin or
banjo. . . .

The face of a calm, mature woman, who is bending over a
man wearing a soutane with the ribbon of the Legion of
Honour in his button-hole. Sister Annunziata, formerly the
Countess Echegaray, one of the most beautiful and wealthiest
women in Madrid Society.

Nossi-Bé. Palms, oscillating dreamily in the soft wind off
the sea. A piercing blaze of fierce light from the tropical sun;
the leper-colony; the man in the soutane has only one eye
left—for the other one has rotted away. His nose has long
been eaten away. So have his ears. Through his cheek the
cavity of his mouth is visible. His feet are bandaged. Sister
Annunziata is busy on his fingerless hand. It is Pére Dupuis,
S.J.

And Fr. Dupuis is speaking:

"I don't, sister, do I? Not exactly look like an Adonis?
In the *Ville lumière* I should hardly be allowed now to ride
on the motor-buses and trams. But the saddest of all is that
I can't nurse my patients now—nor write any articles for the
Ny Feon Ny Marina in Tananarivo. Can't finish my work on
Behaviourism. Ghastly, having to remain so helplessly idle!"

His speech is awkward and difficult—his tongue twisting
distortingly in his wrecked mouth.

Sister Annunziata tears a slit in the end of the gauze
bandage:

"You must pray, Padre—pray, and be patient."

Fr. Dupuis sighs:

"I do pray—but my prayers are as full of distraction as in
my earliest youth. They leave me wearied and exhausted.
St. Augustine has said, 'Our heart is restless till it rests in
Thee, O Lord!' We are all, all of us on earth here, restless,
but——"

His remaining eye begins to glow:

"How beautiful everything will be, beyond——!" . .

In a small provincial town of Central Germany a beer-drinking Philistine in the bar-parlour leaps in startled fright from his drunken broodings.

His pig-like eyes blink suspiciously.

"Beyond—" he grunts. "Where—beyond? In the Golden Goose?"

Beer-froth clings to his walrus moustache. On his waistcoat obsolete coins jingle; he looks at his watch, with a snort.

"Waiter—a portion of sucking-pig, a tankard of beer, and Ludendorff's *Volkswarte!*" . . .

Then the door of the cell is torn open, and jingling with their accoutrements, four armed men march in. Behind them come Mazcorro, the tall, fat chief of the Criminal Police, and the famous detective Quintana. Miguel Agostino Pro-Juarez, S.J., rose from his bed and leaped to his feet.

And Miguel Agostino had a feeling of freedom and untrammelled lightness in his limbs. As if half asleep, he had risen to his feet—he had left off counting how many times his heart had to beat and how often his lungs had to contract for fresh inhalations—he was in peaceful expectancy. As he bade his brother farewell, he pressed his hand briefly—rather as a gesture of solace than of leave taking. They were soon enough to meet again—they were bound for the same destination. Down in the yard, beneath the cross-fire of the Kodaks, Quintana said to him, quietly, disregarding the chief of police: "Can you forgive me?"

Miguel Pro-Juarez stood still for a moment—looked at him with his warm, kindly smile, and replied:

"Not merely do I forgive you—I thank you, many times." . . .

The clear voices of the Carmelite nuns of Lisieux in prayer, vibrating through space.

"And forgive us our trespasses, as we forgive those who trespass against us——" . . .

It was there, blazoned forth in vast letters across the spatial universe. . . .

A small dark cell in the Ogpu building in the Lubyanka, at Moscow.

Shivering and trembling, a prisoner is stripping off his clothes and putting them together. There is a smell of stagnating blood. A Tchekist's voice cries, "Kneel down!" The prisoner kneels down in the dark red, slimy mire.

A hand grasps his hair, and a cold rim presses against the nape of his neck—two seconds later he collapses, with distorted features. . . .

In the electric chair in Sing Sing the outline of a human form, silhouetted against the wall behind. On the air there floats the acrid tang of burned flesh. Low-voiced orders sound. A somewhat distinguished figure, with the face of the well-groomed American gentleman (Colgate's Shaving Stick) is impatient because he is missing a baseball match. . . .

A prisoner in the Balkans. The prisoner is roaring like an animal. There are iron clamps holding him firm. A gendarme approaches with a red-hot iron. . . .

A hangman with a curled moustache, fat, greasy neck, plush hat, a State Official of the Fourteenth Salary Grade, is clutching the feet of the man just hanged, and tugs at the stiffening form of the groaning prisoner, till his face turns blue and his eyes protrude from their sockets.

Again that vast writing:

"As we forgive those who trespass against us." . . .

A young officer is accompanying Miguel Pro-Juarez, the Jesuit condemned to death, to the wall.

"Have you any last wish?" he asked him.

Miguel Pro-Juarez turns his narrow head to face the questioner.

"I should like to pray a little longer *still!*"

The young officer nods hastily.

The Jesuit, in his dark civilian suit, with the light fancy waistcoat, kneels down, draws out his pocket Crucifix and kisses the Stigmata. The prayers of Jesuits are limited as to time—they pray with concentration, not discursively. His prayer is finished. He jumps to his feet, buoyantly and lightly.

Turning to the firing-squad, he blesses them, crying in a loud voice: "Lord Thou knowest that I am innocent. With my whole heart I forgive my enemies."

A short pause follows. Then the young officer, with some embarrassment, asks him whether he shall bandage his eyes.

He thanks the officer, but says that he sees no reason to dispense with the light of his eyes before his death. And then this world and the finite are so beauteous, and the trees that droop their branches down over the wall at his side are, too, simply witnesses of His omnipotence and creative power —no farewell pang embittered his final appreciation of the beauty of this universe.

The officer stood on one side, and the troopers raised their rifles; Miguel Pro-Juarez' earthly, Jesuit career was drawing near to its end. In a few minutes he was to be beyond, with the Saints. Outside the finite scope of the concepts of man and woman, of old and young, the Saints partake of the infinite blisses; with the Saints—with the Martyrs——

The Officer raised his sword, and the flash of the sun on the blade dazzled Miguel Pro-Juarez for a moment. The Kodaks clicked.

"Prepare—to fire!" resounded over the yard.

Miguel Pro-Juarez, of the Society of Jesus, spread out his arms. His pale, slender hands, as he does so, touch the eerie, bullet-riddled target-figures that stood to his right and left and looked like idols.

"Hail, Christ the King!" came, half-aloud, the happy murmur of ecstasy from his lips.

"Hail, Christ the King!" And the officer lowers his sword, and a volley sweeps across the yard. Miguel Pro-Juarez is still standing—but his hands are trembling, and his knees slacken. And then his figure crumples up. The Jesuit's life is over. His knees touch the ground, and the body, wearily, heavily, sinks backwards.

The officer beckons a soldier to him.

The soldier advances with his rifle, and stares down at the quivering body. Stares and stares.

The officer calls someone to him.

He raises his rifle and takes aim at the temple. A hollow, sharp report, and one last tremor runs through the body. Then all around is quiet. Even the Kodaks are silent. Only the cinema-cameras continue cranking.

And now it is hot, broiling hot, in spite of the imminent approach of winter.

Now comes Segura, and with him Mazcorro and Quintana.

Quintana has turned up his coat-collar. They slacken their pace. Only Segura goes forward. He advances smartly, with soldierly gait, as a warrior of the Church Militant who is marching across from the arena of this planet to the Beyond of the Church Triumphant.

He is asked if he has any last wish. But he shakes his head.

He makes the Sign of the Cross. He will not have his eyes bandaged.

With a rigid pose he proffers his bosom to his executioners, placing his hands behind his back.

With a vivid, cool clarity, the man who was hastening down the swift declivity to death in the temporal world, became conscious that he must give thanks to the One above that he was not to be tortured to death like his young friends out in the country districts and the provinces.

"God," his heart whispered up to the infinite heights, "I have served Thee as it has been granted to me to work. I have explored the laws of nature of this universe, I have studied how to put out to the usury Thou willest the talent of gold entrusted to man in his brain——!"

He stiffened his jaw.

"I am ready," he cried. . . .

In the Red Week, from May 1st to the 8th, seventeen priests are standing before an open grave in the cemetery of the little town of Dolores. A volley is fired.

Dead and wounded are tossed together into the open grave. The captain orders the gravedigger to cover the bodies. But suddenly this man bursts out laughing, starts dancing, whirling round on one leg like a drunken man, and tearing his hair. He has gone mad. . . .

Picture follows picture. Jalisco, the Sacristan of Tototlans Abbas Reyes is seized by the soldiers, undressed at the entrance of the church and whipped. Beneath his feet a fire is lit—but he does not betray the hiding-place of his priest. In the cemetery he is shot down.

In Mira Y Salas two priests and a communicant are being shot. They fall together, crying: "Hail, Christ the King!"

In Guadalajara the advocate Gonzales is being stabbed with bayonets.

In the forests of Para nine young factory workers are being hunted down and shot.

In Zamora, Joachim Silva and Manuel Melgarejo, members of the A.C.J.M., and of the sodality, are shot by the orders of Calles. Joachim Silva cries, "Hail, Christ the King! Hail, Virgin of Guadaloupe!" A soldier screams, "I will not shoot! I am a Catholic, like you!" This man does not survive that day. Manuel Melgarejo falls unconscious and is shot as he lies there, on the ground.

In Victoria, in the province of Guanajuato, Maria Guadaloupe Chairez is subjected to a severe cross-examination—scourged. General Saturnino Sedillo orders her to cry, "Hail, Calles!" "Hail, Christ the King!" the woman cries. Then Sedillo has her tortured. Her fingers are broken, her arms dislocated. She is buffeted with blows about the face.

Under the kicks of his soldiers, with the tortured cry of "Hail, Christ the King!" her face streaming with blood, she breathes forth her soul. . . .

"I am ready!" the engineer Segura cries. And the officer lowers his sword. The volley is fired—and Luis Segura's eyes distend. His body quivers with little throbbing impacts. And, suddenly, there is nothing but a frenzy of pain. The sack of the heart is torn—his stomach lacerated, his lungs flooded with blood, his kidneys perforated, his spine broken, his feet paralysed. The pain threatens to rend his body to shreds—and Luis Segura's face is, for a moment, distorted with anguish. His fingers grab groping at nothingness—his knees give way—a curtain of darkness veils his eyes—everything fades out, slips away, is gone. And, suddenly, he feels a great lightness.

Again come Mazcorro and Quintana. The Criminal Police Chief's cloak hangs slipshodly over his paunchy figure. Between them there walks, with short steps, Humberto Pro-Juarez, in his hand a medallion of Our Lady at which he is constantly gazing. Over his face there comes an indecisive look of mingled piety and embarrassment.

Automatically he advances to the wooden target-figures, and sees the corpses of his brother and the engineer. He puts one hand to his side—his tennis pullover shines in the sunlight. To right and left of him the bodies are lying. . . .

In the twilight that lies over the dirty ground in the neighbourhood of Bobigny, a suburb of Paris, a priest beaten almost to death by Communists. His ribs are broken, his soutane torn, and blood is trickling from one corner of his mouth. He turns up his eyes towards the night sky, and his lips murmur, "*O très sainte vierge! Dire non? fuir la parole du représentant de Jésus Christ? Que répondrai-je à l'heure du jugement? Dire non? Ce sera la vie commode—mais dire Oui, ce sera doucement mourir.*". . . .

The officer lowers his sword. And Humberto Pro-Juarez sees the rifle-muzzles flash. Then the little throbbing impacts. Then that pain and weakness that paralyse and make all dark.

Above, in the cell, there remains to the last the worker who has fever—Antonio Tirado. On his forehead there had formed a jelly of cold sweat, and the menacing shadows of a cruel death brought his whole life passing before him in brief, palpitating pictures. Soul-killing work at the factory levers, a few visits to the cinema, and a few girls, a few draughts of pulque and mezcal, a trip to Vera Cruz, and a pilgrimage to Guadaloupe, a silent father, blinded in the factory, who lives out a joyless existence with Antonio's mother, in the workers' settlement, and that old mother, with her quivering voice, and creased hands, racked with toil, over which the skin is stretched taut like dry, brown parchment.

Here they are coming, already, to fetch him. Antonio Tirado's Way of the Cross is beginning. . . .

Out of the darkness the face of the cobbler's son, from the village of Didi-Lilo, in Sakhartvelo, grows to a monstrous size. He screams—and his voice seems to resound through the spatial universe, "Comrades, Comrades! We shall destroy the bourgoisie of the world! *Mooi budem unitchto burzhuaziu!* Comrades, comrades, the turbines of the Dnieprostroy will gain 810,000 horse-power from the dam, the Ford factory in Nishni will deliver 100,000 cars yearly! The Stalingrad tractor works will deliver 40,000 tractors a year! To us belongs the future! The building up of the Socialist State is growing! *Poidyom, tovarishtchi poidyom!*" . . .

Suddenly the Holy Father is standing before the microphone of the ultra short-wave transmitter in the Vatican City, speaking in clear, slow, measured accents: "Our heart is distressed because the economic position of Europe brings millions of our beloved children into material difficulties. Vain was the warning of our predecessor Leo XIII. Now it is necessary to call your attention to the duty which devolves upon every employer to pay his workers a just wage, for the withholding of a just wage is one of the sins that cry to Heaven for vengeance, classed together with premeditated murder and sodomy."

All round the earth is filled with the whirling voices of all nations—the voices of the Catholic University professors in Washington, Pekin, Freiburg, Tokio, Milan, Louvain, Wilna, Salzburg, Ohio, Beyrut, and Namur. . . .

And now the officer asks him his last wish. "His mother—he would like to see her again," he murmurs. That is refused him.

He stood bowed when he was shot. The fever had weakened him. The officer lowered his sword, and he lay quivering like a slaughtered beast of the field, on the ground. The soldier gave him the *coup-de-grâce*, but that wretched, agonised huddle of human flesh was obstinately clinging to life, and with scalp shot to pieces, still whimpers softly, and the suffering eyes are not yet extinguished. The soldier once more raises his rifle, and aims at the back of the neck. Now he is at last to be destroyed. The blood-drenched cloak, with the scalp and head shot into an unrecognisable shattered pulp, are lying still.

A quarter of an hour later, the ambulance cars drive through Mexico City, and force their way with difficulty through the massed hosts of people kneeling and praying.

The corpses of the brothers Pro-Juarez are laid out in their parents' house. Their sisters are weeping. "Children," says their father, a tall, white-skinned creole, "you have no reason to weep."

The next day, the brothers Pro-Juarez are buried. Traffic is paralysed in Mexico City. Houses are decorated with flowers and flags. Tens of thousands follow the coffins. Again and again the masses break out with the cry, "Hail Christ the King! Hail, the martyrs! Long live the Pope!" For hours the street cars are held up.

When the funeral is over, the father of the murdered men intones the Church's great hymn of thanksgiving, the *Te Deum Laudamus*. Tens of thousands join with him in the singing of it.

Segura was buried at the same time in another cemetery. Antonio Tirado is buried on the following day. Six young workers carry the coffin. Once more the traffic is paralysed. Flags flutter, and, from the close-packed onlookers, there resounds the cry, "Hail the Martyrs of the Working Class!" He is interred by the side of Segura. Shoulder by shoulder lie the mortal remains of the working man and the engineer who are resting together in Christ.

More and more chaotic became Nikalai's visions as the fever burned. Once more he saw "Koba," the "little father" Stalin, standing before the microphone, but a voice cried, interrupting, "This is something that good society will not tolerate!"

Then, suddenly, he was in Sir Ralph Eagerley's study at Morston Hall. Sir Ralph was leaning back in his armchair, stroking the well-kept white moustache that breaks the redness of his face, and speaking to his son.

"——to be a gentleman. In business life, in family matters, in dealing with women. A gentleman never gets emotionally carried away. He cultivates the traditional repose of his caste, is a true son of his native country, and of the Church of England, pays his taxes punctually, is always just, sober, and——"

Like a flash the picture was gone. The Budapesth beer-house on the Vàno'mház-Körut, where fat Philistines were talking excitedly at one another, sprang back into his vision. They were all members of the Turanic Archers organisation.

"We don't want any Hapsburg on our throne!" cried Mr. Bendeguz Bodrogközi-Bemmerlſeind, "We want a Mongolian prince!"

"That's right!" said Mr. Csaba Würmsieder, banging his fist on the table. "The future belongs to the Mongolian race!"

Meanwhile, the Sokols are marching through Prague, singing:

> "*Tak vám vojna lidozerna vládce*
> *tak vlast neroztrhnou chytráci*
> *a vas národ prvnî bude v krátce*——"

And in Berlin the soldiers:

> "*Deutschland, Deutschland, über alles,*
> *Über alles in der Welt*——"

And in Guatemala, schoolchildren with their feet and brown calves bare, are singing the State Hymn, before the Emblem of the Parrot:

> "Higher than the eagle shalt thou soar,
> First 'mid all the lands of earth, Guatemala——"

A shooting-range in Turkmanistan. Kirgisian women are manning machine guns. The instructor's voice sounds above the infernal noise:

"Lift your sights, women comrades!   Number three, attention! Ready! Three hundred rounds. Fire!" . . .

The Holy Father: "——economic position of millions of our children in severe material difficulties—Leo XIII—*Rerum Novarum*—*Quadragesimo Anno*—duty of every employer to give his workers a just wage——" . . .

The Catholic professors: "——prohibition of usury—regulation of Capitalism—Canon Law——" . . .

The sun over Santa Catalina on the cost of California. The multi-millionaire S. Goldfeather's villa. A film actress bathing in champagne. A few figures in evening dress among the guests are eating caviare with a soup-spoon. . . .

China.   On the banks of the Hoang-Ho forty million people are threatened with death by famine. . . .

Brazil.   Two million kilograms of coffee are tipped into the sea. . . .

Chicago. Speculators are deliberately inflating the price of corn. . . .

Versailles, Trianon, Neuilly, St. Germain. Madmen and criminals are devising a satanic new order of things for Europe. . . .

Operetta in Vienna. Husband is deceiving wife. Wife catches him. They take up their positions side by side and sing together. The music cuts in. Captain of Hussars, Baron, Jew. Six girls come on to the stage and kick their legs up. Grins under their corpse-like make-up. A man with black coat-tails, top-hat, and small walking-cane bawling behind the prompt-box to create atmosphere. A bedroom. Cami-knickers. A tenor. Reconciliation. Monocle. Curtain. Public—enthusiastic. . . .

Miguel Agostino Pro-Juarez, S.J., stretching out his

arms. Steel-cased bullets. Death. "Hail Christ the King!" . . .

The Corso of a great city. Young sirens in hats adorned with the plumage of birds are swaying from the hips. A terrible tension prevails on the pavements. Of the elegant murmurs only a few words are distinctly audible:

"Hullo, how are you, fellow? I was with a wonderful little woman yesterday. Do you know, dear, she had such a piquant Paris combination—a *good* woman, I tell you. So charmed to have met you, dear lady—is that so? The engagement is already announced! They were given 'noble' rank as long ago as the thirteenth century—give me the satisfaction of a gentleman, of course—to-morrow there is a bridge at-home at Winkelmeyer's." . . . .

Miguel Agostino Pro-Juarez, S.J., stretching out his arms. Steel-cased bullets. Death. "Hail Christ the King!" . . .

Voice: "Three no trumps——" Answer: "Pass!" . . .

Nearer and nearer draws the singing of the Internationale: "Arise, accursed of the earth——" . . .

The Fascist hymn breaks in: "*Giovinezza, Giovinezza, prima-vera di bellezza!*" . . .

The Nazi march: "*Der Furcht so fern, dem Tode so nah, Heil Dir S.A.!*" . . .

The Papal hymn: "Thou who dost bear the torch of truth——" . . .

The voice of Stalin: "Comrade, comrades—six million kilowatts! Thirty million motor-cars! Ten million tractors! Five million tons of coal! A hundred and eighty thousand horse-power! We will destroy the world-bourgeoisie—we are collectivist building-stones on the collectivist road to the collectivist future! Comrades, comrades, comrades——"

A voice intervenes, remarking: "We didn't learn that at school, most respected Herr Kommerzialrat!" . . .

The earth quakes. . . .

The voice: "That's all a lot of exaggeration. Waiter! A black coffee!"

The Kremlin is bathed in red light. Above the Vatican glows the Cross. A voice: "I kiss your hand. Shall I cash the draft?" . . .

The Heavenly Hosts moved forward to the attack. . . .

Voice: "And the police do nothing to forbid that sort of thing——! What do we pay taxes for?" . . .

Louder and louder swells the roar of the Papal Hymn.

Voice: "Interdenominational peace in religion should be maintained. I don't give more than fifteen bob for a night, miss!" . . .

The hosts of Christ and the hosts of Antichrist clash in conflict. . . .

Voice: "Frau Pilaffke, the wife of the Director of the Sirius Co., Ltd., and the mistress of Joe Falkner, wore, at the Press Ball, a red velvet coatee with ermine trimmings." . . .

Terrifying noise. Singing through the whole spatial universe. . . .

Voice: "Lord, man, this'll put guts into you. Down the hatch!" . . .

The Cross is irradiating the entire world. The Papal Hymn merges into the *Te Deum Laudamus*. Nikalai hears the concluding chords.

"He that is not with me is against me." . . .

Everything fades out and is gone. Gone are the Berlin and Pesth and Vienna and Prague cafés and sport clubs. Only the Cross remains.

Ave, o Crux, spes unica!

Mass was being celebrated on the ocean steamship *Saturnia*, off Gibraltar, in the sometime hall of the Sieten barracks at Berlin, in inns and hotels, in gymnasiums, exhibition halls, and negro kraals, and on the Canadian Express. High up in Canada, on the shores of the foaming Yukon, Fr. Bernard

Hubbard, S.J., on his geological expedition to explore volcanic action, offered the sacrifice of the Mass under the open sky. But Nikalai was tortured, now, ever and anon, constantly, with pictures inspired by the Evil One in the exhaustion of his fever. He was conscious of nothing. He heard nothing of the prayers which the priest pronounced as he bent over the altar in the Chapel of the *Charité* to which had gone the not yet completely exhausted but already death-doomed patients of "AC" barracks. The visions that he had seen before in unquestionable clarity and realism and had so fully comprehended, had now vanished—and the confusion of utter chaos broke over him. Scapinelli stood before him, a "corpse of Loyola"—as Foma Efremovitch always designated the Jesuit—stood before him with cheeks rotted away, eye-sockets worm-eaten, and hands putrescent like soft cheese. Half-naked women danced around before him and called out bawdy words at him. And then he was delivering Communist speeches, arm-in-arm with Bludova, before St. Hedwig's Church in Berlin, and singing the Hymn of the Hundred and Fifty Millions, drinking the pledge of fraternity with Stalin in a café of a Viennese suburb, struck him in the abdomen, where green-slimed water gurgled, and then ran away, pursued by a bolting horse on two feet—ran, with feet heavy as lead, and legs that dwindled ever shorter and shorter, as far as Lachistan where, screaming and bellowing, he implored the protection and help of old men who were eyeing him with suspicious glances.

Then he saw the summit of the Vartchembek. He began to climb the mountain—but the mountain-side was smooth, ice-covered, glassy, oily. He kept slipping back and down again. He broke his finger-nails—lived through all the grades and stages of fear—almost died from discomfort and terror and despair—until, eventually, they arrested him.

"They" were Tchekists, disguised as romantic ghosts, with veils, rubber gloves, pointed shoes, and black tights painted with skeletons. He was standing, suddenly, in his nightshirt, before the judge, who was an unpleasant Near-Eastern Asiatic, with curly black hair, and a military, and yet oleaginous, reedy, shrill voice. His was a real, West-European, long, white nightshirt. He lost sight of the judge —and was dragged out to be tortured and beheaded; and the excitement made him red, though he had soft, swollen hands, and hoofs for feet. Then he began screaming shrilly and automatically, like an iron siren. Along this unmusical monotone he groped his way, as along a rope, into the realm of completely pictureless unconsciousness. Like a ruffled sea, his blood rustled in his ears. Then shadows drifted down over him—and with the shadows came silence, emptiness, nothingness.

When he awoke he opened his eyes with difficulty—and stared straight before him, up at the ceiling of the room. The sombreness of the wooden planks reminded him of his deserted state, of the remoteness of everything that was dear, precious, and congenial. Not even gratitude to the Almighty One above, who had left him his life, had saved him from the worst crisis of the fever, and the persecutions of his enemies took possession of him who lay there, "with half a propeller" (as Sonnenschein once expressed himself) on sweat-moist, torn linen, stained with blood and squashed vermin. His gaze was still fixed rigidly on the ceiling, when there came to his mind the words of the psalm: "*Sudi mi, Bozhe, i, razsudi priu moyu, o yauzika neprepodobna . . . . Judica me, Deus, et discerne causam meam de gente non sancta; ab homine iniquo et doloso erue me. Quia tu es Deus fortitudo mea: quare me repulisti? et quare tristis incedo dum affligit me inimicus?*"

This was no prayer that came from him—it was but a reflective echoing of a quotation. He turned his head aside, and saw Bludova. She sat in concrete reality beside his bed, on a chair, and had gone to sleep. Her head drooped forward, chin resting on her breast, and her breathing fluttered over the surface of her blouse.

"She must have been sitting there a long time," he thought. Anna Andreyevna did not stir him. He was filled with bitterness and homesickness. A nausea at Russia seized him. He began pitying himself and complaining. He would have liked to weep now, over himself. He had come there young, audacious, high-spirited, to this grey country for a lightning-trip of six weeks' duration, had stayed here two years, had suffered, for two years, hunger and bugs and suspicions and the fear of death, spotted typhus, prison, the convict settlement, the third degree, temptation, boredom, uselessness; and in exchange for all that he had two things: the bitterness of experience, and his love for Gertrude, of the outcome of which, and the part it was to play in the shaping of his future life, he knew nothing. In this "comfort-my-soul" mood, the affection of Anna Andreyevna was a matter of utter indifference to him. Her presence only brought his thoughts to Gertrude. And to remember Gertrude, full of longing, full of despair, impotent, meant longing to get away from this place, to flee, to return to his native land, to make his way into the realm of unfulfillable desires, of castles in the air, of unsatisfied yearnings.

One day the fever suddenly subsided after a violent rise. The red spots paled, the doctor was satisfied. He was on the road to convalescence. When he got up for the first time, and, accompanied by Bludova, returned with trembling feet to the barracks, where he eyed the furnishings and appointments with gloomily and hostilely appraising eyes, he was addressed by a strange man, carrying a queer-shaped box, and shown an authorisation signed by the camp Governor for him to take "while-you-wait" photographs of the "respected citizens in the camp" at a rouble-and-a-half-each.

"The other citizens have already had themselves immortalised in this way, long ago," he told Nikalai.

Nikalai did not want anything to do with it. But Anna Andreyevna urged him to agree.

"I do so want to have a photo of you," she said, "I have nursed you—and I think you might make a small 'sacrifice' for me."

Nikalai made the "sacrifice." He sat down by the window, with his legs crossed. But he was forced to change his position, because his leg began trembling convulsively. He set his hands on his knees, and tried to sit up straight. After a short pause, Anna Andreyevna received the photograph. He took a hasty glance at it, and asked for another one for himself.

Towards evening the men returned from the factory and congratulated him on his convalescence.

Nikalai sat apart from the others, on the edge of his bed, and was holding the still damp photograph in both hands.

"That is you!" he said to himself. "In Arabic, *Tat twam asi!*" The photo showed him a grey, embittered, gloomy criminal, with unshaven cheeks.

"On the evidence of my appearance alone, I deserve four weeks' imprisonment," he told himself, "or even the torture-chamber. Or even the cemetery."

Self-pity brought a choking lump into his throat. His eyes were moist.

"Away!" he thought, as he undressed. "Simply to get away from here!"

The bed creaked. With his heart full of unjust feelings of hatred for Anna Andreyevna, who was trying to make life pleasant for him, he went to sleep. He did not want to feel under any obligation to anybody.

"Let the ruin fall in!" he murmured, shivering beneath the blanket. The hunger for Gertrude gnawed at him. A Cossack played, in spite of the furious hissing and curses o a few tired workers, on his balalaika, a very "suspect" song, by Lermontov, in which even God was mentioned and racial hatred for the Tchetchenstses was inflamed.

> *"Spi mladenetz moi prekrassny*
> *Bayushki-Bayu*
> *Tikho smotrit messiatz yassny*
> *V Kolybel tvoyu. . . ."*

The song cheered Nikalai with a grateful warmth. "Hail, our life, our sweetness, and our hope; to thee do we cry, poor banished children of Eve, to thee do we send up our sighs, mourning and weeping in this valley of tears."

CHAPTER XVI

DELIVERANCE

WHEN he awoke one morning, and the sun, a shy, dull, early spring sun, shone with accustomed boredom, sombre and in conformity with rules, through the uncleansed window-panes of the barracks, he had no intimation of the alteration in his destiny that this day was to bring him. The day before he had violently quarrelled with Bludova, and had tried to prove to her that a Christian even was capable of doing just as much work as a Red work-obsessed neurotic Bezbozhnik, to which Bludova obstinately replied that the Christians only want to be always going to Church, but recoil from every job of work, as a result of inner conviction and innate cowardice. The dispute had been carried on very excitedly—neither of them had conceded an inch.

In the morning he went to the factory as usual, and returned in the late afternoon and wanted to withdraw into his barrack. Then Khrapov come towards him, and told him that they were to betake themselves to the pool. An order had been issued announcing that a "big bug" from the Gossplan was delivering an address. The Udarniki were to be decorated, and so on. In the vicinity of the pool, where under other circumstances there was often a good deal of fun going on, as it was where they went skating in the winter, the convicts stood, silently craning their necks, and listening to the speech of the man from Moscow, on the timber harvest in the North, and the part played by the woodcutter in the scheme of the Piätiletka.

The lecturer stood on a chair, round which stood a number of other men from Moscow, with the Governor, the President of the Camp Soviet, and Bludova. The men eyed one another with suspicious looks. Why did the emissary of the Gossplan talk about the lack of workers in the North? That did not bode well for them. A few Tchekists, too, were sitting round, with revolvers, under the eaves of the wooden summer-house. The speaker, however, did not spin out his words, but soon brought his appeal to a close with a few inflammatory sentences.

"Therefore, comrades," he said, "it is obvious, from what I have already said, that the welfare of the State depends on the successful carrying out of the forest work in the North. The whole Soviet Union follows, with bated breath, the victorious labours of the working proletariat in the northern governmental district. The timber worker is the true hero of labour. Therefore he lives a better life than any other worker, and gets the highest rate of pay in the U.S.S.R., 225 roubles. Comrades, join up in the ranks of the hard-working Proletariat of the Forests!"

Then the Governor spoke, and announced to the men that it was open to everybody to join the army of the working proletariat of the timber and sawmill industry. Bludova, too, delivered a speech, shrilly declaimed something about the victorious conquests of the world bourgoisie by the proletariat in her tinny voice:

"With every tree that you fell, you kill a Capitalist—with every forest glade, a family of Capitalists—with every thousandth Desyatine, a capitalist State!"

But it was all without effect.

"Should I go?" asked one young convict, in low tones, of a comrade.

In reply the latter only tapped his forehead.

"I'd sooner go back to the Butürka!" exclaimed another man near Nikalai.

The men made sullen faces.

Bludova began to speak again. Just flung a few sentences at the crowd. But not a soul stirred. A few smiled mockingly, and thrust their hands into their pockets.

Then Nikalai stepped forward.

Bludova's words of the day before were still in Nikalai's mind. With shoulders hunched onesidedly he thrust his way through the close-packed crowd of listeners, and took up his position, with feet spread wide apart, before the speaker's chair.

"Where is this trip to, anyhow?" he asked, cheekily.

"You can choose, comrade," replied the emissary from the Gossplan, glad to find somebody showing interest in his proposal. "Kem, the Upper Kama district, the Syriänan district, the Petchora . . . ."

"Kem!" exclaimed Nikalai, "how lovely it is there. By the sea. In the summer, under the midnight sun. In the winter, polar lights, good food. Beautiful Karelian women!"

Bludova looked at him in astonishment.

The workers, too, were in the dark as to what Nikalai was getting at.

He was supposed to be an enemy of the administration, and now he was talking as if he were a paid propagandist.

"Do you see, comrade?" He turned, now, to the emissary of the Gossplan, "I can tell you why none of my comrades volunteer for this work—they are all lazy, stinking lazy! And do you know why they are lazy? No?"

The Governor and Bludova eyed one another with amazement.

"They are lazy because they are atheists," Nikalai continued, in didactic tones. "I have warned the Governor often enough that he ought to stop the propaganda of the Bezboshniki. The men are all demoralised."

The Gossplan man was intensely irritated.

THE GATES OF HELL

"What is it you actually want?" he asked dryly.

"I volunteer for work in Kem," said Nikalai.

"You?" asked Bludova, from the chair, "*You?* Surely, not *you!*"

"Yes—I!" replied Nikalai.

"Bravo!" said the Governor, under his breath.

Bludova almost fell from her chair. Her eyes grew moist.

"You're doing this to me on purpose," she whispered, almost inaudibly.

"She's in love," the men whispered to one another.

"I'll come with you at once," said Nikalai, with malicious matter-of-fact simplicity.

He turned round there and then and went into the barracks to get his things. The snow crunched beneath his heavy footsteps.

Feverishly he grabbed his things together in the barrack-room, and tied them up in a bundle with cord. In the doorway he collided with Anna Andreyevna, who had chased breathlessly after him.

"You've done this on purpose!" she gasped.

"Certainly," he said, mockingly.

"You've gone mad! "she exclaimed. "I shan't let you go away. You're not going to be allowed to do for yourself, for the sake of a mere pose. At the timber work the men die off like flies."

"You should have mentioned that in your speech," he replied, maliciously. "I am rather lusting for Bolshevik martyrdom. Farewell!"

He wanted to go, but she stood herself in his way.

"I can have it all cancelled!" she cried, desperately. "Simply on account of that silly argument last night, you're not going to . . . ."

He shoved her mercilessly to one side, and departed.

An hour later he was already seated in a carriage of the

electric train to Moscow, and leaned out of the window. Outside Bludova was standing, the tears running down her cheeks unchecked.

"I love you—I do love you!" she sobbed.

"Love, Comrade Anna Andreyevna," he instructed her, in a dry tone, "is, as you told me yourself, nothing more than a physical process determined by the nervous system, nutrition, and inner secretions. You must find sexual satisfaction—how, is a matter of indifference—"

The train moved off, leaving the weeping woman alone. And he sat back in his place, and stacked his bundle beneath the seat. The train was hopping over the joints in the line, between patches of forest, and there came to him, too late and uselessly, a deep pity for Bludova. It was only now that he realised how harshly and vengefully he had treated her, a fellow-being, a sister; doubly pitiful because of her lack of God. Only the thought of the possible opportunity for flight, for returning to freedom, for meeting Gertrude again, crushed down in him the welling up of a feeling of regret and sorrow at his own action.

A miserable life, as they had prophesied for him in Bolshevo, began, high up in the North, on the upper course of the Kemi-Joki. Of the promised 225 roubles he was only paid out 25. Most of the workers, however, considered this perfectly natural. They eagerly signed the receipt for the full sum, and were then glad to get the ninth part of it. Nikalai showed his dissatisfaction. For his toil-worn hands and knees, his rheumatism, and hunger, he wanted better payment.

"Why do you put up with this?" he asked the workers.

A syphilitic with his nose missing remarked that everything was in order.

"We only have to sign the paper, and then we get twenty-five roubles," said another man.

"Twenty-five roubles for a signature; that's quite nice!" remarked the man without a nose.

"But it is written on that paper that you've had two hundred and twenty-five roubles," Nikalai urged, provocatively.

"Really?" asked one man. "I've never read it through properly."

"I can't read or write," confessed the syphilitic.

"That's just for the statisticians at Moscow," observed a third man. "For their purposes, they have to have large figures." And with that the conversation ended.

The reason he wanted to go to Karelia was that this country was supposed, among the "observers" and international spies, to be a "way out" of the Soviet Union. From the Finnish side it was easy to strike one's way through the woods. But it was dangerous to "arrive," to show oneself in any village, to approach the railway line, or, above all, to make any use of the railway. The south and the east of Soviet Karelia were overrun with Tchekists, and anybody who was not a native and yet did not belong to the G.P.U. was, from the outset, a highly suspicious character. But to pass as a native it was absolutely essential to be master of the Karelian dialect of Finnish. And that demanded at least three times as long as the study of Russian. For those, however, who had offered themselves as volunteers, it was child's play to get across to Finland. All one needed was an authorisation, good feet, and a bag of dry bread, to dip into water before eating it, and a knuckle-duster for possible frontier-guards. With every step of ground one covered one was getting farther away from the haunts of the Karelian G.P.U., and penetrated deeper and deeper into the realms of forests, bogs, lakes, and uninhabited waste-lands.

As the crow flies, the Finnish border was not more than 115 kilometres away, and during the winter any attempt at flight seemed senseless. They could pursue one with dogs, and then one was done for. In the spring, after the snow had melted, wild woodlands were covered with slime, the lakes often overflowed their shores, and progress was extremely difficult. In summer, one would be devoured by innumerable mosquitos.

All the same, the summer was the only season in which Eugen could chance the flight. On a June evening, at ten o'clock, scantily supplied with provender, he crept out into the bright northern night of the forest. In a safe spot he unfolded the map he had with much difficulty obtained, laid his compass on it, and set off walking, putting forth all his energies, along the shores of the Kuitti Lake towards the land of the Finns, towards freedom and Europe.

Antilla is a small village in Northern Finland, not far from the frontier. In front of the wooden huts of this little market hamlet a starving tramp, whose body was only covered with a few scanty rags, collapsed silently. The peasants picked him up, succoured him, let him sleep, and then asked him questions. The vagrant first said his name was Nikalai Sergeyevitch Kisseleff, then thought better of it and said it was Yevgheni Robertovitch Düring. This did not seem a clear or straightforward case. One always had to be careful about fugitives from the country across the frontier. The village mayor understood a little Russian. But Nikalai's story was a little too confused for him. Two stalwart men brought him to the Kianta Lake and from there along by the water to Suomussalmi. The Pastor there even spoke German, had once been to Berlin, and could not conceive that Eugen could be a German, a "Saksa." He shook his white, curly head. What Eugen spoke was a

mixture of German and Russian.   And, besides that,
Eugen was a "katolilainen," a Catholic; that was really too
"suspect."   He asked him whether he could read, and
showed him the Holy Scriptures. Eugen not only read, but
even cited the parallel passages; that made him still more
suspect.

The good Pastor observed that it must be forbidden to
good Catholics to read the Bible.

A few hours later Eugen was seated in a car, being driven
along a rough main road through pine and birch-woods.

In Kontiomäki he was transferred to the railway; his fair-
haired taciturn companions marvelled at his high spirits
and gaiety.   The wooden seats were hard, but everything
was clean, bright as a new pin, aired, and sweet. They had
given him clothes and allowed him to take a bath at Antilla.
He felt himself wonderfully re-born, and began whistling,
whereupon his companions made severe faces, and cried
out, "*Eiole.*"

In the evening he was in Kuopio. At the police station he
was interrogated. Telegrams were dispatched to Berlin and
Helsingfors.

At midnight the replies came, and Eugen was set at liberty.
Through the bright nocturnal streets he went, accompanied by a police officer, into the "*Seurahuone*," the leading
hotel in the city.

The next day he wired for money, ordered new clothes
from a tailor's, went for a walk on the green peninsular of
Väinölänniemi where the sports grounds, bathing pools, and
casino of the city were situated, spoke to a girl student with
a short skirt that blew about in the wind, a white cap
decorated with a lyre, and long flaxen hair, and invited her
to come and eat with him, eventually having supper with
her at the Casino.

"You look just like Gertrude," he assured her. But she

did not resemble the latter in the least; she merely had a
clear skin, healthy teeth, and a slim body. But that was
sufficient for Eugen, absolutely. She was something beautiful,
white, human. And after his two years of wretchedness
among the heretics that completely fascinated him.

"Who is that Gertrude?" she asked him.

"Something like a sweetheart of mine," he told her, and
laughed to himself with some embarrassment.

As he did not dance, they soon rose, and went out into the
bright night. Her face, her hair, her dress were in white
contrast with the dull darkness of the trees and bushes.
Between the gaps in these the glittering night sky was
reflected in the lightly rippling waters of the Kallavesi. He
took her arm, whispered to her, that for him she was now
Gertrude, and drew in the perfume of her cheeks and hair.
The dried fir-cones from the trees crackled on the ground
beneath their elastic tread, and, now and again, she would
look questioningly into his face. The eyes that were turned
towards him were of such a rare limpidity and translucency
that he began telling her about himself, his experiences and
his feelings. She lived at the end of the Maaherrankatu, in a
spacious stone house. She invited him inside, but he refused,
for he was afraid of the glare of the artificial light. So they
sat down on the stone steps that led up to the door of the
forecourt, and talked together in soft tones. He immersed
himself completely in the world of his bitter experiences.
But as he did so his mouth expanded more and more in a
smile expressive almost of happiness. It was all over—yes,
all over! All past and done with—and not a trace was left,
as if a ghost had vanished after the stroke of midnight.

"You tell of such terrible things," said she, "and yet you
are laughing at it all."

"Because I am so happy," he said.

"Because it is over?" she asked.

"Because it is over and I am with you again," he said "with you—you women and girls."

She laughed softly.

"There!" he said. "Now I am going to do something that is not quite proper—and I hope you're not going to mind!" And, with that, he laid his head on her lap, and looked laughingly up in her face.

"There you are, Miss Ilma Koskinen," he said, and drew the astonished girl's face down by one curl of her hair. "Now I will go on telling you——"

They did not part until they had almost fallen asleep, leaning over one another as they sat there.

He went with Ilma Koskinen up on the Puijo, a low granite hill overgrown with woods, north of the town, from which could be seen a magnificent panoramic view stretching far across the country. Up to the distant horizon nothing was visible but lakes and forests, with only here and there a modest pool or two. But the soil here was not sand, as it is in North Germany, but granite and some quartz, on which lived a clear-sighted and sober people, conscious of their purposeful trend. After the forced sojourn among the sectarians, these people were for Eugen veritable angels. They were neither fixed in their groove, nor did they persecute to death those of another persuasion, nor did they spy on and denounce one another. To Eugen they were absolutely angels, neither more nor less. In their land one did not notice, at every turn, at every street corner, the menacing fist of the State, the State's militarised women with police revolvers, the officious and tyrannical State officials, the office Napoleons of bureaucracy. Tcheka informants, street speakers, State poets, billposters, vermin-hunters, and instructors; rich, full-bodied sea air seemed to blow into the most remote quarters of Finland. Lofty buildings were

constructed of granite, men loved clear-eyed women,
delighted in ski-ing, yachting, aviation, motor-boating,
lived in friendly sobriety, and had a quiet joy in all these
inventions of modern times.

Ilma Koskinen accompanied Eugen back to Helsingfors.
He went with her to the Evangelical Hostel, immediately
called the porter's attention to the fact that he was a convinced Papist, which the porter generously forgave him, and
that he had a special reverence for the Jesuits, which this
man' did not readily find credible. Yet he felt thoroughly
comfortable among the Protestants in the "*Kristillinen Matkailijakoti,*" the Evangelical Hostel. In his present mood
he would have fallen on the neck of even an orthodox
Mohammedan or a Jew. But here there breathed—and he
could most distinctly feel it—the *anima Christi.* Here, in the
chapel of this hostel, a very Protestant Christ was painted in
fresco on the wall, above a harmonium. But nevertheless it
was Christ, Jesus Christ, not Ordshonikidse, or Molotoff,
Lenin, or Bakunin. In this Protestant house Eugen found,
for the first time, a Bible, again. And although he did not
understand the language, he turned the leaves feverishly.
He was touched, too, by their friendliness. The female
employees, who, during the day, silently and servicefully,
lived for their work, in aprons and caps, but in the evening
donned silk stockings and enjoyed social pleasures. He was
utterly happy at the opportunity of living among these
people, and, sometimes, he had the feeling that he would
like, sentimentally, to fall on the necks of the people in the
house, in order to tell them that he forgave them everything,
their sectarianism, and their heresy; he thought it beautiful
that they should be so good and that they ought to endeavour,
if it could not be otherwise, to become saints in their own
way. He visited with Ilma the big multiple stores, cashed
some drafts in a Osake-pankki, a Joint Stock Bank, and

strolled round the German Legation, drank tea with a family of Ilma's friends, ate in the café-Fazer, and went—this time by himself, without her—and turned his mind inward on himself, in St. Henry's Church, in the Vuorimie-henkatu. For a long while he knelt there, with his hands in front of his face, in one of the empty pews. For the first time in two years he had approached the Saviour in the Tabernacle. A sorrowful path that had been from the Lazarist monastery at Trebizond to the church of St. Henry at Helsingfors.

On the day before his departure he went with Ilma Koskinen out to Klippan, an island with a hotel, facing Helsingfors. They ate and drank, went out into the night, watched the searchlights of the lighthouses, and sat down on the steeply shelving shore, on which the sea waves struck and rebounded, wearily and heavily, their force broken by the tumbled and scattered cliffs.

The breeze wafted, cold, across from Suomenlinna, and he rubbed his stiffening fingers.

"Are you cold?" she asked him, and, when he assented, she laid half her mantle across his shoulder, and put her arm about his neck. He felt in his heart a great peace—its only remaining longing, for reunion with Gertrude, to see her again, and for the sisterly love that she gave him. Otherwise, he was so completely without desires, that his inclination was to move neither forward nor backward along life's road, but to sit on for ever, here on the smooth stone, motionless and without thought, and let time brush gently past him, and, as sole nutriment, to taste the gifts of the present moment, and drain them to the last dregs.

On the following day, he crossed over to Reval by boat, admired the beautiful old Gothic cathedrals of Catholic days, and then journeyed further south, to Riga, where, for the first time since his days in Lefortova, he heard the sound of

Lettish words.   From there, he went through Dünaborg and Wilna to Warsaw. The straight road to Germany was forbidden him, for the Lithuanians were not well-disposed to him, owing to his articles on the persecution of the Ataiti-ninkai, a Catholic Guild of Youth.   On the way to the Polish frontier, fine sand seeped through the cracks of the doors and windows, into the compartment. The uniform, of English khaki, worn by the Esthonians, had been suc-ceeded by the Swiss accoutrements of the Letts. A queer country was this Latvia—a Prussianised, Socialistic-Nationalist, militaristic, democratic, naval, flat Switzer-land.   At Krustspils came the beginning of Latgal, and with it—on the same latitude as Edinburgh—the un-broken continuum of the Catholic population of Europe. Further and further the train penetrated into the heart of Europe. He was drawing nearer and nearer to the huge capitals—to Warsaw, to Berlin, to Prague, to Lódz; to the factories and the unemployed, the cafés and the gasworks, the publishing offices, the hospitals, the crematoria; to sexual crime, to central prisons, to street-women, stock-exchanges, mental defectives' institutions, slaughter-houses, and police stations. With his yearning to see Gertrude again, there was mixed a timid homesickness for Suomi, the Canada of Europe, the land of the thirty thousand lakes, of the pine forests and waterfalls, and sparkling nights—for all that he saw here reminded him again, remotely, of Russia, and anything that recalled the U.S.S.R. filled him with an almost morbid nausea and hatred. In Berlin he stood still awhile before the station exit, dazzled by the glare of lights, as though spellbound; and then only did he carefully set one foot before the other.   •

It was about half-past eight. And on the Friedrichstrasse the night-life was already in full swing. He was confused, excited, horrified—the excess of eroticism struck him with extraordinary force—the vast numbers of prostitutes, the placards, the clothes, the gestures and movements of the people, the books in the brightly-lit shop-windows. Uncertainly, and oppressed with a sense of inferiority, he moved along the pavements. Crimson-lipped mouths whispered words in his face—electric sky-signs flashed on and off, silk-stockinged feet tripped to and fro before him. Posters announced the appearance of a female impersonator—metal signs recommended contraceptive appliances—and, in a book-shop near Unter den Linden, there was a special display of flagellantic, masochistic, and sadistic books and pictures. Eugen suddenly felt himself a nobody, a little wisp of humanity buffeted about and never asked for his opinion, who had to obey the traffic-policeman's signals, and pay the utmost heed to the deadly rush of the infinite variety of motor-buses and cars, if he valued his life. He had to use all his strength of will to go his own way and not be carried along by the murmuring, whispering, unknown crowds. First he meant to call on Scapinelli, hoping not to find him in, then to embrace his mother briefly, and then, at once, to ride out on his motor-bicycle to Brühlau, that very night, and, if need were, to arouse Gertrude from her sleep.

Sooner than he had imagined possible he was standing before Scapinelli's house, and hurried in with long strides, taking two stairs at a time, up to the Jesuit's apartment.

He gave a slight knock at the hall door, merely to assure himself that his knock would not be answered. And he was already on the point of turning away, when, out of sheer conscientiousness, he tried the handle of the door—and, to his great disappointment, the door opened. He knew, now, that he would not see Gertrude that evening. In that disappointment, afforded him by the open front door, there lay the whole premonition of a great disaster. The destruction of his anticipated time-table by some unforeseen chance

already seemed to him like the prologue to a series of un-
welcome surprises that would cut deeply into his life.

Softly he opened the door of Scapinelli's study, and looked
cautiously through the slit. Yes, there sat the Jesuit at his
writing table and, on hearing the gentle noise, he raised his
head in surprise. That placid smile at once flitted over his
face. He rose, and hurried towards Eugen, who had come
inside the room. With a glow of warm cordiality upon his
face, he shook his hand.

"What do you think of seeing me here?" asked Eugen,
chaffingly.

"We knew, of course, that you were back," said the
Jesuit, "from the German Legation, at Helsingfors."

"Oh, did you?" said Eugen, and was once more disappointed. He did so enjoy surprising people, and now even this
pleasure had been frustrated.

"Sit down," said the Jesuit, pointing to a chair.

But Eugen swung himself up on to the writing-table. It
was an attitude in which he had often talked to the Governor
of the Lefortova prison. The Governor had put his feet up
on the table and thrust his cap into his face. This absence of
formality had often led to his forgetting their relative
positions.

Now, Scapinelli, too, crossed one leg over the other, and
told him to "fire away."

Eugen began talking about the Bolsheviks and Bolshevism.
But the Jesuit remarked that he could only deal with that
theme by delivering a few lectures. He was much more
anxious to hear something of Eugen's personal experiences.
Eugen leaned on his elbow, and started telling of his fortunes
in the U.S.S.R. soberly, in matter-of-fact style, and tersely.

Scapinelli rested his head to one side, on his slender
tapering hand, and did not once interrupt him.

While telling his story, Eugen had the strange feeling

that is known to all who have had an exceptional experience, and, in reporting it, have to do battle against the inexplicable sensation that what has happened to them is hardly credible, that life has here, once more, outdone the most lurid fantasies of fiction and that their experiences are lacking in any truth or reality, even to themselves. Now he was sitting with the Jesuit again, here in this room, listening to the dreary noise of Berlin rumbling through the double windows of the study, looking at the picture of St. Ignatius, hanging there unchanged on the wall—and yet a gap of two years lay between this meeting and the last. In that interval he had been in police prisons, in convict gaols, in a penal settlement; had fought cheek-by-jowl with a manlike woman; had starved, drudged, and frozen; got over a typhus exanthema; had felled timber in East Karelian forests; had argued with a Jew near Moscow on psycho-analysis; and had offered in expiation for a dead wife-murderer the sufferings of a cheerless solitude. And even when he drew from his pocket his while-you-wait photograph, showing him after his recovery from the disease, with the corners of his mouth drooping, and his famished cheeks sagging inwards, it suddenly struck him that he must be showing the Jesuit a cunningly faked forgery. But Scapinelli held the picture a long while in his hands.

"This will hang in this room, as its sole decoration," he said, finally.

Eugen lowered his eyes. He knew that this was the highest mark of appreciation that Scapinelli could have shown him. He was embarrassed. To hide his confusion, he began talking about Russia again.

"They are in a most unenviable condition, those fellows over there. If they don't overrun Europe, they will completely ossify and rot in their ideologies, while their bodies are still living. But if they do overrun Europe, they will meet with the same fate as the Goths, who tore down the Roman Empire, and then took over Catholicism, Roman law, and the Roman cultural heritage. They are lost——"

"You will now have to learn German," Scapinelli interrupted him.

"Oh, what nonsense!" replied Eugen, with the impudence of a Soviet Russian convict. "I don't yet rightly know who I am, even—Kisseleff or Düring. But—what I was about to say, was, we've a damned lot to learn from the people over there in economic, social, and humanitarian ideas——"

"In economic, social, humanitarian ideas," the Jesuit interrupted him bitterly, "which are our Catholic heritage. Our mistake, you see, lay in our having committed ourselves to the Beast of State, taken Capitalism tolerantly, and rooted out, by means of the Inquisition, the sectarians who were hostile to the State. All this will be different, now, Düring——"

Eugen began asking questions about the general state of affairs in Europe, lacking the courage to ask outright about what was most on his mind. The Jesuit gave him a chance to come to it.

"You mother will be very glad to see you again——"

"And what is Gertrude doing now—Fräulein Gertrude Garrieter, I mean?"

It was out. A few of his words had issued softly—others appallingly loud. And, withal, he had been trying to seem indifferent.

There ensued a brief, agonising pause. His fingers were tremulous, tapping on the table-top, and he could hear the roar of his blood in his ears.

"Whom do you mean?" asked Scapinelli, in a matter-of-fact manner.

"Gertrude Garrieter," replied Eugen, and his eyes clung anxiously to the Jesuit's lips.

"Oh—*She!*" said Scapinelli, recollecting. "Why, of course, you once brought her in yourself. Oh, she's gone completely crazy. She raves for the New Thought movement, Anthroposophy, Annie Besant."

Scapinelli had risen to his feet, and opened his file.

"But how can she——?" exclaimed Eugen. "How did that happen?"

"You seemed to be terribly fond of that girl, at one time," said Scapinelli, looking across from the file. Eugen made no reply.

"In the case of Gertrude Garrieter, one must say '*Cherchez l'homme*'," Scapinelli remarked, coming back, with a paper in his hand, from the dimly-lit corner of the room where the filing-cabinet stood. "She, too, seems to have thought a great deal of you. For, at first, she used to besiege us with enquiries——"

"And—then?" asked Eugen, in a flat voice.

"Then? When you were not back by Christmas, we all thought that you had died."

"And—then?" Again Eugen's question.

"Then came the other man, with his New Thought movement——"

Eugen stiffened himself. He thrust his hands into his overcoat pockets and decided to ride out to Brühlau that very minute.

"You are losing your head, Düring," said the Jesuit. "She sold the villa at Brühlau ages ago—she is living with her husband in England, now——"

"With her—husband——?"

"Yes, of course—with her husband. Dr. Zechmeister has a position in a chemical works over there——"

"She is—then, so to speak—she's—er—married then?"

"Certainly—in fact, she is married by the Catholic Church, at the—— But, Düring, what's the matter with you?"

With swift strides he approached Eugen. The latter had almost collapsed. All the life was extinguished in his face. Where his eyes had been were two dull, dead buttons looking from their sockets. His white lips had withdrawn involuntarily from over his teeth. His hair drooped over the wrinkled forehead of an aged man. He looked as wretched, and presented as melancholy a picture as a seal that has been violently clubbed over the head.

Even Scapinelli was touched. He guessed everything. He laid aside the paper which he still held in his hands, and put his hand on the unhappy man's shoulder, while Eugen, like a wretched bubble of flesh, lay sagging against the writing-table.

"We all thought you were dead——" he said. It sounded like an apology.

Eugen straightened himself up, and raised his haggard face towards Scapinelli.

"Yes," he said, "if only I had died—if only I were dead!"

In those moments of illimitable weakness, he was very near to cursing God, from the depths of despair, lust for revenge, helplessness and baseness.

Then, however, his better nature was victorious again—that Nikalai Sergeyevitch Kisseleff who had voluntarily made expiation for a murderer in the Church Suffering. And so Eugen offered himself up, with his great festering wound, just received, by God's decree, supported himself on the top of the writing-table, and threw back his tired head. In the angular awkwardness of his movements was expressed the anguished weight of the destiny that had spread itself like a black pall over his soul, a soul too young for so much affliction. In his position and attitude he so completely resembled one of the icons which, at the time of his arrest, used to be burned in the market-places of Russian cities amidst satanic screams of mockery. His eyes were dry and expressionless. Only his chin still trembled. Otherwise he had gone utterly stiff and lifeless. Now he would most gladly have gone on his knees in the Lubyanka, in Moscow, awaiting the cold touch of the revolver muzzle at the back of his neck. But here there was nobody who would render him this service of love. Eugen Düring was weary of life. For the first time in this world, *in hac lacrimarium valle*, tired of life.

PART III

CHAPTER I

THE PROSPECT OF ENGLAND

In the *Katholische Reichswarte* there only appeared a small notice about Eugen's return, in the column headed "Local Notes." "Herr Eugen Düring," it read, "has returned to Berlin once more after an absence from the capital of almost three years. He has resumed his work on the editorial staff of the *Katholische Reichswarte*." Brief and terse, these lines stood out on the greyish-white paper. In truth, however, Eugen was fighting to force himself back to his former ways of life, wearily, clumsily, painfully. He no longer saw any reason why one should shave daily, if one did not happen to be looking for a sweetheart; why one should have one's shoes resoled in summer if they were worn through, since there was neither ice nor snow on the streets. Things that were once a custom, and even a necessity, with him, had lost their meaning, and the terroristic constraint that the people about him (who suffered from fixed ideas) exercised upon him, caused him an intense irritation. But it was not merely the neglect of his appearance, and the absolutely shameless audacity, presumptuousness, and lack of manners, often even towards elderly people, but also the Tcheka-psychosis, the constant fear of a disastrous detection, that, even here, still held him in its grip. If he spoke of his experiences in the U.S.S.R., he mentioned even harmless fellow-prisoners only by fictitious names, which he confused when repeating his story. In the streets, he would often turn round, was

cautious, suspicious, and distrustful of everybody. Mingled
with people's pleasure at seeing him again there was always
an element of embarrassment and discomfort. Even those
supposed dead, who come back from the realm of extinction,
and return to the fullness of life, find heirs who are unpleasantly surprised, and even those who would have had
no earthly advantage from his demise, often meet the home-
comer with uncertain, confused embarrassment. And many
a one feels exasperated at finding he has wept or sorrowed
for nothing. That was how it happened in Eugen's case.
In many circles his memory was revered as a martyr's—
suburban priests had said votive Masses for him, and a few
friends of his mother's looked on him with almost accusing
eyes, not because they for a moment suspected that for two
long years he had strayed from the straight path in some
unknown by-way, but from a sense of indignation that a corpse
should be coolly passing along the side-walk in broad daylight.

When Eugen returned he found all the duties that he had
been accustomed to fulfil in his Berlin days allotted to
others. In the *Reichswarte* offices there sat at his table a
young man with a thinly sprouting moustache, gnawing
uncomfortably at a pencil. At the "Church Tax" office
there was even somebody working much more successfully
than he had done. His sitting-room in the villa had been
turned into a card-room. His motor-bicycle had been sold.
His suits had been partly given away, and partly eaten by
moths. The women were wearing long evening dresses.
His mother had had her hair dyed. The monks of St. Bernard, among whom he had friends, had been transferred to
the Himalayas. In place of Pacelli, Cesare Orsenigo was
at the Nuncio's palace. The National-Socialists had 107
empty seats in the Reichstag. The world had gone on, while
he, in the Russian dungeon, like something kept in pickle,
had lived two years of arrested existence. People hastened

to obliterate, as unostentatiously as possible, the traces of this interregnum—and the more complete and the more forced the silence that they practised in the process, the more he noticed it. Even when a man apparently dead awakens, people are careful to remove all the candles, wreaths, in memoriam cards, letters of condolence, and mourning apparel, out of the house, in doing which such an air of flurried activity prevails that it moves the man suppos- ed dead either to rage or to a melancholy smile.

Eugen would have found his way back quietly, after a certain lapse of time, into the regular ordered routine of life, if the loss of Gertrude had not driven him into an utter torture of restlessness. Here in Berlin a number of churches, squares, houses and streets reminded him of Gertrude, and once when he, after a long inward battle, had resolved to ride out to Brühlau, for the sake of craning his neck and peering over the hedge at her villa, now occupied by strangers, his misery returned in full force, and the wound bled afresh, more than ever. In addition to all this, he knew that Gertrude was in fateful proximity—he could get to Brühlau by train in three quarters of an hour, London in nineteen hours; for such a journey he had always the means and the time. Only indecision prevented him from starting on that journey immediately. Added to this was a certain cowardice and lack of self-confidence.

Sooner than he guessed, he was to cross to the big, humid island in the equably warm Gulf Stream. The paper had sent him out to Tempelhof for the blessing of aeroplanes, and so he was soon strolling among the Priests of the Dias- pora, who had assembled there with their motor-cycles, and the spectators, children, reporters, policemen, and aerodrome officials, with his Kodak, staring dreamily around. He asked Köhl a few questions, and jotted down the answers in pencil in his notebook.

Meanwhile, prayers were being said around the new machines, and the 103rd psalm recited, ". . . Who makest the clouds thy chariots, who walkest upon the wings of the winds. . . ."

A cool breeze blew, and set the skirts of the priest's vestment fluttering.

"Familis tuis," their praying voices continued, *"iter aeréum peragentibus, angelum bonum, de coelis, comitem benignus adiunge!"*

Otherwise, all was silent on the Tempelhofer Feld, the wind wafted the words to and fro, now near and distinct, now remote and half-heard. Only a small child seemed to be crying somewhere in the background.

"Pour out Thy blessing over this machine," the prayer ran on, in Latin. "So that those who entrust themselves to the aerial journey, under the protection of the Holy Virgin, may reach their destination unharmed."

The sky that day was blue, with a wonderful blueness. Only at its rim did this blue merge into the brownish exhalations of Berlin.

"All things in this world Thou, O God, hast given over to mankind . . ." Eugen heard. And these words echoed in his mind again: "Bless, O Lord, this aeroplane that it may serve to the swifter conveyance of earthly things without danger—for God has created everything that is in the world for Himself, He is the last end of all things that are. . . .May it carry His praise and His glory far out into the lands. . . . May the technical wonders of it awaken in all who entrust themselves to this aeroplane a yearning for the things that are of eternity."

After the ceremony had ended, when the people were overflowing the broad plain, Eugen got into conversation with an English pilot.

Eugen spoke of flying as it was in the Soviet Union,

whereupon he got to talking of Bolshevism itself, and eventually the two completely lost themselves in their conversation.

"I am flying back to England to-morrow," the pilot said finally. "Perhaps you would like to come with me? I have room for another passenger—and in England, of course, you will stay with me. We've a house near Downside. You probably know Downside, don't you?"

Eugen nodded mechanically, and made no answer. He was gazing fixedly away into space—to fly to England, that very next day! To be there the same evening! To be living on an island along with Gertrude! With, of course, forty-two million other people—but still, England, England——

"Well, what do you say?" the Englishman asked impatiently. "Are you coming? My people will be delighted to meet a real German."

He had decided—not to cross, but to fight down this hopeless love inexorably. But now came something that one might just as well call a "temptation" as a "finger of fate."

Undecidedly he glanced at the pilot, of whom he could not for the moment make up his mind whether he was acting as an instrument of the Devil or of God. At last, however, the all-too-human tendency to read doubtful things in their most favourable sense won the day. And so he turned, with unexpected excitement, towards the tempter:

"Right you are," he said, "I'm on! I'll come! I'll be here to-morrow morning."

With eyes aglow with restless excitement, he held out his hand, which the other took in some astonishment. Eugen had spoken as a trapper or a gangster might speak, when making a compact with a comrade, to enter on some great adventure.

That evening he met Scapinelli, and told him of his

decision. The Jesuit took the Atlas Hierarchicus from his bookshelves, and turned up the map of England.

"See?" he said. "Here is Downside—here, Frome—here is Wincanton—and here is Castle Cary. Do you see how nicely compact it all is?"

Eugen bent over the map.

"If you meet Frau Zechmeister, first look after yourself, and then, of course, look after the woman. Either you're disappointed and everything is all right again, or else your feelings will become more intense and poignant, and then the danger of your going to pieces will be infinitely increased. So, in that case, promise me you'll clear out at once."

"But, Father," he objected, "England is a big place—I've not the slightest intention——"

"You're a *gran' fanciullo, mio caro!*" Scapinelli broke in with a smile. "Just a big baby, my son!" This was the first time Eugen had ever heard him mix Italian words in his speech. "England is large—but the county of Somerset is small; don't I know you, Düring? I know——"

Eugen lowered his head, and over his face there fell long shadows. His own little, shabby dishonesty annoyed him.

"You are going to stay at Burley Hall," said Scapinelli, dryly, "but Frau Zechmeister lives at Gordon House, near Castle Cary, about eleven miles off."

"I didn't know that," murmured Eugen, rather put out than pleased. But then something began to seethe within him—only eleven miles, eleven miles. "The pointing finger!"

Now he knew, quite certainly, that he was going there. But not as Scapinelli thought, to experience a disillusionment and thus be cured of pain, but to see her, to be near her, to be aware of her again.

In his boundless longing he completely overlooked the ultimate sterility of his plans. Disillusionment he did not want. And a renewed contact could only mean for him a fresh wound and fresh despair—and not only that for him, but for her also, perhaps, a disastrous upheaval of her peace. But in his selfish yearning for her presence, he did not think so far ahead as that.

He got leave of absence from his paper. With the pilot he ascended in the morning, landed for a few minutes at Croydon, and soared high over the Great Western Railway to Bath. As in most cases, this air-journey was not particularly exciting, and the surface of Germany, in a bird's-eye view, showed a difference of appearance from the fields of England only in so far as the partitions of fields by hedges and stone walls expressed the consciousness of private ownership so much more distinctly than anything in the lands of Central Europe. At Bath the aeroplane was taken into a wide, roomy hangar, and from a corner of this structure a small car was drawn out into the full light of day. Unceasingly they travelled, up hill and down dale. The asphalt roads took the most incredible corners and curves. Attachment to the soil and the blind obstinacy with which the street planners opposed the estate-owners were the causes. Again and again the clattering car flitted through ancient and yet brilliantly clean villages, with inns of grey stone, petrol-filling stations, respectable business signs, starched white curtains behind the flower-decked windows that pierced the walls of little red-brick cottages, and, at the beginning and end of each hamlet, gossips' benches for maritime-bearded old men and knitting old women. Between these villages grew rank green, lush pastures and meadowlands, with innumerable flies, and mosquitoes even more numerous than in the marshy jungles of Karelia near the polar region.

CHAPTER II

COUNTRY HOUSE CONVERSATION

BURLEY HALL, which they reached at tea-time, was one of those typical English country houses, half villa and half castle, with large sash windows, rising above the gentle slope of a hill of soft soil crested with a little wood. Ivy climbed up the dry but scarcely weather-worn walls a little awkwardly. In the garden grew rhododendrons, wild roses, and pelagonias, obviously tended by an expert gardener. Behind the building were to be seen the garage and out-houses, and, further back, the tennis-lawn.

As the car advanced, driven through the shady avenue over the crunching gravel, and with a sudden jerk stopped before the sunny main entrance, a number of people came, one behind another, out from the hall into the open. First, a butler, who looked more like a German office employee; then a young flaxed-haired girl with a clear, open counten-ance that reminded him of Finland's art-gallery dream-world; an elderly gentleman with greying moustache, whose source of income was for ever to remain a riddle to Eugen Düring; another young girl, rather small, with laughing pearly teeth and mischievous eyes; and, finally, the lady of the house, Mrs. Jeffries, wearing a grey walking costume and beige scarf, who had just come in from a stroll.

After the introductions, when he had been shown to his room, where Eugen passed a brush over his hair and washed his hands, he came down to the hall, where tea was already served. Over a spirit-flame the water hummed in the silver kettle. Outside clouds were gathering, and turned the sunlight a sulphurous yellow. He looked at the furniture— and became aware of the fair girl who had greeted him on his arrival, now seated at the foot of the bookcase. She seemed, however, not to notice him, but sat there, her knees drawn up, bending forward, on the soft carpet, with her hair hanging down over her forehead and in her eyes, gnawing at a pencil and making notes from time to time on a piece of paper. Just as women, when engaged in any masculine occupation, always create an ungainly and grotesque impression, which, according to the nature of the occupation, may be either fascinating or repulsive, so it was in the case of this fair-haired creature, apparently engrossed in some topic either of reflection or of study.

"Why, there you are," she said, shortly, when she noticed him.

"Here I am," he assented, with a bow. "May one ask what you are puzzling your head over?"

"Certainly—if you care to help me," she said hesitantly. "I am not sure whether the *musculus digastricus* is situated above or below the *sterno cleidomastorideus.*"

"You are a medical student, then?" he asked, in surprise.

"Yes," she said, "but I must give you the hint never to mention it to mother or father—it's a constant annoyance to them. Mother says that I can't be presented at court now, anyhow."

"Then you *will* be missing something!" he said, ironically.

"Are you a Catholic, too?" she asked him.

He said he was.

"Herbert never picks anybody up except Catholics. He is a very zealous convert. You should know there is one convert in every family of any size in this part of the world, who upsets the peace of the household. But I quite like them, the people who belong to the Roman Church. They bring some touch of variety into our English lives. I'm not a Catholic myself, of course. But tell me, what are you, really? Dutch?"

"German," he replied.

"Good gracious! You mustn't tell anybody *that*. Mother would have a fit——!"

He suddenly felt the same pride that he had felt at Bolshevo during the epidemic, when Foma Efremovitch had voiced the suspicion that he had come from "over the way." His vanity delighted in passing for something extraordinary. But the mouth beneath the fair head of hair was laughing, too.

"I'd better pack up," he said.

"No!" cried the daughter of the house, emphatically. "You stay where you are. It seems to happen like that, in our house—we have to be having a constant strain in the atmosphere. Last time Herbert brought the general secretary of the Catholic Coloured Federation home here—an American negro. You ought to have seen papa then! And when all's said and done, Roberta is a 'case,' too."

"She is not your sister, then?" he asked.

"There are only the three of us—my brothers, Herbert and Oliver, and myself. Oliver is in London, and gone to the bad altogether. You must never mention him here, under pain of death! If anybody does, all domestic peace is done for. If you do, I'll stick my dissecting scalpel into you while you're asleep, one night."

"Nice prospects," he said.

"Yes. Oh, what was I going to say? Roberta is another 'case.' She's an American girl, that I got to know in town, a very clever girl, got her degree, and she's writing a highbrow political book about Europe. She has faults—a bit of a nymphomaniac—and after dinner she'll ask you if you'd like to sleep with her. But if you're as ascetical as my Roman brother, you needn't mind saying 'No,' but neither papa nor mamma must ever hear anything of this little weakness of Roberta's. I'm responsible for her—I brought her here."

Meanwhile, Herbert and the others had come in. Tea was poured out, Eugen nibbled sweet cakes, and crisp toast, put some butter and jam on his roll, and listened attentively to the somewhat moralisingly flavoured discourses of the master of the house. He talked about pernicious reading matter, that was only allowed to be published in France, which was destroying the taste of the British public. Then Herbert talked about the McKinlays, and his father, thereupon, remarked that they did not pay enough honour to the sabbath-day. The father, he said, even played bridge, while the young people danced! Roberta then observed that Weininger was undoubtedly right when he regarded the Jews and the English as people with pronounced psychological affinities. Both were mercantile, sabbatarian, puritanical, and egotistic by disposition, and regarded themselves as Chosen Peoples.

At this point the mother took umbrage, and asked Roberta whether, perhaps, the Americans were the Chosen People? Besides, it was ridiculous to mention the Jews and the English in one breath, because the Jews were an Oriental people, like the Indians, and England had to train India. Roberta smiled sarcastically, because she had a number of photos of Gandhi stuck up on the wall of her room, and a *de luxe* edition of the works of Tagore was lying in her trunk.

Then the father joined in again, with his resounding officer's voice, and began citing passages out of *Mother India*. The mother, who subscribed to a missionary paper, thereupon declared that only the Scottish Episcopal Church, but not the Wesleyans, on any account, were fitted to release the Indians from their dreadful superstitions. But Herbert remarked, maliciously, that this privileged part could only be played by the United Free Church of England with a Presbyterian-Calvinistic trend. Then Major Jeffries protested: it was not Christian superstition, he considered, that was called for, but the Light of Science that led to progress. Then the whole family began shouting at once. And from the confusion of voices one could only pick out those two words, "superstition" and "progress."

Mrs. Jeffries tried to restore order, and postulated emphatically that Major Jeffries was quite at liberty to enunciate his hyper-modern view that Christianity was a superstition, but he must admit that it was not a *horrible* superstition— but rather a *nice* legend. "And good material for nursery tales," put in Herbert dryly. That view, however, was far from being hyper-modern; it was the fossilised chatter of dilettante ignorant saurians from the Tertiary period. Major Jeffries had to enter a protest here. He brought forward Sir Arthur Keith, Darwin, Macaulay, and Havelock Ellis.

Eugen remained silent, and did not contribute a word to the dispute. In any case, it was really too funny that Major Jeffries should first advocate strict observance of the "sabbath" and keep a watchful eye on the reading matter provided for the young, and then dub Christianity a horrible superstition.

"Tell me, Mrs. Jeffries," he turned to the lady of the house, to give the conversation a new turn, "how far from here is Gordon House, near Castle Cary?"

"Gordon House?" questioned Mrs. Jeffries, in surprise. "What made you think of Gordon House? There are P.G.s there! Lady Cynthia Bexley takes P.G.s. You can get across in the car in forty minutes."

Eugen did not know what P.G.s were. Were they " Partei-Genossen," party comrades, of the Nazi Party? Or "Prisonniers de Guerre," French prisoners of war? No, explained Herbert, that expression meant "paying guests."

"There's a German married couple, among others," remarked Mrs. Jeffries. Eugen stared down at his cup, and was silent.

In the evening they dressed for dinner. He had to put on what he knew as a "smoking," but what over here was called a "dinner" jacket, and to go down, with freshly shaven cheeks, into the drawing-room, where the ladies, dressed to dazzle, stood about in groups, talking in reverently hushed murmurs. Then each gentleman selected a lady, and marched majestically, like an undertaker's horse, into the dining-room, where the imitation candles were already alight. A few more young men whom he had not seen before had joined them. One wore a thin moustache, like Douglas Fairbanks, and with his padded shoulders looked like a pirate lieutenant out of a story for schoolboys. A second was more like a rosy sponge with water-coloured blue eyes, that looked as if from those soft translucent globes he could weep only honey-sweet tears.

The imitation candles were glowing, throwing a brilliant light on the festive faces. A glittering sparkle was reflected in the glass and cutlery. The gentlemen's moustaches took on a more and more elegant curl. The indications of human feeling soon died away in the countenances of the ladies, and Roberta's feet, encased in shoes of gold brocade, made a wearisome round of reconnoitring. Before Eugen's eyes there appeared dark shadows—a picture painted in grey on a grey ground: Russia, a Stalovaya, hunger prison—and cutting right through all, a face, Gertrude's face. Dishes come and go. Red wine gurgles into the glasses—Gertrude. The clear open feminine face is shining somewhere—Gertrude's face. Then came a sudden pain, gnawing savagely at him.

After a sleepless night, tortured only towards morning by a fugitive dream, there followed an empty autumn Sunday. Herbert was already down outside, by his car, with his hand on the steering-wheel, waiting for Eugen.

"Hullo, hullo!" he said as the latter arrived on the scene. That was the morning greeting.

He got into the low-roofed car, and so they rolled over the ashphalt to the Abbey Church of Downside. They had a little time to spare before Mass, and they walked about the place. Eugen never ceased marvelling. Such, then, was the work of the Catholics of England! The Catholics of England and Scotland a hundred years ago—just a few thousand—hidden, whipped, frightened, outlawed faithful sons of the Church—and to-day over three and a half million souls, might well be regarded as the most stalwart Udarniki of the Church.

Eugen was now walking, lost in reverie, by Herbert Jeffries' side across meadows, along gravel paths, through passages, up and down stairways, expressing his admiration again and again.

"But," said Herbert, "what does all this amount to, by the side of your German Catholics?"

Eugen contradicted him. This cheerful readiness to sacrifice—this sense of community—this organisation. . . .

"It is nothing compared with your depth, your profundity and breadth of vision," objected Herbert.

Again Eugen wanted to protest, but they were already in the Church, with its lofty white nave, and its marvellously flexible organ.

After the Mass Eugen was introduced to Fr. Franz Schmitten, a German Benedictine, and a special friend of Herbert Jeffries.

Eugen expressed his admiration for what he had seen.

"Ours is not an easy task," Fr. Schmitten agreed. "You must not forget, England is a planet to itself; not situated on this earth at all, and having nothing whatever in common with Europe."

"Do you still find England so puritanical?" asked Eugen.

"No," said Fr. Schmitten. "The reaction has now set in. By imperceptible degrees England has long been becoming materialist. The German cultural ideal is the scholar, starving in a garret, the poor genius, the ascetic intellectual the book, the professoriate, the consumptive poet, the frozen painter, the woman artist who practises free-love, but here in England things are different. The culture here has become purely material. Culture lies in good clothes, wonderful gardens, furniture, houses, and the bindings and paper and print of books. In matters of education the 'gentleman' is far below the standard of the average German workman. You are sure to find M.P.s who cannot distinguish Budapesth from Bukharest, and who fancy that Austrian is a language derived from a mixture of Slav and Greek! One of the worst evils, however, from which England suffers, is the fact that the Puritan culture, or rather, negation of culture, from which America, too, was born, has long rotted away beneath the materialist reaction. All the same, the conquered Puritanism has remained the backbone of England and is current everywhere as the official stamp that gives a certain decorum. This decorum has become a thin veneer—English literature of to-day is still more or less fit reading for countesses, but the countesses often talk more like pornographic authors. There are families that cannot bear to hear the names of Lawrence or Joyce mentioned, but in which the daughters could write encyclopædias of *demi-viergerie*. Consequently, to use the language of Freud, a great 'discomfort' in their cultural consciousness. The antitheses between the generations seem to be irreconcilable.

Amateur Bolshevism, amateur Fascism, the people of the 'better classes' stiffened in traditions, atheistic, severe, and isolated, unspeakably isolated, freezing in their material culture. On the other hand, the Intellectuals are stultified by their immersion in a welter of retrograde scientific rubbish, tortured by visions of progress, enmeshed in a philo-Bolshevik enthusiasm for birth-control, Rousseauish ideas and technical gadgets. In addition, a feminine culture, feminism as an accompanying symptom of their materialism, a reaction against the 'pater-familias' obsession of Judaising puritanism. To every ten men here, you'll find twelve women. The mental, spiritual and sporting achievements of the women are more and more overtaking those of the men. That has been established beyond reach of contradiction. But that leads, on the other hand, to an enormous superficiality in the nation's intellectual life. Over in America, that one-time puritanical colony of the Pilgrim Fathers, things are much the same——"

"And the 'gentleman'? What is *he* doing?"

"There you have the great brake on our development," cried Fr. Schmitten. "The 'gentleman' is cool, detached, uninterested and uninteresting, self-contained and reserved, and obsequious to women. You know what I mean? The 'gentleman' is just as nationalist as the Prussian German '*Herr*,' the Spanish '*caballero*,' the '*cavaliere*,' the Hungarian '*Ur*'—only he is, of course, softer, he is ' *gentil homme*'—he moves more discreetly, and with more restraint. But that makes no difference to his unlimited sense of 'what he is'— the 'gentleman' is a traditionalist, an adherent of the State Church, pays his taxes, and would never kiss the Fisherman's Ring of an Italian Pope, let alone a coloured Pope, kneel down in the confessional, and reveal to a mere fellow-man the most secret privacies of his soul; say a Rosary or a Litany——"

"Pride is our unhappiest characteristic," assented Herbert.

I don't know if you've visited our colonies—but if you've
ver been to an English, then to a French, colony, in Asia,
ay, or Africa, I expect you've noticed the difference. The
Inglish Colony, with its wonderful streets, and its motor cars,
ts spacious stations, its perfectly trained policemen, and
ts scrupulously clean government buildings, but the natives
egularly vaccinated, converted, registered, schooled, cultur-
ally 'uplifted.' In the French colony, more of the haphazard,
laissez-faire spirit prevails—the brown-skinned policeman
pawls all over the place, just like his instructor, the streets
are a little neglected, but there is a comparative freedom
from the 'ten-paces-from-my-body' regime for the natives;
hey intermarry without restriction; and the authorities
shut their eyes to it if the natives tend sometimes to live
according to their own customs. In return, the natives come
to feel that they are Frenchmen. Look here, I was in Goa,
a filthy Indian, bug-ridden town under Portuguese rule.
The Indians of Goa were all Catholics, and felt that they
were completely Portuguese. In Goa there is no difference
between brown and white. Fifty kilometres away English
officers have Indian merchants turned out of a compartment
by the conductor, if the English officers want the compartment for themselves. What's the good to us of damming the
Indus, of having universities and hospitals and concrete
roads and aerodromes, if we are proud and unloved—
arrogant, upright, with well-groomed moustaches, holding
a cricket-ball and an illustrated magazine in our hands,
and insanely striving to 'keep smiling, and exercise self-
control and commonsense'—and sink away in the engulfing
abyss of world history? German Catholicism is what we
want."

"You dreamer!" said Fr. Schmitten. "No, my friend—
we, too, are far from up to the mark; it's French Catholicism
that——"

Then Eugen felt compelled to object again.

But it was time to go home.

Then came a heavy lunch, with a good deal of silence and complete surrender to the pleasures of eating. Eugen only noticed that Major Jeffries stood at the sideboard and carved the joint, self-sacrificingly, whilst Herbert, the young buccaneer, and the rosy lump of flesh, busily carried the plates backwards and forwards. The womenfolk kept their seats, and chattered gaily together. This was really odd. Here, in feminist England, the men were already beginning to wait at table. Then he got up himself, and helped with the plates. He could not understand what had happened to the servants, till he remembered it was Sunday. Finally, the lady of the house set a towering pile of plates before her, and cut up the pudding, in the distribution of which Eugen ran to and fro with an absurd bustle of activity. Florence watched him rather mockingly, with her improbable blue eyes.

CHAPTER III

BACK TO ALL THAT

AFTER the meal Herbert approached Eugen.

"What would you like to do?" he asked him.

Eugen shrugged his shoulders.

"Whatever you're doing."

"You must realise," Herbert explained, "that an English Sunday is a deadly business."

"Very likely," replied Eugen indifferently.

"I say," began Herbert again, "don't you know some people at Gordon House? Foreigners? Americans? There's a crowd of P.G.s there mostly not English. And the Bexleys—are very hospitable. They have lots of people to tea every Sunday."

"Really?" Eugen looked at him suspiciously.

"If you like, you can have the Morris," Herbert suggested. "Drive over there and give my kind regards to the Bexleys."

That was how the Serpent must have spoken in Eden.

Eugen thrust his hands in his pockets, and looked down before him, undecidedly. Staring at the maze-like pattern in the carpet, he reflected: would it not be worse than suicide, to drive over there, and thrust his finger again into his open wound? "But," said the tempter's voice within him, "what did you come to this country for?" Moreover he was, nonsensical as this may seem at first sight, too much of a coward to face the fact of his own cowardice. "Perhaps," the tempter went on, "she may have acquired a double chin by now and a sagging figure; perhaps she will disillusion you so completely that you'll only have an indulgent smile for the memory of how you used to feel. Perhaps she will seem such a stranger to you, since you have drifted apart for three years, that you will just conventionally kiss her hand and address her as '*Gnädige Frau*'."

"Good," he said, after a long pause, "I'll go."

"Supper is at eight. You needn't be back till eight, as we don't dress on Sundays," Herbert explained.

"Not on *Sunday?*" he said in surprise.

"A Witches' Sabbath of the Puritans," said Herbert, with a laugh, "with primitive matriarchal service arrangements. Picture after Bachofen."

Eugen had to smile, too.

"O.K.," he said, "in an hour, I'll run over there."

Herbert then told him the way.

The hands of his wrist-watch rotated slowly. Meanwhile, he lay on a sofa in the library, and browsed in the *Encyclopædia Britannica*. The more often he looked at the time, the more slowly the time seemed to pass. Sometimes his eyes wandered from the printed page, and he gazed into vacancy, reflecting whether it might not, after all, be better to stay where he was, and let that most perilous of all his adventures remain untried. Once he heard a loud burst of laughter, outside in front of the house. It was Florence and Roberta walking arm-in-arm. He felt really inclined to jump up and join them, postponing indefinitely his drive over to the Bexleys. But an invisible power restrained him. One may say to oneself a hundred times, "I wish to stretch my finger," and yet the finger will not move—but the tiniest act of will is sufficient to make the muscles obey the command of brain and nerve. So it was with Eugen. With the book on his lap, he lay and craned his neck in the direction of the two girls—but his body remained lying there, utterly motionless.

His heart beat as he got into the car and started the engine. He was soon on the road, and he let the fresh wind blow round his forehead. His thoughts were filled with memories of Gertrude.

"What an ass I must have looked, that time when I said goodbye to her, putting on airs like an old maid—instead of taking her in my arms and asking her to wait for me." Then, "Nonsense!" he said to himself, "at that time I wasn't in love with her—and, if I had been, I was supposed to be dead—it's a wonder they let me travel on the railway without making a fuss about it, and without demanding a permit for the conveyance of a corpse, from the Ministry of Transport, at the frontier." Then: "A useless visit, this, for if she still loves me it will be ghastly for us both; and if she doesn't, then I shall be disappointed." Once more he resolved to turn back. He was tortured, torn, undecided; the expedition gave him no pleasure. He was obsessed with innumerable anxieties and fears, and his dejection grew and deepened, his foot pressed less and less upon the accelerator. But he knew, too, that if he returned to Burley Hall of his own accord, with nothing tried, he would bitterly regret his decision, and be driven to a fresh attempt to see Gertrude again. That would mean prolonging his restlessness and anguish of mind for an indefinite period, black with self-reproach. He asked an A.A. patrol whom he met whether it was far to Gordon House. "Just past the next bend," was the reply. And, indeed, scarcely had he negotiated the next turn in the road, at a hesitant speed, when Gordon House leaped into view, like a building springing out of the ground before his eyes—a country house like any other in England, overgrown with ivy and creepers, with vast lawns and clumsy large chimneys, with avenues, gravel paths, sheds, sash windows, and rhododendron bushes. Eugen drew up before the entrance, his heart and lungs labouring with a slow, heavy rhythm.

He got out, and looked over the position. The drive up to Gordon Hall was on the west side. On the other side there were tables set out, figures in white leaping to and fro before a tennis-net, and the wind carrying a few words across to him—but he could not make Gertrude out among those figures. So he resumed his seat in the car, and drove forward up the avenue. The gravel scrunched, and the brakes screeched a little. An elderly servant, who this time looked more like a grandfatherly figure in a coffee advertisement than a pensioned office employee, adopted an interrogative air.

Eugen swallowed before he spoke.

His mouth felt parched. He felt as if his feet were weighted with metal plates.

"Does Mrs. Zechmeister live here?" he asked, eventually.

"She is at tea," said the manservant. "What name, please?"

"Tell her a friend from Germany."

The servant led Eugen into a small drawing-room. On the table lay a copy of *Country Life* and a few back numbers of *Punch*. But he had no senses and no eyes for the arrangements of the room. He stood stiff and awkward, by the large table, resting on it as against a firm barrier that was to protect him from any unexpected attack. He had little time in which to think of his position. He could already hear Gertrude's voice, Gertrude's voice for the first time in three years of horror, of uselessly eating his heart out, while he built air-castles of hopeless love. She was speaking to the servant, outside the room—he could distinctly hear every word she said, with an unreal, clear-cut, sharp accuracy, like the prosecuting counsel's voice that day in Moscow.

"Then he didn't give his name? In the drawing-room?"
he heard her say. "Oh—isn't there a looking-glass here?
I'm all untidy." She stopped somewhere. She did not come
nearer the door. Not a movement was to be heard.

An insensate terror and cowardice came over him—he
felt sick. He was in utter misery. And, suddenly, he realised
that something more than love was at work here—there was
now simply a horrible torture of the soul that seemed to
have an affinity with death. He felt that he must be looking
green with pallor. He did not know what to do with his
hands. A fit of trembling shook him. Then he heard her
step—only one step—for, the next second, he *saw* her. And
the sense of sight instantly dismissed the sense of hearing
from his consciousness. He saw her now—her face, her form,
her hands and arms, framed in the doorway. He did not
know whether she had become more beautiful or less. He
did not notice that she had just been playing tennis, and
wore a white frock, that her hair was done differently, or
her startled fright at the sight of him. He saw nothing but
the abstract concept, "Gertrude." He was engrossed with
the bare fact that he could see her, was near her, could speak
to her. There was no room in him for the thinking and
reflective faculties—what he experienced held him tied to
the passing moment.

But she was in the grasp of the same terror that seizes any
one of us who sees, among the living, one we have believed
to be dead.

"Eugen!" she exclaimed.

She had spoken.

This one word broke the spell that held him. It was his
signal to act and speak. He advanced towards her and saw
her in nearer perspective, larger, more distinctly, looked
into her eyes, that were fixed and distended with terror,
felt her breath, and caught hold of her. Unresistingly she

let him kiss her. Her knees seemed to be giving way. She fell back against the wall and he with her—he buried his lips in her hair, kissed her temples, her eyes, her ears, laid his head against her neck, pressed her face against his cheek, groaned, pressed her to him till she could not breathe. His hand, behind her, could feel the warm, delicate flesh through the thin material of her dress, and, beneath that flesh, could feel her ribs individually, while his lips felt the hard outlines of the bony structure of her head—her eye-sockets, her cheek-bones, her jaws, her shoulders. Like a madman, he caressed this body, till his movements grew slower and slower. He raised his head, let his arms fall, and stepped back.

He crossed to the opposite wall, where he leaned his head against the tapestry. Like two exhausted boxers in the corners of the ring, they stood facing one another.

Without a word, she passed her hand over her ruffled hair.

Then he, pressing his palms flat against the wall, began to speak. The paralysis of his tongue passed off, his vocal chords began to vibrate, the dry fixedness of his eyes relaxed, and life began to flow back in him in its fulness, with all the melancholy bitterness of mortal existence. He talked, bab-bled, laughed. He spoke of the fortunes of Nikalai Sergeye-vitch Kisseleff, of the bug-ridden tourists' hostel at Batum, and right up to that unhappy blow of disappointment that had destroyed all his joy in life, in Scapinelli's study.

She had listened leaning against the wall, her face clasped in her hands. But he, his excitedly recited narrative concluded, had let his head fall forward, and stared at her, with a gaze of frightful understanding, then looked away, looked through the open door into the hall, and through the hall on to the sunlit gravel of the drive, where cars were standing, their tyres slightly spreading beneath their weight. His eyes roved to and fro between the half-light where a

BACK TO ALL THAT

woman was clasping her hands over her face, and the
brightness of the sunlit front garden.

Gertrude did not speak, did not move, waiting for some
supernatural power to release her tongue, and gently remove
her hands from her face.

Eugen took a few steps towards her.

"Here is the half-light, the blind alley, where one can go
no further, death. Outside, light and the sun, roads, paths,
nfinity," a voice said within him. And then realisation came
to him—in whom the memory of the moist warmth of her
ibody, fatigued with her game, the body that his arms had
embraced, and the firmness of her bones slumbering beneath her flesh, had not yet faded—an intermittent and spasmodic realisation, that a look from Gertrude's eyes or the
thawing of her voice, would be just as fatal for him as a
careless scrap of evidence when he was being questioned in
the land of the Eastern heretics. Were she to speak now, he
would have to answer. One word would lead to another.
They would draw near. And that would mean fire, ruin, the
end. That would mean a trembling, deadly torture, deadly
fear, the ultimate boundary-wall of the blind alley in which
their feelings trapped them.

The end with terror was preferable to the terror without
end. There was but one single way out—flight. Flight
now, immediately—flight without reflection. Eugen's knees
began to cave in—he felt as if he were about to sink, to
collapse, as in forgotten dreams of childhood, when he was
chased by dragons highly charged with electricity, or bright
red-painted locomotives, through gloomy forest ravines;
with glaring eyes he measured the distance to the lower
steps that led to the front garden, and took a few more paces
towards the middle of the room. His hair clung clammily to
his forehead, and his heart seemed to have stopped beating.
He had not only drawn closer to the door, but also to her

motionless form. Once more, he wanted to embrace her, then, overpowered with a sudden impulse, he recoiled, rushed outside, halted once more in his flight, turned round twice in the hall, and went down the steps. He had forgotten his hat, but he did not notice that. As if followed by a deadly spectre, he leaped into the car, pressed the starter, put in the clutch, gave it gas, gripped the steering-wheel, and sent the Morris bounding forward in great leaps. He did not stop till he was far out on the grey road. He drew one breath then, and let his hands drop. Powerless and huddled up he sat there on the upholstered seat, like a little child at a big desk. He kept asking himself what had happened to him—whether what had occurred was still anything at all to do with "love." As saccharine is to sugar, that scene had been, perhaps, to his original feelings; for all that was left was simply poisonous rage and misery—and, above all, unrest. A number of things came into his mind—things that he had meant to say to Gertrude, or to ask her. But what had happened? He had rushed at her; had kissed her, and held her body in his hands; had roared his pain at her; and had run away, utterly broken up. Now he was lying in a Morris car, on the hard main road, surveying the field of his ruins, and casting himself into the arms of despair.

He could not go back to Burley Hall like that, so torn and beaten. Aimlessly he drove about the roads, and did not notice that grey-blue clouds had gathered in the sky. He only noticed that it was raining, when the thin spray of comet-like drops had changed to great pouring splashes of water. He put up the roof, and raised his coat-collar, huddled down still more deeply behind the steering-wheel, and changed gears to a lower speed, to mount the summit of a lengthy stretch of rising hillside. At the top, in a pass-like cutting, there was, hanging out in front of a grey house, a coloured signboard suspended above the grey street: "Rose and Crown Inn," it read. Eugen put on his brakes.

He was sitting alone, now, in the cleanly guest-room, and an elderly, lady-like looking woman, with a cap and a black silk blouse, brought him tea in an earthenware pot under a woollen cosy. Sugar in shapeless broken lumps lay in a little bowl; orange marmalade shone, golden yellow, in a glass dish; and the butter was displayed in little salted balls. For a long while he sat before these viands, motionless, a county paper resting across his knees, and looked out of the window, down which the rain-water trickled, and listened to the gurgling of the water in the gutters, with his wet hair dragging over his forehead. Then he decided to eat, after all—poured out some tea, buttered his rolls, but stopped short in the middle of spreading them, and felt like weeping. He dropped the hand that held the knife, and huddled up. Meanwhile it was growing darker and darker. And not until the lady-like woman switched on the electric light did he attempt to make his attitude less expressive of his feelings. Wearily his jaws worked over each mouthful, and even to swallow the tea was a matter of difficulty.

When he had finished tea, and the empty soiled crockery stood before him, dejection came over him in ever-increasing intensity. The glare of the electric light disturbed him, so he moved towards the switch. The guest-room suddenly became almost completely dark—only through the windows did a faint vestige of rainy twilight penetrate. He took up a position at the window, and looked down at the slippery wet asphalt of the road, where the car stood, solitary and beaten upon by the rain, with unlit lamps. Across the meadows, a few leafy trees were swaying in the wind, and in front of the door there rustled a little damp foliage.

Memory-pictures, from the days of the camp at Bolshevo, beset him. Bolshevo, where, in the night, in the late northern twilight, he had pressed his famished face against the small square windows of the barrack-room, half fancying he could see the figure of Gertrude forming among the shadowy trees of the partially cleared woods. How much happier he had been there, than he was to-day, in his supposed freedom! But then Gertrude appeared before him with imploring eyes and dishevelled hair, as he had seen her on that sunny afternoon in Brühlau, where she had spoken of her love for him, with such big-hearted frankness. "Like a stiff, old-maidish high-priestess, I behaved!" he told himself—and repeated the words. Then he calculated the day on which she must have been married, and concluded it could only have been a few weeks after his final return to the Lefortova.

He staggered back to the table, took off his wrist-watch, and set it with its luminous dial before him on the table. Then he rested his chin in his palm, and watched the slow movement of the greenish phosphorescent hands—waging the while a ghastly, vain battle against the rush of thoughts of Gertrude. At a quarter past seven, he drove back through the wet night.

He got in just before dinner, changed only his shoes, washed his hands, brushed his hair, and then hurried down to the dining-room. As it was Sunday he was obliged to keep running about with plates and cutlery, and to offer the ladies the various vegetable dishes, with polite phrases. After the dessert, however, the ladies were ceremoniously turned out—one gentleman even opened the door for them, to get them out more quickly. Then Major Jeffries, to the accompaniment of a cigar and port began to deal with high politics.

After that the gentlemen went into the large drawing-room, where, in the meanwhile, the ladies had been heartily

bored, and bridge began.   There was one too many, so
Eugen expressed his readiness to sit by the fire, with a "good
book." He took a book by Christopher Hollis, on America,
and a collection of Essays, by Chesterton, from the library
and began reading.

When it was already very late, after the sixth rubber, they
all went to bed. Roberta, however, came and joined Eugen
by the fireplace, and asked him whether he would like to
come to her that night. "Herbert need not know."

"But, tell me, must you have that every night? Besides,
there are other people at your disposal," he said softly, with
a jerk of his head in the direction of the buccaneer and the
red-sponge-like youth.

"You'd find it boring, too, to eat plum pudding every
day," she said. "But the main thing is, I'm young, and I
have a taste for it. One sleeps better the next day, and one
has a clearer head. If you look at the matter objectively, you
must certainly see that I'm right."

"So you take everything you have a taste for?"

"Certainly. One must experience everything. Everything
that is pleasant," she said, in a lower voice than before.
For the "pirate" was approaching them.

"I am rather worried about you," Eugen said, aloud,
"for as you know, people who eat everything that they have
a taste for, often thoroughly upset their digestions."

Roberta raised a hand, with red-enamelled finger-nails, to
straighten the shoulder-strap of her evening dress, which
had slipped down.

"You Catholics really are the most terrible Puritans!"
she said, amused.

"We are the pre-established harmonious mean," he said,
tauntingly. "You sectarians oscillate hysterically between
Calvin, John Knox, and the college-girl complex. In the
seventeenth century, we were supposed to be the last word in

moral corruption, and to-day we run about this little island rubber-stamped with the word 'Puritan'!"

She laughed.

"So I'm another little bit of evidence for your theories?"

"Certainly."

"Then you ought to be grateful to me, and open my door cautiously at twelve o'clock to-night, and poke your snub nose inside my room."

"Nothing doing!" he said, and thrust both forefingers into his waistcoat pockets.

Then she leaned over him, and whispered a few delightful *cochonneries* that did not even sound coarse, into his ear.

"I'll soon have you, you little Hun! Cruel darling Hun!" she said half aloud, letting her breath fan his face. "Don't you dare try to thwart me, you awful Pharisee, you butcher of Belgian babies. You won't escape me. I'll enjoy you this very week. I'm curious to see what you taste like, my darling Hun with the snub nose!"

Then she squeezed his hand, where it lay passively on a cushion, and vanished.

So he was left, the last one in the drawing-room. Now he got up. What was he to do? Go up to his room and lie in bed, sleepless, staring open-eyed into the terrible darkness that produced those torturing pictures? Groan into his pillows, after this ghastly day? He had nobody to whom to turn, on this day of heaviest defeat. Neither Herbert, who looked up to him and admired him, as Foma Efremovitch had once done; nor Florence, with her clear-sighted, straight-lined nature; nor yet the others. So there was left nothing for him but to take refuge in the night, "his" night. In the hall he slipped into his overcoat, turned the key in the front door, quieted the dogs outside, and stepped forth into the damp darkness of nocturnal England.

It was still raining. And single drops splashed like spattered ink upon his forehead. Neither stars nor clouds were discernible in the sky. There was merely the rustle of grass beneath his feet, and, in the gutters, the measured, monotonous, drum-like pattering of the raindrops.

Weightlessly he seemed to glide through the black wetness. He compared the coldness that struck against his face with the fire that blazed in his heart—that brought back his introspective awareness of himself. The cool air inflated his lungs, he advanced further and further into the darkness— he walked ever more quickly. The way was familiar to him. His feet broke into a running gait—and, suddenly, he was speeding like an arrow. Not a tree impeded him on his way.

CHAPTER IV

A DIFFERENT BERLIN

At Downside they said to him, in so many words, "Clear out!" He thought the same. He had the urge to see Scapinelli once more. For Scapinelli was the only man who really *knew* him, and could successfully advise him. He decided, therefore, to take the express that same afternoon from Bath to London, and there carry out the instructions of his paper, then at once start back for Berlin.

Florence gave him a friendly handshake, Mrs. Jeffries made a friendly lady's face at him, and Roberta, oddly enough, was ashamed to look him in the eye. "Remain strong, my son!" she whispered softly, her eyes cast down.

"Become stronger!" he replied just as softly.

By evening he was in London, passing through the noisy bustle of Oxford Street. The characteristic street stench o London, a mixture of the smell of sweet cigarettes, used petrol, and spilled motor oil, offended his nostrils. An excess of electric signs, billowing up and down on the walls of the houses. Only in Kensington, Chelsea, Belgravia and Mayfair did it seem a little quieter. A sleepy monotony of rows and rows of one-family houses, built, whole streets of them together, by a single architect, with brass door-knockers, servants, physically a little infirm, called by some old family surname; elderly gentlemen with cheque-books, milky-cheeked daughters, slight "corporations," extensive wardrobes, and uncomplicated philosophies. Here and there, a petrol or electric car would roll through these residential streets, but otherwise a hushed stillness prevailed. Late in the evening, when the theatre performances were over, he was back in the centre of the town. Women in the most sumptuous evening frocks, accompanied by proud-looking men, rustled over the pavement; ladies in brightly lit motor-cars rode by with jewels sparkling on their naked flesh. Nowhere else in Europe could one see such a pandemonium of splendour and extravagance in the streets. Berlin, with its Kurfürstendamm at evening, seemed, by comparison, a shabby, overgrown Oriental village.

On the evening of the following day he left by the train from Liverpool Street and crossed from Harwich to Holland, then through its Catholic districts, which thrust northwards like a wedge, into Germany, reaching to within a few kilometres of the North Sea, and back to Berlin.

This journey from Burley Hall to his home he had made in a state of dreamy twilight. Here and there something he saw or experienced attracted his attention for a few moments, but then, despite all his prayers for strength and comfort, he huddled up weakly within himself, incapable of stepping outside his own sensations.

On the train he was monosyllabic, and tried in vain to join, for the sake of distraction, in the conversation of his fellow-travellers, and with befogged eyes he watched the shaking and tossing of the passive articles of luggage in the rack. In the dining-car he left the food almost untouched, and simply chewed up a few toothpicks. His London impressions, too, were vague, like the memories of some uncertain dream.

The streets of Berlin by night did not distract him from his thoughts, rather did the return to those streets, squares, roads and buildings that reminded him of hours spent with Gertrude before his trip to Russia—increase his unrest and pain. At home in his villa he had suddenly become an affectionate son to his mother, making her forget the way they had drifted apart for more than ten years. In the evening he hurriedly telephoned to the Jesuit, outlined the failure of his journey in a few words, and said he would probably call on him soon. Scapinelli advised him to plunge into his work, to go at once to the editorial offices of the *Katholische Reichswarte*, and on no account to remain idle.

At the *Reichswarte* office a number of cheerful young people worked, who bustled about in the corridors, in their rolled-up shirt-sleeves. Stegelin, the old philosopher, and inventor of the "Black Front!" greeting, now in common use by almost everybody, had died, and Eugen did not work very easily with the younger generation. Moreover, he missed Rudolph Medek. Once when he entered his office before working hours, a whole crowd of these newcomers were sitting on his table, chairs, and window-sill, smoking, and snorting with laughter.

They did not bother about Eugen, who meanwhile had hung up his raincoat on its hook, and they showed no indication of leaving his room. He went out into the corridor, and strolled round, with his hands in his pockets, thinking of Gertrude—again and again of Gertrude. In hundreds of pictures he depicted to himself just how he would have spoken to her, all the things he would have said to her, the journeys he would have taken with her, what he would have shown her, given her, written to her, if everything had not just happened as it had.

The central-heating radiators sent their warmth out into the air, the telephone operator plugged in and out, clocks ticked, pencils rustled, scissors clattered, and bells jingled, in the various offices. He *must* speak to Scapinelli—now. He stepped out into the cool, caressing evening air, and flung himself into the midst of the whirling traffic of the

streets. He could no longer bear it, in the newspaper office.
With lips tightly compressed, hat in hand, he hurried past
the crowds in the road. At last he was at the Jesuit's house.
Lightly he bounded up the stairs, and, without knocking,
burst into Scapinelli's study.

"You've just come at the right moment, Düring," said
Scapinelli. "The first part of your report has already been
worked through. But we want you to supplement it with
replies to no fewer than a hundred and twelve questions on
details."

Eugen leaned across the writing-table.

"Don't imagine for an instant that I am capable, now,
of doing any kind of work," he said.

"Düring, you're a sick man," said Scapinelli, with his
soothing voice. "Don't be offended, but you've become
neurasthenic."

"You're not surprised, are you?" Eugen broke out. "If
one is tied up in one place two years and a half and can't
get away—if one is kept quivering for two and a half years
with the more or less ever present fear in one's mind that one
may be seen through and put to death. Now it's all over, it
seems senseless, but it's true, I can swear it's true, in one of
the deepest recesses of my heart the dread lurked all along,
that this would happen with Gertrude. Yes, just this. Oh,
I know it was my fault—yes, I know, my fault, mine, and
mine alone."

"One must face the facts," said Scapinelli. "Building
castles in the air means getting fixed ideas, cutting oneself
off, sidetracking oneself. You're building up an harmonious
world of misery for yourself, in your imagination, à la 'Sorrows of Werther.' And you are ranting and groaning around,
in this morbid world of yours. I'd like to tear down the
walls of this imaginary third class waiting-room for moaning
old women. . . ."

Eugen was silent. The dry speech of the Jesuit seemed to him, the obsessed man, to be of a positively insulting frivolity.

"You must bring more of the Christian spirit into the way you bear your suffering. One cannot deny the existence of a suffering, if it does exist—that would be playing the ostrich. But the first thing to do is to realise properly the true relative magnitude of that suffering. Any misconception means distortion, all sorts of distortion, disharmony, absurdity, and worrying. In the second place comes the question of deportment—the physical and the psychological have deep-rooted correspondences. This means discipline, control, steering one's course. In the third place, there is the proper integration of the suffering with one's ego, at the right point and in the right way. Above all, however, there is the question of suffering in its relation to Christ, suffering as a Cross, suffering as—'a grace'."

The Jesuit watched Eugen closely as he said this, and then went on.

"Your trial, however, is not really so intolerable, my dear Düring. Put yourself in the place of the girl, once Sonnenschein's protegée, growing old in North-East Berlin, who lives in a garret, her whole body paralysed; she earned her living addressing envelopes with her pen gripped between her teeth, till they fell out. Yes, I know you were shut up 'in pickle' for two years and a half, but, after all, they didn't torture you. You are not lying in one of the AC wards of the *Charité*, as a hopeless case. You are not one of the *Ligue des Gueules Ecrasées*, who have to drag out their existence without face, eyes, mouth or nose, isolated from humanity, ghastly victims of war. You have every prospect of recovery—the certainty of recovery, in fact."

Eugen made no reply. His heart was too full, and he resented Scapinelli's words. But the mechanical workings of

his reason admitted that they were right. The Jesuit, however, allowed him no time for reflection.

"You must get away," said Scapinelli. "Spend four
hundred marks on a new motor-bike, and take a trip round
Europe. That will do you a great deal of good. But mind
you keep to the Continent—and avoid a certain island in
the Atlantic!"

The Jesuit had spoken very forcefully.

Eugen shrugged. He was silent, for he could see that,
although Scapinelli's advice was well meant, it would get
him nowhere. But in spite of that he followed the advice.

CHAPTER V

EUROPEAN SCRUTINY

In Paris he saw that the views he had formed in Russia, of the peasants, were further confirmed here. The French peasant, in the middle and southern parts of the country, had become a rigid anti-clerical, and joined forces with the half-educated undenominational school-teacher against the priests, who became more and more isolated. On the other hand, the great cities, Paris, Lille, Lyons, were being Catholicised on a very extensive scale. In the "Bled," and among the chiffonniers of the *banlieue*, and in the endless suburbs they had, since the war, built over seven hundred churches, chapels, dispensaries, club-houses, children's homes, and schools. A Jesuit to whom Eugen spoke described the migration from the soil as a fortunate circumstance—it is only when he reaches the town that the peasant learns the real greatness of Catholicism.

He passed through Switzerland on his way to Austria. The sight of the mountains—which he had not seen for years—cheered and exhilarated him. On the other hand, as soon as he was alone, the memory of Gertrude provoked a terrible melancholy and sense of futility. In Paris the force of his experiences had shaken him up so much that he had no time for introspection and return to the realm of morbid yearnings and desire.

One day he stood on a steeply ascending mountain road, and looked down at the deep blue Lake of Zürich. The

feeling that nobody stood by him on whose shoulder he could
let his hand rest, brought his thoughts back to Gertrude with
a painful violence.

When he lay down in a meadow and dozed, he would
wake up with the confusion of sleep still veiling his mind, and
find his arms stretched out, his hands groping for—nothingness. There was nobody by his side. He was alone. Then he
compressed his lips, to restrain himself from screaming aloud
in the solitude. The wind sent a tremor through the waving
blossoms and the long grasses around him, and dried up
the moisture of his lips. Brother wind and sister sun were the
only ones who stayed with him, and kept him company on
his wanderings.

The motor-cycle sped on towards the East, his route
passing through the deep-cut valleys of the Tyrol and
glorious Salzburg. Then, through alternations of sun and
rain, he passed on into the romantic world of laughing lakes,
the Salzkammergut. Years had elapsed since his last hurried
tour in these districts, and it seemed to him now that when
he had stayed in these lands before he must have been
visited with blindness. Over the Pötschen Pass the motor-
cycle's two cylinders struggled along into Styria. He strolled
round on foot, climbed the Tressenstein, tackled the Sarn-
stein, bathed in the lakes of Altaussee and Odensee, tramped
with his rucksack on his shoulder along dusty roads, and
climbed the slopes of the Loser. From the summit of the
Loser the Lake of Altaussee sparkled like a friendly, twinkling
eye, and the Trisselwand, which usually rose so loftily,
proudly, rigidly, with its smooth wall, beyond the lake,
seemed to subside in bashful modesty. Before him the still
unconquered Dachstein stood, its glacier glittering crystall-
inely in the sunlight.

Once he sat down on a cool seat before the Kurhaus at
Bad-Aussee, and listened to the rustle of the flowering Traun.

On the post-house there still appeared the two-headed Eagle of the Hapsburgs. One of their race had once, eighty years before, married the postmaster's daughter. The Berliner, Düring, loved the Hapsburgs. There had been men of distinction among them, great Catholics in whom the fire of faith burned fiercely, like Charles V, who ended his days in retirement and humility in the monastery of San Yuste, in the Estramadura, though on his empire the sun never set; or like Ferdinand II, Franz Ferdinand, who was murdered in Sarajevo; Maria Theresa; or Charles I, who had died like a martyr on an African island far from his native land. As a Prussian citizen, Eugen was a republican—for his aversion for the Hohenzollern would-be Popes and Cæsars, who had their hands kissed and did nothing to check the *Kulturkampf*, had been implanted in him by his father. His avowed republicanism was, for him, not a question of philosophy, but a reasoned conclusion from the current situation.

Here, before the post-house with its lovely two-headed eagle and the Hapsburg arms, by the murmuring Traun, and with the Trisselwand beckoning in the distance, he, the cosmopolitan, for the first time fully realised all that was meant by the love of one's native land. They did not really feel Austrian, still less did they feel Pan-German, these peasants and wood-choppers in the valleys here, but only Styrian, Salzburgian, Tyrolean. They loved their corner of the earth—and that was all. And they would, of course, all resent the coming of a strange people who would take their land from them, and force them to speak Esthonian, Czech, or Chevsurian. Their language here was "*Stoasteirisch.*" It was part of the landscape, just like the Loser or the Trissel-wand.

Here everything was natural and clear. Life here seemed to him simple and transparent. A wave of horror swept over him when his thoughts reverted to Berlin. Was not that

city a madness, was not that city a fantasy of the fever-
maddened brain—in spite of the city's lamenting and yet
ardent enthusiast in clerical garb, Karl Sonnenschein, the
author of those *Notizen*, with their madness and yet their
genius, who had celebrated that city, sung over it and wept
over it, in a new style that did full justice to this theme, and
who had become for this city what Heinrich Lersch had long
been to the world of factories? But Eugen knew that the
great cities were inevitable necessities, real creators of culture,
and that no constructive movement could spread from
country to town. The towns were the sources of culture and
intellectual activity, of communal consciousness and development. The peasant, in fact, remained the *"paganus,"* the
heathen, the egoist, the obstinate reactionary, the man of
the earth, earthy. He had heard it from Scapinelli—and not
only from him—he had realised it himself—that the revival
of Christianity and the Church, the Great Offensive, could
only emanate from the great cities, from the factories and
offices, from the professorial chairs of the universities, from
the night-shelters, slum quarters, and meeting-halls. On
the other hand, the townspeople were the martyrs, the men
without sunshine, without room, who stood, close packed,
one beside another, so that they must perforce hold one
another's hands. They lived together in monstrous buildings,
rode together in cramped tramcars, worked, table by table,
in offices and factories, and were all dimly, subconsciously
aware that they lived only by virtue of one another, depend-
ent on one another, drawing on one another; the workman
and the factory-owner, the domestic and the housewife, the
buyer and the trader, the taxi-driver and the passenger; and
even if they hated one another they could not separate.
They were tied together—chained together. Life, for them,
meant service. But the peasant ploughs his fields and milks
his cows, the peasant is free, the peasant is master, and his

only fear is of the weather, of rain and thunder, of drought and hail, of frost and flood. The earth is ever fruitful, and the abundance she yields him he drives to market and sells —barters it for a few clothes, and withdraws into his cottage. The peasant stands alone, hates service, bonds, obedience, humility, the city that tries to give him orders. The city means service to one's neighbour—the peasantry, service to oneself. The townsman is creative, the peasant sterile.

A few stars were already twinkling above the dark contours of the Zinken. The Kurhaus band was beginning its performance, the notes blending with the rustling murmur of the Traun. A cool September breeze blew down from the steep mountain sides, and a few girls in summer dresses were walking, arm in arm, across the gravel. He turned sideways, and saw, near the bench on which he was sitting, a courting couple who leaned over the iron railings along the bank of the river, and stared down into the Traun. Neither of them was speaking a word—the man had placed his arm around the girl's corsage, the wind filled out her coloured skirts a little and rustled the chamois tuft in the lad's hat. They both remained motionless, gazing after the foaming waves of the mountain torrent, and it seemed to them as if they were gliding unconsciously upstream whilst the water frothed, stationary, beneath them. Further and further up-river—to a legendary land where love and restful leisure let the heavy centuries lumber past unheeded.

When Eugen saw these two young people leaning over the iron railings, the memory of Gertrude rushed back on him, and he had to get up and walk about, and fight down the torturing unrest. He left the laid-out park, roamed about the town, went part of the way up to St. Leonhart, and came back; passed the municipal hospital, where once more he noticed a great two-headed eagle with outspread wings, painted in fresco on the chapel. From without, he could find no way into the chapel, and he was athirst once more to kneel before the Tabernacle and to pour out his heart to Him. The painful beauty of the wooded, lake-filled world of the mountains had burdened his soul with such a weight of thoughts and questionings, that he felt an urge to be in communion with Him again. He entered the courtyard of the former municipal hospital, seeing that it had become a home for the indigent aged who, with mumbling jaws and bent backs, hobbled about the courtyard, croaking and chattering. They were men and women with old faces, such as can be seen about nowhere at the present day, countenances that reminded him of St. Vincent de Paul. Easily he found his way to the chapel, and, in the deserted interior, he knelt before the altar.

CHAPTER VI

OUT OF DARKNESS

HARDLY had he reached Vienna when he received a wire from a priest in Upper Silesia asking him to deliver a lecture, on the Monday evening, on the significance of the encyclical "*Quadragesimo Anno*." It was a Saturday evening, when, in a half-dark hotel bedroom, Eugen tore the telegram open. He knew that, despite his sojourn in the U.S.S.R., he did not hit on the right tone in his contact with the working classes. And yet it always gave him a quiet pleasure to be among the workers, to talk with the workers, to advise them, to guide them, and also to listen to them and learn from them. Eugen's favourite poet had always been Heinrich Lersch. With him he had passed through the gradual change of viewpoint, with regard to nation, state, class, war, and it had been Heinrich Lersch who had made clear to him, for the first time, the cosmic and creative position of the worker in the world to-day. It was the worker who had freed himself from the condition of a creature of the earth, from the limitations of soil and latitude, in order, somewhere and somehow, to earn his own bread. Lersch it was who had mastered modern technique, technology, had seen its soullessness, because he had assembled the machines and dismantled them, and knew that there was nothing mystical or spectral concealed within them. He did not, like the Russian peasant, kiss the tractors, did not fall to his knees before screeching gramophone records. He himself was a creator of such things—he had kept for these products a cordial, indulgent smile, and, in the guise of a siege-engineer from a past century, he had stood side by side with the Church, whilst, behind the work of the machines, had seen something vaguely satanic. It was the workman, too, who embodied infinite patience and complete absence of jealousy and envy. The man who has once tried to bring workers to strike knows how much effort it requires—for, so long as the worker and his family are not exactly starving, contentment reigns among them. Whoever has at some time, in carnival time, seen a motor-car arrive in front of a bar or dance-hall, and ladies and gentlemen in gala dress slip from the brightly lit car and past a uniformed commissionaire, into the warmth of the buildings, with their noses in the air, and at the same time watched the men on the pavement standing round gaping, will have seen the distinction between the workman, laughing, childlike, at such ridiculous behaviour, and the bourgeois, writhing with fury, exasperated and tortured with morbid longings and discontent with tawdry elegance. Yes, one can safely assert that, if the tension between the different social grades were measurable physically, the contrast between the worker and the factory owner would be far less than between the municipal councillor and the councillor of state. In his constant ideals, less subject than any other man's to the changing vagaries of the period, the workman always keeps in view the general community, the common good. Always clear, calm, patient, logical, ordered development. While the bourgeois dashes along, restless, selfish, idealless, godless, holding ever before his own face a mirror. And so the workers are the true "children of God," even if they may perhaps vote Red, even if they err, even if they sometimes let themselves be turned away from their immutable paths, by the intoxicating catchwords of power-greedy bourgeois. It is the worker who puts his last farthing aside to give it to the Church, the Party, the bookseller—who does not freeze in the glacier coldness of scepticism—who, in spite of his matured mind, which he has formed and moulded for himself during wakeful nights, bent over an opened book, does not fall a victim to arrogance and gloomy, sterile, bourgeois intellectualism, but views the future with child-like faith, in the spirit of those words of Christ: "Unless ye shall become as little children. . . ."

Glad as Eugen was to meet these men again and to work with them, this unexpected interruption of his leisure, and the prospect of travelling back to Germany, were not particu-larly welcome. On the same evening, he was meeting a Hungarian in Vienna, and he went to the Hungarian wine-house. But the gipsy music drove him, soul-sick man that he was, into such a state of melancholy and restlessness—for him synonymous terms—that he was forced to get up, breath-ing heavily, pay his bill, and, with his friend, go out into the cool street.

The next day in the early morning, he went to Mass at St. Stephen's. There he knelt, praying, in the midst of a varie-gated throng of worshippers, before the representation of the Greek Catholic Mother of God by Pocs—the "servant girl's Madonna"—and petitioned for rest and recovery. It seemed to him as though the picture of grace had promised him an early healing.

The broad sweep of Catholicism, here, he had already become conscious of during the Mass. Vienna, Austria, the Danube—these were Catholic names. During Mass the people stood or knelt in the church with relaxed bodies. They went to visit Him with love and longing in their hearts. But, back there, on the northern Front, each unit encased in the iron armour of a glacial Protestantism, had to be melted through with the flame of a tempestuous love and a glowing faith. Over there, in Berlin, Copenhagen, Oslo,

Edinburgh, Reykjavik, and Riga, men stood to attention in church, like recruits in the days of the army of Frederick II of Prussia. There, men had not yet penetrated into the depths; there, men only worked horizontally—Divine Service was not simply synousia with Him, but also a parade for review, a demonstration, the Ecclesia of the catacombs. "Happy men, these!" thought Eugen, with envy. "They have the time and opportunity to make penetrating investigations into the correspondences between the *Corpus* and the *Anima Christi*—write about the *Economia Perennis*, on Scholasticism and liturgy. But we are only an excited debating society, a Jacobin meeting, a *Fronde* huddled together."

The unopposed sovereignty of Catholicism in Vienna fascinated Eugen so much that he resolved to make a round of the places of amusement, seeking it out—and as on this last October Sunday the sun was shining, he rode on a densely packed electric tram out to the Prater, and let the movement of the crowds carry him along and decide his route. But his disappointment was immense. This false gaiety, in the sharp autumn wind, this ageing that he felt around him, the cheap loudness of the violent colours, the screeching and rattling of the old, worn-out, almost unserviceable mechanical amusements, in this paradise for soldiers, cook-generals, children, apprentices, subordinate employees, and other suppressed types of mankind who here find "life," patronising the "shilling hop," working the automatic machines, trying their strength on the mechanical punch-ball, steering little electric cars for themselves, and having while-you-wait photos taken, in a Napoleonic pose, were not calculated to raise Eugen's spirits. The corpse-smell of the nineteenth century seemed to float over this Fun Fair of the Commonplace. And while not wishing to turn his thoughts back to the past, the picture of the "*Park Kultury i Otdykha*" in Moscow arose before his mind's eye.

And now even the atheist melancholy of that spot, peopled with obsessed heretics, seemed to have a deeper and more serious significance than the present living sea of banalities and its surge of pleasure-seeking. With the picture of the Park in Moscow, however, there came the house in the Afanasievske Pereulok, Lefortova, Bolshevo, Anna Andreyevna, Gertrude. . . .

Filled with nausea, he rode back to the hotel, spent the rest of the afternoon sitting on his divan, rejected contemptuously any idea of taking a stroll round the beautiful city, read Mauriac's *Souffrances et Bonheur du Chrétien*, and then laid the book aside and dozed a little. When he next awoke, it was quite dark. His mouth was dry, his linen stuck to his body, and, in spite of the warmth of the room, light shivers ran through him. The glare of the electric light hurt him, and, with sleepy, puckered eyes, he shuffled round the room. The waiter had to bring him some black coffee. Then he plunged his head in cold water, packed his suitcase, bounded down the stairs, shouted round in a garage, and examined the petrol-feed, dragged an oilcan about with labouring steps, sat on a packing-case talking to a motor mechanic about the economic crisis and the U.S.S.R., and finally, when all the preparations were finished, sat down on his "steel horse" and, with buzzing engine, sped out on to the dry asphalt, steered cautiously through the streets, and, as the lights about him became more scattered and fewer, he depressed the accelerator more and more. Outside on the main road whence, as the last trace of the great city, was to be seen only a strip of rusty-red sky, the motor-cycle, with icy-white beams of light from its head-lamps and with the accelerator "all in," shot forward like a spurred horse, swift as the lightning, and with a perfect smoothness.

Sixty—sixty-five—seventy—eighty kilometres.

The pillion-seat behind Eugen was empty. This emptiness

around him—this emptiness of all humanity—this it was that drove him on to an ever-increasing restlessness, and an ever-accelerating speed. Only the frontiers made any halt in his tearing rush.

When he reached the workmen's village near Bobrek in German Upper Silesia, he involuntarily remembered the story of the sectarian Khrapov, of the wretched hole in the mining area of the Don valley. Certainly, owing to its more westerly situation, the village here looked cleaner and better cared for than that hamlet of death in the Ukraine. Eugen arrived, with his motor-cycle, just as the priest coming from Mass was sitting down to breakfast and dipping his roll in his coffee. Eugen sat down with him at once, drank a few cups of the black-brown beverage, to banish the returning sleepiness that threatened him, then went with the priest (a little thick-set Pole who had studied divinity at Breslau) up and down outside the presbytery, and discussed the programme for the afternoon. Coal waste and clinkers crunched beneath their feet. All around, the cranes rose, their dangling pulleys and wire hawsers rotating on their pulleys. Smelting furnaces emitted thick columns of smoke, workmen went half-naked, often with only a jacket thrown over them, to their pits, huts, and factories.

While Eugen gazed with longing eyes up at the dirty sky of Upper Silesia, the priest kept fussing about Eugen's coat with his fingers, removing a thread from his collar, blowing a speck of dust from his shoulder, and talked and gesticulated. But Eugen could offer him in return nothing but the indifferent nods of a man in ecstasy. Here, again, under the dull German sun, he realised how little his feelings for Gertrude had diminished. They had, perhaps, become kindlier—less tense, and less rigidly outlined. But they had lost nothing in force—save only that now, occasionally, the image of Mary would appear to him, and he was seized with the vain fancy that Gertrude, too, stood close to Our Lady, and that the heart of Mary was the only point of intersection where they could and might meet.

In the afternoon, his lecture in the club-house took place. His discourse, this time, sounded a little confused—his ideas were vague, and his construction lacking in clarity. Not until he began speaking of the emotional side of the problem did a few young workmen who hitherto had been chattering, bored, in the background, thrust themselves forward; and, after the conclusion of his speech, they applauded enthusiastically.

The priest invited Eugen to spend the night at his house. But his restlessness drove him to ride on. This did not please the priest. He told him, outright, to his face, that he was already exhausted with fatigue; he need only look in the glass. Dr. Sirower, who had come from Berlin, and was going to deliver another talk the next day in the same schedule of lectures, urgently advised him, too, to lie down, and not spend another night in the saddle. Eugen hesitated; he wanted to go back to Vienna, he wanted to go to Prague, to call on the "Akkord" people, Jaroslav Durych and Arch-bishop Kordáč. He wanted to get away from here—away from Germany. But sleep asserted itself so strongly that, after insisting in every way he could that he positively must go, he had to yawn, and already too tired to raise his hand to his mouth, he yawned right in the face of the man who was eagerly talking to him. Finally he let them lead him, passive and somnolent, to a bedroom, where a high, hard, short bed awaited him, and the quicksilver was peeling off a mirror.

Sirower wanted to tell him something more about Berlin, about Fahsel, Scapinelli, and Orsenigo. But he was already so tired that sleep fell upon him like the lid slamming down upon an empty box.

He woke late in the morning, washed, dressed, and went

outside the house. Heavy, gloomy dreams had tormented
him during the night. He was oppressed with an un-
accountable feeling that there was something here, in the
house, that was not right. He had passed through the
kitchen, through the sacristy, into the yard. Everywhere
was empty. Only in the front room a cat had leaped,
frightened, from a table, and snarled at him hostilely. Even
Dr. Sirower was nowhere to be seen. Now he was standing in
front of the house, and noticed that the crane above the
nearest pit-head was standing idle. A crowd of people, men,
and, in even greater numbers, women and children, were
thronging noisily about the mouth of the shaft. And, a
little to one side, on the straggling, scanty grass, stood an
empty police waggon. In a dust-coat, with hands in pockets,
Eugen strolled up, more curious than perturbed. Somebody
was delivering an address to the men. He was calming the
crowd. Eugen asked what had happened. A pit disaster?
Fire-damp? Seepage? Gas leaking? Subsidence? Fire?
Nobody yet knew.

With white, distended eyes the women stood there.
Cowering, they peered into one another's ashen faces, their
teeth chattering. The children's knees were shaking. Then,
again, some of them began to whisper, and the whisper
became a scream, the scream became a great clamour of
yells. Like maniacs, the women began shaking the bars of
the shaft-head railings, until, with moistened foreheads and
frothing jaws, they had to desist from sheer exhaustion. But the
men stood aside, and only now and then did a dull muttering
break out. A few excited men, dressed like townsmen, hats
thrust back on their heads, pushed a way through the crowds
of women, jotting down notes in their books, and gesticulating
excitedly, and laughing noisily, then making sympathetic
faces; reporters, Communist agitators, pit officials. At one
of these men Eugen cast a sharp look.

"Hi, there, Krawuttke!" he called to him. "Are you trying to fish in troubled waters again, eh?"

The man addressed was just then talking, near the priest, who stood on the corner-stone of the drive of the administrative offices, to two women, and, on hearing Eugen's voice, turned round like a flash. Four years ago he had twice run into Eugen. Once, at a debate where Eugen had thoroughly out-talked him, and the second time in Wedding, when Eugen, at the head of a party of Catholic Storm Troops, was returning from the Protest Demonstration procession against the Communistic town council of Neukölln. Krawuttke left the women standing there, thrust his hands to his hips, and confronted Eugen.

"Nice of you, honoured sir!" he said mockingly, "to have come here yesterday on the *train de luxe*, to give the people some blarney about eternal blessedness!"

A few women and two half-naked workmen were standing round him, listening closely. With screwed-up eyes they looked, now at Krawuttke, who, with his tousled hair and grotesque lip-movements, began inciting the crowd against Eugen; and now at Eugen, who, pale and smiling with difficulty, stood there in silence; and now at Dr. Sirower, who was trying to make Krawuttke look ridiculous by interjecting exclamations in Polish.

The priest attempted to intervene, and soon all four were surrounded by a large circle of people, screaming wildly together. A policeman tried to disperse this mob with his baton, but he had little success. Now Sirower was engaged in a tussle with the Communist, and Eugen stood a little to one side. He knew one of the half-naked workmen. He had talked to him after the lecture. It would be a good thing, the latter whispered to him, in a low voice, if one of the gentlemen would take part in the rescue work.

Eugen raised his head.

"Quite a feasible suggestion," he said, quietly. "Where could one volunteer?"

"My name is Górecki," the fellow introduced himself somewhat formally. Then he pointed to the second man, dressed as scantily as himself. "And this is Waniek. He's a member of the socialist trade union, but a good fellow. We both belong to the rescue party. You could join us."

Eugen dropped his eyes.

"I will come with you," he said quietly.

"We've just been saying 'good-bye' to our girls," said the one with the darker face. "In five minutes, the side door of the administrative offices will open, and then we'll slip in."

"I'll go with you," Eugen repeated.

"Have you said good-bye to your girl yet?" asked Waniek, whereupon Górecki gave him a nudge.

"I have no girl," said Eugen quietly.

Then something touching occurred, that nearly brought the tears to Eugen's eyes.

Górecki drew from his naked chest, and held out to Eugen in his calloused hand, a dented silver medallion of the Mother of God of Tchenstochau.

"Waniek will laugh," he said, "but anyhow, it's true enough—we may be a rough lot but she looks down at us all."

But Waniek did not even laugh when Eugen kissed this medallion reverently.

At last they were all standing in the courtyard of the administrative offices. Waniek and Górecki were freezing in the autumn winds. Dr. Sirower, of course, also wanted to go with them, but Eugen laughed at the frail little fellow.

"Is your insurance still in force?" the doctor asked him.

Eugen nodded.

The priest gave the men his blessing, and then they went, through passages and sheds, downstairs, and through

basements, into a spacious room. Eugen undressed mechanically. An hour ago he had been gargling and cleaning his
teeth, guessing nothing. Forty-eight hours before he had
still been promenading disgustedly through the Wurstalprater,
in Vienna. Someone handed him a long, greasy pair of
cotton trousers. That was, of course, more suitable than the
gay plus-fours that he hung up on a hook. He also changed
his shoes. Brown shoes are not suitable for pits. A few of the
men looked at the clothes he had hung up and fingered the
neck-tie. "Pure silk?" they asked, among themselves.
Meanwhile, a gigantic foreman got busy with him, and
tightened the massive leather belt about his loins. The white
skin of his chest contrasted oddly with the others. But he
had little time for reflection. The foreman came again—
this time with a gas-mask—suspended it round his head,
screwed in a tin-box-like mouthpiece, tightened the separate
straps till Eugen thought he must suffocate, and invested him
in a tin helmet. Then, once more, the foreman tugged at
the straps. Eugen felt himself being handled like a piece of
passive flesh. It was like that time, three years before, when
he was being strapped down on the operating table in St.
Hedwig's Hospital, and his abdomen opened. Inside the
gas-mask, he had no longer the proper sensation of belonging
to the world, of standing with both feet on the ground. A
feeling of infinite helplessness had come over him. He knew
that a little child, now, could bowl him over like a tin
soldier. The sounds of the outside world came muffled to his
ears, and his forehead was covered with innumerable tiny
globules of sweat. He was now once more at the "Front"—
a real "Front." Someone gave him a push from behind.
That meant "Quick March!" The miners were huddled
together in a corner. He could recognise Górecki by his
medallion of Our Lady. But they were all wearing gas-
masks, and with those large dark-coloured glass goggle-

lenses instead of eyes, and the dangling mouthpiece, they looked like mortally melancholy pigs in a slaughter-house. Naked, dirty, with a tin proboscis, the time had come to face death. His breath came heavily, and the glasses threatened to cloud over. Apart from his dentist, Dr. Hermann Feigelstock, who, incidentally, was the cleverest and most painless dentist in Germany, and the Soviet Secret Police, he was afraid of nothing. The turning of the concrete roads he used to take without relaxing his pressure on the accelerator, but now—with the straps biting into him every-where, now that he had been tied up like a bundle of wretched flesh trussed for sacrifice, undressed, deprived of his hearing, and half suffocated, he was seized suddenly with a terrible faint-heartedness, such as the Evil One sometimes visits even heroes with, in the hour of peril. This faint-heartedness became a panic fear. Had it rested with himself, he would just as soon have torn the pig-like snout from his face, taken to flight, leaped upon his cycle, and whizzed away, never to return. The fact that he did not draw back now was by no means due to his fortitude or courage, but solely to the fear of being taunted with coward-ice. Fear and weakness possessed him—the idea of having to face death in a form in which it could not be averted either by courage or cunning, filled him with despair. He sat down with the miners, and gazed before him, panting. Not being able to breathe, nor to see much, and the pounding of his heart seemed the forerunners of dying. His flesh, his heart, his lungs, his sweat-glands were jibbing and struggling against something—against some hostile power—against death. Outside the mask, men approached him—(inside the mask nothing happened; inside the mask there was only a chill, oily sweat running down)—and handed him a large, heavy object of ice-cold metal. The others, too, were given things to carry. He rested this lengthy implement across his shoulder, so that his clavicle ached painfully, and he tried to stand upright. He was surprised to find that he could feel that pain, outside the mask, and was conscious of this outer casing of the drilling-machine as if it had been a weapon, a gun. Then they got up and formed into a squad. Clumsily he staggered after them; he was the last. What he was carrying was not a weapon, not a gun; it was a Cross. When he was in the hatch going down the shaft, he once more saw the priest and Dr. Sirower. "Black Front!" the latter called to him. He tried to raise his left hand—but at that moment the rope was already beginning to clatter through the pulleys, the basket was going down, down, daylight was simply a circle of brightness that dwindled smaller and smaller overhead; the pit-lamps they had lit began to be effective with their pale radiance, their spectral red luminosity filling the black narrowness of the shaft and transforming the naked torsos of the miners to things of rusty-red, earthy stone.

On landing at the bottom he noticed how many pit workers, without gas-masks, were throwing barometers and other measuring instruments about, and busying themselves at switchboards. Work seemed to be in abeyance. Eugen could make out nothing that was going on—all he knew was that his work was to be dangerous, that he had to drill. Nothing more. That was all. When the party set off, and had put their tools in a mine-trolley, pushing this truck along its rails before them, he trotted unthinkingly after them. He had now become a little better accustomed to wearing the gas-mask. But suddenly the men stopped. And now he, too, looked up.

The wooden props which had supported the stulms, shoring up the sides and sustaining the roof, had snapped and crumpled up like match-sticks, and the electric wires were hanging in confusion. The rails had been wrenched out of shape by some almost supernatural power. Eugen felt his heart in his throat, pounding, where a rubber band belonging to the gas-mask was choking him. So here was destruction, here was death. One of the miners rested his lamp on the ground, looked at it, and shook his head, and then raised it to the ceiling. Eugen could distinctly see how the flame increased.

So there was a gas on the ground, a heavy gas, a deadly gas. "Fire-damp," he told himself. He struggled to recall what he had heard about this at school, in his final year before matriculation. Only confused, disconnected scraps of terminology whirled round his aching head. Then, once more, he saw how Górecki was pressing his head, in its gas-mask, against the side of the excavation. He did the same, and could hear a gentle crackling noise. The miner had noticed him, and laid his mask against Eugen's:

"The coal is crabbing!" he heard him say.

He pondered over this word, but could find no meaning in it. In the meanwhile the salvage party crept, without their apparatus, sometimes squeezing themselves flat against the sides, sometimes crawling on their bellies, through the shattered woodwork. They did not get far, for the stulms seemed to end blindly. Then Eugen saw the bent rails on the ground disappear into the rock, and understood everything. So this was where the passage had caved in, to what extent nobody knew. A miner tapped the wall with a hammer, and then again pressed his head to the rock. This rock seemed to be something mysterious. It crackled, exhaled gases, yielded coal, crumpled up wood like paper, and devoured human lives. And, after all, it was all so nonsensical—what were tree trunks doing down here, hundreds of yards beneath the surface of the earth? Was it not madness to build stables down here, to catch wild ponies from the steppes, to tame them, bring them here down below the earth, and make them work till they were blind? And men, hungry for air and the joy of life, as they were, why should they hammer out of the rock those prehistoric, black, hard fragments of trees, that they called coal, at the risk of their lives, instead of living above ground a life of light and freedom? Must not these men be convicts, or idiots, or— saints?

The leader of the party removed his mask, and the others followed his example. Eugen did not ask any questions, but let his own mask also hang down on his greasy chest. And now the work began. The ceiling had to be shored up again, the electric wires repaired, the cables laid afresh. The heat was infernal. Eugen clenched his teeth. "Capitalism is a work of Satan," he thought to himself. "But a socialist society will also construct mines, and it is of no consequence whether the mountain crushes one as a state employee or as a private capitalist's workman." When the preliminary work was finished they refreshed themselves hastily with their provisions, thoroughly lubricated the drilling appliances again, and at once began their ear-splitting work.

Close packed together, they had already been working with their drills for six hours. They were once more wearing the masks, and Eugen was almost blinded with the sweat that ran from his sponge-like forehead down over his eyelids. The drill was not hard to operate, but Eugen's forearm trembled as in the days of his earliest youth in Riff, when he had held, clenched between his fingers, the handle-grips of a machine-gun. As then, so now, his bones, ligaments, tendons and muscles hurt like liquid fire, from the vibrating recoil of the machine. His ears already seemed deafened with the unceasing, grinding screech, and the shrill, intermittent screaming of the electric drill.

The new boring that they were making was scarcely a yard high, and every stretch of freshly won ground had immediately to be shored up. The air was so full of gas, that the pit lamps were almost completely extinguished. Eugen realised that he had over-estimated his bodily strength, and was in imminent danger of collapsing. His bent spine and the strained tendons of his thighs pained him excruciatingly. Finally, they were working with only two drills; Waniek and another man withdrew to rest, creeping back and then remaining lying like two slain seals, near the entrance of the new boring. Eugen saw, in the dim light of their lamps, how the men's sides heaved and fell in a frenzied tempo. Like machines working under high pressure, these two chests heaved. But Eugen went back to his work, pressed on the switch, and made the hard metal screech shrilly against the rock. They were all exhausted, but it was Eugen's persistence that made them reluctant to give in. Eugen, however, knew in what capacity he was toiling at that drudgery down there; there he was not merely a man out to save the lives of others. . . .

When his turn came to rest, he was already too worn out to drag himself to the nearby exit. Twelve paces from the spot where they were working he collapsed and fell on his face. He re-awakened with his tin proboscis grating on the coal dust—he did not sleep—he did not faint. A rattle sounded in his throat, and he was only conscious of the lungs that seemed to be bursting in him. He now had no desire but to stay motionless where he was, and end his days there. A few panting sighs to Him escaped from his parched, chapped lips. Then he stretched out his arms and his feet, and did not move again. Trivial thoughts trailed before him in procession—expressionless faces looked at him and vanished. He saw numbers, geometrical figures, a kitchen, a room with a table and four chairs, a cow, pictures out of a children's drawing book. . . .

It might have been about an hour that he lay there,

when suddenly an enormous explosion, accompanied with an infernal crashing and splintering, resounded. He was tossed aside, flung with his head against the coal, so that he was lying on his back. At the entrance of the boring a bright glare of fire flickered like forked lightning. His lungs ceased to function—a ghastly scream echoed—and then the rending, crashing, roar recommenced, together with a subterranean rumbling, lumbering noise, that finally gave way to a yet more terrifying silence and darkness.

With a convulsive movement of his hands, he tore the mask from his face—coal-dust trickled from the ceiling into his mouth. He felt a retching nausea—he groped with claw-like fingers in the air—tried to move—and collapsed, fainting.

When he awoke again, nothing was to be seen but darkness, nothing to be heard but that deep silence. A few steps from him the boring had caved in. The whole party had been killed—crushed or burned or suffocated; Waniek and all the other miners. He did not try to think why or how—this had just happened. And slowly it came to him, as he laboured for breath, the realisation that he, too, was destined for death. The air, saturated with fumes, smarted in his palate, his throat, and forced him to close his eyes tightly. It was only due to the fact of his not moving that he did not suffocate. He had laid one hand on his heart. He had reached the end of his earthly journey—and although many men might die more beautifully than he, yet he was grateful that he had been allowed to fall at the "Front," while still young, and not too completely absorbed in the habit of living, not too vitally alive—and not too suddenly, so that he could bid farewell to the body while still conscious.

Stegelin stood by his side, and said:

"Do you see? The sad part of it is, that we are all simply a stage in the great fight—units in the sector of the infinite battle-front of trenches. We never get a view of the end.

We are born somewhere amid the tattoo of the drums, we are stationed at some particular position on the Front, fight for a few decades, and then, somewhere amid the beating of those drums, we go under——"

But he who, with heart wearing out, lay there in the coal-dust, knew, at that moment, more of death at the Front—he knew that he must die, but, hardly a mile as the crow flies, from his body, Dr. Sirower was alive—barely a mile from the spot where his soul was to part from his body. Dr. Sirower belonged to Scapinelli, and Scapinelli was the fighter, the bayonet-sharp intellect, the minister of truth, of eternal truth. He would die; in Rome the Holy Office would continue to work, the Sacred Rota would go on with its labours, the Congregation of Rites, the Eastern Rites of the *Propaganda Fide*. He had to die, but in the glass, concrete, and steel churches of the Rhineland the Litany of Loreto would still be recited, and the glorious Rosary. The Fathers of the Church would still be translated into Chinese. The lepers would still be cared for in Molokai and Makogai. The great cities of France would still continue to be Catholicised. *He* had to die, but he knew that tne wonderful fight of the Church Militant would continue. The heretics of all grades, of all tendencies, of all lands, would rot intellectually, other Popes would follow Pius XI, a Leo XIV, a Benedict XVI, a Pius XII, a Clement XVI, and so on, until the end of days.

His heart often stopped functioning, but here, three hundred yards below the surface of the earth, he had nothing in his heart but sunshine, nothing but gratitude and joy. Through his faith, he had been able to comprehend the world, fully and completely, been able to enjoy it truly and rightly. As, when his sight was going, he looked back over his life, he was compelled to acknowledge how much suffering had been vouchsafed to him—but this suffering had been

so full of significant meaning, it had enriched him, it had
brought him closer to God. He could not help thinking of
his mad, sinful youth, of which he had so often repented,
with that joyful sincerity that only Catholics know. He could
not help thinking of the many girls to whom, in the days
when the words of St. Augustine as to our "restless heart
that only finds peace in God," were especially applicable,
he had approached with a pure heart, and gladdened and
warmed himself at the dual diversity of the sexes. He
thought of the nights, which he had always enjoyed, and
of the multiplicity of lands and mountains, of peoples and
towns, which God has willed and given. He thought of the
innumerable gifts of God which he had never before fully
realised to be such—the power of loving, of praying, of
laughing, of gladness, of suffering, of seeing, of thought, of
comprehension, of weeping, of dreaming. He, now lying
there on the ground, strengthless, was so happy that he
began to weep.

The creeping gas came and paralysed him completely,
but a smile remained upon his lips. His consciousness he
lost, but not the smile.

A quarter of an hour later, his heart still trembled beneath
his ribs. All else, everywhere, was silence and darkness.
Pictures, distinct and unclouded, came before his eyes.
And then the heart's tremors seemed to pass over into a
throbbing, a vibrating. His blood stopped circulating—he
felt a hitherto unknown buoyancy and freshness in his
limbs. He felt nothing more of the physical left in him—
neither warmth, nor cold; it was like a mild summer night.
Neither clothes nor limbs. He was gliding along, and, turn
about as he would, neither did his blood go to his head, nor
did he see earthly things. His consciousness had changed.
That which prevailed in him now was the intimation of a
joy; and *that* filled him completely—filled his entire ego.

He perceived a light, and, obeying a super-terrestrial law, he strove towards it. He told himself that this Light was the true giver of all warmth and all light. There were no more inner voices—voices that stirred in him as in earlier days. *This* inner voice in him, this Being in him, that was glad and that mourned, that prayed and expressed itself in tears, that longed for God—had become his new self.

EPILOGUE
Roma locuta, causa finita

NINE months after the death of Eugen Düring Father
Scapinelli was driving through the summery roads of Brandenburg. To right and left of the road extended flowering
meadows, and in the air hung a scent of sage and mint.
Directly overhead the sun blazed down, and set the landscape, shading away into dirty half-tones of colour on the
horizon, aquiver. The Jesuit was weary of sitting in the
closed car—he let the engine stop, put on his brakes, and
got out. It was already half-past ten, in half an hour he
had to celebrate a late Mass in the Zieten-Hussars' barracks,
on the Hollmann-Strasse. He sat on the mudguard of his
car, lit a cigarette, held up his face to the sun, closed his
eyes. The longing for the mountains tantalised him. There
seemed to be something or other dimming his joy of life.
It was not the thought of an approaching transfer from
Berlin, but something immediate and present. It must
certainly be the cigarette. He took the half-moist, half-
glowing stump from between his gripping lips, and tossed it
disgustedly down on the road. Now there was nothing left
to stand between himself and the landscape. He leaned
his head against the coachwork of the car, and reflected
how pleasant it would be to be able to sleep now, and
participate in the divine rest that Eugen was now enjoying.
But hearing his blood hammering at his temples, the consciousness came to him that his heart was still functioning
quite regularly, and that here, on this planet, rest was
nothing but a dream and a vain wish.

After the Mass he did not trouble to change, but went home in his soutane, and at once settled down to work. Scapinelli always worked simultaneously at three or four books: he had an extensive report to write on the Church in German Encyclopædias; a novel with its scene set in Vienna in the eighties; a theological treatise on the Church among the Negritic-Philipinos in general; and the Aglapayitic schisms of Luzon in particular, from the point of view of national psychology; an article for the official organ of Catholic Prison Missions. He was bending over the Meyer-Lexikon for 1896, which thus dated from a time when people were, after all, walking on their hind-legs, as the Darwinians would point out, stuffing food into their mouths with their front paws. And he read as follows:

"The Jesuits. A spiritual Order founded in the sole interests of the Papal supremacy, progressing from beginnings of fantastic enthusiasm, to the study of world-wide diplomatic policy. The novices' fixed order of the day from four in the morning till nine at night includes a deadening monotony of gloomy exercises in meditation, menial services, fantastic reading, and severe disciplinary austerities, calculated to break down all healthy individuality and complete that mental warping which led the young man into the noviciate. . . . The Jesuit goes about in a long black habit and cloak, with a black, four-cornered biretta, or the flat clerical hat. He is supposed to carry his head forward with a gentle movement, his eyes are supposed to remain directed towards the ground, and to focus only on the lower part of the face of the person addressed. As a fruitful principle of all sensual and supersensual superstition, the cult of Mariolatry is carried to its utmost extremes."

Scapinelli almost laughed aloud.

"And it's people like that," he said, "who have the leonine courage to exclaim about fantastic reading!"

It was towards five o'clock in the afternoon when the sun, which in the morning had burned down searingly from immediately overhead on to the fields of Brandenburg, now diffused its softened rays like a tamed beast of prey, subdued and humbled, glowing softly on the window-sill; and the Jesuit looked out a number in the telephone directory. When he had found it, he took up the receiver, and set the forefinger of the right hand into the appropriate aperture in the dial. Then he thought he heard a noise in the entrance hall and so put the receiver back on its hook. The door of his room opened, and he rose to his feet, with the kindly Jesuit smile on his lips. Cordially he shook hands with the lady who came in. He was facing Gertrude Zechmeister.

Her expression remained rigid and hard.

"I have only come because I happened to be in Berlin," she said, "and I wanted to see how you were."

"I am as well as ever," said Scapinelli, with unchanged friendliness.

"So I see," she said, slowly accentuating every syllable. "You are very well. Probably driving about in your car, and enjoying yourself."

She would not look him in the face, but gazed past him, then began to look at the room, at the books, which were lying open on the writing-table, looked out of the window, turned on her heel and then stood still, in front of the wall, as though fascinated—the wall where, small and inconspicuous, Eugen's photo hung, showing him after his recovery from spotted typhus in the prison-camp of Bolshevo. With trembling fingers, she took it down from its nail, and looked at it by the window.

"Why have you never shown me this?" she exclaimed, "You have always kept this picture hidden from me."

"But I have not seen you for some years," he said quietly.

"You always have some excuse," she broke out. "Just look at him! His cheeks! His eyes!——"

Her words gave place to sobs, and finally, tears ran down her cheeks. She lifted the picture to her lips, kissed it, and covered her eyes with her hand.

Scapinelli stood, motionless, behind his writing-table.

"And how are you?" he asked her suddenly, in his clear, calm voice. "Are you still a theosophist?—or, perhaps, anthroposophist——?"

She let her hands drop from her face, and laid down the photo on the writing-table.

Her eyes narrowed, and the Jesuit noticed that a hatred of several years' standing must now find its expression. Not a muscle stirred in his face.

"Yes," she said, grimly, "I have become everything—theosophist, anthroposophist, new-thought disciple. I believe in Christian Science—Mazdaznam—Buddhism. I am a pacifist, Protestant, Liberal, Communist—*everything*. Anything and everything except a Catholic. If I could, I should like to unite all non-Catholics into one body and lead them into the field against Rome, against you, you slave-drivers. Through you, Helga Düring died—Rudolph Medek buried himself alive—Eugen, my poor Eugen, for whose sake I would gladly have let myself be divorced to make him happy—you allowed to languish in prisons for two years, then made his life a misery, and sent him to his death. No, there are only two worlds, the Roman and the non-Roman. And never—do you hear? never, never, never! —will Rome get this world into its grip again. For that, the rest of the world is much too big, too strong, too powerful. High and powerful stand the walls—Marxism, socialism, the awakening nationalism, pacifism, the——"

The Jesuit felt that her attack had left him unscathed.

To him it was no new thing that the Church Militant had a "busy cemetery." Only the other day a Militant Atheist had stabbed and killed a young friend of his on the *Reichsbanner*. These were accidents inseparable from the business in hand.

"Listen," he said. "So you don't believe that we shall once more unite the world in the name of Christ?" He pointed to a small globe filled with lead, which he used as a paper-weight. "It is true we were 'in pickle' four hundred years, and the smell of the passive preservative still clings about us. Look at our Catholic literature in Germany, and at a few South-German and Austrian weeklies—where only 'fundamental things' are written by hereditary princes, university professors, men of rank and title, and prelates, and which raise, from their first line to their last, the soul-stirring cry, with dismal lamentations, of bathing-beach indecencies, the modern care of prisoners, the abolition of capital punishment, Jewish writers, and trashy plays. Then one notices, at once, that we are living at the present day in a period of flux—when Catholicism (to express myself cynically for once) is being hammered into shape, from being an old women's union for controlling the length of bathing costumes, to become a living embodiment of the essence, the *summa* and the meaning of this world. We see that, since 1517, we have been sitting in a 'preserving tin,' and silently watching a schizo-phrenic, monomaniac, paranoic humanity, setting up their home in Europe.

"The sectarians suffered permanently from the fixed idea that they knew better than we what true Christianity meant. But we have already been standing two thousand years, and all the other Christian sects are forgotten, rotted away, gone into putrefaction, fossilised, bureaucratised. Everything began with a great, enthusiastic *élan*, and ended in the mire. The Puritans entrenched themselves in the Old Testament, and in pharisaic hypocrisies. And, where once it was forbidden to hang our feminine underwear, there prevails to-day a jolly *demi-vierge* promiscuity. Where is Protestantism, Luther's world of ideas, to-day? Where are Protestant literature, culture, politics, philosophy, and sociology——"

"You are crassly practical, you must take account of idealism."

"Of course. Always the monomaniacs of the left, and the monomaniacs of the right, come along, and the ones say, 'Rome is unworldly, Rome is ascetic, Rome is the enemy of progress, Rome is against matter.' Thus spoke and ranted the Protestant Liberal government officials' ladies, with their cul-de-Paris, in the eighties, and travelling Englishmen with check trousers and horsy faces, the infuriated pseudo-scientists and professors, simply raving chimpanzees in shirt-cuffs, with sidewhiskers, brains like chemical retorts, and Jaeger shirts. And now, to-day, sentimental, enthusiastic, raw-food faddists, with Buddhistic, occultistic 'soulful' eyes, are croaking: 'Oh, that terrible, materialistic Rome!' The epileptic Dostoevski was right, after all, it is 'earthy, materialistic, political, practical, worldly.' Then the Protestants come and clamour for free private interpretation of the Bible, while the socialists scream themselves hoarse that we're a gang of individualists, and east of the Elbe, forty years ago, we were still supposed to be the reactionary foes of education, and the obscurantists. To-day we are depicted as anti-capitalistic friends of the socialists, as the next-of-kin to Little Father Soso in Moscow. The Orthodox attacked us as soulless intellectuals. The Bolshevik reactionaries attack us as derivatives of opium and morphine, 'dope for the people.' The pantheists, as theological monarchists, with the wickedest onesidedness. The Protestants as terroristic collectivists and religious polytheists, with fetish-worship and image-cults. The same farce, in the case of the

Orthodox Easterns, with the dualistic God-Devil system, matter versus spirit, Ormuzd against Ahriman. The Ormuzd-proletarian fights against the Ahriman-bourgeois. The basic error was, of course, already inherent in Orthodoxy—for man is not a pendulum between God and the Devil, but something that by his nature strives directly to attain to God, only subjected by the activities of the devil to greater or lesser aberration from the path of salvation."

"Enlightenment will come," protested Gertrude.

"Enlightenment will come," he said, mockingly. "And from whom, if not from us? For a while these worthy citizens, romantics of the Grand Orient, have been the 'big noise' in Europe. One must have seen them to know what they're like—small, ill-washed business men, with fat little tummies, with pince-nez, attaché-cases, down-at-heel shoes, and dilettante, slimy ignorance. To-day they are stranded high and dry, because the masses have slipped away from them. With toil and labour they have built up the U.S.S.R. By way of thanks, they have been put to death, exiled, banished —just like the Nihilists, who had pitted their lives against the Beast of State in its Czarist form. Now gradually, Capitalism is failing, Bolshevism is ossifying, Nationalism is undergoing its last burst of frenzy, whilst Liberalism in civic outlook is exhaling such a corpse-like smell that one has to hold one's nose. Yes, war is to be abolished—and we have prepared for that with our *Treuga Dei* seven hundred years ago. We had great plans, but non-Catholic humanity wanted to do everything better—the egg wanted to be wiser than the hen. And there you see the result. The brightest achievement of those psychopaths, the U.S.S.R., is the way they are armed to the teeth. *Si vis pacem, para bellum!* All the dirt of the Pagan Renaissance and the little bog-flower of Macchiavellianism is blossoming over there among the heretics with redoubled vitality in the darkness. These men outside the Church wanted to make democracy a reality, in their own idiotic way, and the result has been—plutocracy. They overthrew the thrones in order to strike at the altars—and they have landed themselves with dictators. The Beast of State is mightier than ever it was in the Middle Ages. And with you 'free spirits,' the 'emancipated thinkers,' man is simply a civically-organised mammal. We shall create pacifism, for only from the starting point of love can war be abolished. And we shall throttle war, make it ridiculous, pillory it, destroy it—just as we have reduced the duel to a ridiculous foible of the students in the beer-gardens. Your pacifism will only remain the screaming and weeping of the hysterical weakling. Never forget that you are illusionists, and there are hundreds of thousands who stood willingly, even enthusiastically, in the trenches, laughing themselves sick at your humanitarianism. But we have— for the first time and finally—made democracy real, in the Sacrament of Holy Communion, in the Papal conclaves, in the Religious Orders.

"There is also a 'nationalism' in a form pleasing to God, that represents the love of one's native environment, love of language, custom and atmosphere—a nationalism that aims, not at conquest, but at the preservation of man's right to remain what he is, to talk the language one learned from one's mother, to dress in the costume of one's fathers, to sing the songs that have belonged to the country for centuries; while the 'nationalists' who cried out against the 'ultramontane betrayal' roared themselves hoarse against us in all countries. Our priests fought for the rights of the people: in Flanders, in Ireland, in Alsace, in Southern Tyrol, in Slovenia, in Croatia, in Slovakia, in Poland, in Lithuania, in the Latgal, and in the Basque country. But what have you, outside, made of this love of home? Imperialism; mass-psychosis; mass-murders, in which German soldiers are destroyed on French battlefields by the English with fuse-caps made from a German patent; and English soldiers, in the Boer War, were mown down with English munitions inported via Laurenço Marques. A dirty murderous business —but the world is seeing through you more clearly everyday —and from Macchiavelli to Ghandi, from the German Orders of Chivalry to the Fight for Culture, and the ban-lieux of Paris to the 'Bled'—is a way that has led nearer to *Christus*.

"You have always used the catch-phrase of the 'develop-ment of personal individuality,' and, with it all, it is really only Catholicism that let the national individualities be realised. The Gothic style of the Teutons was, of course, Catholic; the Renaissance of the Italians; the Baroque of the Austrians; the Tudor style of the English. With the Reformation and Puritanism, art, architecture, and music died out in Protestant countries. The Dom, in Cologne, stands in contrast to the Kaiser-Wilhelm Memorial Church. Rothenburg-ob-der-Tauber is there to contrast with the late Victorian style. Fischer von Erlach against the builder of the German Reichstag. With the Modern movement there began again the impoverished striving for beauty, instead of for Catholic grandeur. So, back to the antique pæderasts of ancient Hellas. The people outside have nothing left but to go into the cemeteries—to dig up corpses, to galvanise and modernise corpses. The Church of the Sag-rada Familia in Barcelona, when it is finished, will not be 'beautiful' in the Greek, classical, pagan, æstheticising sense—and yet it will look majestic——"

His figure straightened up, his features became more placid and his voice was again calm and quiet. He did not look at her, did not look into her eyes, but rather seemed to be apprehending supernatural numbers and symbols on the whitewashed wall beyond her, as if her body were transparent, as if he were seeing visions.

"You must follow us, and go our way," he said quietly. "For there is only one way—and on that way our feet are set. We are the civilians, the normal, the man-in-the-street —but you, outside, are all absurdly stencilled, maniacally depressed; you run round in brown, black, red, blue shirts. You sit in infantile, romantic secret societies, and if one knows your programmes one's head reels at such a backstairs standard. Just look at the Bolsheviks of the younger generation, with their criminal bovine faces: Old Believers with their somnambulistic, twitching eyelids, and their troglodite beards; the Hungarian Calvinists, with their sad, severe, schoolmasterly faces; and the agnostics of the West, with their little Napoleonic, chauffeur faces; the nationalists in their uniforms; the members of organisations with their badges—all like a herd astray, all Rayah, all bewitched children running ecstatically after the demented ratcatcher of Hamelin. But we are civilian and inconspicuous. The Catholic man is not a type, he varies from St. Anthony of the Sahara to Alexander VI, from La Trappe to St. Philip Neri and St. Ignatius, from St. Francis to Brüning, from Mary Stuart to Sigrid Undset. Everything else is stencilled ——"

"Inquisition——"

"Thanks," said Scapinelli. "You ought to be better informed on that, having once worked with us. You must be aware that we ourselves have never burned or mutilated people. That only happens in popular novels for servant girls in the provinces. It was our duty to determine whether the individual was a heretic or not—the State put them to death. We performed a menial service for the State. That was a sin, and God punished us. As punishment He sent us into 'pickle' for four hundred years. But now the Kairos is

come—the 'time' is come—when we shall intervene between
you who are mutually fighting, to take over the reins of this
world again, in our own hands, for what is happening in
this tormented world to the men ground down like cattle.
It's come to be a bit too thick for us. The fear of death,
which Christianity seemed to have removed from the world,
has come back. Those standing outside cannot disguise
from themselves, either by a developed technical equipment,
or by medicine, or by a simplified scheme of government, or
by an artificialised sexuality, their dread of death. How
different it was in the joyous later Middle Ages, when St.
Francis spoke of 'Brother Death,' when death was just such
a popular figure in the theatre as, at the present day, the
soldier coming back from the front after he has been thought
dead, or the 'noble doctor and friend of man,' who performs
cheap abortions. The skull was a widespread symbol, and
dying a process looked forward to with a solemn reverence,
the introduction and the entrance to something great and
wonderful—but to-day people cling to the oracle of statistics,
and reduce figures of mortality, full of an ashen terror of
death. And their death is a death of fear and shame. With
no Sacrament, with distended eyes and distorted face, they
die in hospitals and sanatoria, in horrible orgasms they clutch
at life, throb, whimper, whine. And when they are dead,
there comes a black-enamelled, six-cylinder car, and speeds
through the streets, swiftly and quietly, so as not to be
noticed. Crematorium. Urn. Sealed up. Despatched.
Room disinfected. Death-duty paid. Quickly, soundly,
silently, inconspicuously.

"For a while we were amused, at Rome, over the way
those outside spoke and acted—people who were simply
filling their mouths with what they took, and producing
nothing in return. And the plaints of the tortured sufferers
have frozen the smile from our lips; the liberal omnipotence-

of-the-state crank; the communistic-militarist; the national-ist-materialist; the humanitarian who wants to exterminate the grievously sick like rats; the 'progressive' who refuses to see in man anything but an evolutionary relative of tape-worms, gorillas, may-flies, salads, beans, fruit-trees, and rats; the whole hotch-potch of monomaniacs, schizophrenes, and sexual monists, not only has a humorous aspect, but also an aspect of the ghastliest terror. For what is significant about the people outside? The Guillotine and the Colt revolver in the hand of the Tchekist, torrents of blood, tortures, state tyranny and bureaucracy, capitalistic mass-misery, mass-stultification, mass-slavery. Their longings are nothing more than to take possession of men as the Capitalists do, to starve them out, to drill them, to kill them morally, to agitate them as the anarchists do, to send them to man barricades, to bleed them to death, to hypnotise them, obsess them, befog their minds, to mould them bolshevistically, to sharpen them like knives, to intimidate them, to destroy the unborn child, to imbue them with a sense of inferiority, to drive fear into them, to preach the reversion to the brute, to rob them of self-respect, to make them melancholy, un-self-reliant, to let loose the world of instinct; and then to be pharisaical, to stop up holes and then tear open others, to lay traps, to experiment all round stupidly, ignorantly, impudently; to sacrifice generations, breed wars, rake in dividends for contraceptive appliances, for films of filth, for books of trash, to exploit meanly or else act insanely, either business or madness, arrogance or cowardice. For do you know, you need a fantastic fund of impudence, after these failures, after these defeats, after driving the cart of history so far into the ditch, to want to go on leading the great world, and not to cast oneself down in the dust, whining and begging pardon before the Church and the misled millions of humanity. Let us hope that these people are only madmen, obsessed men, blinded, erring members of the *anima Christi*, ignorant dilettanti or dilettante ignoramuses —that they are in good faith, and that they are not what they look like: filthy—brutes."

The last word sounded like the lash of a whip. Gertrude had recoiled. But she made no reply. The Jesuit leaned on the top of the writing-table, and took a deep breath. Then he began speaking again. His voice had become lower, and he had recovered his calm.

"We first emerged in the form of Jewish raw material, and then gradually filled the whole world, to persist to all times, right to the end—they attempt, donning their thinking caps again, to go their own ways, as obstinate as donkeys. But the earth will not become happy until humanity, in its preponderant majority, follows *us*, that is to say, Christ. The protagonists of class-warfare can just as little achieve world-peace as can 'soft-hearted' pseudo-humanitarians. World-peace will see the light on the day when, at a signal from the ringed hand of the Holy Father, the soldiers throw away their guns. Peace will not be brought about either by terrorism or cowardice or fine talk, but only by love of Him. And only because 'He is,' because He exists, are we able to love one another. Otherwise we remain hungry animals, desert wolves or pariah dogs, devouring one another in time of need. *We* do everything gradually, progressively, methodically—not hysterically and in jerks. As far back as the nineteenth century, when the military barracks were invading the universities, Leo XIII opposed conscription. We work step by step, exactly, precisely, and it is we who will stop the games of the people outside. We shall destroy everything that is worthless, build up and integrate everything that is significant, that has purpose, and belongs to the *anima Christi*. With our love we shall take the people away from them; with our understanding, take science out of their hands; our organisation, the State."

"You will do nothing, nothing!" Gertrude suddenly cried out. "Look at the apostasy—the millions of Buddhists, Brahmins, Confucians——"

Scapinelli laughed dryly.

"The apostates, the people with no religion, are the physiological waste-matter excreted by our community. Catholicism in the Middle Ages just happened to perish through uræmia. Often they are quite good people, who step outside, but they never have distinction—never yet has a Catholic of eminence become an atheist; and those who now stand outside do not, as the statistics tell us, increase in a natural way. They are dead. And the Bolsheviks have become as transparent, for us, as window panes. We are already playing with our cards on the table, and these childish clowns and muddlers of the Lubyanka-Plosh-tchadya can stand on their heads—but we shall hold out. You cannot keep the truth down with Chinese walls and electrified barbed wire. The books of Mauriac and Bernanos, of Fleg and Bazin, of Maritain, are lying with cut pages on the bedside table of Menzynski. The feat of separating itself wholly from Catholicism, from the *essentia hujus vitae*, will prove beyond the powers of even the stubbornest heresy. And Stalin is to-day not much more than a wretched bogey-man for intimidated ration-card holders, a mantelpiece ornament of morose countenance from the best parlour, out of the history of Oriental sectarian frenzy. Times have changed. The statistical graphs of the losses of the hidden Church in Russia show steeply falling lines—and the absurd tricks of sectarians of all shades to discredit Catholicism with the charge of out-of-dateness will no longer hold water. 'Who eats of the Pope dies,' says a well-known proverb. And Brahminism and Buddhism are dead, too; snowed up, rigidly frozen. The line of development turns from Kali and Vishnu to the Christianised Ghandi; from Confucius and

Buddha to Hungli, Sun Yat Sen, Eugen Cheng, and Alfred Sze. The future belongs to us. Everything that the sectarians imagine they will achieve in the way of appropriating doctrines that belong to Christian belief, *we* shall translate into reality. But, just as they have tackled the idea of peace, starting at the wrong point, so they have made a mess of the social idea. They set up soft-heartedness side by side with egoism, and thus threw the battle away at the very outset. The gruesome sin of Capitalism, too, does not consist in the fact that the workers did not *receive* their just wage, but in the fact that the Capitalist would not *part* with it, but retained it—for poverty in itself is not an evil, but avarice is, and the withholding of the just wage is a sin crying to Heaven for vengeance. But what we want to create is, in spite of our striving for organisation, in spite of the visibility of our Church—what we want is not an apparatus of officials, policemen, and gendarmerie, with prisons, courts of justice, executive officers, spies, enactments, registers, and departments for officially watching over peace and social justice, such as those outside want—what we need is a Catholic atmosphere so strongly concentrated that a war would be an impossibility in it. As a frightful example, there stands Russia. A country where a few Christian principles are thrashed into the people with terrorism and bloodshed and dirt and meanness. Eugen Düring called the U.S.S.R. an 'obligatory monastery with furiously locked-up monks, and a Prior obsessed with collectivist mania.' But our Church is the central focus, the universal circumference, the true, the natural, and the real higher liberty. We are neither collectivist nor individualistic. Neither faith-healers nor fatalists. Neither fanatical admirers of technical developments, nor machine-wreckers. Neither legalistic formalists nor anarchistic sentimentalists. We see no antithesis between the here and the beyond, between matter and spirit. All else is vain—symbolic harmony must——"

"But Eugen had to go to his death——"

Scapinelli was almost forced to smile at this dismal, feminine face.

He opened the window, sat on the window-seat, and looked down at the street. Then, with his hand, he beckoned her to approach. The sun was already setting, but in the street it was still quite light. Motors were hooting busily, boys crying newspapers, windows were glittering with the reflections of the evening sun, children scampering noisily in a nearby playground, and people walking on the warm asphalt slightly bent and with moist foreheads, yet pleasantly fatigued with so much summer weather, and the memory of the Wannsee and the Grunewald, or the Lakes of the Havel.

"Do you see?" said Scapinelli, with a certain joyousness and glow in his heart that made a contrast with the passionate indignation that had formerly sounded in his voice, "there they are—the people—the people themselves. They think little, they would like to enjoy much, but '*qui trop embrasse mal étreint.*' They are good, a little petty-minded, and, in so far as they have no faith, they have a monstrous terror of death. But they are good fellows. Formed after the image of God. And for all these, without exception, absolutely without any exception, the *ecclesia militans* is fighting. And in the first rank of the *ecclesia*, the 'Front.' For, to fight for man, and to fight for the Son of Man, are one and the same thing. An eighth part of these people here are Catholics. Rather slipshod, a little indifferent, here and there frequenting the Sacraments, or else living very intimately with Christ. Of this eighth perhaps only one in a hundred is 'at the Front,' only one working himself to death for others, and for the rest, the word of St. Paul is true: 'Everyone, as

the Lord hath called him, so let him walk.' The highest
criterion with us Catholics is the conscience—and if conscience bids Catholics to join the Weissenberger sect and
eat soft cheeses, so must he act. And he whose conscience
bids him go to the Front, at the Front he must stay. In the
monastery, in the priesthood, in the workers' union, in his
own national life, in the Catholic Action movement, and
on stonier, harder paths he will reach the same goal as the
millions of souls from the back lands and the outposts—those
children of our Church, often so joyous and sunny, who are
married and have children, who, in love, are so devoted to
this beautiful world, and, reverently, with hands folded in
their laps, approach God."

Scapinelli was already speaking more to himself than to
Gertrude. His eyes rested on the sparse Sunday afternoon
traffic of the streets, and his face bore an expression often
seen in the faces of collectors when looking at their treasures
—but Gertrude was rummaging among a pile of photographs, indifferently and absent-mindedly glancing at one
photo after another.

"Isn't that in America?" she asked softly, merely for the
sake of saying something. And she showed Scapinelli the
picture of a gigantic concrete building with a skyscraper-
like tower.

"No," he replied, just as softly, "that is the Seminary of
St. Gall for native priests, Ouidah, Dahomey."

"And this man, here?"

"That is His Excellency, Jacques Réné Lu-Tsien-Tsiang,
formerly Chinese Minister for Foreign Affairs, a Benedictine
since 1927."

"And where is this church?"

"That is the Cathedral of Rejkjavik."

"And this?"

"That is Monsignor Liou, Chinese Bishop."

"And this?"

"The Cathedral of Our Lady of China, in Tong Lü."

"And how are you, personally?" she asked, somewhat hesitantly, after a while. The tone of her words sounded like a reconciliation.

"Thank you for asking," he said, and looked full in her face. "I'm staying here till July 1st—but then I must go back to the House of the Order. On the 1st of September I am going to Rome, and by then my successor will have got used to the work." He drew a breath. "You have no idea," he continued, "how sorry I am to leave Germany—Germany, the great synthesis of soul and matter, the heart of Europe, Berlin, Mayence, Cologne, Upper Silesia——"

"So you are leaving?" she repeated, breaking in on his musing. "And, if one may ask and it is not an official secret, what will you do in Rome?"

"I am being transferred to the Greek, or rather the Old Slav rite, and put in the Collegium Russicum. For that I am sorry. You must know that I am an Italian. I was always very Roman, and have always had a great preference for everything simple, juridical, direct and plain, just like Eugen Düring. And now it is all over. I shall have to read Mass in the Old Slavonic tongue, and say my breviary in Old Slavonic. It will cost me great pains to break myself into this new atmosphere——"

His voice expressed a poignant regret, and this sadness, this self-revelation of human feelings, so unusual with him, touched Gertrude a little.

"Shall you teach in the college?" she asked.

He shook his head.

"For six months I stay in Rome," he said, "then I go to Pogost——"

"I am a little weak in geography," she murmured.

"Pogost is a very modest village in the Roknito marshes, in Polish territory," he explained. "In winter, six hours by sledge from Rafalovka, the nearest railway station. In summer, almost inaccessible. I am taking over the priest's duties there."

He was silent. But she sought for words.

"Really," she said. And in her words there was a scarcely hidden triumph. "Really, you are not being promoted, but rather——"

"Moved down?" he completed her sentence genially. "You've guessed right. But that is being done by my superiors with perfect justification. These five years in Berlin have made me a vain, conceited man. Nearly everybody who works in publicity becomes as I. The day before yesterday, for instance, I caught myself standing, by chance, in front of the looking-glass, and posing. A sojourn in the marshes will do me a lot of good——"

"And after that?" she asked with interest. "After that, you are sure to become General of the Jesuits, or something like that."

"After that," he repeated mechanically—then smiled indulgently and shrugged his shoulders. "After that I shall not be good for much. Played out, worked out, burned out, used up. I have aged mentally a good deal too quickly. I have lost my elasticity. Intellectually I have stagnated for three whole years. I have lost my sense of 'touch.' In England, perhaps, I might get on, but I am not equal to the future in Germany. Parliamentarian, diplomat, salon-abbés have no longer any place here." He drew a deep breath, and continued: "I shall probably finish up where one needs no diplomacy, where one does not have to move with the times——"

"With the heretics?" she interrupted, impatiently.

"With the sick," he replied, correcting her.

"Here—in St. Hedwig's Hospital?" she asked.

"Well, here or—abroad."

A delicate pallor flowed into her face. She bit her lips and only now remembered a few accusations which she had meant to launch against him. But when she looked at him again, she lacked the courage. She looked at Eugen's picture, where it lay on the writing-table, and then at the long black soutane of the Jesuit. And now she felt how Eugen belonged to Scapinelli, and she, *she* was perhaps only a painful episode in his life. Unwillingly she admitted to herself that these men stood for the meaning of this world, that this black cloth that Scapinelli wore was a symbol for that unique synthesis of physical and material, by the mediation of the spirit, that had been intended by God. Once more words struggled to pass her lips—and yet she could not utter a sound. The realisation of her powerlessness and futility came down on her like a high wall falling—and thus it came about that she suddenly held out her hand to the Jesuit, who shook it and, without any word of leave-taking, with drooping head, she turned to go.

With one of those awkward movements that sometimes characterise women's bodies, she slipped through the wide-open door.

Scapinelli no longer looked down on the street. He was gazing thoughtfully after the woman who had just gone, and staring at the open door. Slowly the smile returned to his lips—and yet a little sadness lingered in him like an echo.

"*Multi qui intus videntur foris sunt, et multi qui foris videntur intus sunt,*" he murmured unconsciously.

He slid down from the window-seat, and suddenly, unexpectedly, stood before the writing-table, and could not remember at what point he had interrupted his work when Gertrude had come into the room. When at last he had recovered the thread of his work, he looked up the telephone number of a bookseller in the Französschen-Strasse. He now took up the receiver of the telephone and inserted the forefinger of his right hand in the aperture of the dial. Rattling, it rotated on its axis. He had still to wait a few seconds before he started to speak. At first he spoke softly, and a little unintelligibly. Then a little more loudly, and more fully; and, finally, his beautiful clear voice filled the bare, sober study, penetrating to the farthest corners of its empty whitewashed walls.